CW01460479

THE DARK THING

A NOVEL

JOHN ASHLEY

The characters and events portrayed in this book are fictitious. Any similarity to real persons, living or dead, is coincidental and not intended by the author.

Copyright © 2024 by John Ashley

All right reserved. Without limiting the rights under the copyright reserved above, no part of this publication may be reproduced, stored in, or introduced into a retrieval system, or transmitted in any form by any means (electronic, mechanical, photocopying, recording, or otherwise) without prior written permission.

For more information on this book and John Ashley's other works, please visit johnashleyauthor.com.

Cover Design: Christian Storm

To my wife for supporting me along this journey,
to my mom for being my biggest fan, and to every
reader who takes a chance on this book.
Thank you.

VOLUME
1

ONE

MONDAY, MAY 29TH

Staring down a hallway dark as dreamless sleep, a long-dormant fear awoke in the pit of Jared Gordon's stomach and crept like spiders up his spine. How long had it been since the dark had frightened him? Almost three decades had passed since those haunted, moonless nights in a farmhouse that felt closer to the nearest star than streetlight. But the fear brought back the memories, and the memories a strange sense he was still that same frightened child.

Never mind that he was a father to four children of his own now. Never mind that the hallway was his, in a house he'd watched the carpenters frame with his own eyes. None of this brought any comfort. Not after the nightmare he'd just woken from that seemed even now like it had not yet truly ended.

Why hadn't he grabbed the phone off his nightstand? It would have taken half a second. He thought about going back for it, then thought of his wife, Melody, asleep on the other side of the bed. What would he tell her if she woke? The truth was no good. And Jared was no good at lying.

It was a straight shot, he assured himself. Just a few steps down a path he'd paced a thousand times before. And once he made it to Elena's room, there'd be a window to let the moonlight in.

The window, Jared thought. Any nerve he'd managed to gather was washed away on a rising wave of dread. In his dream, it wasn't just the moonlight that the window had let in.

He shuffled forward, running his fingertips along the wall as a guide. How had it turned this dark? Jared felt the knot of fear in his gut twist tighter. There should have been ambient light from the stairway, at least, or from underneath the bedroom doors. His eyes should have adjusted. Yet he might as well have been blind the way the darkness suffocated the hall.

Finally, his fingers brushed against the ridge of a doorframe. Jared felt for the knob but was startled when his hand found it. It was cold as ice, stinging against his bare skin. So cold it seemed to travel up his forearm and morphed into a shiver. Eager to let go of it, he twisted the knob and pushed open the door.

Light spilled through the doorway, a soft silver-blue glow that chased the darkness and offered Jared some small relief. Peering into the room, he could see all the way across it to the window on the far wall where the light originated. The *open* window.

Elena's butterfly-patterned curtains fluttered up and down. Wind whistled through the opening and around the walls of the room, sounding just as it had in his nightmare when he'd reached this point. Jared felt suddenly dizzy and braced himself against the doorway.

He darted his eyes across the dimly lit room, saw Elena's mirrored dresser with a half-dozen porcelain animals arranged across its top, and the bookshelf beside it with books all stacked neatly in a line, and the full-size bed on the other side of these, it too undisturbed. Undisturbed and vacant.

"Elly?" Jared whispered into the empty room. His voice sounded piercing in the silence.

A whine of wind was the only response. Jared stood frozen in the doorway, panicked but unsure what to do next. Intentionally or not, he had retraced every step of the dream that had shocked him awake and left him gasping as if someone had tossed his sleeping body into cold water. Now, he couldn't remember what had happened next.

Something awful—that was the only surety. Only the horror of it still lingered in his mind, like smoke from a fire that had been doused the moment he opened his eyes.

Where had she gone? No. Where had *they* taken her? If he could just remember, then maybe it wouldn't be too late.

The creak of a floorboard somewhere close behind him broke Jared's concentration. He whirled around, stumbling back into the bedroom and almost tripping. Every muscle in his limbs seemed to turn liquid.

Elena stood in the doorway, her wispy blonde hair framed around a face as pale as the moonlight reflecting on it. Yet where should have been small, crystal-blue eyes were twin pools of midnight black. They swallowed all the light that touched them and ripped through Jared's soul like butcher's blades.

The unfathomable thing that wore his youngest daughter's skin stepped toward him, and Jared collapsed to the floor. It smiled at him, and he closed his eyes and screamed.

TWO

WEDNESDAY, JUNE 6TH

He should leave. The thought came to Jared like a flash of inspiration. Imagining getting up from the leather loveseat and bolting out the door without saying a word, he felt his heart start to race. If he just got up and left, then maybe none of it would be real. If he went home and pretended everything was okay, maybe it would be.

"Can you tell me more about them?" Dr. Stewart asked. He was sitting in a matching leather chair across from Jared's own. He had light black skin with solid white hair, but there were still a few sprinkles of color in his Balbo beard.

"I'm sorry?" Jared said.

"Your nightmares. What are they like?"

"The nightmares. Right. They're uh…" Jared trailed off. Truth be told, he was stalling for time. He let his eyes wander around the small yet upscale room. On the wall behind the doctor's chair hung a diploma from Clemson University and a certificate from the American Psychiatric Association. A large seascape hung on the wall to his left, and a window with beige curtains let sunlight stream in from the right. The air was chilled and smelled subtly of lavender thanks to a diffuser seeping vapor in the corner of the room. Jared could tell that the doctor had gone for a décor both sophisticated and welcoming. And yet it didn't change one bit the fact that he'd dreaded places like this his entire adult life more than the gates of Hell.

"Why don't we start with the most recent nightmare? Can you tell me about it?"

"I don't remember it all. But I was sleepwalking during it. I went into my daughter's bedroom. Something bad had happened in the dream and I...I wanted to check on her. The next thing I remember is waking up screaming on her bedroom floor."

"Do you often sleepwalk during these nightmares?"

"Sometimes. Most of the time I never make it out of the bedroom, but...." Jared trailed off again.

"It sounds like what you're experiencing is night terrors."

"What's that?"

"They're a type of parasomnia. Intense nightmares often paired with sleepwalking or flailing in your sleep."

"Night terrors then," Jared said, rolling the term around in his mind. "I knew they couldn't be normal nightmares."

"And how often do you experience them?"

"Once, maybe twice a week," Jared lied.

Three times a week would have been the true answer. No more, no less, no need for estimates. But he couldn't very well tell the doctor that his nightmares—*night terrors*—ran on a schedule as reliable as the constellations' rise and fall. It sounded absurd even in his own thoughts. How much crazier it would sound if spoken aloud.

"Can you tell me about when this first began?"

Jared drew a long breath in. "I think it started when I was a kid. I know I used to sleepwalk when I was little. Mom had a handful of stories she used to tease me with. Stuff like thinking the broom closet was the restroom or stumbling around our kitchen mumbling about how I had to save the president. Those were just the ones she told her church friends about, though. We didn't talk about the ones where I would scream so loud it woke everyone in the house, but I can remember them too. A little, anyway.

"I'm not sure exactly when they stopped. Probably around ten years old, or maybe a little before. Then it was never a problem again. Not until I had the first one since then about a month ago. From then on, it's been way worse than it ever was as a kid."

"Is there anything that happened around that time, or since for that matter, that could have triggered them to return?" Dr. Stewart asked. "Any losses in the family or issues at home or any other unordinary event in your life, big or small?"

"No," Jared said. "None at all."

Nothing except the letter in his breast pocket. But that had come in just a couple days ago. Far too after the fact to have been the trigger of his nightmares. Horrible though it was.

In a moment of clarity, Jared wondered why he was being so cagey. It wasn't like the doctor was going to have him institutionalized. Jared's experience with the mental side of medicine ran deep. He knew better than to fall for such tropes as the psychiatrist ready to lock up his patients and throw away the key at the first sign of instability. He had seen firsthand just how far they were willing to let a person go before they intervened.

"Is there any history of mental illness in your family?"

As if on cue, Jared thought. No sense in lying. There'd be no point in coming if he lied here. "Yes," he said, making little effort to hide the resignation in his tone. "My father was schizophrenic. He killed himself when I was seventeen."

"I'm sorry to hear that, Jared."

Jared wasn't sure which part he meant: the part about his father hanging himself from the storage building rafters or the game of genetic Russian roulette that was Dad's only legacy.

Thirteen percent. That was the game's odds—the odds of a person developing schizophrenia when one of their parents was diagnosed with the condition. Those odds had been seared into his mind through witness of their consequence. They had hung over his existence like a storm cloud that any moment might conjure a bolt of lightning and burn life as he knew it to the ground.

"Let's get the elephant in the room out of the way then, shall we?" Dr. Stewart said. "I want to start by saying that it is uncommon for a person your age to develop schizophrenia."

"Uncommon, but not unheard of."

"Correct. Only about twenty percent of schizophrenics experience onset of the condition past the age of forty. It is uncommon. But not unheard of."

Twenty percent. Thirteen percent. These seemed like such manageable odds. Yet how many times at the casino or the horse tracks had he won a bet with lower odds than these? How many times throughout his life had the unlikely come to pass?

"Are you experiencing any other symptoms? Agitation, compulsive behavior, visual or auditory hallucinations?"

"Just anxiety. Nothing else besides the night terrors."

"Well, there's a lot of different factors that can cause those. Their frequency is some cause for concern, but I don't want you to be too alarmed, Jared. What I would like for you to do is start keeping a journal. Nothing too elaborate. Just a record of your nightmares, any interesting observations you might have, things along those lines."

"I've never been the journaling type."

"Try writing in third person if it helps," Dr. Stewart said. "Some studies show journaling actually offers more therapeutic benefits that way. Also, I'm going to give you a prescription for Risperdal. It'll be a relatively small dose, but enough to help with the anxiety and hopefully the night terrors too."

"Any side effects?" Jared asked.

"They're uncommon. And mild. Digestive issues are the most frequently reported. I'm just writing you a one-month prescription, though. I want you to come see me again when you run out. We'll reevaluate from there."

Jared nodded. Maybe he would come back, if the medicine helped. And if it didn't, if this past month turned out to be just the beginning of a downward spiral into a condition intimately, horrifyingly familiar, what then? Would he crawl back here, begging for a cure that didn't exist? Or would he take the same out as his father? Save himself the two and a half years of torment that poor man endured before he chose a noose as the kinder alternative.

"I'll see you in a month," Jared said. And he meant it. There were four beautiful children and a loving wife whose lives were welded to his own.

"Take care, Jared. I'll see you then."

THREE

WEDNESDAY, JUNE 6TH

By the time Jared made it out of his car and up the driveway, a sheet of sweat had already formed on his forehead. For the past week, Georgia's take on what June should feel like had been especially cruel. The thermometer on the Bank of America sign had read 97 degrees. The air felt like the inside of a bathhouse, so thick and sticky that his lungs protested each inhale.

Jared reached into his pocket and fished out his keys to open the front door. The cool indoor air rushed out to meet him, carrying with it a muffled harmony that was coming from somewhere upstairs. Grace's room most likely. She was the only one of his children who preferred speakers to headphones. Ever since she'd come home from Georgia Tech for the summer, music always seemed to be playing in the house. Some of it Jared even enjoyed.

He walked through the living room past the arched entryway that led into the kitchen. He opened the refrigerator and plucked an IPA from the bottom shelf. With his skin still radiating heat, it tasted just like heaven.

Not that Jared believed in such a place. Once upon a time, maybe. Back when Sunday school was a weekly regimen and everything adults said was taken as gospel. It didn't take long after his father's diagnosis for him to kick faith to the curb. It sounded cliché, but the God of love and mercy everyone talked about sure hadn't shown up then.

His brother must have seen it differently, Jared had long ago accepted. The image of the letter in his breast pocket—close to the heart and heavy on the mind—flashed before him and soured the taste of beer on his tongue.

Just three years younger than Jared, Jeremiah had seen all the same horrors. And the same suffering—its very existence to the degree they witnessed—that had turned Jared to naturalism had sent Jeremiah running to the foot of the cross with arms open wide.

This was far from the main reason that he and his brother hadn't spoken since their mother's funeral six years ago, but it didn't help. Six years without so much as an email. Then, two days ago on a morning that was quite splendid up until that point, the letter had arrived.

Jared had carried it with him ever since, afraid that Melody might find it and read it if he left it lying around yet not willing to destroy it. Even now, he could feel its folded corners poking through the fabric of his shirt.

So formal, to send a letter, in this era of instant communication. Such a difficult thing to ignore. Jared imagined that was probably the point. He turned his wrist and glanced at his watch. It was a quarter past three. He had taken half a day off at work, and it would be a few hours still before Melody got back from her job at the bank. On any other day, her return was something Jared would have looked forward to.

She knew about his appointment with Dr. Stewart. She had insisted on it, in fact, after what had happened in Elena's bedroom. What she didn't know was how it went. And what was said. And how he felt about it. And a whole list of other questions sure to be forthcoming.

But when six o'clock rolled around and Melody came through the door, the inquisition he'd dreaded never came to be. There'd been questions about the appointment, but they'd been more patient than probing. Helping her in the kitchen to get dinner started, he felt a sudden pang of guilt for assuming the worst from her. A strand of auburn hair fell across her face as she diced onions on a cutting board. When she pursed her lips and blew it to the side with practiced grace, he couldn't help but smile.

"Can you dice the potatoes now?" Melody asked.

Jared shook himself from his daydream, realizing he'd been staring at the chef's knife in his hand for what must have been more than a minute. He tended to do this, his mind retreating within itself and leaving his body on autopilot for the extent of its vacation. "What's that, Mel?"

"The potatoes. For the stew. Can you get started dicing them?"

"Yeah. Sure."

By seven o'clock, the beef stew and store-bought rolls had finished cooking. Emily and Elena set the table while Grace poured lemonade from a pitcher into five glasses and one sippy cup. Timmy, still young enough to enjoy a life absent any responsibility, played with his toy cars on the living room floor.

When six ceramic bowls had been filled with stew and placed on plates alongside butter-glazed rolls, the family took their places at the dining room table. Each one slid into the upholstered chair designated over the years through an unspoken rite as their own. It wasn't often these days that all of his children were able to gather for dinner at the same time. It was particularly uncommon for his older daughters, who seemed to spring eternal from one obligation to another.

"You girls don't have any big plans for this evening?" Jared asked, looking down the table to where Grace and Emily were sitting.

"Not until nine," Emily replied. "We're picking up Lauren and Tiana then going to the movies."

"You too, Grace?"

She nodded.

"Did you invite Elena?"

"It's R-rated, Dad," Grace said.

Jared sighed and nodded. He and Melody had never been especially conservative as parents, but they did believe that some things were best kept from younger eyes. They'd decided when Grace was a child that the age restrictions recommended by the movie's rating were as good a rule as any. Thirteen for PG-13, seventeen for R—allowing, of course, for the occasional judgment-based exception.

"Tomorrow we're going to the pool, though," Grace said. "Would you want to come, Elena?"

Elena shrugged. "Hmm. Maybe. I'll have to see." She spoke as she so often did, with a cheerfully distant tone. One of satisfied indifference.

Elena had always been such a delicate child from a physical standpoint. It was something that dated all the way back to her premature birth. Nine years old now, she was still as thin as a piece of paper, with small, blue eyes and a narrow face framed by hair as airy and golden as clouds at sunrise.

From an emotional standpoint, the girl was as solid as a stone wall. Quite the opposite of her outgoing older sisters, Elena kept mostly to herself aside from the odd playdate every now and then. Jared tried to get Grace and Emily to include her in their plans whenever possible, but there was only so much you could ask of a girl in high school and another in college when it came to inviting their middle school sister to tag along. Not that Elena seemed to care one way or another. She was unshakable. Wholly content with her own little world of paintings and books and daylong daydreaming. It concerned Jared more than it should. He had been the same way as a child. And that, he figured, was likely the very reason for his worry.

"What about you, Dad?" Emily asked. "You and Mom have any big plans?" She was smiling, already knowing the answer. There were dimples on her cheeks brought on by the grin and crinkles touching the corners of eyes as big and brown as her mother's. Gentle waves of jet-black hair, the likes of which appeared nowhere else in his or Melody's known family tree, were pulled back into a ponytail.

"Your mom and I are going to plant ourselves on the couch and watch a few shows. Then we're going to plant ourselves in bed no later than eleven because that's what you do on a Friday night in your forties."

"Not me," Grace said. "I'm living it up all the way to the retirement home."

"Pappaw!" Timmy proclaimed, reacting to a term he associated with visits to Melody's father.

"Get back to us when you've raised four children, sweetheart," Melody said. "It might change your mind."

One by one they filtered away from the table. By the time Jared and Melody finished putting the dishes in the sink, Grace and Emily had left and Timmy and Elena were upstairs in their bedrooms, leaving him and Melody alone on the living room couch. They watched television for a while, opting for a new Netflix documentary about John Wayne Gacy. The two of them had always enjoyed the true crime genre. Tonight, though, Jared was struggling to keep his eyes open. He'd had a beer before dinner and two more during, and though far from drunk, he was feeling quite sleepy.

"What do you say we call it, Mel?"

Melody, who had sprawled across the couch and laid her head on Jared's lap, sat up and stretched. "Fine with me."

She followed him up the stairs and down the hall to the master bedroom at its end. Jared crawled straight into bed, having changed out of his work attire and into a pair of shorts and a t-shirt several hours ago. Melody shut the bedroom door, then began undressing. Jared watched as articles of clothing dropped from her body one by one. First a robin-egg blue smock, then a black bra that landed on top of it, then a pair of jeans that she shimmied down and bent over to slip off her feet. She disappeared below the foot of the bed.

Then she stood up holding a familiar piece of paper in her hands. "Someone sending you love letters?" she asked playfully.

Jared felt his heart skip a beat. Not thinking earlier, he had tossed his shirt haphazardly onto the floor. The letter had probably slipped right out of the pocket and into plain view.

Before he could think of any good way to stop her, Melody began to read. He watched her eyes move across the page, the humor in them fading with each passing moment.

"When were you going to show me this?" she asked. There was nothing so harsh as anger or accusation in her tone. Just the subtle inflection of disappointment that stung even worse than these.

"Eventually," Jared said. "I was just still getting my head around it, honey."

Melody sat down on the bed beside him. "Are you going?"

"Yes," Jared said, surprised as soon as the word left his lips by his sudden resolution. "I think I should."

"Okay," Melody said. She laid her head down next to his on the same pillow and placed her hand on his chest.

No more was said between them. Melody drifted off to sleep in a matter of minutes, her chin tucked against his shoulder. He could feel her breasts against his ribs and the beat of her heart just inches from his own. For the first time in much too long, Jared relaxed. He closed his eyes and willed this welcome sense of peace to last throughout the night. Yet the moment that sleep took hold and flushed his mind with darkness, clearing the way for a different darkness to rush in and fill the void, he knew that it would not.

FOUR

SATURDAY, JUNE 9TH

Dear Jared,

I want to start with an apology. With the help of Clarice and God above, I've come to recognize that I have myself to blame as much as you for the death of our brotherhood. I should have reached out long before this letter became necessary, and for that, I am truly sorry.

I need to meet with you. Sometime soon, if possible. I think it would be best if you came here. You know where I live, and that's where I'll be when I'm not at work or church. Come by whenever you are able.

I have things to tell you. Things that can only be spoken when the two of us are in the same room.

I hope to see you soon.

Your brother still,
Jeremiah Gordon

Jared folded the letter back in half and tucked it away in the glove compartment of his Toyota Camry. He couldn't say why he read it over again so often. Each word was fuel for his nightmares. Nightmares that had shown up last night on schedule and in force.

They had come one after another, each one nested within the last like some ungodly Matryoshka doll. False awakenings followed each abhorrent episode, giving way each time to the start of a new nightmare. He had lain in bed for well over ten minutes upon actually waking—wide-eyed and white-knuckled from gripping the fitted sheet—before he accepted that morning had actually come and the night was truly over. Even now, it felt as if some part of the nightmares had followed him out into the daylight.

The pharmacist said it would take at least two weeks for the Risperdal to reach its full effect. Jared had swallowed the day's first dose with his morning coffee and would take the second sometime before bed. Two a day, every day, for four to six weeks. Was it a recipe for deliverance or a futile exercise? Only four to six weeks of time that couldn't possibly pass quick enough would tell.

He started the Camry and shifted it into reverse, backing out of the drive and onto Cherry Street. A GPS was built into the car's infotainment system, but there was no need for it today. Every stretch and turn between here and his destination was branded on his mind. For the first time in twenty-four years, Jared was going home.

Jeremiah had never left there. At least not for very long. He had lived with their mother Linda after their father's passing until he was twenty-nine. Then he had married Clarice Honeycutt, the youth minister at the church he attended, and moved into her apartment. When Linda Gordon died three years later, Jeremiah and Clarice took possession of the home.

Their mother's will dictated that the property was to be shared equally between her two sons, but Jared had ceded his claim. He had zero desire for the place and no real need for the money to be gained by selling it. And giving it away was just a drop in the bucket of atonement that he owed.

It had been a pleasant enough place to grow up. Before their father's diagnosis, Jared and Jeremiah had enjoyed their childhood in Allen Hill as much as any small-town American children. The town was like most in the heart of the South with a population of less than ten thousand. Friday night football games and Saturday morning Lion's Club meetings composed the bulk of the social scene. A tight-knit community made up for most such deficiencies but created plenty of problems of its own. People were friendly yet private, except when they weren't. Life there seemed so isolated from the outside world. Like the town was a macrocosm all its own.

Or at least that's the way it used to be. A relative lifetime had passed since Jared last visited his hometown. He'd realized at an early age that there were two kinds of people who lived in places like Allen Hill: those who were living out their small-town minimalist dreams of peace and simplicity and those who dreamed only of the day they could leave. He had realized not long after that he belonged in the latter camp. Yet he never imagined when he finally did leave—even under the awful circumstances at the time—that it would take him this long to return.

For the next four hours, Jared cruised down I-65 toward Savannah. He exited the interstate just before reaching the city onto US-17 toward Allen Hill. He had cranked the radio for the entire trip, alternating at each ad break between a pair of classic rock and contemporary stations. He didn't care much for the silence these days. It offered too much of a void for unpleasant thoughts to fill. Passing by the Allen Hill city limits sign, though, he turned the dial all the way down.

Allen Hill High School would be up ahead on his left. Surely that hadn't changed. Brunson's Hardware was still where it had always been, though Jared doubted it was still Old Man Brunson running the place. Probably his son Daniel now. He had been on the baseball team with Jared in high school. Hell of a shortstop, but a bit of a prick.

The elementary school was where it had always been too. The playground had been renovated and the buildings given a fresh coat of paint, but otherwise, it looked mostly the same. It was a place that Jared hadn't wanted to be more days than not. Yet thinking back on it now, only fond memories surfaced.

The Walmart and Dollar General were still across the street from each other near the center of town, locked in a competition that Dollar General lost nine times out of ten. But next to them were new stores that hadn't been there before. A Sassy's Salon next to the Walmart and a Chinese buffet named Cheshire Gardens.

So much of the town remained the same that Jared had the eerie feeling of stepping back in time. The small things here and there that had changed made it even more eerie. Like stepping back in time and into a different reality all at once.

Only the vehicles on the road gave away that it was still 2021 and not the era of his childhood—those late eighties and early nineties when neither he nor any of his friends ever stopped to question if the world really was their oyster.

Another stoplight, one of the only two in Allen Hill, and another few blocks of mom-and-pop shops, and Jared was leaving the city limits. Allen Hill was a "blink and you'll miss it" town. And, much more than he had expected, Jared had indeed missed it.

But when he turned off the highway and onto a gravel street called Dizzy Dean Road, these feelings of nostalgia began to fade, replaced with a sudden knot in the pit of his stomach. There were dark evocations at the end of this road. Two years of fear and misery that had blackened every memory of the sixteen preceding them.

He had a strong impulse to turn the car around. It would be a shameful waste of time and gas, but surely not as shameful as what awaited him at the last house on Dizzy Dean Road.

"*Why did you come, Jared?*" he remembered his brother saying at the funeral. "*You weren't here when she needed you. When I needed you. Eighteen years without a word. And now that she's dead, here you are.*"

That was the last time he had spoken to Jeremiah. Six years ago at Oliver's Funeral Home in Savannah. Mom had written in her will that she wanted to be buried there next to her mother and father. There'd been whispers at the time about why she chose this instead of the plot next to her husband in Allen Hill. But Jared understood the reason. It was the same reason he had left and never returned until now. The same reason the urge to turn the car around was so compelling.

It was too late now, though. He'd become too caught up in his recollections, and the opportunity had passed. He had already pulled onto the dirt driveway leading up to a modest 1960s farm home. Jeremiah, and his wife if she was home, had no doubt spotted his car already. Having lived on this road for well over a third of his life, Jared knew that traffic was rare and always drew attention. A series of barks and howls from inside the house ensured they hadn't missed his arrival.

His throat felt dry. Jared tipped the bottle of Powerade he had purchased when he stopped for gas up to a ninety-degree angle, but only a trickle came out. Just enough to wet his lips.

The empty bottle trembled a little in his hand when he set it back in the cupholder. Jared steeled himself and drew a deep breath. He couldn't show up at the front door shaking like a leaf. His pride wouldn't allow it.

He unbuckled his seat belt without any tremble and opened the car door. The smell of pine trees and honeysuckle carried on the breeze, transporting him back in a way far more profound than any sight he had seen to this point.

He crossed the gravel walkway to the home's front porch in a dazed disposition, struck by the déjà vu of so many dreams over the past twenty-four years that had mirrored this very moment. Was he dreaming now? For just an instant, Jared considered the possibility.

He ascended onto the porch and stopped in front of the door, curbing his impulse to turn the knob and walk inside. It felt strange to have to knock at this door—a door he had come and gone through unchecked ten thousand different times. He reached out his hand and rapped it against the wood.

The barking inside intensified. Jared heard a female voice shout at the dog to shush, then footsteps approaching the door. He watched through the door's glass panes as Clarice turned into the hallway. Good God, would she even be expecting him? Had Jeremiah told her about the letter? He thought about turning and sprinting back to his car. There was the click of a retracting lock, then the door swung inward.

Surprise creased the corners of Clarice Gordon's round face, but it quickly melted into a soft smile. "Jared, I'm so glad to see you. Why don't you come inside?"

He followed her through the door and down the short hallway that connected the washroom and entry area to the home's kitchen. She rounded the corner well ahead of him, and Jared picked up his pace. There was an urge to linger at every footfall. Moving forward with all the memories washing over him was like trying to swim against the tide.

Plenty of minor details about the home had changed from what he remembered. New décor and appliances. New paint and new photographs on the walls. But the soul of the house remained the same. Stepping into the kitchen, Jared had expected for a moment to see his mother standing behind the stove preparing the night's dinner. His father would be outside in the garden or tinkering away in the garage that doubled as his workspace. Jeremiah would be in his bedroom playing with his assortment of hand-me-down toys. And Jared was coming in now from a game of touch football with a group of neighbor kids in Trenton Crowley's large backyard. Walking into a perfectly normal and nurturing home that was still a few good years away from being ripped apart at the seams.

A set of paws thumping into the side of Jared's hip broke his trance. He stumbled a little, then caught his balance. A brown lab walked circles around his legs, sniffing them vigorously.

"Annabelle, that's a bad girl! You know better than to jump on people!" Clarice said. The wag in Annabelle's tail subsided, and she retreated a few steps, walking sideways so as to keep him in her gaze. "She doesn't meet a lot of new people these days. I'll put her in the kennel if she doesn't behave."

"She's no problem."

"Please," Clarice said, gesturing toward the kitchen table. "Have a seat. Jeremiah is out back watering the garden. I'll go tell him you're here." Jared sat down. Annabelle sat down on her haunches beside him and started to whimper. "Shush, Annie. You be a good girl," Clarice said as she left the kitchen.

Jared heard the back door in the living room open and close. He exhaled and rubbed at his temples with the tips of his fingers.

Why did you come, Jared?

He'd been unable to answer the question then and was no more able to now. From the moment he'd first read the letter, it never felt like he had a choice. If his sense of indebtment had not made him come, it would have been sickening curiosity instead.

He heard the back door swing open again and straightened up in his chair. The boards of the living room floor creaked as heavy footsteps trod across them. The footsteps drew closer, and Jeremiah Gordon rounded the corner into the kitchen.

He was bigger than Jared remembered. Once he'd made up the age difference, Jeremiah had always been the taller and broader of the two brothers. Now, though, he was sporting some new pudge that stretched his gray t-shirt a little tighter than the white dress shirt he'd worn to the funeral. A Kubota baseball cap covered all but a few stray tufts of his sand-colored hair and shaded his oval face.

He stood there at the entryway. The silence between them started to grow. Six years it had gone unbroken. Being the first to break it now felt suddenly difficult. Jared tried to swallow, but the saliva wouldn't come. He wondered if the warmth he felt rising in his cheeks was visible and hoped it wasn't. Finally, Jeremiah started forward into the kitchen.

"Good to see you, brother. I wasn't sure you'd come," he said. Then, as if realizing somehow the dryness of Jared's mouth, "Can I get you something to drink? Maybe a beer?"

Jared cleared his throat. "Yeah. That sounds great. Thanks."

Jeremiah opened the refrigerator and pulled out two dark bottles. He handed one to Jared, then sat down at the table across from him. "Pardon the dirty clothes," he said, glancing down as if just noticing the splotches of mud on his shirt and jeans. "I've been out in the garden since lunch."

"How's that going?" Jared asked, unsure what else to say but anxious to avoid another silence.

"Be going better if we'd get some rain. Clarice and I do our best to keep it watered, but between her job and mine, it gets a little hard to keep up when the ground's this dry. But we should have a nice crop of squash and okra and whatnot come the end of the summer. And there's cherry tomatoes ripening already. I'll send a bag home with you."

"You don't have to do that."

"It's give them to you or give them to someone else. That or let the crows have 'em. I don't know what possessed us to plant three full rows of the darn things."

Jared knew this last part wasn't true. When his mother and father had been the ones to tend the rather large garden that took up the bulk of the home's backyard plot, they too had always grown much more than they could ever use themselves. Always for the purpose of sharing it freely.

"I'm sure my daughter Emily would love to have them. She's always after us to shop more at the farmer's market."

"Smart girl. Can't beat homegrown vegetables. Don't tell her they aren't organic, though. It's nice and all 'till you have to get down on your knees and pull weeds all day because you can't use herbicide."

Jared nodded. He had helped out in the garden enough times as a kid to know how much of a chore it could be.

"How was the drive?" Jeremiah asked.

"Fine."

"Good. It's a long trip."

Jared's heart began to beat a little faster. It was time to get to the point of his being here. The silence was threatening to build again, and the elephant in the room could be ignored no longer. "It's really good to see you again, Jeremiah. It's been way too long. And I'm sorry because I know that's my fault. But you know the reason I'm here."

"It's not your fault alone. But yes, brother, I know why you're here. There'll be plenty of time to get to all that later, though. Have a couple more beers with me. We've got a lot of catching up to do. Then, after dinner, we'll get to the letter."

"I don't think I can stay that long, Jeremiah. Like you said, it's a long drive."

"Don't tell me you were planning on going back today?" Jeremiah said, blinking incredulously at him just like he used to as a kid. "That's too much travel for one day. We've got two spare bedrooms with comfortable enough beds. You can take your pick."

"I can't impose on you like that."

"It's no trouble at all. Clarice and I have planned all along on putting you up for the night when… and if…you came. And I've got a bottle of Blanton's I bought just for the occasion."

"Isn't whiskey against your religion?" Jared said, stalling for time to make a decision. He was exhausted, and the idea of being on the road for another four hours was none too appealing. His reluctance to turn his brother down was a strong factor as well. Yet the thought of staying the night here, in this house, chilled him in a way he couldn't fully explain.

"'He causes the grass to grow for the cattle and vegetation for the service of man that he may bring forth food from the earth and wine that makes glad the heart of man'. That's Psalms 109. I'm not much of a wine person myself, but I'd imagine it applies to beer and whiskey too."

Jared heard only parts of this. If he could come up with the right excuse, he would turn the invitation down. The thought of the nightmares that sleeping here might conjure was far more dreadful than a four-hour drive. But he couldn't tell Jeremiah this, and any other excuse he could think to offer felt so hollow.

"Melody is at home, though. She'll be waiting for me." One last desperate attempt.

"I lived with you for thirteen years, Jared. Trust me when I say that poor woman would probably love nothing more than an afternoon to herself."

Jared couldn't help but smile. It felt good, despite it all, to be joking again with his brother. To break first the silence and now the eggshells they'd been walking around.

"Come on, have a few more beers, and then you can decide," Jeremiah said, grinning at the implication; a few more beers and the decision would already be made.

Jared sighed. At this point, only honesty would do. "It's the house, Jeremiah. It's uh… bringing up a lot of memories, I guess you could say. And, to tell you the truth, I don't know if I'd be able to sleep here. I've been having a lot of nightmares lately…" He trailed off. The less was said about those the better.

Jeremiah studied him for a while before taking a long sip of beer, then pushing the bottle away emphatically. "Tell you what. I've got a hunting cabin about six miles from here. It's a property I lease along with a few men from church. But nothing's in season now, and no one's gonna be there. What do you say we put the beers away for now, then I can take us there after dinner? It's a single-room cabin, and you'll have to use the woods for a restroom. But it's got two beds and a brand-new window AC. And there's a firepit where we could get a campfire going. What do you think?"

"Okay," Jared said after some consideration. "Sure."

"It's settled then. We'll stay for dinner first, though. There's a lasagna with homemade sauce in the oven that should be ready in about an hour."

"Sounds great," Jared said and truly meant it. For the first time since he opened the letter, he considered the idea that this visit—this reunion—might actually be good for him. Perhaps this was just what he needed to erase some of the troubles from his mind. At the very least, the chance to spend another night in the forest out under the stars just like they used to on so many fall and summer nights seemed blessedly cathartic.

This *was* just what he needed, Jared decided. This trip and this night would be far better medicine than anything Dr. Stewart could prescribe. "You remember what happened last time we went camping, though, right?" he asked.

Jeremiah groaned. "What a disaster."

Jared grinned and relished in the joint retelling of the time the two of them had gotten themselves so lost that the park rangers had to come looking for them. And the letter was far from his mind.

FIVE

SATURDAY, JUNE 9TH

Jared snapped a twig from one of the branches they had dragged next to the firepit and tossed it into the fire. It slid through the crumbling teepee of burnt logs and landed on the red embers beneath, flaring up like a match. A few blinks and it was embers too. Glowing embers and a thread of smoke that joined the rest ascending into the star bespangled sky.

A pack of coyotes howled somewhere deep in the forest. A gust of wind bent the campfire's flames and lifted a sprinkle of cinders up into its stream. Jared closed his eyes and breathed it all in. He had gone too long without such primeval pleasures.

He grabbed the bottle of bourbon from the ground next to his chair and poured another splash into his tumbler. Jared offered the bottle to Jeremiah, but he shook his head.

"No thanks. It's getting late. And there's still something we need to discuss."

For the first time in hours, Jared's anxiety crept back in. He and Jeremiah had spent the entire night lost in conversation. Swapping stories and reminiscing. Healing decades of wounds in hours of time the way two estranged men are prone to do when given the right reason to meet again. But never once until now had that reason come up in conversation.

He glanced at the tumbler of whiskey in his hand, then sat it on the ground. Noticing this, Jeremiah straightened in his chair. He seemed on edge now too. For a long time, there was only the sounds of the woods and the hiss of the fire between them. Then, finally, Jeremiah spoke.

"It's funny, I've always had a hard time remembering what it was like in those days when Dad got sick. But, for some reason, the older I've got, the clearer it's become."

For Jared, the opposite was true. Memories of those times had faded little by little with each passing year. Now, all that was left were fragments and scars.

"Do you remember much of those years?" Jeremiah asked.

Jared shook his head. "Not much. I never *tried* to forget, so to speak. But I think I've buried a lot of the memories all the same."

"Do you remember what he used to say toward the end? On the bad days."

"No," Jared said, almost choking on just this one short word. Part of him remembered. An old fear his brother's words had roused like breath on a fading ember. Something Jared wanted nothing more than to bury again at once.

"He used to tell us that *they* were here," Jeremiah said. If he had noticed the ashen color of Jared's face, it didn't stop him from continuing. "Not that they were coming. Not that they were out there somewhere. It was always 'they are *here*.' Have you ever wondered what he meant by that?"

"No," Jared said again, this time emphatically. "And I don't want to know. Nothing Dad said back then means anything, Jeremiah. He was sick. It was the disease talking when he said things like that. And nothing it had to say is worth dwelling on."

"I've had the same thought a lot of times over the years. That dwelling on it isn't worth the cost. But I've never been able to keep my mind away from it for long."

They went silent for a while, both men gazing into the flames. Neural pathways not traveled in years were flickering back to life in Jared's mind. New slivers of memory burst into existence one after the other. Jared could feel them starting to come together. Starting to form a bigger picture that he *did not* want to see.

"I remember a lot of things from back then," Jeremiah said, still staring at the fire. "I remember them as clear as if they happened yesterday. And you know as well as I do there were things that happened back then no disease could explain."

Jared felt drunk suddenly. Too drunk. The few splashes of bourbon he'd downed probably amounted to little more than three or four shots spread out across as many hours. But the stars overhead were spinning, and it felt like he was going to be sick. He tried to focus on his breathing. A swell of anxiety simmered through his body, threatening to boil over into full-blown panic.

Jeremiah must have noticed his sudden deterioration. There was no way he could have missed it; Jared's face was blanched and slicked with sweat, and each breath he took was deep and purposeful. There was some empathy in his brother's voice when he continued, but he continued all the same.

"You were there, brother. You saw the same things I did."

With no consideration for this, Jared shook his head. Rejecting it at once felt vital. Vital to his entire view of the world. To his sanity. "We were little kids," he said. "Kids with our lives turned upside down by something we didn't understand. So our minds played tricks. We came up with a monster we could understand to make sense of the one we couldn't. That's what I remember."

"I was twelve when Dad was diagnosed. That'd mean you were sixteen, right?"

"Even adults can convince themselves of some wild fantasies in the right situations. There's no age limit on coping mechanisms. Calling us children might have been a stretch, but we sure weren't mature enough yet to deal with all the shit we had to. I doubt anyone would be, really."

"So what then?" Jeremiah asked. "We just imagined it all? Imagined it all and played pretend and yet twenty-six years later, I still somehow remember it as the most real and terrifying thing I've ever experienced."

Though he'd never admit it—*didn't dare* admit it even to himself—Jared was starting to remember too. The voices from their father's bedroom. The constant feeling of being watched. The inexplicable fear that haunted every waking and sleeping hour. Oh God, why had he come back?

Why did you come, Jared?

"It was real to us then," he said, compelled to still argue his case if only to reaffirm it to himself. "I'm not saying we played pretend. I'm not saying we made it all up. It was a real and awful experience for us, but that does not mean it actually happened."

"A shared delusion then? That's what you're saying. That you and I and Dad were all paranoid about the same fantasy at the same time. Mental illness might be genetic, but it's not contagious."

"For Dad it was schizophrenia. For us it was trauma. We believed the things he told us when he was in psychosis because he was our father and we didn't know better. And our imaginations ran wild from there. I don't understand your hang-up here, Jeremiah. What I'm telling you really isn't hard to believe. I can guarantee it's a hell of a lot more plausible than whatever it is you're driving at."

"I hope you're right," Jeremiah said, seeming to mean it. "I really do. But it just doesn't feel like the truth. It never has."

Did it feel true to Jared? Before this trip, it would have seemed like the only possible explanation for what few bits and pieces of inexplicable memories remained accessible. In the dark of the woods just miles from the house where it all took place, Jared wasn't quite so sure. "What's the point of all this, Jeremiah?"

Jeremiah sighed. "I said in the letter that I had things to tell you, but I've got something to show you too. I've told you what I have to say. That I'm not convinced all the things that happened back then were trauma-induced delusions like you and every shrink I've ever visited keeps telling me they were. What I have to show you is this." He turned around in his chair and reached behind him, turning back again with a backpack in his arms. He unzipped it, then reached inside. Jared felt his heart begin to race.

Jeremiah pulled out a book. A short but thick volume that was leatherbound with brass adornments at the corners. Jared recoiled at the sight of it, his breath catching in his throat. It was his father's journal. The one he'd purchased soon after his diagnosis to catalog his symptoms. The one he had scribbled in all hours of the night, talking to himself loud enough for his sons to hear in the other room. Speaking to life the very delusions that fueled their waking nightmares.

"Put it away," Jared said. "I can't believe you'd ask me to read that. I can't believe you'd read it yourself."

Jeremiah kept the journal in his hands. "I know it can't be easy coming back here. Remembering all these things that I'm sure you'd rather leave forgotten. I wish that I could continue to spare you that. But ignorance is only bliss when you are safe. It is no longer bliss when the wolf is at your door."

"What do you mean by that?" Jared asked. Then, pivoting to another question that seemed suddenly more important, "Why now? You must have had that journal ever since Mom passed. Maybe before. So tell me, why now?"

Jeremiah's eyes dropped down to his boots. This was a bad sign. He'd made it this far unabashed. No telling how preposterous what's coming next would be. "I, uh…About two weeks ago I had a vision."

"*A vision?*"

"Yes. That's exactly what it was, Jared. A vision. It wasn't a dream because I wasn't sleeping. I was stacking boxes in the garage one second, then the next I was somewhere else. It's the sixth time it's happened to me, and it's damn near impossible for me to explain what it's like when it does. But what I saw this time was you and your entire family in danger. I don't know much else, but I know it has something to do with what happened to us back then."

Jared could hardly believe what he was hearing. Was this a sick attempt at a prank? Some kind of revenge for past wrongs? Whatever it was, it was the exact opposite of what he'd hoped to find by coming here. The opposite of everything the entire night had been to this point. Confusion instead of closure. Fear instead of peace. And Jared had had enough.

"I want you to put that thing away, back in your pack, and don't say another word about it. I refuse to read it, and I'm done talking about it. I mean it, Jeremiah. I'll walk back to the highway and call a cab if I have to."

Jeremiah seemed to consider this. He studied Jared in the dying fire-light, and Jared stared back at him. It was no bluff. He wouldn't listen to another word.

Finally, Jeremiah slipped the journal back into his pack. For a while, neither of them spoke. They watched the fire's last embers slowly flicker into ash. They listened as the crickets and the night birds and the faraway coyotes filled the silence's void. The night was all but over, with midnight fast approaching, and there would be no salvaging what remained.

"I think I'll turn in," Jared said. "I'd like to get an early start in the morning. Try and get back home before lunch."

Jeremiah nodded. "I'll try not to wake you when I come in. I'm not sleepy yet. Think I'll see if I can get this fire going again and hang out here a while longer."

But when Jeremiah crept back into the cabin well after 2 a.m., Jared was still awake. When dawn broke near 7 a.m. and pale light filtered through the room's sole window, his eyes were open to see it. The horrors that the world of dreams might bring on this night and in this place were too terrible to risk.

SIX

SUNDAY, JUNE 17ᵀᴴ

"Higher!" Timmy yelled between giggles, gripping the swing set's plastic-covered chains in his hands. Jared gave him another hard push.

He rose into the streams of a sprinkler Jared had positioned carefully in the backyard for just this effect, squealing and shouting when the swing reached the top of its arc and left him suspended for an instant within the chilly spray.

"Higher!" he yelled again the moment the swing began to descend. But this time Jared let it continue its return sweep untouched.

"It's Sis's turn, little buddy." Jared glanced toward the picnic table where Elena was sitting, but she didn't seem to have heard. She was crouching on the bench with her chin in her hands, her eyes tracing the path of a caterpillar inching across the table on sixteen tiny feet.

Jared walked over and sat down across from her. "Whatcha doing, Elly?"

Elena kept her eyes on the caterpillar. "Daddy, do you know how to tell the difference between a caterpillar that's going to turn into a butterfly and one that's going to turn into a moth? Ms. Huntley told us that moths come from caterpillars too. But how do you tell which is which?"

Jared observed the insect still charting a determined course toward the table's edge. It was long and thin and a yellow shade of green with hairy spines sprouting out in organized clusters across its body. "I don't have any idea, sweetheart. That would be a good question to ask Ms. Huntley when school starts back."

"This one's going to be a butterfly," Elena said resolutely.

"Oh? How can you tell?"

She shrugged. "Just by looking at it, I guess."

Jared took another look at the caterpillar and frowned. From examining the creature himself, saying what would come out of its cocoon would have been a toss-up. Yet if there existed a bookie offering toss-up odds on this strange wager, Jared would have bet the farm.

It was uncanny how often Elena was right about trivial things like this. Eerie even, at times. He had long ago concluded that his youngest daughter's mind somehow worked differently than most—accessed little tidbits of information that were hidden from everyone else. To take it any further than this (perhaps, if he was honest, to even give the appropriate name to the very thing he was describing) would be to violate his rejection of all things fantastical. Ever the naturalist, this was something Jared could not accept. Yet nothing had ever challenged this resolve more over the years than his youngest daughter. Her very survival after being born fourteen weeks premature was the kind of thing that even the moderately religious would've proclaimed a miracle.

"You want a turn on the swing?" Jared asked.

"No thanks, Daddy. Timmy can go again."

Jared watched her for a while as she continued to watch the caterpillar, searching for any sign of discontent. It had taken quite some time for him to adjust to Elena's withdrawn nature. Even now after nine years of acclimation, he mistook it sometimes for sadness. Yet Jared had come to realize over the years that rare were the occasions when Elena really was unhappy. If she was withdrawn, it was only because whatever world she had fashioned within her imagination was where she preferred to be.

And so it was now, Jared accepted, getting up from the picnic table and leaving Elena to her daydreams. "You want one more turn, bud?" Timmy cheered and hopped back on the swing.

After pushing the swing for so long that his shoulders grew sore, Jared went back inside, showered, and poured a bowl full of potato chips to take with him to the living room. He'd eaten lunch not two hours ago, but entertaining Timmy was always hungry work. At least that's what he told himself as an excuse; the furnace of a metabolism he had enjoyed as a younger man was starting to fade, and his days of guilt-free indulgence were officially over.

He sank down into the cloth recliner known collectively by all the household as "Dad's chair" and sighed. It had been a long five workdays to make it to this Sunday, each one of them bringing some unique new pain in the ass. These stresses at work made it hard to tell if the medication was helping yet after his first full week of taking it, but it didn't seem to be. The knot in his chest was still as tight and toxic as ever, and the nightmares still came on their inexplicable schedule as fierce as always. He had been able to keep two out of the three secret from Melody, with her only knowing of the nightmare on Wednesday night when he cried out in his sleep loud enough to wake her. She didn't know how often they afflicted him, and she certainly didn't know that they came on a schedule.

The nightmares always happened three nights a week but with no pattern beyond this. At the start of a new week, there was no way for him to know which nights he'd be spared. Sometimes they would be spaced out so that he was forced to go to bed almost every night of the week dreading what might come. Other times they would hit him three days in a row, right from the start, pummeling him into submission. Jared didn't know which was worse.

What he did know was that there was nothing to gain from telling Melody this. All it would do was frighten her. So, when he heard the sound of someone coming down the staircase and glanced up to see his wife gliding into the living room, his heart sped up a little. As if even thinking about it in her presence would somehow give it away.

"Hey, honey, have you seen my mouse? I had it last night, but now I can't find it anywhere."

"Try putting out some cheese. Maybe you can coax it out."

"You're so hilarious," Melody said, deadpan. Jared winked at her. "But really, though. Have you seen it?"

"Not since last night. Should be somewhere in the bedroom still."

Melody sighed. "Not anywhere that I looked. It's not that big of a deal for now, anyway. I was just wondering if you knew where it was."

"Sorry."

"So whatcha up to for the rest of the day?" she asked, still hovering near the foot of the staircase.

"Absolutely nothing," Jared said with a grin. "In fact, why don't we order a pizza or something tonight? We can cook the pork some other night and just be lazy today."

"Sounds good to me. I've just got a couple things to finish up for work. Shouldn't take more than an hour or so. I'm surprised you're not busy with your new printer thingy. Wasn't that supposed to come in today?"

Jared perked up. "Damn, I honestly forgot about it."

He had ordered a desktop 3D printer from some science website a couple of weeks ago. It seemed like it would be a fun thing to tinker with and a good way to keep himself occupied for a while during the times when there was nothing better to do. The website had sent him an email on Wednesday saying that it had been shipped and was scheduled for a Sunday arrival—an email that had since slipped his mind.

"Might be on the porch," Melody called back, now halfway up the stairs. "They don't always knock."

Suddenly eager again to try out his new toy, Jared rose and walked to the front door. When he opened it, there were two packages sitting next to the potted plant they kept on the porch. One about the size and shape of a large microwave and the other a small, rectangular box. He had ordered a few rolls of plastic filament along with the printer, and the company must have shipped it separately.

Jared knelt to pick up the larger box but paused. It wasn't unusual that the company would ship the products in separate packages. What *was* unusual was how different the two packages looked. The bigger one was brown with beige packing tape and the company's logo stamped onto a big, white shipping label. The smaller one was white with clear packing tape and no shipping label. In the place where every company large enough to sell a full catalog of scientific supplies would certainly have put a shipping label, there was instead handwritten text.

Jared felt the ever-present knot in his chest squeeze tight around his heart. He knew even before he picked up the smaller package and read the return address what it was and who it was from.

It was heavier than he expected. A sickening heft suggesting a volume thick with ink-filled pages. Holding it in his hands felt suddenly wrong, even with the tightly taped package obscuring it from view. He glanced across the lawn at the trash bin near the end of the driveway. He could throw it in there, stuff it down deep so that Melody wouldn't see it if she took the trash out, and never think about it again. Burning it package and all seemed the more appropriate option, but there was no way to do that without getting caught.

Yet when Jared rose back to his feet with the package still clutched in his hands, he turned without thinking back toward the door. He stopped in front of it. Was he really about to bring this awful thing into his home? Was he really going to open it and read what was inside? The urge to do just those things was strangely sudden and strong. It felt almost as if the book inside the package was beckoning to him with some unheard siren call, bending him to its will.

The thought sent a chill down Jared's neck. He turned away from the door and marched across the lawn to the trash bin. He shoved the package deep beneath the pile of bags inside, then closed the lid. The garbage truck would come on Tuesday. And then it would be gone forever.

He took a moment to collect himself before he went back inside. To calm the shakiness in his breath and the tremble in his hands.

"Fuck," he swore under his breath so the neighbors wouldn't hear. It would be bad enough already if one of them were to see him leaning against the trash bin and looking like he'd just laid eyes on a demon.

It wasn't healthy to be getting worked up like this. The nights brought too much fear for him to suffer it in the daylight. He hated his brother for sending it to him. He thought of reaching for his phone to call him and curse him out right there on the lawn, neighbors be damned. Instead, Jared opened the bin one more time to make sure the package was well hidden, then went back inside.

SEVEN

SUNDAY, JUNE 17ᵀᴴ

It had taken only six hours for Jared to break down and retrieve the package from the trash bin. Truth be told, he would have done it much sooner if not for having to wait until Melody and the kids had gone to bed.

The moment he'd turned away, the urge to pull it back out of the bin had been impossible to ignore. Normally, Jared was good at pushing back against self-destructive compulsions. Good at not letting emotion or even curiosity get the better of him. But not this time. This time, the compulsion was overwhelming. So unnaturally overwhelming that it made his stomach turn.

If he could have burned it, then none of this would have been a problem. He could have mustered the few moments of resolve it would've taken to douse it in gas and set it ablaze. That would have been permanent. Would have left no room for temptation.

But it was too late now. He had already fished it out of the bin and brought it back inside. He had already opened it and found exactly what he'd been afraid to see. Now, the leatherbound journal that Greg Gordon had used to catalog his two-and-a-half-year plunge into madness was sitting on Jared's workbench in the garage.

Driven by impulses that didn't make sense, Jared flipped open the book's front cover and began to read.

FROM THE JOURNAL OF GREG GORDON
ENTRY #1: DATED 11/11/1993

I've never been one to keep a diary or a journal or anything like that. It always seemed to me like nothing more than a good way to get your secrets exposed. But Dr. Haywood says it might help.

It's been twelve days since I was diagnosed with paranoid schizophrenia. I'd like to think that I've come to some kind of terms with it by now. I know there are meds I can take. Dr. Haywood says that there are lots of people with my condition who go on to live normal, happy lives.

It's difficult to say when my symptoms started. Sometime this year, for sure. I've been feeling anxious and irritable for several months now. Borderline hostile at times. But I did a good enough job of keeping these feelings suppressed, and the thought of seeing someone about it never crossed my mind.

Then the paranoia and the nightmares came. That started sometime around August. I'd spend the whole day convinced someone was following me. It felt like I was being watched everywhere I went.

The nights are the worst. I dream all manner of horrible things when I sleep. The only mercy is that I'm spared from remembering most of it. I wake up in a panic with only the most fleeting recollection of the nightmare that caused it. The fear subsides after a while, but it never really goes away.

Three weeks ago was when I started to hear the voices. It hasn't been a constant thing. The doctor calls the times when I hear them "psychotic episodes." He says that the condition can come and go like that. It's been happening more often lately, but he says the medication will help if I give it time.

I will not let this disease destroy my family. I will do whatever is necessary to keep that from happening. For now, that means taking my pills, keeping this journal, and trying my damndest to keep a positive disposition.

Jared heard the sound of footsteps in the kitchen approaching the door to the garage. He shut the journal and tucked it away into the workbench's drawer. The door opened.

"How's the printer?" Melody asked, then noticed the 3D printer still in its unopened package atop the workbench. "Oh. Never mind."

"I was just clearing off a space for it."

It was a feeble excuse. The workbench was still a clutter, and the words had come out a little more strained than Jared had intended. But Melody took it in stride, probably not really interested enough to question it. She had never been much of a tech junkie.

"Try not to stay out here too long, okay? I don't want to fall asleep by myself."

"You know what, I'll just finish setting it up tomorrow."

Melody smiled. Jared stood up, casting a quick glance at the drawer where he'd hidden the journal. Tomorrow he would find an opportunity to slip away into the woods behind the house and burn the thing.

He couldn't have it here, so close to where he slept. And if burning it was the only way to stop the strange allure that had made him bring it back inside in the first place, then burn it he would.

He followed Melody back into the house and up the stairs to their bedroom. They made love—even though his heart wasn't really in it. He had been distant ever since the nightmares started. Uninterested in intimacy. Melody had been too patient and understanding to say it aloud, but he could sense the longing in her he had lately been failing to fulfill. So when she brushed her hand against his chest and let it trail down his stomach, Jared couldn't bring himself to deny her.

She fell asleep with her head on his shoulder, breathing softly against his neck. Before long and despite it all, Jared was sleeping soundly too.

EIGHT

MONDAY, JUNE 18TH

Jared groaned and rolled over onto his back, confused when he opened his eyes and saw that the bedroom was still dark. He had a recurring alarm on his phone set to wake him up at 7:30 every weekday, but the sun had evidently not yet risen. As he grew more awake and aware, he realized that the sporadic ringing that had woken him wasn't coming from his phone. The tone was different, and the noise came from downstairs instead of the nightstand by his bed.

It's the doorbell, Jared realized, a spurt of adrenaline bringing him fully awake. He glanced at the clock on his nightstand. It was 2:45 a.m.

He looked to see if the noise had woken Melody as well, but her side of the bed was empty, the covers kicked down to the foot of the mattress. Where was she? Surely she hadn't gone to answer the door at this time of night without even waking him first.

Downstairs, the doorbell continued to ring. Jared rose, not bothering to throw on more clothes than the boxers he was wearing, and headed out the bedroom door. By the time he made it across the hall to the top of the stairs, the frequency of the chimes had increased. There was no pause between rings now. They came one right after the other—the rings of a person who desperately wanted inside.

Across the living room, the door loomed large in front of him, both it and the doorbell's constant chiming seeming such menacing things at this late hour of the night. Jared strained to see if he could make out a figure behind the small pane of glass in the door, but all he could see was darkness.

Don't open it, a voice inside his head warned him as he set his hand against the deadbolt. *Turn around and go back to bed. Let them ring all night if they want, but do not open it.*

Jared turned the lock and opened the door.

His eyes widened and he let out a startled cry. Standing on the porch in front of him was his mother. Or what remained of her at least. Her skin was shriveled and riddled with rot. Only a few clumps of brown hair still stuck to her yellowed scalp, wet and matted with fresh mud. She gazed at him with milky eyes and continued to ring the doorbell with one decaying finger.

Jared stumbled back and fell to the living room floor. A jolt of pain shot through his hip. Seeming to notice him for the first time, the corpse of his dead mother followed him inside.

She leered over him. Her mouth stretched open impossibly wide—a cavern of toothless decay. "They are here, son," the dead woman moaned, kneeling in front of him. Jared could feel her breath against his face, cold as winter wind and smelling like rotted meat. "They came for your father. Now *they* are coming for you."

She reached out and placed a shriveled hand against his leg. The feel of cold, leathery skin and twig-like bones was more than Jared could bear. He screamed, lunging up with as much force as he could muster and swinging blindly.

His left fist struck something solid. Pain erupted in his knuckles—somehow much more vivid and real than anything he'd felt thus far. The room began to swim, and Jared's vision faded.

When he opened his eyes again, he was alone in the living room. The front door was closed and locked, and the soft, orange light of sunrise shone through its glass pane. Beside the door was a fist-sized hole in the drywall, and Jared's left hand throbbed. He could feel a small stream of blood running from his knuckles down the back of his arm.

"Jared?" he heard his wife say. He turned to see her standing at the bottom of the stairs, her eyes wide.

"I, uh…there was someone at the door, and I…"

"You had another one, didn't you?" Melody asked. Then, before he had time to respond, "Come on. Let's get a bandage on that cut."

Still drowning in confusion, Jared followed her back up the stairs.

NINE

MONDAY, JUNE 18TH

The day passed by with all the sluggishness of a typical Monday compounded by a heaping dose of sleep deprivation. Jared had accomplished next to nothing at his job as a financial analyst for Cox Enterprises. He had drifted off at his desk and slept for a substantial part of the morning, then had spent more time in the afternoon staring at the clock than working on the risk assessment reports that were due Thursday.

His manager—a pompous but effective woman named Shirley Stein—had surely noticed; she'd passed by Jared's office several times throughout the day. But today, Jared didn't care. The memory of his early morning night terror was all that he could think about. Most of the nightmares slipped from his mind like melting frost the moment he woke, but somehow every detail of this last one had been branded into his memory. He remembered the smell of mold and decay that grew strong enough to choke him as the corpse crawled closer. He remembered the inhuman sound of her voice, nothing at all like the soft and cooing voice that used to read fairy tales to him and his brother.

It had been as real as anything he had ever experienced. He felt ridiculous even considering such a thing, but Jared couldn't shake the feeling

that it hadn't been a night terror at all. That it had all actually happened. That the reanimated corpse of his six-years-deceased mother
really had visited him in the night and that he had passed out from the
fear only to be found by Melody hours later after the sun had risen.

It was a theory so absurd that it shouldn't have required counter-
evidence for Jared to dismiss, but there was indeed a strong point of
evidence against it. Melody claimed to have woken from the sound of
him punching the wall and come downstairs at once. It had been dark
when he answered the door and daylight when Melody found him. If
little to no time had passed between those two events, then the first one
couldn't have been real.

Driving home, Jared scolded himself for running through this point-
less exercise. Of course the nightmare had not been real. He'd have to
be a lunatic to think it was. So why was he having to work so hard to
convince himself it wasn't?

Because it felt real, Jared thought.

That was the answer. And if something felt real—if it was experienced as an event that was as real as any other event that a person has
ever experienced—didn't it become real in all practical senses? Jared
saw his dead mother last night. He smelled her rotting breath and felt
her rotting skin. Whether or not all that took place within the agreed-
upon realm of reality had no bearing on how horrible it had been.

Jared cranked the radio in the car a little higher. His street was just
another mile down the road. Unless she had some errand to run,
Melody would be there when he arrived. Jared steeled himself for what
was sure to come. He hadn't felt like talking in the morning after it had
happened, and Melody had taken the cue. But she'd made no attempt
to hide her concern, and a long conversation was surely forthcoming.

Jared wasn't often one to shy away from hard conversations, but this
one didn't seem to have any point. Either the medication would work

or it wouldn't. Either the nightmares and the anxiety were temporary, fixable symptoms of stress, or they were permanent—symptoms of a disease chronic and impossible to cure. Melody knew this as well as he did. So what more was there to say?

He would find out soon enough. Pulling into the driveway, he saw Melody sitting on the front porch. She rose and met him at the car.

"Hey, babe," Jared said when the driver's side door was open. "What's up?"

"Just been waiting on you to get home," Melody said. "I was thinking we could go for a drive. Grace said she'd watch Timmy and Elena."

"Where to?"

"Nowhere in particular. Just somewhere that we can talk without little ears listening in."

"Right," Jared said, resisting the urge to sigh. "Hop in." He slid back into the seat he'd just left, and Melody sat down in the passenger seat beside him. Once she'd buckled in, Jared pulled out of the drive.

There was silence between them for a while before Melody finally broke it. "What happened this morning, Jared?"

"I had another night terror, Mel. That's all there is to it."

"But you sleepwalked again. It's the sleepwalking during them that worries me more than anything."

"Dr. Stewart said it might take six weeks for the pills to start working."

"Maybe you need a stronger prescription?"

Jared shook his head. He didn't like the way the medication made him feel even on its current dose. It made him groggy and dulled, thus far without much positive trade-off.

"I'm worried about you," Melody said, putting words to a feeling that was already etched across her face.

"I'll be okay, Mel."

"Jared, you punched a hole in our wall. In your sleep."

"And I'll fix it too. I can do it this afternoon if you want to go pick up the supplies."

"That's not the point," Melody said. "What if next time you end up really hurting yourself? Or hurting me or one of the children."

"That won't happen," Jared said, a little offended. "You know I wouldn't do that."

"You wouldn't punch a hole in the wall either if you could help it. These new night terrors are getting dangerous, Jared. Just look at your hand."

"It's just a cut. And yeah, I know. I know. That's not the point. But I don't know what you want me to do about it, Mel. We've just gotta hope the medicine does what it's supposed to."

The next question went unspoken, but Jared could tell it was on both their minds. What if the meds didn't work? What if Jared's genetic dice had come up snake eyes and this was only the beginning? Only time would tell, and until then, he preferred to think about it as little as possible.

"I know it isn't your fault," Melody said. "I don't want it to seem like I'm coming down on you. I'm just worried, sweetheart."

"I get it, Mel. I'm sure it hasn't been easy for you. Or the kids either, for that matter. And it definitely hasn't been easy for me."

"What were you dreaming about anyway? What is it you were punching at?"

"A rabid dog," Jared lied. "I was being attacked by a rabid dog."

"Like Cujo?" Melody asked, stifling a smile.

"Bigger. It was more of a rabid wolf, really. I know it sounds kind of silly now, but it was plenty terrifying at the time, trust me."

He felt guilty lying to her so baldly. But the truth was just too grim. Even more, it was wholly unnecessary. Telling her the truth in this situation helped no one. Softening it down to something that even King couldn't make all that frightening only served to make things easier for them both.

"Do you want to go pick up the stuff to fix the wall?" he asked.

"We might as well. I certainly haven't enjoyed looking at it today." Happy to shift focus to a problem he could actually solve, Jared turned the Camry left onto Cherry Street and headed toward the hardware store.

While Jared focused on installing a new square of drywall, Melody and Emily were in the kitchen cooking dinner. Timmy was in his room playing with his toys, Grace was out with her friends, and Elena was helping him fix the wall, per Jared's request.

"Would you hand me the spackling, sweetie?" he asked.

"This one?" asked Elena, presenting him with a small tub of DryDex.

"That's it." Jared took the spackling from her hands and tore open the seal. He dipped a putty knife into the thick, white goo and began spreading it over the new square of drywall he'd placed in the wall.

"Can I ask you something?" Elena said. Something in her tone told him she'd been building up the courage to ask even this.

"Sure. Ask away."

"Is there a God?"

Jared stopped what he was doing. He'd expected her to ask why they were having to fix a hole in the wall and already had a white lie prepared. But this was a question he hadn't been expecting. "I don't think I can answer that, Elly. I don't think anyone can. But I will say that Mommy and I don't believe in God."

"What about the devil?"

"No, Elly," Jared said, a little bothered by the question for reasons he couldn't pinpoint. "We don't believe in the devil either." Elena seemed to consider this, then said no more. "Would you hand me that can of paint and the paint roller? We're almost done here."

She did, and Jared applied a coat of paint over the patch of repaired wall. Before long, the repaired section blended almost perfectly with the rest of the wall. Once the paint dried, Jared was confident that it wouldn't be noticeable at all.

"Dinner's ready," he heard Melody call from the kitchen.

"Perfect timing," Jared said to Elena. "Wash your hands and let's go eat."

"I have another question first," Elena said.

"What's your question, Elly?"

"Who was at the door this morning?"

"No one was at the door," Jared said. "Daddy just hit the wall on accident because he was having a bad dream."

Elena looked confused, her small face scrunching up a little as if she had analyzed Jared's response and found it wanting. "But I heard the doorbell. And when I looked downstairs, I saw a woman in our living room. She didn't seem very nice."

Jared felt like she'd just kicked him in the balls. "No one was at the door, Elly," he said, though it felt now like he was trying to convince himself more than her. "I had a bad dream, and I was probably talking in my sleep. I bet that's what you heard. And it was probably just me that you saw too."

"Okay," Elena said. But she didn't seem very convinced.

Jared cleared his throat. "Let's go eat, okay?"

Elena nodded and followed him into the kitchen. A few minutes ago, the smell of taco meat coming from the stove had been tantalizing. Now, though, Jared had lost his appetite.

TEN

TUESDAY, JUNE 19TH

Tuesday morning came far too early, with the sound of Jared's 7:30 alarm heralding the arrival of a day he wasn't ready to face. When the ringing first started, he had jolted awake, thinking he'd been sucked into a repeat of the previous night's night terror. Once he realized it was his phone making the sound and not the doorbell, it took longer than it should've for the feeling to pass.

Jared groaned and turned off the alarm. The night may have been nightmare-free—dream-free for that matter—but sleep had still not come easy. He'd been plagued all night with thoughts of Elena and the details from his night terror she had fed back to him with inexplicable accuracy. It didn't make any sense. It wasn't rational. And yet it had happened. She had somehow peered into his mind and retrieved information that only he knew.

It wasn't the first time she'd done something like this—only one of the more extreme instances. Elena had always exhibited a piercingly keen sense of awareness. She would guess with little trouble at all what she was getting for Christmas or her birthday no matter how hard he and Melody tried to keep it a surprise. The day before the family cat was killed in the street by some punk teenager driving faster than he should have been, Elena had cried all night, convinced beyond consolability that something bad was going to happen to Muffin. Now, absurd as it sounded, she seemed to have peeked into his dreams—as if his mind was a theater and his nightmare a film she snuck in to watch.

Maybe there was some perfectly logical explanation besides this, but Jared couldn't see one. Ultimately, the explanation that Elena was somehow able to tune in to the mental frequency of others in a way that let her catch a stray signal now and then was much less disconcerting than the only other explanation: that his daughter really *had* heard the doorbell ringing. That she really *had* peered down from the top of the stairs and seen a dead woman in their living room.

Coming to a conclusion he could live with was an exhausting exercise that'd taken Jared half the night. Deliberating on what it meant for his youngest daughter—or anyone, for that matter—to be capable of such things had taken up most of the other half, so that by the time sheer mental and physical fatigue finally pulled him down into a shallow sleep, the sun had already begun to rise outside his bedroom window.

Now, Jared felt a body not near as resilient as it used to be protesting its lack of rest. He showered and dressed and drank a cup of coffee. It would be another long day at work, that much was clear. With the risk assessment reports due in two days, he had no choice but to be productive. But the longing to crawl back under the blankets and stay there until lunch was almost strong enough to make getting fired worth the trade-off. He could call in sick, he supposed. He didn't do that very often. Except that wouldn't do anything to change the fact that the reports were due Thursday and there was no way he could get them all done tomorrow.

Jared took a long gulp of coffee and resigned himself to his fate. He plucked his car keys off the counter and went into the garage. He fumbled at the button on the wall, and the garage door squeaked and rumbled open. The tangerine light of early dawn filtered in through the door's widening gap. Jared squinted against it and made for the door of his Camry.

He stopped before he opened it, peering over the top of the car at the workbench on the other side. The journal was still there in its drawer. After his night terror, then Elena's troubling observations, Jared had forgotten about it.

Maybe it was the cause of his night terror. Perhaps not the cause of the dream itself, but almost certainly the cause of its subject. He should have destroyed it like he'd intended to. He never should have brought it inside, and he certainly should have never opened it.

Jared let go of the door handle and walked over to the workbench. He slid open the drawer and took out the journal. It felt vile to hold it in his hands. Like holding the very rope that ended his father's life. Yet the pull of the words inside was still as strong as ever. It was strange how a thing could be so alluring and so revolting at the same time. Such a queasy paradox that it set off the ring of some alarm deep inside his mind—like a tuning fork struck hard and left untouched.

Jared tucked the journal underneath his arm and got into the car. He was being foolish letting it get his anxiety ramped up like this. The journal was an awful thing that reminded him of awful times. But nothing more. He'd swing by the dumpster behind work and throw it away there. Then all he'd have to do was forget it ever existed.

With the journal tucked inside the glove compartment, Jared backed out of the garage and drove away.

ELEVEN

TUESDAY, JUNE 19TH

FROM THE JOURNAL OF GREG GORDON
ENTRY #9: DATED 12/02/1993

I knew this wasn't going to be a bed of roses. I understood that there would be dark days ahead before things had any chance of getting better. But this is more than I can bear.

My symptoms defy all reason. Audible and visual hallucinations. Terror that never goes away. Nightmares that last from the moment I close my eyes to the moment I open them again. But worst of all is the feeling like the whole world is rotting. I see it in the eyes of my sons and smell it in my wife's hair. It permeates everything, everywhere I go.

Dr. Haywood insists that all this is nothing the medication can't at least dampen down to tolerable if I'm patient. But in the two weeks since I've been taking it, I've only been getting worse.

There's a seed growing in the pits of my mind. An idea of what's happening to me that is far different from Dr. Haywood's diagnosis. I can feel it starting to take root. I still know that I am sick. I still know that this seed and all the horrors I'm experiencing are symptoms of my disease. But it is there, and it is growing. And if I'm not able to snuff it out soon, it will take over my mind like ivy strangling a tree.

What will remain of me if it does? How much destruction can a mad dog cause? Already, I feel nothing but inexplicable fear when I look at my family. God forbid the day comes that I can't keep myself from acting on it.

A knock against the car window caused Jared's heart to leap. On impulse, he slammed the journal closed.

The freckle-faced KFC employee standing beside his car blushed a little, seeming embarrassed for having startled him. Jared rolled down the window.

"I'm sorry, sir, but would you mind pulling into a different space? These three spaces here are reserved for customers who are picking up an order."

"Sure," Jared said. "No problem. I was just finishing up anyway."

"Sorry again that the dining room was so crowded. Can I throw that away for you?" the young girl said, gesturing to the crumpled brown bag on his passenger seat.

"Thanks. I appreciate it." Jared handed her the bag. He wondered if she'd be able to tell from its heft that there was still a barely touched meal inside. From the moment he'd gotten into his car to go out for lunch, all that he'd been able to think about was the journal in the glove compartment. He had taken only a single bite out of his sandwich before the temptation took him and he spent the remainder of his lunch hour reading from where he'd last left off.

Reading this latest entry brought up memories of the holiday season his junior year. There'd been nothing merry about that Christmas. Right as the nights were growing their longest and the days their coldest was when his father's condition had really started to deteriorate. It had been just after Thanksgiving when his father started to question whether he was actually ill at all—*the seed*, as he'd described it in his journal. And just as poor Greg Gordon predicted, it had indeed germinated into a ruinous thing.

Jared put the journal back inside the glove compartment and drove back to the office. Mustering a much-needed second wind of motivation despite his trepid lunchtime reading, he was able to finish a little more than half of the reports by five o'clock. His head was throbbing by the end, and his fingers were stiff. It felt like staring at a computer screen for another minute might cause his eyes to melt.

He drove home slower than normal, fearing that any moment he might drift off and stray across the yellow line. When he finally made it home and through the back door, Melody was there in the kitchen to greet him.

"Long day?" she said.

"That obvious, huh?"

"Well, I was about to start dinner, but on second thought, what do you say we go out tonight? Maybe Puesta De Sol? I can drive if you want. It's up to you."

Jared considered it. He was exhausted enough to curl up right there on the kitchen tiles, but hungry too. Puesta De Sol made a fajita platter that sounded mouthwatering after having only a cup of coffee for breakfast and a single bite of chicken for lunch. Plus, he hated taking naps even on days like this; they always seemed to screw with his sleep later that night and thus create a vicious cycle.

"Sure," Jared said. "Mexican sounds great. Just let me shower and change and I'll be ready."

"I'll go tell the kids."

The shower turned out to do Jared a world of good. He stayed in there longer than usual, but there was no rush; in a house with four women, he was never the last one to be ready for an outing.

He dried off and put on a pair of khaki shorts and a gray polo shirt, feeling at least marginally refreshed. He put on deodorant and a spray of cologne, then went back downstairs.

It took another thirty minutes before the entire family was able to load into Melody's Chevy Tahoe and drive to Puesta De Sol. By the time they were seated, Jared's stomach was starting to snarl.

"What can I get you guys to drink?" a waitress with short, dark curls and a name tag that read "Olivia" asked.

The six of them ordered drinks, then a few minutes later their food. Olivia came back to the table with a basket of corn chips and a bowl of salsa, which Jared went after with enthusiasm.

"So your dad and I were talking earlier this week about driving up to Lake Lanier Saturday," Melody said. "Pack a lunch, do some swimming, get some tans. What do you guys think?"

Jared had forgotten about that conversation. At the time, it had seemed like a good idea. He'd thought maybe a few hours of warm sun and cool water might do him some good. But now the week had already exhausted him to the point that spending the weekend doing anything other than relaxing at home was nearly unthinkable. Perhaps he'd feel different by Saturday, but if not, he'd have to be the one to disappoint the kids, and he wished Melody hadn't brought it up.

"Can we invite Jackson?" Emily asked.

Again, not something Jared wanted to hear. He didn't have any real reason to dislike the guy. Nothing other than the fact that Jackson was the pimple-faced high schooler dating his sixteen-year-old daughter. But that was more than reason enough.

"We'll talk about it," Melody said, glancing at Jared.

"I'm definitely down," Grace said. "I actually just bought a new swim-suit yesterday."

"What do you think, Elena?" Melody asked.

Elena looked up from the straw wrapper she was twisting and tearing between her fingers. If she was excited about the idea of a weekend lake trip, it didn't show.

"What's the matter?" Melody asked.

Elena sighed and dropped her eyes back down to her lap. "Do you think it would be okay if I stayed home?"

"Why would you want to stay home, Elly?" Jared asked. He wasn't any more thrilled about the trip than she was, but her lack of enthusi-asm bothered him. She was a kid. Normal kids weren't supposed to ask if they could stay home when the family was going to the lake.

"I'm just not supposed to stay gone for very long is all," Elena said.

Jared chuckled despite his creeping unease. "Says who, honey?"

Elena didn't look up at him. She continued to worry at the straw wrapper. "He just told me not to stay gone for very long."

"Who told you that?" Melody asked.

Elena's face flushed a little as if she'd said something she shouldn't have. Jared watched her with an eagerness that bordered on anxiety; the way she had recited details from his previous night terror was still heavy on his mind.

"Who told you that, Elena?" Melody asked again. Jared noticed a touch of concern in her voice now as well.

"His name's Ronny," Elena finally said.

"Who's Ronny?" Jared asked.

Elena shrugged. "Just someone I play with sometimes."

"Is Ronny a real person, Elena?" Melody asked, "Or is he…"

She trailed off, but Jared knew that "imaginary" was the word she'd left unspoken, likely afraid their daughter would grow defensive if she suggested that her friend wasn't real. Elena shrugged again. She looked from the straw wrapper she was still picking at and gave a wan smile.

"I don't think he's a person," she said and giggled a little. "He looks really funny most of the time."

Grace rolled her eyes, but Melody shut down any further remarks with a glancing look. "Well, Ronny will just have to be okay with you going out for a while this weekend," she said. She glanced at Jared, flashing him a look of mild concern. At nine years old, Elena should have been past the imaginary friend stage, especially since she had never had one in her younger years. It was something that Jared would have expected more from five-year-old Timmy than her. Still, she had a creative mind, of that there was no denying, and Jared knew better than most that creative minds sometimes express themselves in odd ways.

He noticed that Elena had grown distant again. Her smile was gone, and, having shredded the straw wrapper into pieces that littered the floor beneath her feet, she stared down at her empty hands. "He won't like that very much," she said.

"Well, I'll just have to have a talk with Ronny, then," Jared said. "Straighten him out." He tried to keep his tone jovial, but the worry gnawing fiercer and fiercer was hard to ignore. Perhaps under normal circumstances, he would not have taken Elena having an imaginary friend too seriously. But after the things she'd known about his nightmare, he couldn't help but see it through a different lens. Even before this conversation, just looking at her had made him uneasy—as much as he hated himself for it.

Elena met his eyes, her own suddenly wide. She shook her head. "He wouldn't like that either, Daddy."

A chill made the hairs on Jared's neck go rigid. He swallowed a mouthful of soda and let the shiver pass. There was no point trying to explain his simmering fear. There was almost certainly no rationale behind it. Either way, he was done talking about Ronny.

"Okay, Elly," he said. "But we may go to the lake this weekend and that's that. We'll talk about your friend later, but I don't want to hear any more about him tonight, okay?"

Elena nodded, and the waitress returned with their food. The sound of sizzling fajita meat still cooking in its cast iron skillet filled the air, and Jared could feel the heat coming off it. His mouth watered a little when its spicy scent hit his nose.

"You guys enjoy," Olivia said. Despite it all, Jared intended to.

TWELVE

FRIDAY, JUNE 22ND

FROM THE JOURNAL OF GREG GORDON
ENTRY #13: DATED 12/14/1993

Something is watching me as I write this. I know that it is here. The hairs on my arms stand up every time it enters the room.

I believe its voice is the one that I'm hearing. It speaks to me somehow in a way that no one else can hear. Day and night, it murmurs unspeakable things.

I have read every book on psychiatric disorders that I can find. I have listened to cassettes of lectures from the world's most prominent psychiatrists. The symptoms they describe when they discuss even the most severe cases of schizophrenia psychosis pale in comparison to what I am experiencing.

I have seen things. Shadows that move in the corners of my eyes. Shadows that loom over the shoulders of Linda and the boys just long enough for me to blink before they're gone.

I can feel it inside of me. It's growing like a tumor in my brain, leaching toxins that infect my every thought.

Something has come for me. I do not know its true nature. Maybe it is indeed just what Dr. Haywood insists. A severe case of psychosis that will become less severe in time. Or maybe it's something else entirely. Whatever it may be, it has come for me with more rage and hatred than I could have ever imagined. And the worst of all is knowing for certain that the worst is yet to come.

ENTRY #14: DATED 12/18/1993

I had a dream two nights ago. A nightmare really, but all my dreams are such these days. I dreamed of Jeremiah. I saw him floating in the sky, just above the tops of the trees near the woods behind our house. His shoulders were slack, and his head was drooped. It looked like he was sleeping.

There was something in the forest behind him. I couldn't get a look at it, I'm not sure there'd be anything to see if I did, but I could feel it. It was the same thing that I feel watching me all hours of the day, but stronger now. Big enough to cover the entire woods in its shade.

Then I saw Jeremiah lift his head and open his eyes. His face was as white as fresh bone. It looked like he was dead. And when he opened his eyes, I saw in their place two voids of solid black. Empty and infinite like portals to another universe.

He started speaking to me then. Speaking to me in the same dark language as the thing inside my mind. It felt like I stood there barefoot in the grass listening to him for hours. And it felt like the words he spoke might drive me mad.

Yet when I woke, it was just another nightmare. No more terrible or more meaningful than any of the rest. By midday I'd forgotten it, too caught up with present terrors.

It was only this morning near six a.m. as I sat watching the sun rise from my bedroom window that I remembered my dream. Through the window, I saw someone emerge from the forest. When I rubbed my sleeve against the glass to get a clearer view, I could tell it was Jeremiah.

There were no chores for him to be doing at this early hour. Most certainly none in the dense and overgrown thicket behind our house. There's nothing out there at all but briars and brambles and poison oak.

He lied to me when I asked him about it at breakfast. He looked me in the eye and lied to me with his mother and older brother watching on. My boys don't lie, and they sure as hell aren't supposed to be good at it. But when I asked him what he was doing in the woods this morning, he pretended to have no idea what I was talking about in a manner so convincing that I almost began to question what I'd seen.

I don't know what it means seeing him come from those woods two days after dreaming the same, but I can feel its importance.

Something terrible happened last night while he was out there. Something permanent and devastating. I can still feel the fallout from it in the air.

I have to know what happened. If I'm going to have any chance of stopping what's coming, I have to know what he was doing out there. I feel as if much more than just my own life depends on it.

ENTRY #15: DATED 12/21/1993

I know what anyone who might read this journal someday is sure to think. In this moment of relative clarity and peace, I can't help but wonder myself if I am insane. But the things that follow such brief and rare moments are things too real and too awful for any psychotic condition to explain.

I have been targeted by something. Someone? I don't know their complete nature, but I do know that there is more than one. They told me that. I am cursed by the knowledge of the things they tell me.

I don't know what intentions they have for me or the purpose of their torment. Of that, they have said nothing. I can only pray that whatever it is involves only me and has nothing to do with my family. But I already know that Jeremiah is involved some-how, and I fear that Jared might be as well.

And, as of last night, I know their name. They showed it to me in a dream, carved into the earth as if by a plow beneath the

shadows of three upside-down crosses where my family hung cru-
cified. They have whispered it incessantly ever since, but to say
or even write it myself is almost too dreadful. I will write it this
once for the record, then no more.

Ra'Tak

Jared closed the journal. He'd made a terrible mistake reading it this far.
What was he thinking? What good could it possibly do to resurface
memories so frightening and painful? Least of all now in his compro-
mised state.

He remembered his father speaking that name. Not often, but once
or twice at the height of his psychosis when there was little left of the
man but a shaking and sobbing shell of his former self. His father's grand
delusion concerning that name was starting to come back to him too.

Greg Gordon had slipped the noose around his neck and stepped off
the stool convinced he was under assault by some supernatural force. A
supernatural force named Ra'Tak. It was a story no doubt born somewhere in the depths of his own diseased mind, but his conviction never
wavered. In just a matter of weeks, he had gone from understanding
that he was sick to hopelessly convinced of things too fantastical for
any sane mind to believe.

The worst was that he had somehow blamed Jeremiah for his imagined
circumstances. Jared too, to some degree. The details of how he and his
brother tied in to the delusion that ultimately took their father's life were
lost on him now, either forgotten or never known in the first place. But he
remembered how his father would look at Jeremiah in those days—with
fear and hate in his eyes. God, what a horrible thing to remember.

Jared found himself growing angry again. Angry at his half-wit
brother for sending him this awful thing and insisting that it offered

anything more than senseless pain. But this anger was misdirected, and he knew it. No one made him open the package. No one made him read and continue reading even as the words sliced open scars in his mind like a scalpel, rendering them again as fresh wounds.

And yet some part of him knew with a sick certainty that he would return sometime soon and read the rest. It was too late to stop now. He could scold himself, distance himself from it for a while, but it wouldn't matter. Its twisted allure was far too strong, and not knowing the rest seemed somehow more frightful than knowing.

But at this late hour, so close to the point when he'd be forced to surrender himself to his dreams, Jared could read no more. He rose from the workbench and turned off the garage light.

The darkness was complete, with not even a light on in the adjoining kitchen to filter through the cracks in the doorway and cast a glow across the garage.

He had just begun feeling his way across the door for the knob when a breeze brushed across his back. It was cooler than the rest of the air inside the room. Cool enough to chill his exposed skin. It whistled through the creases in the garage door, sounding eerie in this dark and otherwise silent space. Another gust pushed against the door. Another erratic whine as it forced itself inside and another chill against the back of his neck.

Ra'Tak.

The sound made Jared's breath catch. He whirled around, but all he could see was darkness. He slapped at the wall behind him in a panic, finally finding the light switch. Fluorescent light flooded the garage.

It was empty. Jared finally accepted this after scanning it corner to corner more than once. The garage door was still closed, and no one else was there.

He could hear the wind whipping and whistling outside, joined now by the pounding of his heart. It was the wind he had heard. It had produced some sound close enough to that horrible name, and Jared's imagination had done the rest. There was little doubt in his mind that this was true.

He turned the lights back off again. And in the darkness, that little seed of doubt began to grow.

THIRTEEN

SUNDAY, JUNE 24TH

Jared peered up at the sky, surprised by a small drop of rain that had splashed against his forearm. There'd been no rain in the forecast last he checked, but a haze of gray on the western horizon suggested an incoming storm.

Thunder murmured somewhere far away. Jared pulled his phone from his pocket and checked the time. It was 4:45, meaning Melody would be back from her dentist appointment any minute. When she'd left, Jared had thought he might appreciate the time alone. But now he was anxious for her return.

He'd spent most of this Sunday afternoon outside in the backyard, the sun and open space providing at least some relief from his growing despair.

Something was terribly wrong inside his mind. He could deny it no more. The entire past week had been marked by staggering depths of darkness. It wasn't just the places his mind went in his dreams and daydreams alike. It was a darkness that permeated his every experience. Turned the air foul and toxic, muted the colors, and cast the world in shades of gray. It cloyed his senses and tainted everything he touched like a spreading rot. And, when all of this wasn't enough, sometimes it spoke.

Such auditory hallucinations were rare thus far and always possible to dismiss as a passing car or a chirping bird. Or wind against a garage door. But they were becoming more common and harder to ignore.

All of it was growing harder to ignore. He had tried to disguise his recent deterioration as best he could from Melody. She knew that he was taking his medication and knew about some of the night terrors, but she had no idea how bad it had gotten. He justified keeping it from her with a promise to himself that he would tell her everything as soon as he was certain. Certain that the disease that claimed his father's life had now wrapped him, too, in its talons.

But how much more evidence did he need? The paranoia and the anxiety and the nightmares had still left room for hope that maybe it was just a rough patch and not the genetic land mine he'd been bracing for his whole life. The moment he started hearing the voices, any such hope vanished, crushed even further by the smothering depths of darkness that had opened up and swallowed Jared's mind.

No, there could be no more denying that something was terribly wrong. And yet the true nature of his circumstance still seemed just short of certainty. It was foolish at this point to entertain any idea other than the reality of his cruel yet perfectly logical condition. Dangerous, even, to entertain those that sometimes crossed his thoughts these recent, black days. But the feeling that there was something more to his downfall still persisted in the catacombs of his mind.

He had continued to read his father's journal even knowing that each entry would be brought to grisly life at night in his dreams. When he'd first opened it, it had seemed like a window to his painful past. Now, it seemed a window to his even more painful future.

The dates between entries in the journal were becoming more spaced apart, and his father's ramblings more desperate and disjointed. There were still plenty of pages left in the thick, leatherbound book, but most had no doubt been left unused. Jared could tell that he was nearing the volume's end.

It would be a mercy to be done with it. His father's crazed recordings were more haunting than Jared could have ever imagined. He wrote of torments no decent mind could conjure, carried out by the invisible hands of a group of beings Greg Gordon dared not write again by name. He wrote of how they molested him day and night, assaulting mind and body both yet somehow never inflicting more than temporary harm on the latter. Even the most gruesome of physical injuries he claimed they inflicted left no trace each time his panic subsided and his wits returned, leaving only the trauma of the experience for him to bear.

Much of what he wrote grew difficult to follow the more fragmented his tortured mind became. But there was one thing that his father rarely penned an entry without mentioning—that all his inexplicable sufferings were Jeremiah's fault.

Jeremiah had let them in. Jeremiah had performed the ritual that granted his tormentors access to the physical realm. Jeremiah had given them access to his family to use as their vessels.

His father wrote about how they commandeered the bodies of Jeremiah and Linda and even Jared to use as instruments in their wicked schemes. Reading such accounts of the things he'd been alleged to have done while his body was under their control made Jared nauseous each time, even knowing that none of it truly happened.

That was the important part. The *crucial* part. None of it had happened. None of it had happened to his father, and none of it was happening to him. With a wall of smoke-colored clouds fast encroaching and blotting the sun from the sky, Jared felt the need to remind himself of this once more. Already, he could feel the call of a voice far different than the voice of logic and reason he had listened to solely throughout his adult life. It was most powerful at night when he lay awake in the silence, staring into darkness and dreading the dreams to come. But even a moment as simple as a storm cloud rolling in to smother the one comfort he drew from this day could be enough to strengthen its hold.

Another drop of rain struck the top of his knee, then a few more behind it before Jared resigned himself to going back indoors. Alone again inside the house, he sat and listened to the sound of quickening rainfall splatter against the roof. Now and then, a sound like that of whispering voices seemed to mingle with the wind and rain. Trying to discern the words they spoke proved a maddening exercise. A senseless one too, Jared thought, gritting his teeth in frustration, for there were no voices and no words being spoken. Only the sounds of a summer thunderstorm, twisted into something else the moment they passed his ears by a clearly defective brain.

In his past musings of what it would be like if he did end up drawing the short straw and inheriting his father's condition, Jared had always imagined himself facing it with dignity and resolve, holding steadfast to the assurance that everything he experienced was nothing more than the product of biological processes gone wrong. But these were the assumptions of a sane mind. If it were so easy for the mentally ill to recognize the nature of their condition, then there'd be a lot less mentally ill. And if Jared was going to make it through this disease without succumbing to whatever fiction it wrote inside his mind, he was off to a horrible start.

At the sound of an approaching car and the sight of headlights shimmering through the rain-soaked living room window, Jared's relief was almost overwhelming. The jumble of voices and music from the TV he had turned up loud could only go so far to break up the silence of being alone and the whispering voices that crept in to fill it. If it was true what he had long feared and now strongly suspected, the coming months and maybe even years would put his poor wife through hell. But he needed her now more than ever before.

The living room door opened, and Melody stepped inside. Elena trailed in behind her, home from a playdate with her best (and truthfully *only*) friend Crystal Heaney. Jared started to speak, to let them know he was happy to see them even if he dared not explain the reason why, when something in both their expressions stopped him short. "What's wrong?" he asked.

Melody shook her head. It was easy to see she was irritated. Irritated with Elena, so it seemed. Elena glanced up at him, then quickly back down at her feet when she realized he was watching.

"Tell me," Jared said.

"I actually don't know what to tell you," Melody said. "You'll have to get Elena to explain because she won't talk to me about it. But when I went to pick her up from Crystal's house, Elizabeth Heaney met me at the door looking white as a sheet. And I could hear Crystal crying in the background. I suppose Elizabeth was trying to be polite by not telling me what happened. Or rather telling me that it had just been a children's quarrel when the look on her face made it obvious that wasn't true. But now our daughter is refusing to talk about it, and, Jared, I'm telling you, I've just about had it."

"Elena," Jared said. "Look at me." Elena lifted her eyes from the floor—eyes that looked much more frightened than defiant. "Tell me what happened. Why were Crystal and Mrs. Heaney upset?"

"I didn't do anything, Daddy," Elena said, her voice hardly above a whisper. "I promise."

"Okay. So what happened?"

It took a while before Elena mustered the nerve to say. But when she finally spoke, her voice was far more confident, as if she knew the words would have to be delivered with bravado if they were to be believed. "Ronny did it."

Jared raised his eyebrows and cast a glance at Melody, who shook her head and frowned. The two of them had meant to discuss Elena's imaginary friend at greater length but had forgotten. Elena kept to herself so much that it was easy sometimes to miss the issues troubling her. Dinner at Puesta De Sol was the first and last time he even remembered her mentioning her friend Ronny until now. "What do you mean Ronny did it?" he asked.

"I think he scared them," she said. "He was being mean today, and I think he did it on purpose."

"Elena, sweetheart," Melody said. "It's wonderful that you are so imaginative. It really is. But Ronny isn't real. Right? Surely you're old enough now to know that."

Elena didn't answer. Jared studied her for a while, deciding at last to try a different tact. "Tell me about Ronny. What's he like?"

Elena looked at him a little puzzled, distrusting, perhaps, of this sudden willingness to take her seriously. "He's just someone I play games with sometimes."

"What kind of games?"

"All kinds. I spy, hide and seek, Simon says. But…" She trailed off.

"But what, Elly?"

"He says he doesn't want to play those games anymore. He says he has a new game for us to play, but he won't tell me what it is. And he's been acting mean too. He scared Crystal and her mom on purpose. He made the chair move and scared them. They think that I was the one who did it, but it wasn't me."

Jared looked at Melody. He hoped she would have some input here, some direction to steer the conversation, but she only looked back at him. Jared too was at a loss for words. Alarms were ringing in the depths of his mind, sounding warnings whose lack of context made them only more alarming. He swallowed and cleared his throat. Whatever Ronny was or wasn't, whatever had or hadn't happened at the Heaney house, and whatever truth or lies might exist in Elena's telling of it now, this was the exact kind of thing he could not afford to indulge. Not when it already felt as if he stood trembling at a precipice, one nudge away from oblivion below.

"Elly," Jared said, his tone serious and firm. "I don't want you playing with Ronny anymore. I don't want you talking *to* Ronny ever again, and I don't want you talking *about* Ronny ever again. I mean it. Do you understand?"

"But, Daddy—"

"No buts. I'm serious about this. Is that clear?"

Elena shook her head, then started to cry. "That's not fair!"

"Jared—" Melody started but Jared cut her off.

"I'm sorry, Elly. That's the way it has to be. You are way too old for this kind of thing, and now it's starting to cause problems. You have to promise me that this is the end of it."

Elena was silent.

"Promise me, Elena."

Still, she was silent.

"Elena, promise me. Now."

"No," she finally said. "You can't make me." It seemed that the words were more observation than insubordination. It was true, Jared realized himself; he couldn't make her stop. He could punish her, perhaps, each time she brought it up, until she kept her fraternizations with this character of hers—imagined or not—a secret from him. But as to stopping the places her mind went when she was bored and alone, there was nothing he could do. This worried him much more than the present, silly situation should have ever warranted. He found himself growing angry with Elena. This, too, much fiercer than deserved.

"Go to your room, Elly," Jared said through gritted teeth. "Now."

Elena did as she was told. Watching her disappear up the stairs, Jared felt the sudden urge to chase after her. An urge brought on by the sense that some unknown yet vital opportunity had been missed.

FOURTEEN

MONDAY, JUNE 25ᵀᴴ

The sound of leaves rustling in the wind was the first thing Jared noticed. It was night, full dark, with not a single star visible through the canopy of trees surrounding him. Everywhere he looked, he saw nothing but bushes and thickets of thorns that made it impossible to move very far in any direction, all shrouded in fog that hung low on the ground and stirred with the wind.

I'm dreaming, Jared thought.

It wasn't the first time he'd become aware in the middle of a dream. Somehow, though, his awareness only seemed to make the dream all the more vivid. The forest around him came alive. Jared could now smell the scent of rich earth and old pine and could feel the suffocating humidity of the air. Suddenly, there was a voice behind him.

"I'm sorry, Daddy."

Jared whirled around to see Elena sitting against the base of a tree, illuminated by a beam of silvery light that seemed to come from nowhere. She was wearing a light blue dress that was ripped and tattered at the hem, and splotches of mud stained the fabric. Her lip quivered, and she looked up at him with tears welling in her eyes. "I let them in," she said between sobs. "I'm so sorry, Daddy."

Jared stepped toward her, but as soon as he did, she disappeared, leaving him alone again in the woods. The light that she had been sitting in was gone as well, and the forest grew even darker than before.

All at once, the previously hot and muggy air turned frigid, freezing the moisture it carried into tiny snowflakes that fell slowly to the ground. Jared felt his skin prickle into goosebumps.

A low, vibrating rumble reverberated through the woods, intensifying until the ground itself began to shake. He stumbled back, bracing his hands against a tree for support. The rumble grew louder, loud enough to hurt Jared's ears and intense enough that even the tree he clung to shook violently. Then, just as quickly as it had started, the tremor passed. The woods returned to silence.

Jared heard a small noise behind him and swerved around, nearly tripping over a root that poked up from the ground. Elena was there in front of him again. She stood just a few feet away, partially shrouded in fog, partially illuminated in silver light.

Her eyes were the first thing he noticed. Eyes as empty and dark as twin black holes. Staring into them felt like seeing past the edge of oblivion and into the madness beyond.

The thing that stood in front of him now bore a semblance to his daughter that was only surface level. Aside from the black orbs that took the place of her eyes, all her physical features remained the same. Yet everything from the way she stood to the way she positioned her brow was somehow shifted, as if the delicate little person supposed to inhabit that delicate little body had been sucked out and replaced with something else.

When it stretched open its mouth to speak, the voice it produced left no doubt that his daughter no longer occupied this form. It sounded like a hundred voices garbled into one, each speaking the same words but with different rhythms and tones.

We are Ra'Tak. This vessel is Ra'Tak. All that we devour is Ra'Tak.

Hearing this cacophony of tormented voices come through Elena's gaping yet unmoving mouth proved more than Jared could bear. He scrambled toward the thing in a wild frenzy, clawing and striking at it with utter disregard for the semblance it bore to the daughter he so loved. He tackled it to the ground and pinned it there with his knees against its tiny stomach. He set his hands around its throat, intent to squeeze until its dark eyes gave some indication that the dark thing inside was dead.

Yet the moment his grip tightened, the darkness in those eyes seemed to rush out like a flood, enveloping Jared at once so that darkness was all he saw. Only an instant passed before his vision returned. He could still see Elena's face beneath him and his hands around her neck. But her eyes were normal now—normal save for the panic and confusion in them—and the forest floor was now instead a tangle of blankets and sheets.

Jared let go of Elena and stumbled back from the bed. A wail escaped his lips, and his legs started to shake so badly they couldn't support his weight.

"Daddy?" Elena said, her voice on the verge of sobs. "What's happening?"

When Jared first tried to answer, he could manage only a stammer. He sucked in air and wiped at the tears pooling in his eyes, then gathered his strength and stood. "I'm so sorry, Elly. I um…I had a bad dream. But there's nothing to be afraid of, okay? I promise. Go back to sleep."

Jared turned away from her and walked across the room toward the bedroom door. He could feel her watching him as he left, still wide-eyed no doubt, and with the blankets still pulled up to her chin as if they would offer some protection. But Jared left the room and closed the door behind him without turning back to see, overcome with a certainty that drove him down the hall and away from that room in a near panic—a certainty that if he did turn and look back into those eyes that watched him as he left, he would find them black and foreboding as a starless night.

FIFTEEN

FRIDAY, JUNE 29TH

Jared sat in the waiting room of Dr. Stewart's office, staring blankly at the beige walls and trying to get comfortable in the hard, wooden chair. He had called to schedule an appointment with Dr. Stewart the morning after the night terror that ended with his hands around poor Elena's throat. But the receptionist had told him over the phone that Friday would be the earliest the doctor could see him. Jared had made the appointment, but much had changed in those four days since. So much so that if it weren't for Melody's insistence, he might not have even come.

Something had settled in him like spores of black mold, growing and spreading and poisoning everything it touched. It had settled in his home just the same. And—so it seemed every time he looked at them or heard them speak—it had poisoned his family as well.

There was no mystery as to what Dr. Stewart was soon to say. His diagnosis held no suspense. Jared's father was schizophrenic, and now Jared was as well. Eighty-seven percent odds you would have dodged that bullet, pal, but looks like you got unlucky. Better luck next life.

And if it were true, Jared could accept it. He'd spent a lifetime preparing for the possibility. But if this was schizophrenia—a possibility that Jared would not yet rule out no matter how wrong it felt—then his expectations for it were wildly off the mark.

"Mr. Gordon?" the receptionist said.

Jared straightened his posture, trying to hide the fact she'd startled him. "Yes?"

"Dr. Stewart is ready for you."

Jared rose and walked past the desk through a glass-paneled door into Dr. Stewart's office.

"Come in," Dr. Stewart said, his knees croaking audibly as he stood from his desk chair. "Sit down anywhere you'd like." Jared chose the chair. Dr. Stewart sat down across from him on the couch. "How've you been doing lately, Jared?"

"Not good." The doctor watched him for a moment, perhaps waiting for more, but Jared offered no elaboration.

"Can you tell me what's troubling you?" Jared had no idea where to begin—something that Dr. Stewart quickly gleaned. "Why don't we address the night terrors first? Are you still experiencing them?"

"Yes."

"Have they gotten better or worse? In terms of both frequency and intensity."

"Worse. On both accounts."

"I'm sorry to hear that. So it doesn't seem that the medication is helping then?"

"It hasn't helped at all."

"What about anxiety and feelings of paranoia? Have these gotten any better since you've been taking the Risperdal?"

Jared considered the ramifications of his next words, but hiding his condition from the doctor didn't seem important anymore. "Doctor, I am terrified every moment of every day. At this point, calling it anxiety or paranoia doesn't even come close."

"I see," Dr. Stewart said. "Tell me more about what you're experiencing."

Where to start? Jared thought. Should he talk about the voices that whispered to him in those vulnerable moments just before slipping off to sleep—a common symptom of that awful disease, no doubt, but exceedingly uncommon that the voices should whisper in a language guttural and inhuman that still somehow made sense when it hit his ears?

Should he start with the shadows that had swallowed the entire world, turning even days when the sun was bright and unobscured dreary and gray? Or should he cut right to the worst of it and tell of how each time he looked into the eyes of his wife or children, it seemed that something else was looking back?

None of that seemed like a good place to start this conversation. Describe any one of those experiences and the doctor's conclusion would be foregone. He might as well just skip to the chase.

"I am experiencing severe hallucinations. Auditory and visual. And the delusions that go with them. Or at least that's what you're going to tell me. But I'm not sure that's true. I'm not sure they're hallucinations or delusions at all, to be honest. And I know people must sit in this chair and tell you stuff like that all the time. But when every fiber in my body is screaming that it's real…" Jared drew a shaky breath. Of course it felt real. He'd be a fool to expect any different from a disease that'd seized stronger men than he. He'd be much more of a fool to believe it was anything else. "This is just so much more than I'd imagined. I wasn't ready for this."

"You're right that you're not the first to feel that way, Jared," Dr. Stewart said. "Far from. These things always hit so much harder than we imagine. But let's not get too far ahead of ourselves. Tell me more about the hallucinations."

Jared sighed. Talking about these things was the furthest thing from comfortable. The idea of getting up and walking out the door without saying another word was a much more inviting thought. "I hear voices, to start," he finally said. "Sometimes during the day but mostly at night. They're worst when I'm trying to fall asleep. They're not in English, and they don't even sound human. But I still understand what they say, in a sense."

"And what is that they say?"

Jared shook his head. "I couldn't tell you. By the time I wake up the next morning, I can only ever remember fragments of it. The night terrors are the same way. And even then, I don't really understand the things they say in the same way I can understand you right now. Thoughts just intrude into my head when they speak. Awful thoughts."

"You mentioned visual hallucinations as well, correct?"

Hallucinations. There was that term again. He'd used it himself, so why did it sound so grating when the doctor said it? Why did it make him feel so defensive when it was so obviously true?

"I see shadows move in ways they shouldn't," Jared said. "Sometimes they seem like they're following me. Everything looks so dark now, too. I've wondered before if I was just slowly going blind. It's like someone turned every light in the world to dim. Sometimes…sometimes I see things moving behind my wife's eyes. Or my children's eyes. Like shadows again, but…different somehow."

"Is there anything that brings on these hallucinations? Any triggers that you can think of?"

Jared's thoughts went straight to the leatherbound journal, its yellowing pages mere footsteps away from where he laid his head to sleep. Wasn't it the nucleus around which all his fears were based? If this appointment were to do any good one way or another, it was time for him to tell Dr. Stewart the truth.

"I don't know. Not in the moment. But there is this one thing. It's uh…it's this journal that my brother Jeremiah sent me a few weeks ago. I drove up to visit him last month, and he tried to give it to me then. But I wouldn't take it, so he mailed it to me and…"

Jared trailed off. There was context behind that journal that he had never shared with Dr. Stewart, and he was getting ahead of himself. Dr. Stewart waited patiently for him to continue, his wizened hands folded in his lap.

"Let me start over," Jared said and paused a long while to gather his thoughts. "I was sixteen when Dad was diagnosed schizophrenic. My brother Jeremiah was twelve. We were still kids, but we weren't little children anymore. Well past the days of worrying about ghosts in the closet or monsters under the bed, you know? But believe me when I tell you that there were things that happened in those years after Dad's diagnosis that I still can't explain. Jeremiah would tell you the same thing. I had forgotten about it over the years. It's shocking, really, just how much I forgot now that it's all coming back to me. The journal I mentioned is my dad's journal, the one his doctor had him keep after he was diagnosed. Jeremiah has been convinced his entire life that what we experienced was real and that our father was never actually sick. That's why he sent me the journal. To convince me too, I guess."

"What kind of things do you and your brother remember experiencing?"

"All things that I'm sure you would describe as trauma-induced psychosis. Or something along those lines. Those years were traumatic for all of us, no doubt. But that doesn't explain me and my brother both hearing the same awful sounds coming from our father's room at the same time, or us both seeing shadows following him up the stairs, or both of us having the same exact nightmares on the same nights.

"Then as soon as Dad was gone, it all stopped. No more horrible noises in the middle of the night. No more panicked feelings that something was watching us. No more anything out of the ordinary at all. Our father had just hung himself and yet somehow that's when the nightmares ended. Twenty-two years went by after that, and nothing happened. But ever since that journal showed up, the same things that happened back then have been happening again. Except last time I felt like a bystander. This time I feel like the quarry."

Jared flinched a little. Had he seen that word somewhere, in the journal perhaps? What a strange word to come to mind, and yet it felt like the perfect description of his now central role in an atrocity that he and his brother had once only glimpsed.

"I want you to think about this next question very carefully, Jared," Dr. Stewart said. "And I want you to do your best to answer it truthfully. Right now, sitting in this chair at this very moment, do you believe that the things you are experiencing are true events, events of the supernatural, if you will, or do you believe them to be symptoms of a mental condition, perhaps schizophrenia or perhaps something else? I want you to answer truthfully, and I promise there will be no judgment on my part. You'll forgive me if my profession has made me quite the skeptic, but that doesn't mean I'm not profoundly interested in what you have to say about the matter."

This was the million-dollar question. One Jared had been grappling with long before this visit and one he was nowhere close to answering. "I don't know," he said. "I'm a skeptic too, Doctor. I don't even believe in God. Much less demons or hauntings or anything of that nature. And logically, at times like right now when everything is calm, it still seems unthinkable to believe anything except the obvious. That I am sick, and that everything that's been going on is symptoms of my sickness. But... can I give you a hypothetical?"

"By all means."

"It's a proven fact that the earth is round, right? Thinking it's flat is about as crazy as believing in the supernatural. Maybe more so."

"I suppose that's a fair comparison."

"Alright, but what if someone took you up in a spaceship and you saw it for yourself for the very first time, and there it was, flat as a pancake? A blue and green pizza dish floating in space right there before your eyes. Would you still believe everything you've been told and assume you'd just lost your sanity the moment you looked out the window? Or would you change your mind?"

"Trusting what our senses are telling us is one of our deepest ingrained evolutionary traits. That's part of what makes mental illness so devastating. But they can't always be relied on. Sometimes, better judgment has to prevail."

Jared wasn't sure what his better judgment told him. He knew what his nerves were screaming—that fight or flight response that knows when it's in danger. Yet the voice of reason that still persisted even when other voices roared over it told him that what the doctor was saying made perfect sense. "How am I supposed to know for certain? I feel like I can't do anything until I do."

"I think the best way to know is to approach your condition for what it almost certainly is. A *mental* condition. Take the medication, trust the process, and if you show improvement, then you'll know for sure that we're treating the right problem after all."

"I thought that's what I was doing when I started seeing you and taking the Risperdal. But it hasn't helped."

"I know patience is hard when you're suffering, but these things can take time. The first medication and dosage prescribed rarely achieves the desired effect. And therapy doesn't work overnight either, I'm afraid. For as far as we've come as a field, much of psychiatry is still a trial-and-error process. But it's a process I have seen yield positive outcomes time and time again for those who give it time. I plan to prescribe you additional medication as well as a couple of therapeutic exercises you can use when psychosis sets in. Trust me, Jared. I remain wholly confident that, in time, we can return your life to some degree of normalcy."

Jared gazed expressionless at the doctor as he spoke. These were the same platitudes he'd heard his first time in this office. Probably the same ones they'd told his father too. Empty assurances recycled at a rate of $200 an hour. Crazy or not—*hunted or not*—coming here had been a mistake.

"But if you are going to begin the process of healing and moving forward," Dr. Stewart continued, "I think it's important to start by putting this business with your brother and the journal behind you."

Jared winced and hated the fact that the doctor had surely noticed. Why did the idea of throwing out that journal seem so dreadful? Was it because the journal was his only lifeline, the only place where answers could possibly be found? Or was it something else? He recalled the day it arrived on his front porch, the unnatural way that it had pulled him in, like a moth to a bulb.

"Do you think you can do that?" Dr. Stewart asked.

The lie rolled off his tongue so quickly and naturally that it left no reason for doubt. "Yes. I think I should."

"Good. I'll submit the new prescription to your pharmacy. I'd like for you to pick it up on your way home and start taking it right away."

Jared nodded and rose from the chair. Waves of nervous energy washed over his muscles as the urge to be away from here grew stronger by the moment.

"Take care, Jared. I hope you'll be feeling much better by our next visit."

Jared made for the door, having to throttle his footsteps down to an ordinary pace when his legs felt like sprinting.

"Ah, one more thing before you go," Dr. Stewart said.

Jared almost didn't stop. His hand was already around the doorknob, his other in his pocket clasping the Camry's keys. But he let it fall away and turned back around.

He gasped and stumbled back, bracing himself against the door to keep from falling. The room—now dark and laced with shadows—started to spin. The muscles in his legs turned to water, and he collapsed to the floor.

Jared gazed up with wide, unblinking eyes as the thing that now wore Dr. Stewart's skin stepped toward him. Its face was twisted into an impossible contortion, as if all the little bones beneath had been broken and rearranged. And where once set gray yet friendly eyes were now featureless black orbs.

It spoke to him, its gaping, disjointed mouth never moving as the inhuman syllables were formed. Thoughts poured in uninvited, a stream of filth so vile it made him gag.

At first, it seemed his mind would shut down. The room spun ferociously, and the darkness was swallowing his vision. But just as he began to spiral around the vortex's edge, a jolt of newfound energy spurred his limbs into action.

He clawed his way to his feet and flung open the office door. Walls and waiting room chairs and the shocked face of Dr. Stewart's receptionist flew past him in a blur. Somewhere, in some unimportant part of his mind, he heard the doctor calling out to him, his voice now normal, as it were, but racked with concern. Dismissing it without a thought, Jared pushed open the exit, sprinted across the parking lot to his car, and sped away.

SIXTEEN

FRIDAY, JUNE 29TH

A repeating reel of nightmarish visions kept playing in Jared's mind as he drove down the interstate. Visions of his family staked to the ground in the front yard like morbid lawn ornaments. Visions of his home burned to the foundation and their black, shriveled corpses buried beneath the ash. Visions of a quiet and empty house where the disappearance of all who lived there but he would go forever unexplained. All things that *they* had shown him.

When Jared squealed into the driveway and burst through the door to find none of it true, it did little to ease his concern. Melody approached him as soon as the door opened, her face full of worry. For myriad reasons, Jared had hidden as much as possible from her. She had known since they started dating the risks his genetics posed. She knew that he was suffering and that something was severely wrong— that he could not hide. But she knew nothing of the true danger at their door.

Part of him wanted to tell her everything. To tell her that something strong, unknown, and malignant had claimed his father's life, stalked him since childhood, and was now ready to pounce again. But how could he possibly convince her it was true? She trusted him, of that

Jared was sure, but she was smart and just as skeptical as he. He'd given her every reason this past month to make her think he was losing his mind, and telling her the truth would only convince her more.

"What happened?" Melody asked.

Jared brushed past her and sat down on the living room couch, folding his hands and resting his forehead against them. He didn't mean to ignore her. There was just no good answer to the question that his foggy, scattered thoughts could formulate. And he was so tired. It seemed almost like gravity itself had been kicked up a tick these past few days; everything from getting out of bed to walking upstairs was so much more tiring than it had ever been before.

Melody, though, wasn't having it. She followed him into the living room, parking herself in front of the couch and engulfing his field of view. "Jared, tell me what happened?"

"I don't know what you mean, Mel."

She looked bewildered. "You don't know what I mean? Dr. Stewart called, Jared. He said you passed out in his office, woke up screaming, then ran out the door. Then ten minutes after I get off the phone with him, you come through the door looking like something was chasing you. And now you're already back to pretending like nothing's wrong. Right back to how it's been this whole time."

Jared closed his eyes. Sleep was what he needed—even if it was sure to bring its own flavor of terrors. If he just leaned back and kept his eyes shut, he could probably fall asleep right then and there.

"I'm not doing it anymore," Melody said. "We are going to talk about this."

Jared opened his eyes. He studied his wife for a moment, weighing his options, then finally sighed and said, "I don't know what there is to talk about."

"Let's start with what happened at Dr. Stewart's office," Melody said, barely throttling her frustration.

Jared gnawed at the corner of his lip. What *had* happened there? Already, the memory seemed so distant. Like a dream forgotten the moment it's interrupted by the dawn. "I'm not sure, Mel," he said, hoping the emotion in his words would convey their honesty.

Melody's features softened. She sat down beside him on the couch and placed a hand on his leg. "Talk to me, Jared. Whatever it is, talking about it will only make it better."

Jared wondered if that was true. Once more, the longing to tell her everything burned like embers in his chest. "Something is wrong with me. I don't know if it's all in my head or…I just don't know. I don't have any answers, Mel. I don't know what to do."

"Dr. Stewart wants you to call him back. You can start there, sweetheart." Jared shook his head, revulsed by the idea for reasons already forgotten but no less sickening. "You have to let him help you," Melody said.

"Not now," Jared said. "I will, Mel. Just not right now."

"He told me he prescribed you some new medication. Will you at least let me go pick it up?"

Jared considered this for a second, then nodded. It would appease her, at least for a while, and there seemed no harm in trying the new meds. After all, if they were as ineffective as his current prescription, then there was no reason they too couldn't be flushed down the toilet one by one each day.

"Would you want to come with me?"

"No, I think I'll just stay here. Maybe take a nap."

"Is there anything else I should pick up while I'm out?" Melody asked, now calling back to him from near the front door as she collected her wallet and keys.

"Huh-uh," Jared said without actually considering the question. His eyes were closed again, and his head was drooped. He heard the sound of the front door opening and closing and the sound of Melody's car backing out of the drive. This and the AC's steady whirring seemed as good a lullaby as any to drift away to; he could feel sleep tugging at his mind like the weight of an iron anchor.

But then, a thought pierced through the thickening fog. Had Melody seemed quick to leave him? Was it strange that she had left his side so willingly, knowing the episode he'd just suffered?

She was grasping for ways to help, no doubt, and picking up his new medications was the only one he'd given her. This seemed the logical explanation. But what if there was something more? If she'd been eager to get away from this house, Jared couldn't blame her; darkness hung in the air here like toxic smog, a sickening presence that assaulted his every sense. Could she sense it too, Jared wondered, to some far lesser degree? What would it mean if she could?

Before his train of thought could steam off the rails any further, a sudden sound snapped it away. Jared's eyes opened, his muscles tensing in surprise. He hadn't always been so jumpy, but these days even the smallest creak or pop caused his heart to skip beats.

At the top of the stairs, where the first noise originated, he heard the sound of small feet bounding up hardwood steps. Jared looked up just in time to see a flash of blonde hair disappear behind the wall at the staircase's landing.

It was Elena. No doubt playing some silly children's game. It couldn't be that she was watching him from the top of the stairs, hurrying away as soon as his eyes opened. And if it was, then this, too, was surely nothing but a game. Just another peculiar expression of a wild and wonderful imagination. Surely nothing more.

When Melody returned from the pharmacy, Jared was still awake and sitting on the couch, staring blankly up at the top of the stairs.

SEVENTEEN

THURSDAY, JULY 5ᵀᴴ

FROM THE JOURNAL OF GREG GORDON
ENTRY #29: DATED 01/17/1994

My death is coming. They have shown me when and how it will happen. Even if I could stop it, I wouldn't. Knowing it is coming soon is a comfort to me now.

I have never believed in an afterlife. The thought of eternal sleep has never frightened me. But the thought that frightens me now more than anything is that they will be waiting for me there. They have told me that once I die, it will be nothing but me and them and darkness for all of time. I hope they are lying. I hope that nothing at all comes next and that anything else is impossible even for them. Hope has only failed me so far, but this is a hope I cannot bear to let go.

Whatever comes next, I hope even more that my curse will die with me. I have asked them what will happen to my family once their work with me is done. But this they will not answer.

It still seems impossible to me that Jeremiah could have brought this evil upon us. Yet I feel it to be true. I know that they have taken over his mind just as firmly as they have my own, albeit in a different way. They tell me that he invited them. They've shown me how it happened. Maybe this too is just another cruel lie. Confronting Jeremiah has got me nowhere. I have to accept that I will die without knowing.

Either way, I fear for him. I fear for all of them. The fact I am told nothing of their futures frightens me even more than the things I hope are lies.

Jared closed the journal. He opened the workbench drawer where he kept it hidden and put the journal back inside.

It occurred to him not for the first time that perhaps it was odd reading it in piecemeal like this. Sneaking away to the garage to read a few pages at a time before shutting it away again. If there were answers to be found in those pages, shouldn't he search for them at once?

But answers were not what Jared searched for in that volume. To be truthful, he wasn't sure he was searching for anything at all. Reading the journal just felt like something he had to do, and he could only bear to do it a little at a time.

No one had the answers he needed. Not Dr. Stewart, not Melody, and not his dead father. No one except…

Jared pushed the thought away. He had already frightened her enough. She had woken from peaceful sleep to find her father with his hands gripping her throat. That would be a memory she had forever, one he could never erase. He wasn't going to create more.

Still, every mention of Jeremiah in his father's journal made him think of her. Was it even imaginable that his precious, innocent daughter had let this evil into their lives? Jared sympathized in ways he wished he didn't each time his father asked a similar, tortured question about his youngest son.

An idea flashed into existence. Perhaps there *was* someone else who might have answers. It seemed inexplicable—worrisome even—that the thought had slipped his mind this long. Almost as if any thought of reaching out to his brother had been somehow suppressed.

Fighting the tremble in his hands, Jared pulled out his phone and dialed Jeremiah's number. He pressed the phone to his ear and drew a shaky breath.

The dial tone rang once, then was interrupted. "We're sorry, your call cannot be completed as dialed," an automated voice said. "Please check the number and try again."

Jared looked at his phone screen and furrowed his brows. He had found Jeremiah in his contacts to place the call, not even bothering to look at the number itself, although it had been so long since he'd last tried to call his brother, it wouldn't have been surprising if his number had changed.

But looking at the number on the screen, Jared realized it wasn't right. Jeremiah's number was a Savannah area code, 912. It always had been. The number on the phone screen was 479. Jared didn't recognize that area code.

He gritted his teeth, hating how uneasy it made him looking at that strange number he knew he'd never entered himself. He ended the call and opened the phone's touchpad. He typed 912 onto the screen and then stopped. What was the rest of Jeremiah's number? He didn't search his memory for long before realizing it was hopeless. He could count on one hand the phone numbers he still knew by heart, and all of them were ones he had committed to memory in the time before smartphones.

He went back to his brother's contact, but the number was still the same. 479-856-2758. A random string of digits he'd never seen before.

Jared swallowed and tried not to think about how they'd got there in his brother's contact. Putting in the correct area code and keeping the rest of the number the same seemed the next logical thing to attempt. Jared scrawled the number onto a scrap of paper, replacing the unknown area code with the one he knew to be correct. There was a time he could count on himself to remember seven numbers long enough to punch them into the screen, but that wasn't the case these days.

With the paper in one hand and the phone in the other, Jared dialed the number. It rang twice this time before someone answered. "Savannah's Secrets Adult Video, how can I help you?" said a husky, female voice.

Jared hung up the call. He looked at the screen and the number he'd just dialed. 912-746-2795.

Was that right? He looked back at the note still in his hand and felt like crying. It wasn't right. It wasn't right at all. Could he have possibly mistyped it that badly? His hands were shaking, sure—nothing he could do about that—but hadn't he checked the number one last time before he dialed? He tried to remember but couldn't and found this just as maddening as everything else.

With the paper on the workbench and the phone flat beside it, Jared dialed each number one by one, checking every entry against the number he had written down. He checked the digits again once he was done typing, from start to finish. 912-856-2758. The number on the screen matched perfectly with the number on his note. Jared made sure of it, then made sure again. Finally, he pressed the dial button.

The phone rang once before a male voice answered.

"911, what's your emergency?"

A gasp was all that Jared could manage.

"Hello? Are you there?"

"I…um, no. I'm sorry." Jared pulled the phone away from his ear and tried to end the call, but it slipped from his fingers. The phone clattered against the garage's concrete floor, and Jared hurried down after it. He picked it back up, oblivious to the new spiderweb of cracks at the top corner of the screen, and hung up the call.

He sat there on the floor for a while, catching his breath and staring at the phone in his hand. The logical person he used to be would assume it was broken, routing calls to the wrong number somehow. But Jared knew this wasn't true.

This was *them* exerting their will. They didn't want him to contact his brother, so they had kept the thought from him for a while. And when that didn't work, they'd resorted to more direct means. Jared didn't understand how it all worked, whether they had changed the numbers in the phone itself or just caused him to type them in wrong, but it didn't matter. *They* were the ones in control either way.

Jared sat back on his haunches and clutched his knees. Darkness crushed in around him, the light from his desk lamp looking impossibly dim and far away. He closed his eyes. Somehow, that darkness was better.

But it didn't stop the ringing in his ears that seemed to climb in pitch on and on continually, never reaching a climax. The sound of it left a nauseous feeling in his stomach and sent the room into a spin. Jared had read once about sound-based weapons that could induce dizziness and nausea in a crowd when they broadcast just the right frequency. Somewhere in the depths of his mind, he wondered if this was something similar.

He kept his eyes closed, certain he would vomit if he opened them to find the room spinning as fast as his other senses seemed to indicate. But then those other senses, those primal senses deep within the mind that everyone accepts but no one ever tries to explain, indicated something else. He wasn't alone anymore. Something was standing in front of him.

Jared's eyes jolted open, a scream already forming in the back of his throat. But the garage was empty. The lamp on his workbench shined adequate as ever, dispelling most of the shadows that had swallowed the space just moments before and leaving nowhere for anything to hide. The ringing was gone now too, and so was the dizziness it seemed to induce.

Jared barely had time to draw a breath before a different ringing snatched it away. His phone buzzed against the concrete floor, its screen a ghostly glow. He let it ring for a while, not sure he was ready to answer it no matter who—or what—might be on the other line. At last, he could stand it no more.

He crawled across the floor and picked up the phone. It felt living in his hands, warm and vibrating and wailing with sound. On the screen were the words "Caller Unknown." Reading this made some of the nausea come back.

The pads of his fingers were almost too sweaty to operate the touchscreen. He had to swipe twice before it registered his touch and answered the call. Not daring to put the phone to his ear, Jared kept it at arm's reach, ready to fling it away from him in an instant. He hadn't thought to put the call on speaker, but alone in the garage with only the sound of his own labored breathing, even the dull static on the other end came in clear.

He leaned a little closer to the phone, trying to make out anything distinct in the garble of white noise. But white noise was all there was. A steady hiss interrupted only by the occasional crackle, like a vinyl record someone forgot to take off the player.

Except that wasn't quite right, was it? The crackles were too sharp and spread apart, more like green wood burning in a campfire than the sound of a blank record. Jared listened closer, the phone now just inches from his ear. Then a voice cut through the static.

He recoiled, almost dropping the phone again. The voice on the line was hushed and warped, sounding like someone whispering inside a waterfall. Yet unmistakable all the same even after all these years. A voice Jared never thought he'd hear again outside his dreams and nightmares.

"*Son?*"

Jared stared at the phone, wondering if the urge to smash it against the floor until its haunting glow went dark was one that he should heed.

"*Son, you have to listen to me. You have to save us. Death isn't the end. Not the end of us. Not the end of them.*"

"Dad?" Jared croaked. "Dad, what's happening to me?"

For a while, the hiss of static and a crackle like that of flames were the only response.

"*There's no time,*" Greg Gordon finally said. "*They're here again. Save us, son. You have to save us all while there's still a chance. It's too late for me. There's no way to fight them from here. But until you cross over, it's not too late for you.*"

"How? What do I do?"

No answer. This time, not even the static came through. The phone had gone dark and lifeless again, showing only his own gaunt reflection amidst a web of newly formed cracks.

But Jared already knew what he had to do. He might not have understood his father's pleas, might not have been certain that those words were even his father's at all, but one thing was clear. There was no more time for half measures.

Rising from the garage floor without even bothering to brush the dust from his jeans, Jared took off toward Elena's bedroom.

EIGHTEEN

THURSDAY, JULY 5ᵀᴴ

"Where are we going?" Elena asked.

Jared took his eyes away from the road long enough to glance at her in the passenger seat beside him. She was still wearing the Mini Mouse PJ's she'd gone to bed in, looking strange paired with the sneakers he had quietly helped her slip on before heading out the door. "Nowhere, sweety. We're just going for a drive."

The clock on the Camry's dash read 3:47 a.m. Melody had gone to sleep hours ago, never having been one to burn the midnight oil. But she had also never been the soundest sleeper, and Jared hadn't wanted to risk waking her. There would have been no way to make her understand why speaking with Elena couldn't wait until morning.

Trees and shadows of trees rolled by just outside the headlights' beams. Jared checked his speed and eased off the accelerator. They were truly going nowhere in particular, and there was no need to get there fast.

"It's really late," Elena said.

"I know, Elly. We just need to talk about something, okay? We're just gonna drive around for a bit, just me and you, and have a talk. Then we can go back home."

He could feel her small, bright eyes boring into him even as he kept his own eyes on the curving white lines of Highway 17. A semi approached from the opposite lane, its entire front bumper alight with neon orange bulbs—the only other vehicle they'd seen at this late hour.

Elena watched it pass by through the passenger side window. For a moment, its lights lit up her face enough for Jared to glimpse her eyes through disheveled strands of hair. They looked wide and full of worry.

Or was this just his own eyes playing tricks on him in the dark? Jared couldn't say for certain. Even looking straight ahead at the well-lit road, the signs passing by seemed to sway back and forth as if moved by the wind. It was indeed really late, and the night's events had left his mind a scramble.

"Elly, I want to talk about Ronny." Jared watched her as he spoke, but she kept her head turned away, still staring out the window at the dark forest flying by as though looking for something amidst the shadows. "Look at me, sweetheart."

Elena turned toward him. Her skin looked pallid in the dim blue light from the car's dashboard, and there was now no mistaking the fear in her eyes. "Daddy, I'm scared," she said.

Jared felt his heart begin to race. This was not the response he'd expected. "Of what, Elly?"

Jared glanced back at the road just long enough to make sure he was still within the lines, then turned his attention back to his daughter. Tears pooled in the corners of her eyes, and her little hands quivered on top of her knees. "Is it Ronny?" he asked. "Is that who you're scared of?"

Elena nodded. A chill wrapped icy claws around Jared's heart.

"Tell me why, Elly. Why are you scared of him? What did he do?" Elena didn't answer. She glanced at the rearview mirror, then dropped her eyes to her feet. "Tell me and we can stop it. I promise I can make it better if you just talk to me, Elly."

Elena lifted her head and wiped her eyes with the sleeve of her PJ's. For the first time in days, Jared felt a flicker of hope. Maybe Ronny was Ra'Tak, and maybe she had let them in. But if she worked with him now, then maybe it wasn't too late. If she had opened the door, perhaps she could close it again too.

"Please, Elly. Tell me what's going on."

Elena opened her mouth, and Jared held his breath. But just as the words began to form, they turned into a scream. "No! You can't!"

Jared swerved, startled by the outburst. He turned the steering wheel to the left, jerking the car off the shoulder and back onto the road. "What is it? What's wrong?"

"Daddy, look out!"

Jared turned back to the road just in time to see the tailgate of a truck stopped in front of them—so close he could see dust on its license plate in the headlights' beams. He slammed his foot on the brake as hard as he could and braced for the collision.

His head snapped forward, and a jolt of pain seared through his neck. There was the sound of metal smashing against metal, crumpling under the force, then a ringing explosion as the airbags deployed. The fabric balloon smashed into Jared's face, rocking his head back against the headrest. Spots of light flashed in his eyes, and his head felt faint and woozy.

He searched for Elena, terrified of what he'd see, and felt a rush of relief when he saw her sitting upright and sobbing. A trail of blood streamed down her nose, and the skin beneath her left eye was red and swollen.

Jared fumbled at his seat belt, finally managing to get it off. He tried to open the door, but it wouldn't budge. He pushed harder. The crumpled door groaned a little but still would not move. He gave up, then remembered the cell phone in his pocket.

"I want Mommy!" Elena cried.

"It's okay, baby. It's all going to be okay."

There was blood on his fingers, and it smudged across the screen as he tried to type his PIN. He wiped the phone and his hand on his shirt, leaving trails of crimson across the fabric, then tried again. It worked, and Jared dialed 911.

This time, the call went through.

NINETEEN

THURSDAY, JULY 5TH

It was well into the morning by the time Jared made it home from the hospital, the sun already a searing yellow blaze. After what seemed like endless X-rays and examinations, they had set his broken nose, put his neck in a cervical brace, and sutured a cut in his thumb with four stitches.

Elena had suffered whiplash and a bruised eye from the airbag. The doctors had ultimately concluded that her injuries were not serious, but they had kept her a little longer to examine her for signs of a concussion.

"You're both very lucky," an RN had said at one point while Jared was waiting on the results of Elena's X-rays to come back. "God must have been watching over you."

Not God, Jared had thought. *Maybe something else.*

The police had come to the hospital to talk to him too. Not the same officer that had showed up at the crash but two detectives wearing slacks and button-down shirts. They told him that the first 911 operator had tried to call him back and had sent a sheriff's deputy to his address when he didn't respond. Fifteen minutes later and another 911 operator was sending officers to where he had wrecked his vehicle with his young daughter inside. At nearly four o'clock in the morning on a road to nowhere with her still in her PJ's. The story must have made quite an impression at the department, Jared imagined, to get them both out of the office at this late hour.

They had lots of questions. Fortunately, Jared mustered the where-withal to give them the right answers. The first 911 call had been an accident, he told them. His phone had been acting screwy and dialing random numbers, and that's also probably why it never rang when the operator tried to call him back. As for his and Elena's late-night drive, that was entirely unrelated to the accidental 911 call. Elena has insomnia, Jared told them, and driving around helps her fall asleep.

The detectives didn't seem very convinced, but it didn't matter. He'd already been given a ticket for the accident, and there was no other law he had broken. They told him that false 911 calls were a serious matter and advised him to purchase a new phone. They voiced their suspicions and told him his was the strangest story they'd heard in some time. Then, finally, they left.

Dealing with Melody would not be nearly so easy. She had sat there in the room listening to every lie he told, never contradicting his account but glancing at him once while the detectives were occupied with their notes with a look that told him his true interrogation was still to come.

There'd been no opportunity for this conversation yet. Melody had been with Elena for most of the night and never in Jared's room with just the two of them alone. The drive home had been silent too. Awkward and silent. Jared could almost sense the questions that simmered underneath Melody's tired, blank expression as she drove them from the hospital, held back only by little ears in the back seat. But now that they were home and Elena was tucked away in bed, those questions would have to be answered.

Jared sat waiting at the kitchen table, staring down at a mug of lukewarm coffee he hadn't yet sipped. Melody would be down the stairs any moment from putting Elena to bed. He wondered what was taking her so long. Was she talking to Elena about what happened? It seemed only logical that she would. He wished he could know what Elena told her.

The creak of old boards signaled her arrival. Jared straightened in his chair. Across the kitchen, a beam of sunlight shone through the front door's glazing, spotlighting swaying specks of dust in the air between the door and staircase landing. Another creak in the stairs, and Melody stepped into the beam.

"How is she?" Jared asked.

"Okay, I think. I stayed with her until she fell asleep. Hopefully, she'll sleep for a while." Melody pulled out a chair across the table and sat down. She looked tired and stressed. Probably not half as bad as he must have looked himself with his nose in a bandage and his face all puffy and purple. But the night had clearly taken a toll on her too. "What were you doing, Jared?"

Jared took his time responding, mustering his nerve. The truth was going to be so much harder to tell than the lies. "There's something I have to tell you. I'm not sure you're going to believe it, but I need you to listen to me. Start to finish. Can you do that?" Melody nodded slowly, her eyes unblinking and locked on his. Jared could see the concern in them growing deeper but continued nonetheless. "Remember last month when I visited Jeremiah? We ended up staying in this hunting cabin of his because I didn't think I could sleep in the house. I think I told you that part."

Melody nodded again.

"We had a few beers by the campfire. Then he wanted to talk about Dad. About what it was like when he…got sick. I didn't want to talk about it. I never have wanted to. Those years have always seemed like a bad dream that I'd just sooner forget. I don't know if I forced myself to forget it or if it happened all by itself. But talking to Jeremiah that night and being back at that house started to bring some of it back.

"He tried to give me a journal. Dad's journal that the doctors had him keep after he was diagnosed. I refused to take it. I didn't even want to look at it. But three days later it showed up in our mailbox. I don't know what compelled me to read it this time. It's impossible to explain, really. But the point is that I read it. I'm still reading it. And all those repressed memories that I talked about are back now. Crystal clear.

"There was something in that house with us back then, Melody. I felt it, Jeremiah felt it, and Dad felt it most of all. The thing that drove Dad to kill himself was not schizophrenia. I don't know what you'd call it, but it wasn't a disease.

"Jeremiah and I didn't know what it was or what it wanted, but we knew it was real. I remember that now. And Jeremiah never forgot. I think he could sense that it was coming for me next somehow. I think he was trying to warn me."

"Warn you of what?" Melody asked. Jared studied her. She had listened this far without interruption, but he could see that her patience was wearing thin.

"It's back now, Melody. I can feel it again just the same as it was back then. Except it's stronger now. I don't think me and Jeremiah were its targets back then. I think Dad was its target, and we just got caught in the crossfire sometimes. Just saw glimpses here and there. But now it's come back for me." Melody shook her head. She opened her mouth to speak, but Jared cut her off. "I know how it sounds. You've got every reason to think I've lost my mind. There's more you have to hear, though. Then you can decide if you still think that's true."

"Go ahead," she said, and Jared did despite the painful truth in her eyes—that nothing he could possibly say was likely to change what she had already concluded.

"I haven't been entirely honest with you," Jared said, determined to get the rest out anyway. "I kept the journal from you, and I've kept most of what has happened since it arrived from you too. It felt like I was protecting you somehow. I realize now how stupid that was.

"The truth is that I have experienced a hell of a lot more than night terrors and paranoia. I've *seen* them, Melody. With my own eyes, right there in our bedroom, towering over the bed and waiting for me to sleep so that they can weave my nightmares."

"Seen *who*, Jared?" Melody asked. Desperation colored each word.

"I still don't know who they are. What they are. If they're even a they. Dad said their name was Ra'Tak, but…"

Jared stopped. The hairs on his arms and neck prickled as the sound of that name seemed to hang in the air. Was this the first time he had spoken it aloud? It had felt so foreign on his tongue—like a sound human tongues were never meant to form. Speaking it for the first time left him reluctant to ever say it again.

"Jared," Melody said, breaking the spell. "What were you doing earlier? Where were you going with Elena?"

"Nowhere," Jared said. "I just wanted to talk to her."

"Talk to her about what?"

"I think she has something to do with it. I think…" Jared stopped. This part of the conversation required the most caution of all, and he was already botching it. His whirlwind of thoughts refused to coalesce into the right words. "You remember that imaginary friend she mentioned? Ronny. That was his name."

"Yes," Melody said, "I remember." Her face was stern, her guard clearly up. She was humoring him, Jared could tell, and she wasn't going to humor him much longer.

"Don't you think it's strange to have an imaginary friend at her age? And I know you can tell she's been acting differently lately too."

"You need to stop, Jared. This has gone far enough."

"Dad said in the journal that they can't come into our world freely. They have to be invited. Jeremiah let them in when we were kids. Now I think that Elena's invited them back. I don't know how or why, whether it was on purpose or accidental. But it's true, Melody. I can feel it."

"Jared," Melody said. "Your daughter has been acting strangely because *you* have been acting strangely. You are not well, sweetheart. It's my fault for not realizing how bad it's gotten."

"No," Jared said. "That's not it. Look, I know…I know it seems that way, okay? I don't blame you for making that assumption. But I *know* it's not true. I know it."

"You can't know that. There's no way to—"

"Do you remember freshman year of college when that asshole tried to roofie you? Your friends just thought you couldn't handle your alcohol. It was like your second time drinking ever was what you told me, and they thought you were being dramatic. But you knew something was wrong, and you made them walk you back to your dorm."

"It's nowhere near the same."

"It's exactly the same. You were the only one who knew what was happening inside your own mind. And you needed your friends to trust you because you were in danger. Just like I'm needing you to trust me now."

"I needed them to believe that I didn't feel right. You're asking me to believe that… that *demons* are haunting us. And that Elena, our sweet little girl, invited them in. I can't believe that, Jared. I'm not sure I could bring myself to believe something so awful and outlandish if I saw it with my own eyes."

She was fidgeting. Jared could tell she was fighting the urge to get up from the kitchen chair and walk away. "You want to know what she did right before we wrecked?" he said. "Her face turned white as a sheet, and she screamed 'no, you can't.' And she wasn't looking at the truck we were about to hit either. She was looking in the rearview mirror.

"She was going to tell me about Ronny. Whatever he is or isn't, she's terrified of him, Melody. She told me so, and I could see it on her face. But something stopped her right before she could tell me why. Just like it's stopped me from doing things before too."

"You're not well, sweetheart," Melody said. A tear trickled down her cheek. "Call Dr. Stewart back and schedule another appointment. Take the new medicine. It's the only way things are going to get better."

"I'm not going back there. I'll take the drugs if it makes you feel better, but I'm not going back to Dr. Stewart."

"He can help you, Jared."

Frustration roiled over into a surge of anger. Jared slammed his fist against the table. "You're not listening! I am not sick, Melody. I'm under attack. I think we all are."

Melody never flinched at this outburst, but Jared could see that it frightened her. It killed him to see her looking at him with so much fear. "Talk to Elena yourself," he said, an idea suddenly coming to him. "Ask her about Ronny. Watch how she reacts. See if you're even able to talk to her about it without some freak accident getting in the way. Then come back and tell me if you still believe he's imaginary."

Melody sighed. Jared's heartbeat quickened; for the first time, he seemed to have actually penetrated her defenses. "I tried to talk to her," she said. "I tried at the hospital and again when I put her to bed. She told me that she and Daddy were just going on a drive. I knew there was more to it than that. But she wouldn't talk about it."

"She's scared. I know you can see it. And she has every right to be." Jared held his breath as he watched her consider this. It seemed to happen in slow motion, each second stretched like rubber bands. The door to her mind had creaked open just a crack, and the doubt he so desperately needed her to embrace had its foot on the sill.

What if that doubt took hold just as it had with him and led her to the truth? With the two of them working together, Elena could be brought around too, he was sure. He didn't know exactly what that meant or what it would look like just yet, but they could figure it out. Just like they had figured out every other problem over the last twenty-three years—together. God, did he need her on his side.

Then, just as suddenly as it had creaked open, Jared watched the door slam closed. Her muscles tensed again, and the conviction in her eyes returned. Jared felt his heart sink.

"You're right. She does have every right to be scared. Two nights in a row you've woken her up in the middle of the night. First the night terror and then a three a.m. drive talking about God knows what that ended with both of you in the hospital. That's not to mention how you've been acting before all that. She can see the way you look at her now, Jared. If I can see it, so can she. You think that doesn't affect her? You know how sensitive she is."

Melody let this hang in the air for a moment before continuing. "You have to get help, sweetheart. For yourself and for me and Elena and all your children. Before something terrible happens."

Jared exhaled and closed his eyes. "Okay," he said. "I'm sorry. I know you're right. I know I'm not well. I just…"

Did he believe it? Did he still know deep down that Melody and the voice in his head that spoke the same reason—the one voice that had been there before the rest showed up—were both speaking the truth? He wished more than anything that he could.

"I'll take the medicine. I'll see someone again. Maybe not Dr. Stewart, but someone."

The faintest relief flashed across his wife's face. It was the best he could hope for. No more point in arguing. Even pleading would get him nowhere. Nothing short of tangible proof would change her mind now, and that he did not have.

"We can get through this, Jared," Melody said, reaching across the table to take his hands in hers. "You can get better."

Jared nodded and lifted her slender forearm to kiss the back of her hand. Even in this embrace, she felt a million miles away.

TWENTY

All things considered, Jared had been having a surprisingly tolerable day. Any movement sent needles of pain up his neck despite the brace that kept him looking straight ahead, and he'd woken up with a headache that still hadn't gone away. He had a gimp in his left knee too, but that didn't hurt all that much anymore.

And that was it. A little pain, but only the physical variety. No nightmares while he slept, no voices when he woke, no dark and toxic qualities in the air. It wasn't that whoever was responsible for these things—*they*—were gone; Jared could still sense them in the distance, watching him from afar. Resting, perhaps. Maybe causing the wreck had exerted them. Jared wasn't sure it worked that way, but it seemed reasonable. Four days had passed since the wreck, and all four had been free of torment.

Taking the opportunity, Jared had rested too for a while. He still had plenty of sick days left for the year and had told his boss that he'd likely need the rest of the week to recover from the accident. Despite the pain and the uncomfortable neck brace, he had slept well the past two nights. After so many nights of insomnia and half-waking dreams, two nights of deep, healing sleep felt like finding an oasis in the desert. But now there was something he had to do.

Melody had taken wonderful care of him ever since the wreck, preparing his meals, helping him up the stairs, and making sure he took his meds. But Jared wondered if the real reason she'd stuck so close to his side was to make sure he and Elena weren't alone; she'd only left the house twice since the wreck and had taken Elena with her both times.

She had gone back to work this morning, and Jared had expected that this would be his opportunity to talk with Elena again. He'd woken well after Melody had already left, but when he did, Elena was gone too. A note on the kitchen table explained that Melody was dropping her off at Crystal's house to play. Jared wondered if that was Elena's idea and figured it probably wasn't.

The note also explained that Grace and Emily had agreed to stay home for the day to look after him and Timmy. Jared didn't feel like he needed looking after—even getting up and down the stairs by himself was manageable now—but he supposed it was a nice gesture. Depending, again, on what his wife's real intentions were; he had felt plenty of warmth and empathy from her these past two days, but not a lot of trust.

Elena being at Crystal's house, however, was only a minor setback. Nothing a phone call couldn't fix. Jared's cell phone had stopped working yesterday, finally giving in to its mortal wounds. Melody said she would stop by the Verizon store to buy another one on her way home. In the meantime, Grace's phone would have to do.

"Hey, Grace," Jared shouted up the stairs. "Can you come down here, please?"

"Coming," Grace called back.

Jared limped past the stairway and into the living room, lowering himself slowly onto the couch. He heard two sets of footsteps coming down the stairs. He saw Grace first, then Emily behind her.

"What's up, Dad?" Grace asked. Emily walked up beside her and slipped her blue headphones off her ears.

"Hey, can I borrow your phone real quick?" Jared asked.

"Yeah, sure." Grace put the phone up to her face to unlock it, then handed it to him.

"You used to babysit for Mrs. Heaney, right?"

"Yeah, back in high school."

"Do you still have her number in here?"

"Should have."

It took Jared a while to find Elizabeth Heaney's name in the phone's sea of contacts. So many boys' names he didn't recognize. A few long months ago, that might have bothered him just a little.

Finally, he found her number and placed the call. The phone rang four times before she answered. For once, Jared was relieved to hear Elizabeth's nasally, New Yorker voice.

"Hello?"

"Hey, Elizabeth, this is Jared."

"Oh. Hi, Jared. How are you doing? Melody told me about the accident."

"I'm doing fine. Hey, is Elena there with you?"

"Yeah, she's here. Melody dropped her off about nine. She and Crystal have been upstairs all day. We bought a new trampoline for the kids last Tuesday, but it's just been so hot lately, you know? Should have bought a swimming pool instead, I guess."

"Great. Listen, thanks for agreeing to watch her today, but I'm going to send Grace by here in a minute to pick her up. It totally slipped my mind and Melody's too, but she has a dentist appointment this afternoon. We've rescheduled twice already, and, well, I just hate to call that place back and cancel again."

"Yeah, no problem. I'll go tell her."

"Thanks, Elizabeth. Bye."

Jared hung up the phone and handed it back to Grace. She and Emily both stared at him as she took it, clearly confused. "Just a little white lie, girls," he said. "I haven't got to see Elly much since the wreck, and I want her home. But that's a little more than I felt like explaining to Elizabeth. Grace, would you mind picking her up?"

"Mom said we were supposed to stay here to take care of you and Timmy," Emily said. Jared turned his attention to her, but she avoided looking him in the eyes. They both seemed apprehensive now. What had Melody told them? Jared felt embers of frustration flare but kept them suppressed.

"Emily, you can stay here and look after Timmy while Grace goes. It's just a few minutes away. Besides, I'm fine. Grace, is that alright with you?"

"Yeah," Grace said. "Sure. I'll be right back."

She turned for the stairs to fetch her keys, but not before sharing a concerned look with Emily. Jared's irritation rose again. "Something wrong, Grace?" he said.

"Huh-uh," she said. "All good. Right, Em?"

Emily nodded and forced a smile. Jared watched them both for a moment, then decided to leave it at that. "Okay," he said. "Come straight back, please. And thanks too. I should be good to drive again myself any day now. Might still be a while before the Camry's out of the shop, though."

"Yeah, no problem, Dad," Grace said, then headed up the stairs. Emily followed behind her.

It took about twenty minutes for Grace to make the trip to the Heaney house and back. Jared waited anxiously while each one passed.

Elena had been so close to confiding in him, to hopefully shedding light on his situation. Barring another intervention, he was sure he could convince her to talk.

He practically jumped from his chair at the sound of Grace's car pulling back into the drive, forgetting momentarily the injury to his leg until the pain reminded him. He caught his balance and hobbled to the front door, meeting Grace there as she opened it.

Elena stood on the porch beside her older sister, her butterfly skirt and matching headband making her still blue and battered little face all the more heartbreaking. Looking at her there, Jared felt a lattice of emotions he couldn't possibly unravel.

Grace raised her eyebrows at him, presumably because he was standing in front of the doorway like a dog waiting for the mailman, then both of them came inside.

"How was the playdate, Elly?" Jared asked.

"Fun," Elena said. "We drew with colored pencils. Want to see?"

She produced a piece of rolled-up sketch paper from under her arm and handed it to Jared. It was a picture of a cartoon dog with bright blue fur and oversized eyes—like all of her art, surprisingly good for Elena's young age. Jared smiled and handed it back.

"That's amazing, honey." In the corner of his eye, he could see Grace watching him. He turned to her and caught her quickly diverting her gaze. "Hey, Grace. Can I have a minute with Elly?" It was rushed and ham-handed, but he didn't have much time; Melody would be home before long, and then he'd have no chance of getting Elena alone.

Again, Jared could sense Grace's apprehension. Again, he pursed his lips and pretended not to notice. Grace wasn't the confrontational type, and if he kept his temper, she'd do what he asked. The fact that she and Emily now distrusted him as much as Melody was a problem for another time.

"Sure," Grace said. She gave Elena a playful smile, then headed upstairs.

"Have you eaten yet, sweety?" Jared asked Elena once he'd made sure that Grace wasn't listening from the top of the stairs.

"Yeah," Elena said, sitting down on the couch. "Crystal's mom made spaghetti for lunch."

"Oh, that sounds good."

"It was yummy. I am thirsty, though."

Jared stepped into the kitchen, leaning to peer through the archway at Elena as he opened the fridge. "Capri Sun or Gatorade?"

"Capri Sun."

Jared grabbed one of the silver pouches from the door rack and limped back to the living room. He put it down on the coffee table in front of Elena, then sat down beside her. "How's your eye?" he asked. The swelling was mostly gone now, but the skin was still a motley purple shade.

"It doesn't really hurt anymore. Crystal said I look like a witch."

"Well, don't tell Crystal, but she looks like a little witch even without a black eye."

Elena giggled a little, and Jared put his arm around her. "Listen, sweetheart," he said. "I'm really sorry about what happened the other night. I should have been paying more attention to the road."

"It's okay. It wasn't your fault."

Jared wondered what she meant by this exactly, whether it was a meaningless consolation or something more. His throat felt dry all of a sudden, and he stole a long sip from her Capri Sun.

"You were going to tell me something right before we crashed, though, weren't you? Something about Ronny." He felt her tense against his arm. "It's okay, Elly," he said. "You can tell me. You *have* to tell me, baby."

She wouldn't look at him, and for a while, she wouldn't say anything. When she finally spoke, her voice was a fearful whisper. "Daddy, I can't."

"Why?"

"Because it isn't safe," Elena said, whispering still as if she didn't want someone else to hear. The thought made Jared feel cold.

"Tell me anyway. Safe or not, tell me anyway. It's the only way we can fix this, Elly."

But Elena wasn't paying attention to him anymore, Jared realized. She was staring beyond him instead, at the empty corner of the living room behind the couch. Her eyes had widened, and the color had left her skin. Jared watched her, terrified to turn around and see what she was seeing.

When he finally managed the courage, there was nothing there. Just the floor lamp and the curtains fluttering in the draft.

"What is it?" he asked, turning back to Elena. Her face was still ashen, but she was looking at him now. To Jared's surprise, she smiled. Even as faint as it was, it looked eerie aside the fear that had still not entirely left her eyes.

"It's okay, Daddy," she said. "It's going to be okay."

"What's going to be okay, Elly? What did you do?"

But Elena didn't respond. She just gave him another weary smile—like she was the adult and he the child that needed to be sheltered. Comforted, but not clued in on all the horrible realities of the world.

Then there was the sound of a car pulling into the drive. Melody had come home early. Before Jared could recover from this strange shift in dynamic, she was walking through the door. Her eyes landed on him and Elena at once, full of suspicion.

"Hey, Mommy," Elena said, her voice as cheery as ever. Jared watched as a little of his wife's concern melted away. Not all, but a little.

"What's up?" Melody asked. "I thought you were hanging out with Crystal today?"

"I had Grace go pick her up," Jared said.

"How come?"

Jared shrugged. "Just felt like seeing her." It was the only lie he could muster. Melody glared at him but didn't press him further. "You're home early," he said.

"I decided not to go to the Verizon store."

"How come?"

"I was just tired. We can go tomorrow if you're feeling up to it." Her lie was almost as obvious as his. He should have counted on Grace texting her.

"Alright. I'd probably rather pick out a new phone myself anyway, come to think of it."

"Elena," Melody asked. "You want to come help me with dinner?"

"Okay," Elena said and got up from the couch. Before she disappeared behind the archway, Jared saw her cast one final glance at the empty back corner of the room.

TWENTY-ONE

THURSDAY, JULY 12ᵀᴴ

Jared sighed and tried once more to focus on the television screen. On it, a leopard held a gazelle in its jaws while a narrator with a British accent spouted off some bullshit about the circle of life. He watched for a while longer, then gave up and turned off the set.

Each minute of the past few days had passed agonizingly slow. The respite from his suffering had been a relief at first, but now it just felt like waiting. Waiting out the calm before the storm. Like rain in the air, Jared could almost sense *them* out there somewhere, preparing their next move. And he could tell it would not be long coming.

Sense it or not, though, there was no way for him to stop it. Days with nothing to do but wrack his brain for answers had only driven home how helpless he truly was.

He had tried once more to talk to Elena. Twice more to talk with Melody. None of those conversations went anywhere. Melody wouldn't hear a word of it and was ready to get Dr. Stewart on the phone the moment he even mentioned the danger they were in. Elena, meanwhile, seemed to know full well that the danger existed—and seemed not to care. In the brief conversation Jared had managed with her while Melody gave Timmy a bath, all she would tell him was that he didn't need to be afraid. Jared wasn't sure if that was a child's unfounded optimism or something more ominous, but it did not comfort him either way.

It had crossed Jared's mind that perhaps these past few days were not, in fact, a respite from his suffering, but rather a new chapter of it. Like a cat toying with a mouse, letting it wriggle and writhe on the ground for a while before sinking her claws in again. Like an inquisitor letting his subject up for air just long enough to keep them from drowning before plunging them face-first back into the water.

Jared's mind whirred through these and a thousand other despairing thoughts. When the sound of Melody yelling from upstairs jolted him awake, the hot afternoon rays coming in through the living room window had cooled to the orange hue of sundown.

"Jared!" she shouted again. Her voice still sounded a little distant in his sleep-muddled brain, but it was clear enough this time to trigger a response. He could hear the alarm in her tone now and felt his pulse quicken.

He leaped off the couch and hurried up the stairs. Melody was waiting for him when he got to the top, standing outside the open door to Timmy's bedroom. She turned back inside the room once he arrived, and Jared followed her in. He expected to see Timmy lying on the floor, sick, or injured.

Or dead...

But the room was empty. Jared scanned it quickly. Toys were scattered on the floor, and the sheets were tangled in a pile at the foot of Timmy's bed. He felt a warm breeze brush across his face, then saw with cold realization what Melody too must have seen. The window in Timmy's bedroom was open. It was open, and Timmy was gone.

Jared prepared himself for the worst when he leaned out the window, expecting to see his son lying in a broken heap on the ground two stories below. It was a long way down for a five-year-old child to climb, and the rain gutter running along the side of the window would have been the only thing for him to hold on to.

But he didn't see Timmy when he looked out the window, nor any sign that he had fallen. Jared broadened his search, scanning the backyard. He saw the swing set, the oak tree, the firepit with grass grown up around it, and the gate to the privacy fence that surrounded the yard, swinging softly back and forth in the breeze—unlocked and open.

"Come on, Mel," Jared said. "Go get Emily. She needs to help us look for him."

"Look where?" Melody asked.

"The gate's open. He's probably close by, but he's not in the yard, and the gate's open." Jared saw the concern on Melody's face grow more severe as realization dawned on her.

She turned to leave, but before she made it to the door, a thought struck Jared. "Get Emily and then call Grace," he said. "Tell her to come home right now and bring Elly with her."

Grace had gone to the mall and dropped Elena off at Crystal's again. Jared wondered if Melody would question the reasoning for calling them home and wasn't sure what he'd say if she did. The storm was breaking now. He could feel it. And having them...no, having *Elena* home felt somehow vital.

But Melody only nodded and took off to go find Emily. Jared followed her out the door and scrambled down the stairs, swiping a flashlight from the kitchen drawer and hoping he wouldn't be out long enough to need it.

The neighborhood was relatively safe, he assured himself as best he could. He and Melody checked online for sex offenders living nearby on a semi-regular basis and always came up empty, and the only predators of the four-legged variety that took up residence in the woods behind their home were coyotes. Jared knew that a pack of coyotes would be more than capable of bringing down a defenseless five-year-old, but he'd never heard of a coyote attacking a human being, especially in broad daylight. Most animals as smart as dogs had learned to stay far away from the vengeful, hairless apes.

Yet none of this reasoning made the dread any less dizzying. Timmy wandering away would have been worrying under normal circumstances. And Jared could feel it in the very air against his skin that these were not normal circumstances.

When he made it across the yard to the open gate, he noticed a small footprint in the mud. It had rained the night before, leaving the ground soft and wet. Jared wondered if he might be able to track Timmy all the way to wherever he'd gone. But when a quick search of the ground outside the gate didn't turn up any more footprints, he gave up on the idea.

He stood in place a few steps beyond the gate and turned in a half circle, trying to decide which direction he should head. To his left and right were more houses. Jared didn't exactly consider any of his neighbors close friends, but he knew any one of them would recognize Timmy if they saw him wandering through their yard and would certainly bring him home at once.

Directly ahead, to the west, was the forest. Looking at it, Jared felt his stomach twist into a ball. Black limbs reached into a darkening sky, blocking from sight anything more than a few feet into the woods. A crow cried out from somewhere in the trees.

Jared heard footsteps coming up behind him, and soon both Melody and Emily were standing next to him.

"Mel, I want you to start going to the neighbors," Jared said. "See if they've seen him. Emily, you stay here at the house in case he comes back or in case someone tries to call. Okay?"

"Where are you going?" Melody asked.

"I'm going to look for him in the woods." Melody cast a glance at the tree line and bit her bottom lip. They must have seemed ominous to her as well. "Did you call Grace?" he asked.

"Yes," Melody said. "She's going to pick up Elly and head home."

"Good," Jared said, satisfied, at least, with this.

Melody grabbed Emily by the hand and walked back through the gate, leaving Jared alone. He still didn't know what direction to take. The track of woods was over a mile thick and several miles long. Straight ahead seemed like the most obvious route, however, and Jared hoped that it would have been the most obvious route for Timmy, too.

He took off at a hobbling jog towards the tree line but slowed down to a crawling pace the moment he entered the woods. The trees were grouped tightly together, almost strangling one another, and thorn-covered brambles were scattered about the ground like razor wire in a war zone. They tugged and ripped at Jared's clothing and skin with every step he took, tearing out strands of thread and opening up small, red lines on his exposed forearms and calves. He did his best to maneuver around the brambles and trees, seeking out small paths into the forest where the foliage was less dense. But the zigzag path combined with the still present ache in his left knee made progress slow.

"Timmy!" he cried out as loud as he could. Up ahead, a crow squawked out its reply. Jared listened for a moment longer, then pressed ahead. He was deep enough into the forest now that he could no longer see through the trees behind him. One direction looked the same as the other, and he took careful note of his bearings to keep from getting lost himself. The woods were suffocatingly dense, and for a moment Jared thought about turning back around, convinced that there was no way his young son could have ever made it through this thicket.

Then, up ahead, he saw something on the ground. It was bright blue—a color out of place against the browns and greens of the woods. Jared inched around a patch of briars and made his way closer to the object, close enough to see it clearly through the foliage that broke up its profile. It was a shoe—Timmy's shoe. It dangled a couple inches off the ground, its laces caught in a tangle of thorns. Jared felt the strongest wave of dizziness yet as he knelt down and began untangling the shoe. He couldn't imagine why Timmy would leave it behind. Why he would continue to press farther into the woods across jagged rocks and briars with a bare foot.

"Timmy!" he cried out again. This time, not even the crow responded. He glanced down at his watch. It was 7:48 now. In less than an hour, it would be full dark. The thought of Timmy in these woods alone at night filled him with newfound urgency. "Timmy!"

No reply. Jared called out again and pressed farther into the woods. He'd never been this far into the forest behind their home, yet somehow it felt familiar. He suddenly recalled the night terror he'd had—the one that had taken place in these woods—and felt like moaning; there was no way to tell one tree from another in this forest, but Jared was nonetheless struck with the notion that this spot where he now stood had been the exact location of his previous night terror.

With no warning, the world around him began to spark and buzz. The branches and ground trembled, and sparks danced across his eyes.

Not now, he thought. *Please, not now.*

That's when *they* returned to him—at once and with fury. Jared's ears began to ring, and his vision swam. He took a step forward, tripped over a root, and fell to his knees, hitting the one he'd injured against a rock that was buried in the ground.

Pain coursed up his leg, seeming to shake up the hornet's nest inside his head even more. His vision blurred, fading away as spots of white light winked in and out of existence. The woods seemed pitch dark now, as if the sun had somehow fully set in the few minutes he'd been inside the forest.

Jared tried to stand, but a flash of pain in his knee sent him back down to all fours. The ringing in his ears was overwhelming now—a roar of noise. Leaves and bark seemed to close in on him, crushing him from all sides. The darkness that had come from nowhere pressed in on him too, making it so that all he could see was the silhouettes of limbs and leaves and the static that sparked in the air.

Jared sobbed. He covered his ears and pressed his face into the ground. He willed it all to go away, the noise and the static and the foul, deathly odor that now filled his nostrils and slicked his tongue.

Instead, it all grew stronger. Jared screamed, pressing his hands even harder against his ears and burying his face deeper into the blanket of wet leaves. Then, as if simply nodding off to sleep, he felt his conscious-ness slip away.

When Jared woke, still face down in wet leaves and mud, his first thought was to wonder if he was dreaming, to wonder if this was simply the start of another brutal night terror taking place in these woods. It took him a few seconds to ascertain that he was not dreaming and that his predica-ment was real. This, Jared realized at once, was far worse.

He rolled over onto his back and stared through the tops of the trees at the sky beyond. It was dark now. Not the bizarre, artificial darkness that he'd felt earlier, but a true darkness that signaled the sun had set some time ago. Jared suddenly remembered the reason he'd come into these woods and let out a weak cry. He pushed himself into a sitting position, then jolted back in surprise.

Someone was standing in front of him. It was too dark to make out anything more than the shadowy figure of a person, but they were close enough for their form to stand out against the trees. A scream caught in Jared's throat, and only a dry, choked gurgle came out.

The figure took a step closer. Jared could see now that it was small—much smaller than a full-grown person. He strained his eyes, and the figure came closer. He fumbled for the flashlight in his pocket and flicked it on. Against the bright beam, Timmy squinted and shielded his eyes with a mud-covered forearm.

"Timmy?" Jared said. Timmy moved his arm and stared at him with a confused, squinting gaze. He was entirely unclothed save for one shoe on his right foot, and his skin was covered in splotches of mud and deep red scratches. Scraps of leaves hung in his curly brown hair, and dried blood speckled his cheek from a cut above his eye.

"Can we go home, Daddy?" Timmy asked, as calmly as if he were making the suggestion from the back seat of their car. Jared was at a loss for words. He scrambled to his feet, ignoring the pain in his knee. Timmy turned away from him and began to walk away, but Jared caught up with him quickly and lifted him into his arms.

"Where are your clothes, son?" Jared asked. It seemed to be the only question he could formulate. Timmy, however, didn't reply. Jared saw that his eyes were closed, and he could hear him snoring softly. He pulled his son tight against his chest and took off walking in the direction he hoped would lead them out of the forest.

TWENTY-TWO

THURSDAY, JULY 12TH

Had a few more minutes passed before the flashlight beam flickering through the tree line signaled their return, Melody would have called the police. She had met them at the gate with her phone in hand, moments from placing the call.

Jared wondered what the cops would have thought watching him carry a naked and injured boy out of the woods after already taking a long look at him just days ago with visions of child endangerment charges dancing in their heads.

It didn't really matter anyway. Paled in comparison to other concerns. But Jared was glad to have avoided the whole fiasco all the same. He assumed Melody must have been thinking the same thing; she certainly hadn't put off calling the police for lack of concern.

None of Timmy's injuries turned out to be serious. They had given him a thorough examination as soon as they got him back inside. The cut above his eye wasn't deep enough to need stitches and fell well within the range of what Band-Aids could fix. The few other small cuts and scrapes did as well.

Patching each one, however, was taking some time. They had given him a shower first, then brought him to his bedroom. Now, Timmy was stretched out on the bed while Melody dabbed Neosporin across a cut on his shin. Jared handed her a Band-Aid when she finished.

"How's that feel?" Melody asked, smoothing the adhesive tape against his skin.

"Fine," Timmy said.

"One more, okay," she said and turned her attention to the scrape on his right shoulder.

Jared watched her work, trying to get a sense of what she was thinking. Was she suspicious of him? Every mark on the boy's body could be explained by the impossible thicket he'd pushed through. She knew that Jared wasn't the one who brought him out there, only the one to find him. But the same sight that would've looked bad to a police officer might have looked a little strange to her too. A few weeks ago, probably not, but now, maybe so.

If Melody held any suspicions, though, she wasn't showing them yet. Caring for Timmy had been her only concern the moment Jared carried him through the gate.

"Let's get some clothes on you now," she told Timmy, leaning in to kiss him on the cheek. She dressed him in a pair of Scooby-Doo pajamas, being as careful as she could not to slide the fabric across his scrapes. Then she pulled the blankets up around his shoulders and tucked him in.

It seemed strange to be putting him to bed so early. He wasn't injured nearly bad enough for bed rest. Was it early, though? For the first time since waking in the woods, Jared thought to check his watch.

It was 10:47 now, he realized. Not early at all. Jared figured about an hour had passed since he made it out of the woods. That meant he'd been in the woods for about two hours. *Unconscious* for all but fifteen minutes of it at most.

Something had happened in those woods while he slept. Jared could feel it. *They* had done something to Timmy. Something Jared wasn't supposed to see. And to stop him from seeing it, they had simply put him to sleep while they worked. He, their puppet to control.

While Melody checked Timmy's body for injury, Jared had searched his eyes for other kinds of affliction. But exhaustion was all he found. Now, those eyes were closed, and his son's breathing was soft and rhythmic.

"I think I'm going to stay here with him for a while longer," Melody whispered. "He's alright, I know. I just don't feel like leaving him right now."

"Mind if I turn in?" Jared was exhausted too. If sleeping was what he'd been doing those two missing hours, it sure didn't feel like it now.

"Yeah, go ahead. We can talk about all this in the morning."

Jared wasn't sure what she meant by that but figured he'd find out soon enough. His knee throbbed, protesting all the activity and the knock it had taken during his tumble to the ground. He hadn't been scratched up nearly as badly as Timmy, seeing as he had remained fully clothed, but there were still angry red lines down his forearms and calves. He needed a hot shower and lots of rest. The rest part most of all.

Jared closed the door behind him as he left Timmy's room, then turned down the hall. Near the end of it, Elena was standing outside her bedroom door. Seeing her, he flinched a little in surprise.

"Is Timmy okay?"

Jared exhaled, but his heartbeat kept its pounding pace. "Yeah, Elly. He's okay."

Elena smiled. "Good." She turned to go back into her room.

"Hey, Elly," Jared said, turning her back around. "Do you know what he was doing out there?"

Her smile faded. He watched her gather her thoughts. "Timmy went somewhere he shouldn't have. But it's not his fault, Daddy. Don't be mad at him."

"Where did he go?" And then, when she offered no response to this, "Have you gone there too?"

"Once," Elena said, her voice a whisper now. "It's okay, though, Daddy. I won't let Ronny hurt you."

Stunned, Jared watched her blow him a kiss, then disappear into her bedroom. The door closed, and he heard its lock turn.

TWENTY-THREE

FRIDAY, JULY 13TH

Sleep tugged at Jared's mind, an indomitable vortex into unconsciousness that felt almost drug-induced. It had struck him in the hallway the moment Elena's bedroom door closed and had almost sent him to his knees right there. Skipping the shower, he'd at least managed to strip off his dirty clothes before collapsing onto the bed.

He surrendered the instant his body hit the mattress. But the waters that unnatural vortex pulled him to were shallow, his sleep disturbed every few minutes by noises down the hall.

A particularly loud noise roused Jared enough for him to raise his head and open his eyes. His vision swam, but the blurred numbers on his clock looked like they said 12:07 a.m. He was alone in the bed and determined in his half-awake mind that Melody must have been the cause of the sound.

Then he heard it again, unmistakable this time. A hesitant knock against the bedroom door.

"Who's there?" Jared managed with some effort. Had he *actually* been drugged? His faculties were coming back to him slowly, but fighting off the lingering listlessness proved a queerly difficult task.

"It's me, Dad," Grace replied.

"Just a second." Jared tossed the covers off his legs, then turned on the lamp. He pulled a pair of shorts and a t-shirt from the dresser and put them on as quick as he could manage. Then he opened the bedroom door.

"Dad, can we talk?" Grace said. Her voice was weak, and her eyes were red and watery.

Jared put his arms around her. She practically went limp when he did. "Honey, what's wrong?" he asked, helping her to the edge of the bed.

"I don't feel right."

"What's the matter?"

"I don't know," she said and started to tremble.

Jared hugged her tighter. She felt so frail quivering in his arms, like a little girl again. "Tell me what you're feeling, sweetheart. Tell me what's wrong."

She started to speak, then it turned into a stammer. She took a labored breath, then started again. "I feel like something's inside me." Another labored breath. "In my head. Under my skin. Oh Dad, please make it stop!"

A violent shudder passed over her. Beads of sweat broke out across her skin, and the color flushed from her face. Jared felt her muscles go slack in his arms, and he had to catch her to keep her from falling off the bed.

She stared up at him, pleading silently with panicked eyes. Jared would have given things a lot more precious than his own life to make it stop. But watch in horror was all that he could do.

Tears poured out of her wide, frozen eyes in a steady stream, but her gaze never moved. Her mouth gaped open as if to form a scream that never came. It was as if she had been struck paralyzed at the peak of terror.

The air whistled out of her throat in a drawn-out sigh. Then she didn't inhale again. Jared pressed a panicked hand against her mouth but felt no breath against his skin. He watched helpless as the life leaked from her eyes like water wrung from a rag.

A wail formed in his chest and roiled up his throat. But surprise cut it short. She had just blinked. Her eyes were still frozen and lifeless, but the eyelids had undoubtedly moved. Jared leaned in closer.

Like time ran in reverse, he watched the color return to her paling skin. Life flooded back into her eyes, and they started to move. She blinked again, then looked to the left. Then to the right. Then up at Jared.

Jared let her slip from his arms as she rose slowly to her feet. Now it felt like he was the one paralyzed. Was this a miracle he was witnessing? Could he even call it such, knowing with sickening certainty the evil that had performed it?

Grace walked around the bed, running her fingers across the linens and her eyes around the room. She took a deep breath in through her nose and exhaled with a sigh. Then she turned to face Jared again.

"You don't look so good, Daddy," she said. Jared stuttered, at a total loss for words. "You should get some rest." She turned her back to him and headed for the bedroom door.

"Grace," he said, jumping to his feet. "Are you... Are you alright?"

"Yes, Daddy," she said without turning around. "We're fine."

"What?"

"I said I'm fine." She looked over her shoulder and gave him a wink. "Go lie down. You need your rest."

Jared took another step toward her, but Grace slipped through the door. "Sweet dreams, Daddy," she whispered through the crack as it closed.

TWENTY-FOUR

FRIDAY, JULY 13TH

FROM THE JOURNAL OF GREG GORDON
ENTRY #33: DATED 1/22/1994

What more do I have to suffer before they will let me die? How great must the offering to my new gods be?

They've taken my boys. Not just Jeremiah but Jared too. It's unspeakable the things they've made them do. It's more than any father could bear.

I am a dead man already. There is no soul left for you to torment. You have taken from me all hope and goodness and life. Now let this husk that remains fulfill your final demand. Please, oh gods, let it be so.

Jared kept his finger at the end of the page but didn't flip it. He checked the date of the entry again. 1/22/1994. Greg Gordon had hung himself the morning of the twenty-third. If this wasn't the journal's final entry, the next page surely was.

A faint sound from somewhere inside the house caught Jared's ears. He tried to ignore it. Tried not to imagine what it might be. Such imaginings had kept him awake for hours and were what had driven him out to the garage.

All manner of strange sounds had been coming from Grace's bedroom ever since she left his. Bumps and moans, sobs and trickles of laughter. All muted, but all impossible to ignore. How Melody had never heard it from Timmy's room where she'd ended up staying the night, Jared didn't know.

Once, in a moment of courage, he had snuck down the hall and rapped gently against Grace's door. But there had been no reply. Just her voice whispering from somewhere at the back of the room. And a second voice whispering back.

After that, he had come down to the garage and turned on the overhead lights; there would be no sleeping tonight.

Part of him wanted to rush back upstairs and break down Grace's door. To try and save her. Wasn't that what any good father would do? But that was where the plan ended. She had been in his arms when they'd taken her, and there'd still been nothing he could do.

Reading the journal seemed the only possible action that Jared could take. And now it was at its end. He wondered if he should close it now and save the hope of a final page. One last lifeline he could turn to the next time he was left helpless.

But the longing to see its conclusion was too strong. Jared turned the page. He saw more writing, and relief washed over him. Why did he need so badly for it not to end?

Something was off, though, he realized. The page was in pencil, while the rest of the journal had been written in the same black ink throughout. Then he noticed the heading and felt his throat tighten.

Dear Brother,

I hope you never read this. I hope I'm wrong and you never have a reason to. But if you are, then that means you've read the rest too. And for that to have happened, I know something must be horribly wrong.

Two weeks ago, I had a vision. I saw them coming for you. The things that killed Dad. Ra'Tak.

I prayed, and talked with Clarice, and searched my soul. I knew that warning you would not be easy. And neither would confessing the truth.

Dad had it right. I let them in. I didn't know what they were or what I was doing. At first, I thought it was just a game in my head. Something I'd made up. By the time I realized what I was doing, it was too late.

I was their connection to this realm. Maybe I still am. Maybe they've found another. But they are back now. I can feel them, just like before.

They are back for you, Jared. And I'm afraid it won't stop there. Their curse is generational. I let them in, and now they will follow our blood down the line until that line is extinguished. It's why Clarice and I have never even dared to adopt, much less have children of our own.

I want redemption. I want to fix what I caused and am willing to do whatever it takes. If I am still their only link to this world, then I realize the sacrifice that might be required. Even that would not be too much.

I am here for you, Jared. Please call me if you need help. I want to help however I can. I don't blame you anymore for leaving. I hope you can forgive me too.

Jeremiah Gordon

Jared turned to the next page but found it blank. Nothing but empty white space between the ruled paper's thin, blue lines. He turned to the next page and then the next. But these were empty too.

They had granted Greg Gordon his wish. Allowed him to die. With no one there to witness his final moments, his scrawled prayer to them would stand as his last words.

Not dwelling on this lest sorrow compound his misery, Jared turned the pages back to his brother's note. He read it again slowly, pausing to ponder each line.

Jeremiah had let them in but not intentionally. Jared had assumed as much of his brother and assumed it of Elly as well. They were both victims, tricked into making a terrible mistake.

Their curse is generational. This was the line that bothered Jared the most. Thinking of his children in the context of these words was agony. If they survived this as he and Jeremiah had done, would it return for them too someday? Someday when they were grown and had children of their own and the dark memories of childhood were distant and dismissed. He couldn't handle thinking about it anymore and moved his eyes to the next section. He could only hope that his brother was wrong.

What if Jeremiah was still their link to this world? Would the sacrifice he mentioned indeed break that link? Pondering this was difficult too, but less so than the alternative. Jared realized in that moment that if all else failed, it was a sacrifice he, too, would be willing to make.

He read the last paragraph and relished in the faint breath of comfort it brought. It felt good knowing that someone else knew the truth. Contacting him might not be possible. *They* hadn't allowed it before. But simply knowing he wasn't alone was more relieving than he'd expected it to be.

Jared rested in that relief for a while, his eyes closed and his head leaned back against the chair. It was almost six in the morning by the time he woke.

When he crept back upstairs and into the bedroom, he saw that Melody had returned during the night and was asleep on the bed. She stirred only slightly when he slipped under the comforter.

When a wail loud enough to wake the neighbors sounded from down the hall, she didn't stir at all. Not then, nor at the burst of laughter that followed, nor at the sound of furniture falling to the floor. He watched her sleep peacefully through it all, as though she hadn't heard a single patter.

Staring at the ceiling with no hope of sleeping himself, Jared lay still and listened. He listened until he could take it no more, then covered his ears with his pillow and waited for the dawn.

TWENTY-FIVE

FRIDAY, JULY 20ᵀᴴ

Jared's phone vibrated against the newly repaired Camry's center console, jiggling the nickels and pennies at the bottom of the cupholder. He glanced down at it, the strange ringtone catching him off guard; he had gone with Melody to the Verizon store to purchase it two days ago in a moment of relative peace and was still getting used to all the newness.

His number and contacts, though, had both stayed the same. On the phone's screen above the red and green telephone symbols, Jared saw the name Shirley Stein. His boss. He listened to it buzz and watched the name on the screen until finally the call was dropped. A few seconds later, a little red notification indicating a new voicemail appeared at the top of the screen.

Jared picked up the phone and clicked on the notification. The message began to play.

"Hey, Jared. I hope everything's alright. I haven't heard from you in a while. I know you said your phone was busted, so I tried sending an email too. Anyway, I need you to get a hold of me. You, uh…you ran out of sick days last Monday. We can work something out if you still need more time to recover. But I just really need you to call me back. The team's been struggling to pick up the slack, and if we can't get you back soon, we're going to have to start looking at a replacement. Just call me back, okay? As soon as you can."

Jared put the phone back in the cupholder. It had been fifteen days since his accident. Seven days since Timmy got lost in the woods and Grace got lost…somewhere else. Had he really not gone into work all this time?

He'd been going *somewhere*. The fact he was parked in the driveway, clearly returning from a trip to some place or another was proof of that. But even now, just moments removed from the experience, Jared couldn't say where that place had been.

Most of his memories from the past six days were just as distant and scattered. Every moment felt like waking from a dream that he couldn't quite remember. What he did remember made forgetting seem like a mercy.

They had taken Grace. His firstborn child. The one who had first shown him new depths of his love. She was gone, and something else had taken her place.

Taken.

Gone.

Jared wasn't sure which word best fit what had happened to Grace. He liked to think that she was lost somewhere. Lost was much more hopeful than gone.

Through the Camry's windshield, he stared up at the house. It looked so foreboding to be just another cookie-cutter home in his cookie-cutter neighborhood. There were no weathered gargoyles perched on top of ivy-covered spires. Just red brick walls and charcoal shingles. No boarded-up windows where candles flickered in the dead of night. Just windows to vibrant rooms where children still played. Even the sky above it was cheery and blue, a few wispy cirrus clouds brushing strokes of white across the cerulean canvas.

But his home was haunted all the same.

He wondered how long he had been sitting there in the drive, putting off going inside. Not that it would matter. Grace—or whatever pretended to be her—would be in there when he came in. It never left.

Melody was in there too, and that offered Jared some hope. The Grace-thing never acted out when she was around.

In fact, it seemed to avoid all interaction with anyone but him. When it had no choice, it mimicked its host's personality with near-perfect accuracy. Only someone who knew her like a daughter and watched closely would have been able to spot the difference. Jared found these moments almost as frightening as the moments when the Grace-thing found him alone and revealed its own, awful nature.

It sounded cruel even in his own thoughts to call what was left of his oldest daughter a thing. But thinking in these terms was the only way for him to cope.

It wasn't Grace that had caught a rat from God knows where and eaten it alive in front of him, grinning with bloodstained teeth as it screamed and writhed in her fist.

It wasn't Grace that had snuck into his bedroom one morning after Melody left and taken off her clothes, sliding under the covers and taking him in her hand before he woke and threw himself out of bed onto the floor.

It wasn't Grace whose eyes turned black as death and whose garbled voice mocked the secret fears and insecurities that he had never told even his wife.

It was the Grace-thing who did all these. He was already teetering on the brink of madness; to think of all that had happened in any other terms would shove him right over.

Jared pulled the key from the car's ignition and opened the driver's door. Hot July air blasted into the air-conditioned cabin. Beads of sweat broke out on his forehead almost at once. The bank sign on the way home from wherever he'd been had read 102 degrees. That memory seemed to come back from nowhere. Another contextless freeze-frame to add to the reel.

He locked the car and headed down the flagstone walkway toward the front door. He paused outside it and pressed his ear against the wood, listening for voices inside. Had any of his neighbors seen him, they would have thought him crazy. But this thought barely crossed Jared's mind.

It was silent inside. All he could hear were songbirds in the trees and the whir of a lawnmower somewhere down the street. Steadying his nerve, Jared opened the door.

The rush of cold air should have been welcome, but it felt more chilling than refreshing. Jared scanned the entryway. He heard the scrape of a chair from the kitchen and held his breath.

Elena walked through the archway. She looked better now than she had the past few days, having woken with a nasty cold the morning after Grace was taken. At least that was Melody's diagnosis. Jared had his own suspicions.

But her skin was a little rosier now and her eyes a little brighter. She smiled when she saw him and ran up to hug his waist. Jared exhaled and placed a tentative hand on her back.

"Where have you been, Daddy?"

"Just out for a drive," Jared said. He searched his daughter's eyes. Did *she* know where he had been? Was she aware that he didn't know himself? But all he found there was mild curiosity. "Where's your mom?"

"Upstairs."

"And your brother and sisters?"

"Emily went to Violet's house, I think. Grace and Timmy are upstairs too."

"What have you been up to?"

"Just about to eat lunch," Elena said. She walked back into the kitchen, and Jared followed her.

He sat down at the table and watched her eat. Even though she did seem better, to look at her closely still told the story of a sick little girl. It was unusual for a child to be ill so long, Melody had expressed to him last night, especially since she'd been taking the antibiotic her doctor prescribed. Jared had reached this same conclusion right from the start; her falling ill the same night Grace had been taken was very unusual indeed.

"We need to talk, Elly," he said.

"I know," Elena said. Her compliance took Jared by surprise. "Something happened last week, Daddy. The night that Timmy got lost in the woods."

"What? What happened?" Jared's heart was thrumming so fast he could feel his pulse in his temples.

"I don't know if I can explain it. But—"

"Try, Elly. Try and explain it."

"It's going to happen again tonight," Elena said. Her voice had dropped almost to a whisper, and some wave of emotion—maybe fear, maybe something else—clouded her features and turned her gaze distant.

"What's going to happen, Elly? Tell me. Right now. Tell me what's going on." Jared's ears started to ring. His eyes burned from staring unblinking at her for so long. His lips had barely stopped moving, yet still it felt like minutes had passed.

But Elena wasn't looking at him anymore. She was looking behind him now, at the kitchen archway. Jared turned around and saw Grace standing at the entry.

For an instant near imperceptible, her eyes flashed solid black. A blink of his own eyes and they were normal again. She smiled wide and strolled into the kitchen.

"Well, you two look serious," she said, still grinning wickedly. "Why the long faces?" She brushed a strand of loose hair behind her ear. Jared saw fresh scabs covering her wrist when she lifted her arm, a couple of the deeper gashes still oozing blood. It wasn't the first time these past six days she'd come downstairs with some horrific injury. Like those, these cuts, too, were sure to have miraculously healed by the next time Melody saw her.

She caught him looking at them and winked, slipping her sleeve down a little farther to cover the wounds. "Elena," she said. "I'm actually working on something I could use your help with." She reached out her hand and beckoned Elena to take it.

Elena looked at Jared first, then back at her sister. Then she took her hand. Jared watched the Grace-thing lead Elena out of the kitchen. He heard two sets of footsteps walking up the stairs.

Standing there alone in the kitchen, he felt a rush of adrenaline for the first time in days. For the first time in days, Jared had a plan.

TWENTY-SIX

SATURDAY, JULY 21ST

In the bed behind him, Melody hummed softly and turned over in her sleep. Jared checked the clock on the nightstand and saw that it was 2:06 a.m., then he turned his eyes back to the crack in the bedroom door.

He had opened it just enough to peer through and had left a lamp on at the end of the hallway. Through the slit, he could see the closed doors of his children's bedrooms. The door to Elena's bedroom, most importantly of all.

Something bad was indeed happening tonight. Jared had been able to sense it ever since Elena spoke it to life. But if he was there to witness it when it did, maybe he could stop it. Or at least learn something useful.

The plan seemed thin now in the dark of night with his knees cramping and his mind fighting sleep. Not nearly as encouraging as it had been in the light of day. Whatever Elena did or didn't do tonight, there was no rule that said she couldn't do it from her bedroom, quiet and out of sight. If there were any rules at all to this awful game, Jared didn't know them.

But with no other hope to cling to, he kept his eyes locked on the empty hall. Eyes that finally began to falter when another hour passed.

A noise startled them back open. All the doors were still closed, but the sound had been unmistakable. One of them had opened and then closed again.

Jared eased his own bedroom door open a little farther and stepped out into the hallway. He tiptoed down the hardwood floor to Elena's door. He pressed his ear against it but heard only the rhythmic swish of her ceiling fan inside.

There was no way of knowing for sure, but intuition told him that the sound had come from farther down the hall. From one of the bedrooms at the end, most likely. Either Emily's or Timmy's room.

But there were no sounds coming from either now, and Jared was at a loss for what to do next. He stood there in the hallway, growing more anxious with each second that passed, until he could take the inaction no more. Letting impulse make the decision for him, he reached out and opened Timmy's bedroom door.

Scanning the dimly lit room, he spotted Timmy beneath the covers of his bed. The blankets rose and fell gently with the rhythm of his breath, and his hand clasped the leg of his teddy bear. Jared leaned in closer, close enough to see that Timmy's eyes were closed and moving back and forth beneath his eyelids as he dreamed.

He turned his attention to the window. The cream-colored blinds were pulled down, obscuring all but the very bottom of the pane. Still, he could see enough to confirm that the window was closed. Closed and locked, best he could tell. And yet the feeling that someone else was in the room clamped around him suddenly like a frozen vice.

Jared felt his hairs stiffen as he imagined the Grace-thing jumping out at him from the closet. Or clawing out from underneath the bed.

He should check on her, he thought. Make sure she's in her room. He'd likely regret it, but the thought of her…it…lurking in the darkness was something he had to dispel. He turned to leave when a strange sight caught his eye.

Timmy's foot stuck out from underneath the comforter and dangled over the edge of the bed. It was covered by the fuzzy blue fabric and rubberized sole of a pajama onesie that Melody had dressed him in after his bath. In the dim glow of Timmy's Scooby-Doo night-light, Jared could see that something was stuck in the small rubber treads.

He took a step closer, and Timmy stirred a little, murmuring in his sleep. Jared leaned in and strained his eyes. The object came into focus. It was a small piece of bark, plastered against the treads of his pajamas with what looked to be a layer of fresh mud. Scanning the floor, Jared traced a trail of small, muddy prints from Timmy's bed back to the window.

Not pausing to consider what it might mean, he reached out his hand and took Timmy by the shoulder. "Wake up, son." Timmy groaned and rolled over onto his stomach. Jared shook him harder.

To his shock, the floor shook too. A dull rumble rose to a deafening crescendo, and Jared grabbed hold of Timmy's bedpost to keep from falling. Toy soldiers sitting atop the turrets of Timmy's plastic castle fell from their posts one by one, clattering to the floor and rattling against it as the house continued to shake violently.

Then, just as quickly as it had started, the tremor ended. An eerie silence took its place, and Jared loosened his grip on the bedpost. He took a step back, stumbled over a toy truck that had rolled off from the top of Timmy's dresser, and almost fell. Timmy, meanwhile, continued to sleep, his slumber somehow undisturbed.

The sound of a creaking floorboard broke the silence. Jared whirled to face the door, alarmed to find it open with two figures standing just inside the room. Two sets of long hair—one blonde and one jet-black—reflected the dim glow of the night-light.

"Whatcha doing, Daddy?" Grace asked. There was a singsong quality to her voice that rose and fell with each syllable. She stood side by side with her sister. And though the light in the bedroom was dim, Jared was certain he saw Emily's light brown eyes flash black.

They were smiling at him, each one wearing a wide and wholly unnatural grin that stretched their lips to seemingly painful proportions. But while Grace's eyes seemed to match her mocking grin, there was no joy in Emily's eyes. Hers were wide and panicked and streaming with tears—the only feature of her face she still seemed to control.

Grace noticed his gaze, then stepped in front of her younger sister, her own smile shifting into a frown. "Don't worry, Daddy. She'll come around. Just give her a little time." Jared groaned and shook his head. It was all he could manage to do. "You really shouldn't be sneaking around at night like this, Daddy," Grace continued. "It's not a good idea."

She drew closer to Jared, yet her legs never swayed. Both stayed square with her shoulders, unmoving. It was only then that he noticed her feet were floating off the ground.

"Because if you keep snooping," the Grace-thing said, its voice growing more twisted and garbled with each word, *"we're going to teach you a fucking painful lesson!"*

It rose higher into the air, leering down at him with eyes so dark and bottomless they seemed to suck in what little light there was in the room. Jared cowered in the corner, dreading whatever nightmare was soon to come.

Emily watched from the doorway, her every muscle frozen and rigid as tears continued to pour from her panicked eyes. Then another figure appeared beside her.

There was a popping sound that seemed to come from inside Jared's own head, like water clearing from his ears. His mind felt fuzzy all at once as if he had just woken from sleep.

Grace was standing in front of him, her feet firmly on the ground. Behind her, Emily and Melody stood in the doorway. All of them wore looks of concern.

"Are you okay?" Melody asked.

Jared didn't know how to respond. He stuttered for a moment, then resigned himself to silence.

"Was that an earthquake?" Emily asked. Her voice was small, but far from panicked. Any trace of the terror in her eyes or the tears that had been streaming down her cheeks was gone.

Jared regarded her with a look of confusion, then noticed that Melody was staring at him. But when she caught sight of Timmy still asleep in his bed, she broke out into a stifled laugh. "I can't believe it," she said. "That kid literally just slept through an earthquake."

Emily covered her mouth and snickered, and Grace shook her head in mock disbelief. Jared turned his attention to Timmy as well but without any sense of humor. The mud and tree bark that had been stuck to the bottom of his foot were gone now, and so too were the dirty tracks across the floor.

"Were you checking on him?" Melody asked.

"Huh?" Jared responded.

"Yeah," Grace answered for him. "We all came out into the hall when the shaking started. When Timmy didn't come out, we decided to check on him. Turns out he's just the soundest sleeper on the planet, apparently."

"What about Elena?" Melody asked. "Is she okay?"

Grace answered again, but this time she was looking at Jared as she spoke. For a moment, the emptiness in her eyes seemed to return, and

Jared felt a chill. "She's fine. Already gone back to bed. We're all fine, Mom. It was kind of exciting if anything."

"Guess I must have been sleeping pretty heavy too, huh?" Melody said. "Seems I'm kind of late to the party."

"Guess so," Grace said. She yawned and rubbed her eyes with the tips of her fingers. "Well, this has been wild, but I'm gonna get back to sleep." She put a hand on Emily's back as she turned to go, ushering her out of the room. "Come on, Em."

Emily turned around and caught eyes with Jared as her sister led her past the doorway. Before she disappeared into the shadows of the hall, Jared thought he saw a single tear streak down her cheek and fall to the floor.

TWENTY-SEVEN

SATURDAY, JULY 21ST

"In other news, residents throughout Fulton and DeKalb counties were woken last night at 2:13 a.m. by what officials are saying is the state's strongest recorded earthquake since 1974," said a female news anchor on the television in Jared Gordon's living room. "The quake registered as magnitude 4.3 on the Richter scale according to a seismograph located at the Atlanta Institute of Technology. No damage or injuries have been reported, but the late-night tremor is certainly one that many of us won't soon forget. Our own Janice Eckles reached out to one South Atlanta homeowner to get her thoughts on what it was like to be woken by an earthquake."

An elderly woman with spiky white hair appeared on the screen and started talking about how all the shaking had scared her poor little dogs. Jared turned off the television. He'd wanted to know if others besides him and his family had experienced last night's tremor. But knowing brought little comfort. Other things had happened last night that could never be explained by tectonic plates.

For better or worse, however, these things had mostly drifted from Jared's memory. There were snapshots still—the image of Grace's bare feet dangling above the ground, the image of Emily's eyes turning to soulless black orbs, and the image of mud on the bottom of Timmy's onesie-covered foot—but these freeze-frames had no context. Jared could recall clearly what had happened before he entered Timmy's room, and he could recall clearly what had happened after Melody had arrived. But the in-between came only in bits and pieces.

Memory lapses or not, he knew one thing for certain: time was running short. His efforts last night had done nothing to shed light on his situation. Or rather, if they had, Jared couldn't remember.

He wondered if hiding such a revelation might be the reason for his lapse in memory and felt the despair in his stomach turn even sourer. If this was true—if *they* were powerful enough to command his very thoughts and recollections—what hope did he have?

Jared leaned back in the recliner and closed his eyes. A dark chorus of terrible noises drifted down the stairway and through the ceiling from the bedrooms above. It had persisted all day, a constant racket of laughter and wails and gibberish that Jared couldn't understand even when it was loud enough to hear clearly. Sometimes it was Grace's or Emily's voice that he heard. Other times it wasn't their voices at all.

It hadn't mattered that Melody had been home all day. He hadn't even bothered to ask if she could hear all the awful things that he heard so clearly and incessantly. He already knew the answer.

She was worried, no doubt. Scared even. That much was clear. But her fear was terribly misplaced. She was afraid for him. Or maybe afraid *of* him. Jared decided it was probably a little of both.

A loud shriek from upstairs jolted his eyes back open. He gathered himself, tried to calm his pounding heart, then closed them again. It was a trap, he told himself. *They* were trying to lure him up there. Trying to get him alone. What other purpose did all the commotion serve?

There was nothing he could do anyway, trap or not. There was only one cure to his suffering that Jared could see, and it grew more alluring by the hour. Had it not meant leaving his family to their fate, he would have chosen it already.

So when followed a moan somewhere between pain and pleasure loud enough for Jared to tell that it had come from Emily, he willed away the thought of it and tuned his ears instead to the sound of Melody humming obliviously from the kitchen.

What song was she humming? Jared could almost place the tune. Maybe he would have if not for the thud of a body crashing hard against one of the upstairs walls. But Melody carried on uninterrupted, never missing a note in the song that—like so many things—rested just on the edge of Jared's memory.

"Are you hungry, dear?" Melody asked some immeasurable time later, entering the living room with a spatula in one hand and an oven mitt on the other. "Dinner's just about ready."

"Sounds good," Jared said. Truth be told, he was weak with hunger. When was the last time he'd eaten? Yesterday, surely, though he couldn't say for certain. Even now, with hunger stabbing his stomach, the thought of eating made him a little queasy. He'd have to fight through it. He needed the energy.

"Kids!" Melody yelled up the stairs. "Dinner's ready!"

Just about to rise from the recliner, Jared froze in place. He fixed his eyes on the staircase. He heard doors open and close and the sound of footsteps coming down. He saw Grace and Emily, then Elena behind them, and felt fear begin to gnaw at the same place as the hunger.

But what was there to be afraid of? Merciful yet maddening, nothing would happen so long as Melody was there to see it.

Once more this proved the rule. The six of them sat at the table and ate pork chops and baked potatoes. They all talked and laughed like nothing was the matter while Jared watched and wondered silently how the things now occupying his daughters' forms could possibly replicate them so effortlessly.

By the time dinner was over, Jared looked down at his plate and realized that he'd barely eaten more than a few bites. It would have to do. The way his stomach continued to turn despite the fact he was alone now at the table meant forcing down any more would come at the risk of losing what he'd already managed all over the tablecloth.

From the living room, he could hear the television and the sound of conversation. He hoped he would be able to sneak by unnoticed. It was only a quarter past eight, but sleep was all that Jared wanted.

Endless sleep, even better still.

TWENTY-EIGHT

SUNDAY, JULY 22ND

A gust of wind carried through the trees and chilled the skin beneath Jared's sweat-dampened t-shirt. He swept a flashlight back and forth in a wide arc, tramping through the underbrush and grateful he'd at least thought to put on long pants this time.

Something had roused him from sleep and compelled him to go to the bedroom window. An instinct perhaps, but it felt more like a compulsion. Whatever the catalyst, he'd seen what he assumed he was supposed to right away—a light flickering at the edge of the stygian forest behind his home. Elena's bedroom door had been open when he crept into the hall to check. Timmy's too. And both of them were gone. The light he'd seen from the window was gone too by the time he'd made it out the back door, leaving no option but to head straight from the point in the woods he'd last seen it.

A barn owl screeched from somewhere ahead, its cry sounding so unnatural even though Jared had heard it countless times before. So late at night and with cobwebs of sleep still clouding his mind, every sound and dancing shadow seemed uncanny.

He stopped next to a cedar tree and turned off his flashlight, as the sharp, woody scent prickled his nose. He searched the darkness for any sign of light but saw nothing and quickly turned his own light back on.

The more he came awake and the less dreamlike his surroundings began to feel, the more his fear grew. He knew what would happen to Timmy in these woods if he couldn't stop it somehow. *They* would take him just like they took his sisters.

And Elena…what would happen to her? Was he saving her too? Or saving Timmy *from* her. It still seemed inconceivable to think of her as the danger. She'd always been an odd little girl, fascinated by the ordinary and often lost in the clouds, but pure and harmless as living creatures come. Was that girl still possible to save, or was she already gone too?

More likely that Jared wasn't saving any of them. All he was doing was wandering aimlessly through the woods, getting bit by mosquitos and tripping over roots while *they* likely watched and laughed from whatever dark realm they inhabited. Or maybe they watched from Grace's and Emily's eyes, stalking stealthily behind him. Jared turned around and shined the light back down the trail he'd followed, but nothing was there.

Nothing but trees and shadows of trees everywhere he looked. Jared felt like crying. His son was in these woods. And if he didn't stop whatever was happening here, what came out would not be him.

Up ahead, the barn owl screeched again. Or so Jared thought at first. It sounded even more unusual this time. When he heard it yet again, a little louder, he realized it was a voice.

Jared pushed forward, fighting through the brambles as fast as he could manage. Limbs swatted at his face and vines grabbed at his ankles. Twice he tripped, staggering to all fours and clawing back to his feet.

Just as he noticed the trees growing a little less dense, Jared saw a light ahead. He turned off his own light and slowed his pace, slipping up to the trunk of an oak tree that bordered the point where the woods broke into a small glade. He pressed himself against the tree and peered into the clearing, watching the yellow beam of a flashlight bounce up and down stalks of brown grass.

He traced the beam back to the center of the glade where he could just make out two small figures beside what looked to be a rotted stump. Urgency overwhelmed him, and he crashed into the clearing, fumbling with his light until finally it came on. "Elly!" he yelled. "What the hell are you doing out here?"

Elena squinted against the bright LED, but Jared kept the beam steadied on her. He could see Timmy behind her, crouched on top of the stump with his head against his knees. Thunder rumbled from somewhere distant in the dark sky, and a gust of wind moved through the grass.

Jared felt suddenly sick. He had seen this place before. Not in person like now, but in his nightmares. The rotted stump, the tall, dead grass, the starless sky overhead, and the strange chill of the wind—all so familiar in the most repulsive ways.

This place was death. Rot and death. And Elena had brought her brother here like a lamb to the altar. Had she brought her sisters here too? Had she also walked them through the woods at night to this place of evil and walked something else back out?

"What have you done, Elly?" He stormed across the glade and grabbed her by the shoulders, gripping her hard enough to feel the bones against his fingers. "What did you do to him?" She stared at him with wide eyes. A thin layer of sweat lined her pallid skin. "Tell me, goddamnit!" He shook her. Harder than he'd meant to. He heard her teeth clack together, then felt her muscles tense in his grasp. "Tell me!"

"I was saving him!" Elena screamed. Spit flew from her lip, and tears streamed from her eyes.

Jared turned to Timmy, who was still crouched on the stump. He let go of Elena and knelt in front of him. "Timmy, wake up, buddy," he said and gave him a shake.

Timmy lifted his head and opened his eyes. He rubbed them with his fists and then looked around, frowning at what he saw. Jared watched him and held his breath.

"Daddy, where are we?"

"Are you okay, son?"

Timmy thought about it for a second, then nodded his head. Jared exhaled. If *they* had taken him, then they were hiding. And hiding well. Not at all like it had been when Grace and Emily were taken. Only time would tell for sure, but maybe he wasn't too late. Jared rose and turned back to Elena.

Words died at the back of his throat as he scanned the clearing. Elena was gone. He shined the light where she'd been standing just seconds ago but saw only undisturbed grass swaying in the breeze.

"Elly! Elly, you come out right now!" He shined the light in a full circle around the clearing. He considered that she might be crouching somewhere in the grass, but she'd probably made a break for the woods as soon as he turned his back. Likely halfway back to the house already.

Either way, finding her wasn't his current priority. Timmy and whatever she'd done to him was Jared's main concern now. He picked his son up and draped him over his shoulder, shining the light one final time around the clearing before heading back in the direction he'd come.

TWENTY-NINE

SUNDAY, JULY 29TH

Thunder cracked, a splitting boom loud enough to rattle the dishes in the cabinet. Streams of water snaked down the kitchen window that Jared sat peering through. The flow gurgled boisterous and constant as the house's drainage system ushered it down the gutters, across the slope of their lawn, and into the ditch that now looked like a moat separating their backyard from the tree line.

It had to fight plenty of weeds to get there, though, Jared noted. Their lawn had grown to an unacceptable state of unkept, and the rain that had been falling for the past four days straight was sure to make thirsty weeds sprout even higher. The HOA would probably start bitching soon. There was a time when Jared would have considered that important, but it wasn't anymore.

One week had passed since he found Elena and Timmy at that terrible place in the woods and interrupted whatever she'd been doing. For a while, there'd been reason for hope. Timmy had woken the next morning acting his normal self, spending most of the day in the backyard, playing with his dinosaurs and trucks. Elena had returned home too, mostly to Jared's relief; some part of him wondered if it would be better if she had vanished that night never to be seen again. Horrible beyond imagination but perhaps better for them all.

She seemed to have come down with another cold the next morning but had otherwise behaved her normal self as well. In fact, the first few days following that night had been nothing but normal all the way around. No voices, no visions, no nightmares of the sleeping or waking variety. Grace and Emily had kept to their rooms those first few days. It worried Melody, but Jared saw it as a positive development; even when she wasn't there, they never once came downstairs those first three days to torment him with acts unspeakable.

For a while, it seemed that Jared had scored some victory against his dark adversary that night in the woods. And for three days, he had relished in this hopeful belief. He took Timmy to the park, watched a Braves game on the TV, and even made love to his wife. Then the storm struck.

The Georgia and South Carolina coastlines got the worst of it. Hurricane Eliot made landfall as a category four storm, assaulting coastal cities with haymakers of wind and water. The storm had weakened and slowed as it pushed inland. It was a whisper of its former self by the time it reached Jared's home outside Atlanta, but a roaring whisper all the same. It seemed to settle over the central part of the state and had been dumping water for the past four days without any sign of dissipating.

Outside the kitchen window, a streak of lightning flashed down from a black cloud, striking somewhere distant within the forest. A clap of thunder, then a loud, fading grumble soon followed, making Jared think the bolt might not have been so distant after all.

From his stomach came another angry grumble. He glanced down at the ham and cheese sandwich on the table with queasy disinterest. He needed to eat—was weak with hunger—but still lacked any semblance of an appetite. When he looked in the mirror this morning, he'd hardly recognized the gaunt face staring back. He hadn't bothered to step on the scale lately but figured he must have lost at least fifteen pounds over the past few weeks. Terror, it turned out, was a hell of a diet aid.

If only the rain would stop. Jared wondered what good sunshine and clear skies might do. Not that *they* had ever shown an aversion to these things, but that first day of dark skies and pouring rain was when it all went to hell.

Melody had woken that first stormy morning with what she said was stomach flu and had spent the entire day tracing a trail between the bed and the toilet. Something hit her hard, and she hadn't recovered since. Far from recovering, she seemed to be getting worse. Jared wondered if they were taking her like they had taken Grace and Emily. Maybe it was more difficult for them since she was older. Maybe her symptoms were a result of her body fighting back against their intrusion.

Or maybe it was just their way of sidelining her so his torment could continue undisturbed. In her relative absence the past four days, Jared had witnessed untold horrors carried out by the vessels that used to house his oldest daughters. He'd watched his tormentors violate the bodies they'd stolen in the vilest ways—Grace in the bathroom carving symbols on her stomach with a broken piece of glass; Emily floating down the stairs toward him, nude and smeared with her own feces; the two of them intertwined on the kitchen floor, moaning in ecstasy.

That he could only remember these episodes in frames and fractions had seemed a small mercy at first. Now, he thought it might be the cruelest part of all. The memory of how it felt—the horror and shame—never went away, so that when something as benign as a carving fork, or a hairbrush, or a bottle of detergent sparked some faint remembrance of an awful event, Jared had no context for the fear and revulsion he felt.

Even now, he couldn't say what circumstances had brought him to the kitchen table, but trying to remember made his blood run cold.

Something terrible had happened, he had tried to stop it, and now he was here. That's all he could say for certain. But that was how it always went.

No matter what he tried, Jared was always powerless to stop the ghastly events unfolding in front of him. Sometimes he would pass out and wake up hours later. Other times it would simply *be* hours later. These disorienting episodes were something beyond Jared's understanding; all he knew was that one moment he'd be shambling forward to stop some monstrosity being committed by one of the girls, and the next moment they'd be gone and he'd be standing in the same spot, bewildered as to why the day had suddenly jumped from noon to sunset. By the time he could gather himself, the memory of whatever he'd been trying to stop was always nothing but a ghost.

On rare occasions these past four days, Grace and Emily had seemed perfectly normal. Jared had watched them closely during these times, always waiting for the mood to change and something nightmarish to happen. Often it had, but other times, Grace and Emily had just rolled their eyes or shook their heads at him and taken their conversation somewhere else.

Last night, even Melody had come downstairs looking nothing like the sickly woman he'd last seen in bed. Since she'd taken ill, Jared had been heating up canned soup—the only thing she could keep down for any period of time—and bringing it up to her for her lunch and dinner. But last night she had come downstairs and made herself a salad. Jared had sat across from her in the kitchen and watched her eat, mystified by how fully she'd seemed to have recovered. When he asked her about it, she'd just given him a puzzled look and told him she was feeling fine. But when he woke this morning, he'd found her hunched over the toilet again, as pale and hollow-eyed as ever.

The only two members of Jared's family who had portrayed any kind of consistency since the storm started were Timmy and Elena. Timmy had behaved like any normal, happy boy his age, and Elena like someone physically ill and emotionally haunted. Timmy played with his toys; Elena stayed shut away in her bedroom. Timmy laughed at the cartoons Jared put on TV for him; Elena had tears in her eyes each time he saw her. Timmy's cheeks were bright and ruddy; Elena's were the color of cigar ash.

Late last night, the storm had taken out the power. It was a little past three in the afternoon now, and the lights still hadn't come back on. Jared wondered how much longer it would be before the food in the freezer and refrigerator started to spoil, then wondered about what to prepare for dinner that night.

Caring for his family while Melody was sick was the one thing that kept him anchored to some semblance of sanity. He couldn't break down into a hysterical mess—his wife was counting on him to warm her up a bowl of chicken noodle soup. He couldn't run out to the car and drive as fast and as far as he could—Elena was sick and needed him to give her medicine. He couldn't tie a rope around his neck and hang himself from the swing set—Timmy was hungry and wanted chicken nuggets for dinner.

Through the rain-streaked kitchen window, Jared could see that swing set now. A memory came to him of the day he had brought the set home and put it together while Melody kept the kids occupied at Chuck E. Cheese. It had taken all of three hours to figure out the pieces and fasten them together one by one, but the squeals of delight from Timmy and Elena when they saw the shiny red swing set that had appeared in their backyard like presents under the tree on Christmas morning were worth every minute and blister. Thinking back on it,

Jared was struck with a painful longing. The sun had been shining that day. It had been a good day.

The sun was certainly not shining today. A sheet of water covered the ground outside, rippling with the impact of a million raindrops and lapping against the feet of the swing set's metal frame. The patches of ground beneath the seats of the dual swings—furrows of dirt kept grassless by the constant impact of small feet—were now muddy puddles. Beyond the swing, a streak of lightning coursed down from the clouds, tributaries of electricity streaming out from the bolt as it snaked its way to the ground. Jared wondered what would happen if the next bolt struck the swing. Would it kill them? Would it be a mercy if it did? Or were they already dead?

He turned his eyes away from the distant spot on the horizon where the bolt had struck and back to the swing. With wind driving sheets of rain against their skin and flashes of lightning reflecting off the water beneath their feet, Grace and Emily swung gently back and forth. Their hair was soaked flat against their heads, and water cascaded down from the swing's chains each time they pushed or pulled against them.

How long had they been out there? There was no way to know; he couldn't even say how long he'd been sitting here watching them. He supposed it wouldn't be long before he forgot this present moment as well. It seemed a buildup to another terrible episode that, for better or worse, he probably wouldn't remember.

Even through the haze of falling rain, Jared could see the blackness of their eyes. They stood out in stark contrast against pale white skin— like circles of onyx set into ivory effigies. While Emily's skin was fair by nature, Grace had always been a little darker than the rest of Jared's children. Now, she and her sister were both as ashen as the dead.

Jared stared at them through the window, and they stared back with soulless eyes. Soon, they would come back inside. Thunder would crack, lightning would illuminate a dark sky that grew darker as night began to fall, and—without a word between them—Grace and Emily would step off the swing and walk across the flooded yard to the back door. Jared knew this somehow, and knowing left the sour taste of dread on his tongue.

This time, though, Jared had no intention of sitting idly by while whatever abomination they planned played out. Never taking his eyes away from the window, he reached down and ran his hand along the waistband of his pants. His fingers brushed against polished metal and a rubberized grip. Satisfied that the revolver was still firmly secured, Jared rose from the kitchen table and walked out into the gale.

THIRTY

SUNDAY, JULY 29TH

"Wish you'd given me a call first," Jeremiah Gordon said, shutting the door after letting Jared in. "Not that I mind the visit, but I would have tidied up some."

"It's not a problem," Jared said. He glanced around the familiar spaces of his childhood home—terribly more familiar now than his last visit with his memories of those younger years now fully returned. Of all the places to find himself, Jared thought. Of all the refuges to seek.

"I'd offer you some dry clothes, but I don't think they'd fit you. You're looking a little thin there, brother."

"I'll dry quick enough."

"Can I get you something to drink? Maybe some coffee to warm you up?"

"Just some water."

Jeremiah poured him a glass, then sat it down on the kitchen table. "So what's going on? Don't get me wrong, I'm happy for the company. Clarice has been out of town since Wednesday with some women from church. But today seems like a strange day for a road trip."

"I think you know why I'm here," Jared said, staring unblinking back at his brother's curious eyes.

Jeremiah laughed a little and shook his head. "No, can't say that I do."

"You were right, Jeremiah. *They* have come for me. They've come for my family. And I need your help."

Jeremiah chuckled again, but there was a nervous edge to it now. "Jared, I don't have a darn clue what you're talking about."

Jared felt heat rise to his face. "I'm talking about the journal you sent me. Dad's journal. And your note at the end. I'm talking about *them*, Jeremiah." Then, when this too failed to spark realization, Jared braced himself and dared to speak their name. "Ra'Tak. That's who I'm talking about."

Jeremiah stared back, his expression now one of iron seriousness. "I never sent you a journal, Jared. Or a note. If Dad even had a journal in the first place, then I didn't know about it."

"Yes," Jared said resolutely. "You did."

Jeremiah studied him, his eyes narrowed and his jaw tight. "You're sick, aren't you?" he finally said. Jared could almost see the realization igniting in his mind. "Dear God, I thought it had missed you. I'm so sorry."

"No," Jared growled. "Not you too. I know you know what's happening to me."

"You're right," Jeremiah said, catching Jared off guard and suppressing if but for a moment his simmering anger. "I do know what's happening to you." Jeremiah stood up then and rapped his knuckles once against the table. "Wait here a minute, will you? I'll be right back."

Slowly, like all things Jeremiah Gordon did, he ambled out of the kitchen and into the hallway. Jared heard footsteps going up old wooden stairs. A couple minutes later, he returned holding an item in each hand. In one was an empty prescription bottle, its once-white cap a dingy shade of yellow. In the other hand he held a leatherbound Bible, it, too, worn and frayed from years of age.

"Looks like the start of the world's strangest show and tell, doesn't it?" Jeremiah said, putting them both down on the kitchen table. "Come to think of it, I guess that's exactly what it is."

"Where are you going with this?" Jared asked. Tired and terrified and now confused as well, his patience was wearing thin.

"Take a look at the bottle."

Jared picked it up and read the worn label.

"You recognize it?"

He did. Thorazine. An antipsychotic commonly prescribed to schizophrenics. "Was it Dad's?" Jared asked.

"Nope," Jeremiah said. "It was mine." Jared looked up from the pill bottle. "I was diagnosed when I was twenty-three. Took meds for three years. Thorazine, Clozaril, Abilify. And more than a few that I prescribed myself, too. I knew when I started shooting heroin that I wouldn't be long for this world. And, at the time, that was fine by me."

"Jesus, Jeremiah. I had no idea."

Jeremiah frowned. "I'd prefer if you didn't take the Lord's name in vain around me, brother. It's like nails on a chalkboard to my born-again ears. And how would you have? Known, that is. You've been three hours away all these years, yet you might as well have been living on another planet."

"I should have been there for you."

"You should have," Jeremiah agreed. "And I should have forgiven you for it a lot sooner than I did. But thankfully I did have people who cared about me. Mom first, and then Clarice. I tell people I met my wife at church. What I don't tell them is that she was helping lead a recovery program I stumbled into one day out of desperation and, I think, divine intervention.

"That's where this comes in," Jeremiah said, tapping his fingers against the leather Bible. "Clarice had a big hand in it, no doubt, but this is what saved me. There were demons inside me, brother. Now I don't know if they were the physical or spiritual sort, but they haunted me every minute. And the drugs didn't touch them. Not the ones the doctors prescribed or the ones I got on the street either. It wasn't until I gave my life to Christ that I was healed. The moment I came up out of that baptistry, I knew that they were gone. And they've not been able to touch me since."

"That's your answer?" Jared said. "Baptism?"

"Salvation is my answer. I can see it in your eyes that there's demons inside you too. They're tearing you apart."

Lightning flashed through the small kitchen window, and the lights flickered. A clap of thunder sounded and dissipated into a fading rumble. "What about the journal?" Jared asked. "And the note?"

Jeremiah shook his head. "I'm not lying to you, Jared. I don't know anything about a journal or a note."

Jared swallowed, feeling dizzy and disoriented all of a sudden. Had Jeremiah not sent him the journal and written the note at the end? Had he not seen it with his own eyes? Unlike much from the past couple months, this seemed like something he could remember quite clearly. But if they were capable of erasing his memories, could they be capable of planting false ones too?

Or maybe it was his brother's memory that they'd erased. They'd prevented him from reaching out to Jeremiah before. Maybe this was their way of doing it now.

Why hadn't he thought to bring the journal with him? He thought of it sitting in the workbench drawer some two hundred miles away—the one piece of proof that might be able to jog his brother's memory—and cursed himself for not being more thoughtful.

"You said you didn't know if your demons were the physical or spiritual sort," Jared said. "What did you mean by that?"

Jeremiah sighed. "When I started hearing voices and having panic attacks, there was no doubt in my mind that I'd inherited Dad's condition. I got treatment for it. Just planned on living with it the best I could. But the treatment didn't work.

"I do remember things from when Dad was sick. Things that a mental condition shouldn't be able to explain. And I might not have believed in them at the time, but I certainly do believe in demons now. The real ones, like Christ himself used to cast out. I cannot tell you for certain whether my affliction was a physical disease or a spiritual attack. All that I can tell you is that the blood of Christ cured it either way."

"I've already tried praying, Jeremiah. I know that's probably hard for you to believe. But I have. I've tried everything. And if your God is up there, then he sure doesn't give a shit about me."

"'He that turneth his ear away from hearing the law, even his prayer shall be an abomination.' That's from Proverbs 28. The book of John tells us that 'we know that God heareth not sinners: but if any man be a worshipper of God—'"

"Enough!" Jared said. "I'm not going to hear any more of it. If you'd seen the things I've seen, then you'd know it's all bullshit, Jeremiah. There might be something out there. Something more than I ever thought existed. But whatever it is, it is *not* merciful and loving."

"Tell me then," Jeremiah said. "What is that you've seen?"

Jeremiah watched and waited with a patient gaze while Jared struggled with where to begin. He'd come here expecting to talk with the one person who would believe him, but Jeremiah's inability to remember the journal had left him spinning.

"I'm going to tell you something," Jared said. "And I know how it's going to sound."

"Like you're crazy."

"Yeah. Like I'm crazy."

"Let's hear it. You forget that I'm a lot more open-minded than you, brother."

"A few months ago, I started having nightmares. Then anxiety and paranoia. Then eventually I started hearing voices. Seeing shadows move. I felt like something was following me everywhere I went.

"I thought at first what you're probably thinking now. I went to the doctor and took the medication, but it didn't help. It just kept getting worse. And now...now it's undeniable. I am not sick. I am not a schizophrenic. I am being hunted. And not just me, my entire family. They've possessed Grace and Emily. My girls are gone and something evil has taken their place. They tried to take Timmy, and I think they're trying to take Melody too. And Elena...I believe that Elena is the one that let them in."

"Let who in, Jared?"

"Their name...their name is Ra'Tak. That's what it said in Dad's journal. The journal that I can *clearly* remember you trying to give me when I visited last month. Then a few days later, it shows up on my doorstep with your return address on it."

"You have to be mistaken," Jeremiah said. "I sent you a letter because I wanted to reconnect. But that's it. The only other person who could have sent you something was Clarice, but she'd never do that without discussing it with me first."

"Dad also said that you were the one that let them in," Jared said, ignoring these defenses. "He said that you were their connection to the physical world back then. Then, in your note, you said that you might be still. And you said that you'd do whatever it takes to stop them."

Jeremiah's expression was steely now. But behind his grave eyes, Jared thought he could see the slightest flinch of fear. "For the last time, Jared, I don't know anything about a journal or a note or anything like that. I'm not trying to call you a liar, but I can't pretend to know what you're talking about when I don't. So if that's all you want to talk about, then I'm afraid I'm not going to be much help to you."

Jared studied him, unsure of whether to believe him. He searched for the fear he'd seen sign of and wondered what it had meant. Was it *them* he was afraid of, or was he afraid of the brother—practically a stranger now—sitting dead-eyed at his kitchen table?

"Let's talk about something else, then," Jared said. "Let's talk about those two years before Dad died."

"That's what it always comes back to, isn't it? For both of us, it seems. Strange how two years so long ago can change a lifetime."

"What do you remember from back then?"

"Everything, I suppose. How could I forget?"

"Specifically. What do you remember specifically about the events leading up to Dad's suicide?"

"Where do you want me to start, brother? Do you want the whole story, start to finish?"

"Yes," Jared said, "if that's what it takes."

"Alright. If that's what you want." There was a resigned sigh, then a pause while he gathered his thoughts. "I remember Dad acting distant and angry. More than normal, I mean. I remember coming home from school one day and finding him crying in the kitchen. That's when I first knew something was wrong.

"I remember him talking to someone when there wasn't anyone there. I remember him telling us that *they* were here. That *they* were taking over his mind. That *they* were going to take us too. I remember being terrified day and night. For myself, and Dad, and you and Mom too. And I remember the morning of January 23rd, 1994, when I went out to the barn to feed Sissy and her litter of kittens and found Dad hanging from the rafters.

"He knew I fed those cats every morning. He knew I'd be the one to find him. I've never understood why he chose that time and that place. At the darkest points in my life, that's all I thought about. And it still haunts me today."

"No," Jared said. "There's more to it than that. Tell me what else you remember."

Jeremiah scoffed, his face flushing the slightest hue of red. "I don't know what you want from me. Do you want me to tell you about how black his lips were, or the way his eyes bulged out of his head? You want me to talk about wetting the bed almost every night for the next three years because of the nightmares? Do you just want to watch me relive every gory detail? Is that it? Because you've put me through enough already."

"I want you to talk about Ra'Tak. I want you to tell me who they are and why you invited them in."

Jeremiah's eye twitched, a subtle reaction that Jared did not miss. "You're not well. You need to get help. The help of the Lord, most of all, and the help of his servants in the medical field too, perhaps."

"No!" Jared said, slamming his palm against the table. "I'm not going to hear it from you too! Not after the things I *know* you've seen. Not after what I *know* you told me."

"You're right," Jeremiah said, his voice still calm. "I saw...some strange things back then. If you're asking if Dad was possessed by demons, I don't know the answer. Demons of some variety, for sure. And I don't know who…whatever you called them are or what you think I told you. But I do know that if those same demons are after you, whatever they might be, there's only one answer."

"Killing you. And maybe Elena too. That's the only answer." The words slipped from his tongue as soon as the thought had formed. Jared paid no attention to the look of horror on his brother's face.

It all seemed so clear now. Jeremiah couldn't remember because Ra'Tak still clutched his mind. Or maybe he *could* remember and had been playing the role of their servant all this time. Either way, it didn't change the solution. He and Elena were their links to the physical world. If Jared severed one, maybe he wouldn't have to sever the other.

"Why would you say something so terrible?" Jeremiah asked, his voice somewhere between a croak and a whisper. "What in the world would that accomplish?"

"Saving my family. Saving them from something a lot worse than death."

"Jared, you're not making any sense. And you're scaring me, to be honest." This was honest indeed; Jeremiah looked almost as ghostly as Jared now. Could he sense somehow what was happening beneath the table—Jared's sweaty palm clenching the revolver tucked in his waistband?

"Why did you let them in? Tell me why you did it."

"I don't know what—"

"Tell me. Tell me, or there's no point in dragging this out any longer."

"Jared, please."

"I'm sorry," Jared said. "There's nothing more I can do for you if you won't tell me." He inhaled and braced himself for the wretched task ahead. He closed his eyes as he drew the gun, hardly more than a blink…

...then opened them again to find himself staring at the ceiling. Jared sat up, looking confused at the blankets over his legs. His hands were empty, the revolver nowhere in sight, and he was wearing only his boxers.

At first, Jared thought he must be back home, in his bedroom. Maybe *they* had brought him back there somehow. Or maybe he'd never left, and it had all been a nightmare from the start. But a quick glance around the room revealed the truth.

He was in his bedroom, alright, but not the one he and his wife shared. It was his childhood bedroom. The one where all the nightmares had originated. Jeremiah had changed the room's décor beyond the point of recognition, but the soul of the place was still the same. Jared felt a chill slither down his neck.

A sudden voice from the nightstand beside him startled him enough to make him bang his elbow against the headboard. Oblivious to the pain, he stared at the glowing LCD screen of a radio on the nightstand that had just turned on by itself.

"That was Maggie May, by Rod Stewart," the voice on the radio said. "Coming up, we've got thirty minutes commercial-free of nonstop classic rock hits. So don't touch that dial, and I'll see you on the other side. You're listening to Cool 107.3." An outro clip of guitar music played, followed by the voice of a man named Randy Adams who promised that his prices were lower than any other used car lot in the county. Jared reached out an unsteady hand and turned off the radio.

Remembrance slowly crept in, and Jared realized why he had woken searching for a gun in his hand. His mouth went dry and his heart began to pound. *They* had stopped him from doing what he'd come here to do in much the same way they always stopped him from interfering.

But this time, they allowed him to remember the effort. Jared wondered if that meant something.

More pertinent, he wondered where Jeremiah had gone. Had they wiped his memory of the afternoon, or would he be waiting outside with an army of police? Or maybe worse.

Jared kicked the covers off his legs and scrambled out of bed. He headed straight for the bedroom door, not bothering to search for his clothes or the revolver. But as soon as his hand touched the doorknob, a voice froze every muscle in his body.

Jaaaarrrreeed….

It came from behind him, from the radio on the nightstand. It buzzed with a staticky whine, it's screen aglow again.

Time to go, Jaarrreeeed…

Jared let go of the doorknob and rushed across the room to the radio. He grabbed it with both hands and jerked its plug from the outlet, just barely resisting the impulse to smash it against the floor. He watched its dark screen, half expecting it to glow back to life even with the plug dangling disconnected in the air.

But when the voice spoke to him again, it didn't come from the radio's speakers. This time, it seemed to whisper in Jared's ear—so horribly close that he could feel cold breath against the nape of his neck.

We…

Jared whirled around. A moving shadow caught the corner of his eye, and he felt a breeze brush the air beside him. And when the growling, whispered voice spoke to him again, it came from behind his other shoulder and breathed into his other ear.

Are…

Jared froze. The energy seemed to drain from his body and, this time, he didn't have the courage to turn and face the source of the chilled breath he had felt against his ear.

When the voice spoke again, it spoke from overhead. Or from inside his head. Or from nowhere at all. It spoke to him as if it were his God, as if it had always been his God, and as if meeting it here this night had always been his predestined fate.

Ra'Tak!...

The voice was booming now. It reverberated through the floor and the walls and the bones of Jared's body. Like Saul on the road to Damascus, Jared fell to his knees.

We...

Are...

Ra'Tak!...

Each word came down like mortar shells exploding inside his head. And when the last booming retort had sounded and left silence in its wake, the air inside the room still thrummed with energy.

Jared lay prostrate, his eyes buried in his forearms. He could smell it in front of him. God almighty, he could *smell* it. And though it was no longer roaring down from the heavens, Jared could still hear it too. He could hear it breathing or growling or whispering to itself in front of him, and he knew that if he lifted his head up from the ground and opened his eyes, he would see it too, and seeing it would be more than he could bear.

Jared had a sudden certainty that he was about to die. It was a certainty that didn't frighten him nearly as much as the other horrors the thing in front of him had already shown him. He only hoped that it would be quick. He only hoped that it would be merciful. And he had no reason to believe that it would.

Behind him, he heard the bedroom door creak open. Still careful to avoid looking at the unspeakable thing towering in front of him, Jared raised up and turned around. He expected to see Jeremiah in the doorway, but there were two figures there, each too short and slender to be his brother. When they stepped out of the hallway's shadows and into the lamplight, Jared's heart dropped.

It was Grace and Emily. Or rather Ra'Tak in its human form. Ra'Tak wearing their skins. A wail escaped his lips, and he collapsed back down to his knees.

Their dark eyes dropped down to the floor where he cowered. They moved in unison toward him. And when they spoke, they spoke in unison as well—their voices a mangled fusion of their own and the voice of the thing that had brought them here. The voice of Ra'Tak.

"...And we have come to take you home."

Unable to help himself, Jared lifted his eyes to meet their coal-dark gaze. But they weren't looking down at him anymore. They were looking above him and beyond him. They were looking at the thing that swirled behind him. The thing that smelled of sulfur and rot and shook the ground with its voice.

For a brief instant, Jared caught its reflection—*Ra'Tak's* reflection—in the inky pools of his daughters' eyes. He screamed. He screamed for what felt like hours. And when those dark eyes finally looked away from their master and back down at their quarry, Jared was screaming still.

Darkness closed around him, and the lamp in the corner of the room that had once lit the entire space in warm yellow light now looked like a distant star. It was so dark and his tormented mind so far away that he didn't notice the butcher knife in the Grace-thing's hand. He didn't notice when she leaned in and pressed its edge against his throat. He didn't look down to see its mirror-polished blade reflecting dim, blue light.

"Time to take you home, Daddy."

The Grace-thing dug the knife deep into the side of Jared's neck, then pulled it sharply across the width of his throat. He had time for shock, time for confusion, and time for little else. In that final moment when his vision gave way to darkness, only nothingness remained. Nothingness and peace. Before his last flicker of conscious thought went dark as well, Jared hoped above all else it would stay that way.

THIRTY-ONE

MONDAY, JULY 30ᵀᴴ

Light filtered through Jared's closed eyelids. They fluttered once, then opened. There was a window to his right with blue curtains that were drawn to the sides, letting in the morning sunlight. But it wasn't in the right place on the wall, and the curtains weren't right either.

The sheets on his legs were thin and scratchy, with no sign of the black and gray comforter he and Melody slept under every night. And there were plastic rails on the side of the bed. Growing only more confused as his awareness returned, Jared pushed himself to a seated position.

He was in a hospital room, he realized. The strong smell of antiseptics, the gray linoleum floor, the monitor on a silver stand next to the railed, twin-size bed—all of these left no doubt.

But why?

He tried to recall the previous night but dredged up only a nauseous feeling of despair. Something bad had happened. Nothing new there, but whatever had happened last night had been especially bad. Still, the gritty details of it all were, as always, just outside memory's reach.

Jared scanned the bed until he spotted a wired remote on the mattress near his feet. He reached for it, then pressed the red nurse call button at its center.

There was a quick knock at the door a few minutes later, then a middle-aged Black woman wearing green scrubs came in without waiting for an answer. "Did you need something, hun?"

"Where am I?" Jared groaned, not realizing the pain in his throat until he started to speak.

"You're in the hospital, Jared. Saint Elizabeth Medical Center."

"Why?"

"You don't remember?"

"No."

The nurse frowned. "Well, that's no good. Dr. Mah will be by shortly. She'll be able to explain it all to you."

"Just tell me why I'm here," Jared said. "Please."

The nurse, Gabriella Taylor, LPN according to her name tag, hesitated for a bit. "I don't want to alarm you, Jared. But you tried to hurt yourself last night. The police were the ones who brought you in. They said you were holding a knife to your own throat when they arrived."

Was it true? Parts of it rang some distant bell, but it didn't feel true on the whole. It felt like another of their tricks. And if he was here at the hospital—separated from his family—then it was because that was where *they* wanted him to be. He had to get home right away.

"I need to leave." He scanned his forearms to make sure there were no tubes connected to them, then swung his legs over the side of the bed.

"You can't leave just yet, hun," Nurse Taylor said. "It's probably going to be a few more days, I'm sorry to say."

"I feel fine. I feel fine, and I'm ready to leave."

"Well, that's great that you're feeling better, Jared. But it's still gonna be a little while. When you were brought in last night, you were committed involuntarily. Your wife signed off on it, and Dr. Mah agreed that it was prudent."

"My wife?" Jared said. "Tell me where we are again. Are we in Atlanta or Savannah?"

This seemed to puzzle Nurse Taylor. "We're in Atlanta, hun. Why on earth would they take you all the way to Savannah?"

Now it was Jared who found himself confused by his own question. Why indeed had he asked about Savannah? His brother lived there, and…

And Jared had gone to visit him. No, not to visit him. To kill him. He remembered the trip and its purpose, but nothing of whatever had happened next.

"Are you okay?"

"Where's my phone?" Jared asked, ignoring the question.

"We've got all your belongings at the front desk. You'll be able to get them back when you're released."

"I need to make a call."

Nurse Taylor smiled. "It's best if you just focus on getting better while you're here. The outside world can be a…distraction from that sometimes."

"You don't understand," Jared said and rose to his feet. Nurse Taylor took a small step back. "My family is in danger. And I'm leaving."

"I'm going to be real straight with you, Jared. You need to lie back down and rest right now or you might have to spend the rest of the day in restraints."

Jared sized up the woman standing between him and the door. Very possible that she weighed more than he in his current state, but he still liked his odds.

Those odds changed when the door opened and two tall orderlies stepped into the room. She must have pressed a silent alarm in her pants pocket, Jared assumed. The two men—both in their thirties or late twenties and both looking to have spent a healthy amount of their lives in the gym—watched and waited. One of them held a pair of pad-ded cuffs in his hand. Jared sat back down on the bed.

"I know this isn't where you want to be," Nurse Taylor said. "But it really is the best place for you. And I'm sure your family is just fine. Hopefully you'll be able to return to them in a week or so a brand-new man."

But Jared wasn't listening anymore. In the far corner of the room, opposite where Nurse Taylor and the two orderlies stood, something had caught his eye. A shifting pillar of shadows— the same dark form he'd seen the night before in the reflection of the Grace-thing's black eyes. Memories rushed back, and Jared stared at the shapeless, dark thing with wide-eyed terror.

Too late to see the way the color drained from his face or the way his mouth dropped slack, Nurse Taylor and the two orderlies left the room. But they did not leave him alone.

THIRTY-TWO

FRIDAY, AUGUST 3RD

"You're looking a little better this morning," Dr. Mah said. "Are you feeling it?"

Like most of Dr. Mah's questions, Jared didn't answer. There was no mirror in the room, but he couldn't imagine he was truly looking better. And he certainly wasn't feeling it.

It'd been four days since he'd woken up in the hospital. Four days in which the dark, unknowable thing in the corner of the room never left. It appeared to him like a slow-swirling column of smoke that settled against the floor. Sometimes, as if in some desperate attempt to make sense of why looking at this ethereal shape smothered him with such terror, his mind would shape it into something else. Sometimes dark horns and slick black fur. Sometimes polished scales and slitted eyes. Always something almost as terrible as the original, but more tangible and familiar.

He knew that these were his hallucinations and not Ra'Tak shifting their form. He knew because *they* had told him. These past three days, they had told him many things.

"You are the silent type, aren't you?" Dr. Mah said. She looked far too young to be a doctor. That was one of the only opinions Jared had cared to form about her. "Listen, Mr. Gordon. I know you aren't going to want to hear this, but I've requested an extension to your five-day commitment."

Jared scowled at this. But what did it matter? They had already shown him what was to become of him and his family. They'd already proven that they were the ones in total control. When they were ready for him to go home and their work with him to proceed, that's when he would leave. Not a heartbeat before.

"I think your time here has done you good, and that a little more time will do you even more good. I promise you'll go home soon, Jared. This is not a permanent solution."

"I had a phone call with Dr. Stewart yesterday evening," Dr. Mah continued when Jared offered no response. "He'd like to come visit with you later today. Is that something you'd be up for?"

"Yes," Jared said, though he still didn't take his eyes away from the thing in the corner of the room. Truth be told and despite it all, he'd come to like Dr. Stewart. The man might not have believed his story, but at least he'd listened.

Dr. Mah prattled on about something or another. Jared only caught a few words here and there. Treatment. Brighter days. Takes time. A normal life. All empty promises from someone who didn't understand his true affliction.

She left the room a few minutes later. Left him alone with his company. Unlike Dr. Mah's misguided assurances, every word that *they* spoke, Jared clung to. If not for the horror of it, it might have been awe-inspiring to hear them speak thoughts into existence. To merely be in the presence of something so confounding and almighty.

They spoke of an eternity that stretched both directions, their existence woven inseparable into its fabric. They always were, and they always would be. They mocked his suffering and its insignificance. *His* insignificance. Who was he to demand a reason from *them?* Who was he to think he could even understand?

A knock at the door sometime later broke Jared from the spell that Ra'Tak weaved inside his mind. This time, whoever stood on the other side waited for a response.

"Come in," Jared said, straining to make sure the words were loud enough. The door opened, and Dr. Stewart entered the room.

"Hello, Jared. I hope I'm not disturbing you. I know they don't always let you get a lot of rest in these places."

"I don't think I could be any more disturbed than I already am, Doctor."

Jared saw a faint smile crease Dr. Stewart's face. "I've been talking with Dr. Mah. She seems to think you are showing signs of improvement."

"That's an interesting opinion. But she does seem like an optimistic person."

"Do you mind if I sit down?" Dr. Stewart asked, gesturing toward the rolling chair by Jared's bedside. Jared nodded his approval. "I'm grateful you've agreed to speak with me again, Jared. Yours is a very interesting case. And to be quite honest, I find you a very interesting person."

"I'm not interesting," Jared said, chuckling the words. "I'm insignificant."

"Is that how you feel? Insignificant?"

"That's what I know."

"I'm sure your family doesn't think of you as insignificant. Neither do I." Jared bristled at the mention of his family. Any thought of them brought thoughts of the future Ra'Tak had shown him. Thoughts unbearable. "Have you spoken with them?" Dr. Stewart asked.

"No. Dr. Mah doesn't allow it."

"Truthfully, I think that's unfortunate. But sometimes it can be helpful to disconnect from everything for a while. Family included. And make no mistake, Dr. Mah is an excellent physician. You really are in the best of hands."

Jared, who knew well whose hands he was clutched within, smiled at the irony. "We're still at the same impasse as before, Doctor."

"Oh? What impasse is that?"

"You…and Dr. Mah, and my wife, and everyone for that matter…you all still think I'm psychotic. And I know that I'm not."

Jared watched for a reaction from the doctor, but his face never changed from the same friendly yet unreadable expression he always wore. "If I remember our last conversation, you said that you believed you were being attacked by a supernatural force."

"Something like that."

"And do you have any proof for that yet?"

"It's been proven to me enough."

"What about tangible proof? Proof that you could show to an old man who is more broad-minded than you might think."

"There's the journal," Jared said. "My dad's journal. It describes the same things I'm experiencing now. And there's my brother, Jeremiah. I don't know what he knows or what he's hiding. Or maybe it's being hidden from him. But I'd be fascinated to know what he would tell you."

"I actually spoke with your brother, Jared. Last night, on the phone. I've been speaking with your wife as well. And I've read the journal. Your wife found it and thought it might be helpful if I saw it."

Jared sat up a little straighter in bed. He hadn't even known for certain if Jeremiah was still alive, still unable to remember most of what had happened after he'd arrived at his brother's house. He'd assumed he would have heard by now if his brother was dead. But knowing for certain that he was still alive brought Jared a mix of relief and concern.

"I hope you don't mind," Dr. Stewart continued. "I'm only trying to understand and help."

"What did Jeremiah tell you?"

"Nothing much, I'm afraid. He seems like a nice fellow. And he's worried about you. He thinks that the devil is to blame for your illness. For your father's illness too."

"Maybe he's right."

"The journal was what I found more interesting, though. There are some enlightening insights into your mind in there."

"*My* mind?"

Dr. Stewart paused and studied Jared for a moment with that curious, calculating gaze so common to those in his profession. "You said that the journal describes the same things you are experiencing now, correct?"

"A lot of it, yeah. Except it's my father's journal. His experiences. They came for him first, and now they've come for me. And when I'm gone, they will come for my children. On and on through generations."

"Ra'Tak. That's who you're speaking of, right?"

Jared felt the thing in the corner of the room pulse stronger at the mention of their name. A wave of nausea rolled over him as the air grew thick and noxious for as long as that name hung on it. When it passed, a sheet of sweat slicked his skin.

"Don't say their name again. They're listening."

"Remarkable," Dr. Stewart muttered. Then louder, "My apologies. I can see that brought you some discomfort."

"Did you feel it?"

"Feel what, Jared?"

Jared sighed. "Never mind. Of course you didn't. They're not here for you."

"Who are they? You say that they came for your father and that now they've come for you. You say you know their name—one I won't mention again, don't worry. But who *are they*?"

"I don't know," Jared said. "I've thought about it a lot lately. And they've told me a lot lately too. And I still don't know. I know that they are powerful. Able to manipulate mind and matter. I know that they are evil. But I don't know what they are or what they want. Maybe just evil for evil's sake. That's my only theory."

"Demons. Is that what you're describing?"

Jared thought of his brother. A memory of a tattered Bible sitting on an old oak table flashed across his mind. "It's possible. Or maybe they're just a force as natural as gravity and magnetism. Maybe they're the force of evil. Its tangible existence."

"That would imply a force of good too, wouldn't it?" Dr. Stewart asked.

"I don't know." Jared sighed. "I've only met the one."

"You've seen them then?"

"I'm seeing them now."

"And what do they look like?"

"Like nothing you'd understand."

"Try me. Surely you can give me some approximation."

"Why don't you turn around and look for yourself, Doctor? They're all around you."

For the briefest instant, Jared thought he saw fear cross the doctor's eyes. Dr. Stewart smiled a little and exhaled. "Alright then. Let's have a look."

Dr. Stewart looked over his shoulder. The thing in the corner swirled and rose when his eyes met it. Jared felt his hairs stand on end as the air pulsed with sickening energy in rhythm with the shadowy form.

"I don't see anything, Jared," Dr. Stewart said. He looked self-assured. Almost relieved, Jared thought.

"Did you expect to?"

"No. If I'm being honest, I knew that I would not."

"So did I. They never reveal themselves to anyone who could help me."

"And how could I help you if they did? How could anyone help you?"

Jared considered this. He'd been so desperate to win Melody, or Jeremiah, or Dr. Stewart, or *anyone* to his cause. But what good would it really do if he did? If *they* had shown themselves, if they had appeared in front of the doctor and reduced him to a sobbing sack of terror, how would that help? Even if convincing him didn't mean anything so dramatic, what good could he, or anyone, possibly do?

"Comfort," Jared finally said. "It would just be comforting for someone else to know the truth. And believe it. There's not much more that you or anyone else could do for me beyond that."

"I hope that's not true. I do believe that I can help you. There's a path forward for you. We simply have to find it."

"There is a way forward," Jared said. "But it's unthinkable." He tried not to picture Elena. Not the girl she used to be, at least. To think of that precious, innocent little girl would rend his heart to shreds. To think of the little girl who brought her brother to the woods like a sacrificial lamb and welcomed the essence of evil with open arms was hardly better but somehow more bearable.

"What would that be?" Dr. Stewart asked.

"Cutting them off at the source."

"Do you mean suicide?"

"Yes," Jared said. "Eventually."

"Is that what you were trying to do the night you were brought to the hospital?"

"I don't remember."

"You can be truthful with me, Jared."

"I am being truthful. I don't remember."

"I probably don't need to tell you that both short and long-term memory loss are commonly documented symptoms of schizophrenia."

"I'm aware."

"And that everything else you are experiencing can be very easily caused by the disease as well. No matter how real or vivid it might seem."

Jared shook his head. "Not like this. There's no disease that could do all this."

"Jared, you have to realize that accepting your condition is your only path forward. You've said yourself that there's no hope for you otherwise. Why not give treatment and a commitment to grounding yourself in reality a try? No matter what the truth of the situation is, can't you agree that's your only hope?"

"I've got to hand it to you," Jared said. "You're almost convincing. I'm sure I would have benefited a lot being in your care if I was actually schizophrenic."

Dr. Stewart sighed. "Well, we'll see, I suppose. You might just benefit some yet." He stood up from the chair and buttoned his suit jacket. "I've got to get back to the office, Jared. I do hope that you will continue to visit me once you are released from here. You've been dealt a terrible hand, but where you go from here is up to you."

"Goodbye, Doctor," Jared said. "And thank you. You've been more comfort to me than you probably realize."

THIRTY-THREE

FRIDAY, AUGUST 3ʳᵈ

Jared's mind slipped into sleep and fell straight through the veil to the realm of nightmares. He knew the moment he laid down his head and closed his eyes that he had made a mistake.

The first couple of days here, he hadn't even tried to fall asleep with that dark thing next to him in the room. Eventually, the drugs and exhaustion won over. He had slept well from then on; they'd left him alone in his dreams these past few days and nights. It was when he woke that they were there to greet him.

But this time *they* were the ones pulling him down into sleep. And they would be there waiting when he fell. He tried to swim against the spiral, to reignite his fading consciousness. But it was no use. Darkness swallowed him like swirling waters and turned his whole mind a void.

And for what felt like time unfathomable, the void was all there was. Just endless nothing and his own tortured awareness. Jared tried to scream, but he had no mouth to form the sound. He tried to run and thrash and fight, but his limbs no longer existed. All that remained were his thoughts and darkness infinite and eternal. Like death with none of death's mercies.

They had told him of this future. This never-ending purgatory that he and his family had been chosen to endure. And it had petrified him. But experiencing it now was even worse than he'd imagined.

This is what awaits you, Jared, a voice within the void bellowed. *This is your life everlasting.*

So strange to hear again after what already felt like eons of complete sensory deprivation. So strange to sense them within the void after so much time spent sensing nothing. But these sensations were far from a comfort. The voice and the presence of them that formed it left him begging for the nothingness to return.

Your time in the living world is almost over, Jared Joseph Gordon. You will soon meet us here. Like your father did before you. Like your sons and daughters will after.

Beneath the panic and pain and his own inner voice that could do nothing but scream, Jared wondered why.

Why don't you ask Elena? the voice responded to this deep-buried thought. *We didn't choose your family, Jared. She chose us.*

She wouldn't! Jared forced the thought to the surface of his tortured mind.

She did. Not your father or his father. Not your brother. Her and her alone. Her invitation stretched forward and backward in time. She rewrote your past and future the moment she welcomed us into your realm.

You tricked her, Jared thought. *You made her somehow.*

She's a very special soul. More special than you could ever understand. And that's why she will be the only one of yours that survives. And someday, when we have used her dry and she, too, takes her own life, she will have a special place in our realm.

I'll kill her, Jared thought, projecting the words out into the void with as much force as his mind could muster. *You need her alive to do all this. I know it's true. I've seen more than maybe you meant for me to.*

You know nothing, the voice boomed back. It was malicious and mocking as always. Still dripping with hate. But there was something else there this time. Something that had never been there before.

Perhaps it was only his imagination grasping desperately at straws, but in this place where all other stimulations and distractions were no more, Jared felt certain that he had heard a new undertone in this dark thing's dark words: fear.

Just take me. Take me and leave the rest of them alone. And I won't do it.

WE ARE TAKING ALL OF YOU! The voice reverberated inside Jared's mind. It seemed to ripple through every corner of the endless void, shaking an entire plane of existence to its core.

"Then I'll kill her," Jared said.

It caught him off guard to hear the words aloud and feel the forgotten sensation of his own tongue forming them. Qualia rushed into his dormant mind, an overwhelming blur of sights, smells, and sounds. He could feel every organ inside his restored body functioning at once. It was all so disorienting that it took him a long while to realize he was standing in Elena's bedroom.

You don't have the spine, Jared, the voice inside his head spoke.

Suddenly, Elena was standing there in front of him. He could smell the strawberry shampoo in her hair and the fear on her skin. She stared wide-eyed down the barrel of the .38 that had appeared in his hand just as suddenly.

"Daddy? What…what are you doing?" Her voice quivered and her little hands shook at her side.

Go on then, Jared. Show us how you'll do it.

"Daddy, you're scaring me!"

Jared was dumbstruck. He watched his arm rise on its own. He watched his wrist tilt down to press the revolver's barrel against Elena's forehead. He watched his thumb reach up and pull back the gun's hammer.

He tried to wrest his finger away from the trigger, tried to throw the revolver to the floor, but neither of these commands went through. Elena was crying now. Her wet eyes tilted up to the gun that was pressed against her head, then focused back on her father. On the man who had put Band-Aids on her boo-boos and told her bedtime stories at night and called her Elly even when no one else in the family did. On the man holding the gun.

We're watching, the voice mocked.

Jared's finger rested gently against the curve of the gun's trigger. His body was paralyzed in place with only the muscles in this one finger and the muscles that moved his eyes left unfrozen. He looked at Elena from behind the revolver's neon sights. She met his eyes, her own pleading and full of fear. Tears began to flow one after the other down Jared's unmoving face. His finger stayed rested against the trigger, never twitching, never once applying more pressure than the softest caress.

Like we said, you don't have the spine.

Jared's rigid muscles went lax at once, and the gun dropped from his hand. It thudded against the carpeted floor. Jared followed it down, collapsing in a heap of limbs he'd been unprepared to take back under his own autonomy. He started to shake.

Elena stood with her back against the wall, her eyes still wide and wet with tears. But now she was grinning.

He watched as darkness spilled out from her pupils in thin, black tendrils, infecting first the blue of her irises and then the white of her sclera until only black remained. "Sorry, Daddy," she said, in a voice barely still her own. "You're just too weak."

Jared screamed. He stood and shoved the thing that looked like Elena away from him. It stumbled back and hit the wall with a solid thud. Without thinking, Jared knelt and picked the revolver up off the floor. Its hammer was still cocked, still poised to strike primer at just the slightest trigger's squeeze and send death flying out the barrel.

Never pausing, he leveled the gun on the thing now wearing his daughter's skin and pulled the trigger. The revolver barked. A burst of fire shot out the barrel's end, and recoil jolted the gun back against his palm.

Jared never saw the aftermath of that shot. Never saw the round, red-rimmed hole appear between the thing's dark eyes. As soon as the gun went off, he found himself back in the hospital bed, awake and breath-ing rapidly. He didn't get to witness his tormenters' reaction when he pulled the trigger. But in those final moments before real lucidity returned, Jared had felt their surprise. He had felt their fear.

With a sudden surge of confident defiance, he turned and looked to the corner of the room where they resided. He braced himself, deter-mined to stare into them unwavering for as long as he could bear. But Ra'Tak was no longer there.

THIRTY-FOUR

MONDAY, AUGUST 6ᵀᴴ

"Do you want to stop for a coffee or something?" Melody asked. "There's a Dunkin' Donuts just ahead."

"I'm fine," Jared said. "I had a cup at the hospital this morning." He watched the flowing lines of interstate traffic through the passenger window. A thousand different people on their way to a thousand different places. Given the option, Jared would've blindly traded places with any of them.

It was about a twenty-minute drive from Saint Elizabeth back to Jared's home, and the first ten minutes or so had already gone by—ten minutes that Melody had desperately tried to fill with conversation. She was nervous, Jared could tell. She always rambled when she was nervous.

"I'm going to make spaghetti for dinner tonight," Melody said. "I know hospital food is never the best, and I figured I'd fix one of your favorites as sort of...uh... you know, a welcome home, I guess. Does that sound okay?"

"It sounds fine," Jared said. It was jarring to hear her speak so normally. She acted like this was an ordinary morning drive and not a trip back from the hospital she'd had him committed to. Just as

205

confounding, she acted as if everything was normal at home. As if the week he'd been gone had passed without incident.

Of course, he supposed this wasn't so confounding after all; everything that had happened since *they* found him had been carefully hidden from her. She was his partner, and they had taken that partnership away. Though he couldn't have explained how, some part of Jared still believed that everything would have turned out okay if only Melody had been on his side.

"The kids are excited to see you again," she said.

"How's Elly?" Jared asked.

Melody turned her eyes away from the road and looked at Jared, but he didn't meet them. "She's doing fine." For the first time, concern crept into her voice.

Jared wondered if it was true. Lately, Elena was the only thing he thought about. Distant memories were juxtaposed against recent ones in a never-ending reel. He thought of the first time he took her to the zoo and the way her eyes and smile both grew wider with each exhibit they came to, then he thought of the first time she mentioned Ronny. He thought of the time he found her pretending that she was a ballet dancer with her audience of stuffed animals sitting in rows, then he thought of the time he found her with her brother in the woods—the time Jared stopped her from doing the same thing to him that she'd already done to her sisters. Back and forth it went like this; dark memories followed pleasant ones in a continual sequence.

They seemed like memories that shouldn't coexist, each set seeming to refute the possibility of the other. How could the little girl who had used her own birthday money to buy her brother a new action figure just because she wanted to see him happy be the same little girl who had willingly invited an unspeakable evil into their lives? How could the daughter he had loved more than life itself have chosen to be Ra'Tak's daughter instead?

The only answer he could accept was that the little girl from so many happy memories was not the same as whatever now slept in her bed. That little girl was gone. Somehow, someway, Ra'Tak had taken her. And now, Ra'Tak was all that was left.

He wondered if they had already taken the others as well. Melody and Timmy certainly seemed to still have a chance. Perhaps it wasn't too late for Grace and Emily either. There were times, after all, when they seemed to return to their prior selves, even if it was only when Melody came around.

It was too late for him, though. Jared knew that for certain. He had seen too much. Endured too much. And if there was any hope at all left for the others, it was too late for Elena too. Accepting something so horrible was as difficult and terrible as anything Jared had endured so far, and coming to terms with what he had to do was a war that still waged in his mind.

She's already gone, he thought over and over. It had become his mantra.

"Did they help you, sweetheart?" Melody asked. So much emotion bled through her voice that it ripped at Jared's heart. He could tell the question had been boiling inside her all this time.

"Yes," Jared lied. "I think they helped a lot." There was no point in hurting her with the truth. What he had to do would torment her for the rest of her life. The least he could do was spare her a little peace until then.

Except when Jared met her eyes, there was no peace to be found. He realized then how unconvincing he must have sounded with the truth scrawled across his face.

"I know that this isn't going to be easy," she said. "I know that there's probably a long road ahead. But I want you to know that I am going to be here for all of it, Jared. I'm not going to leave you. I promise."

Jared turned away. He couldn't bear to look at her. Not when he was the one that would soon be leaving her. And taking their daughter with him.

She loved him now, but how quickly would that love erode once shock and disbelief wore off? Jared could see no future where she didn't go to her grave hating him, never knowing the fate he had spared her and the others.

"I love you, Mel," he finally managed. If the words weren't so heartfelt, he might have never gotten them out.

She smiled a little, and Jared saw perhaps a touch of that peace he so wanted to give her. Soon, they were turning onto Cherry Street. Their house would be just ahead on the left. Jared wondered what was waiting for him there.

They pulled into the drive. The car came to a stop, and Melody shifted it into park. Jared traced his eyes up the walkway and red brick walls to the second-story window. Grace's window.

It was closed, and the curtains were drawn. Jared exhaled. He turned his gaze to the front door beneath it. Soon he would have to go inside. He couldn't put it off any longer.

Noticing that Melody was watching him, Jared unfastened his seat belt and opened the passenger door. The morning air was cool and the sun's beams warm, and squirrels chattered from nearby trees. By anyone else's account, it would have been a splendid morning—the kind of morning that lifts a person's mood the moment they open the door. There was a time when Jared might have taken such a morning as a sign of hope. As a sign that perhaps the darkness was gone and not waiting for him just behind the next closed door. But hope had become a high no longer worth the comedown.

Are you coming?" Melody asked, looking back over her shoulder as she neared the door. Doing his best to steady the sudden shake in his hands, Jared followed her inside.

THIRTY-FIVE

MONDAY, AUGUST 6TH

Jared crept up the stairs, slow and quiet like an intruder in someone else's home. He flinched each time the boards creaked or his sneakers squeaked against the polished wood.

And yet there was no one at the top of the stairs to hear these things. No one downstairs either. Grace and Emily had hung around long enough to welcome him back from the hospital before leaving to meet up with friends. Melody had left not long after to run a few errands, and she had taken Timmy and Elena with her. Any other time, she would have left them in his care. But not anymore.

He had braced himself for what might happen the moment Melody was no longer there. He'd considered going with them, sticking close to his wife to delay the opportunity for whatever nightmares *they* had planned. But delay them was all he would do, and there was no more time for delay.

Except when the front door closed and Melody's Tahoe rumbled away, no nightmare came. He'd had the sickening sense all day that Grace and Emily had never really left. That they were simply waiting somewhere around the block like idle machinery, ready to awake the moment Melody left so that Ra'Tak could formally welcome him home. But this feeling had never come to fruition.

Instead, a different feeling had struck him the instant he heard her pulling out of the drive. It was as if someone had turned on a magnet somewhere upstairs that pulled at his very being. It beckoned him toward it like an unheard siren song, and Jared, knowing well what sirens did to those attracted by their chorus, was still hopeless to resist it.

Somewhere outside, a lawnmower whirred to life, making his heart leap. The surge of adrenaline brought an instant of clarity, and he paused near the top of the stairs. But his hesitation didn't last long before the hypnotic allure beguiled him once more.

When he made it to the second floor, the lure grew even stronger. Sharper and more distinct. Jared could tell now that it was coming from Elena's room, and he hurried down the hall toward her bedroom door, no longer cognizant of the noise he was making. Whatever was behind that door pulled at him now like the current of some great vortex, and he had crossed the point of no return.

And yet, just as his hand clenched the doorknob, the sight of a watercolor taped to the door brought him to a jarring halt. It was a painting of a monarch butterfly perched atop the fuzzy head of a dandelion—incredibly detailed and textured considering its artist's young age. Elena must have finished it while he was at the hospital; her newest works were always given a brief exhibition on her bedroom door.

Why did this seem significant? Jared could ponder it for only a moment before his thoughts were whisked away again. Realigned to the thing behind the door and its irresistible pull.

He twisted the doorknob and gave it a push, any sense of caution long gone. He hurried across the threshold and stopped in the middle of the room, suddenly confused. The feeling of whatever had brought him here was entirely gone now, and even the dreamlike state it wrapped him in had fizzled away like lifting fog.

Jared scanned the room, wondering if whatever he'd sensed in here might still be hiding somewhere. It was dimly lit, the small glow of sunlight that filtered through Elena's dark curtains the room's only source of light. Yet even in the shadows, Jared couldn't help but notice the room's state of disarray.

Colored pencils were scattered around the floor as if an entire box of them had been tossed haphazardly into the air. In between these, the books from Elena's bookshelf were strewn about, each one of them—bizarrely, Jared thought—open and placed on the floor with their spines facing the ceiling like little tents. The drawers of Elena's dresser were all open as well—open and empty, with the clothes they used to store now flung across the room.

Amidst this sea of clutter, Elena's bed stood like a pristine island. The covers were tucked neatly underneath the mattress, and decorative pillows were positioned level and orderly against the headboard. The only thing out of place was a single book in the center of the mattress, closed and aligned perfectly with the bed as if someone had positioned it there. Noticing it, Jared felt a subtle pulse of the attraction that had brought him here.

He stepped around the clutter and picked the book up from her bed. With his eyes still not yet adjusted to the room's dim lighting, he had to squint to make out the single word written in cursive across the book's pink and purple cover: *Sketchbook.*

He recognized it then. Elena rarely went anywhere without it. Yet holding it now, Jared felt a sudden sense of dread. It was heavy in his hands. Much heavier, it seemed, than a book its size should be, and his palms were sweating against its laminated bindings. He fought the abrupt urge to drop it to the floor, then clenched it tighter—tight enough to make one of his knuckles crack and make his heart skip at the sound.

Looking down at the carefully made bed juxtaposed against all the clutter around it, Jared realized he didn't want to be in this room any longer—didn't want to think about what dreams were had in this bed, or what was meeting her there. Driven by a force opposite but every bit as strong as the one that brought him here, Jared hurried out of the room.

THIRTY-SIX

MONDAY, AUGUST 6ᵀᴴ

Jared sat down on the edge of his bed and lifted open the sketchbook's cover. On the first page was a picture of two horses running through a field. He licked his finger, flipped to the next page, and found a drawing of a whale jumping out of the sea. He flipped to the next page, and then the next, and then the next again. There was a sketch of a bird, then one of a blue dog, then one of a garden with an old woman tending it. Jared continued turning through the book.

Midway through, it seemed as if these innocent drawings were all he was going to find. Most of them were sketches that he had seen already—ones that Elena had been all too proud to show him. He flipped through the book's pages faster now, pausing just long enough to confirm their incorruption before turning to the next. But when he came to a picture of a forest's edge, Jared lingered a little longer.

He recognized the woods this drawing depicted. It was the woods outside their home. As if placed there to confirm this, he saw the edge of the swing set in their backyard drawn into the picture's foreground. Unlike the sketches preceding it—each one brightly hued with colored pencils—this one was grayscale. Thick, black pencil strokes formed the trunks of trees and the stalks of grass at the woods' edge, scrawled hard into the paper as if Elena had been grasping the pencil in her fist. Jared stroked a finger across the page, not realizing he was holding his breath, then turned to the next.

It was another picture of the same woods, done in the same scrawling style. This time, there was a girl standing at the forest's edge. Though the quality and detail of these last two sketches suffered somewhat compared to the ones before them, there was no mistaking that Elena had drawn herself into the scene. She stood with her back to the trees, staring blankly ahead with her hands at her sides.

Jared turned the page. At the edge of the woods, drawn for a third time now, a second figure joined her. It was much taller than the depiction of the little girl next to it and was sketched in solid black. Tiny tears marked its profile where the pencil had been pressed too hard into the paper. It had no clothes, no face, no features. It was barely in the shape of a silhouette at all. Yet Jared recognized it at once.

His teeth began to chatter. His hands were shaking so badly now that it was all he could do to turn the page. He saw the trees first, then Elena and the figure beside her. This time, she was facing the woods. Jared turned to the next page. On this one, Elena was holding the figure's hand.

The urge to fling the book across the room came back to him suddenly. Instead, Jared turned to the next page. The background of the picture had changed, but its subjects remained the same. Elena was sitting on the edge of a stump in the center of a circular clearing surrounded by trees. The figure stood over her, its long arms stretched up to the sky.

Jared flipped through the sketchbook at a feverish speed, stopping only an instant at each new page. There was a picture of Elena leading her little brother by the hand into the woods, then a picture of the figure waiting for them both at the clearing. The sequence repeated, once with Grace, once with Emily, and once with Melody. They were all gathered at the clearing in the next picture, the figure joining them there. And all their eyes were dark.

Finally, after rifling through scene after terrible scene depicting his family and the figure now leading them, Jared came to the sketchbook's final page. On this one, Elena had drawn the front of their house. Behind the house, the figure loomed. It was even taller now than before—so tall that it tilted its head down at the roof below it. Its arms were stretched up into the clouds, disappearing out of frame. In front of the house, five dead bodies littered the yard. The bodies of his wife and children.

Jared slammed the book closed. This time, the urge to fling it was more than he could overcome. It struck corner-first, punching a small hole in the drywall before falling to the floor amidst a shower of chalky dust.

It landed open, somewhere near the middle. Breathing heavily, Jared watched it. He would have to pick it up and put it somewhere safe before long, he knew. Melody would be home any minute. But the thought of touching it again made him queasy.

He glanced at the clock on the nightstand. Forty minutes had gone by since Melody left. Clenching his teeth, Jared stood up from the bed and took a step toward the book. He could see the page that it had opened to now. It was the very first sketch of the woods outside his home. He reached for it, then jolted back when the pages began to move.

They riffled forward as if blown by a breeze, sending the pictures into motion like a terrible flip-book. Jared watched dumbstruck, his mouth agape. Finally, the riffling pages reached their closing scene. But as they came to a stop on that final, stationary page, something else—something within them—started moving.

The figure that overshadowed his home and dead family in the book's concluding sketch lifted its gaze up from the gore-littered ground and looked at Jared. He let out a choked cry as he watched it come to life. It rose from the page, growing in size as it did and expanding into three-dimensional form. Jared stumbled back, and the figure—now tall enough that its head grazed the ceiling—took a step toward him. It reached out a long arm that ended in spindly, black fingers. A mouth tore open in its head, slowly ripping and stretching wider. Jared felt his bladder let loose.

From outside the room—distant, as if it had come from downstairs—he heard a door open and close. At once, the nightmare in front of him was gone, vanishing in an instant with no trace left behind. Quivering, Jared stumbled back until he was seated on the edge of the bed.

"Jared?" he heard his wife call from downstairs. His chest was heaving. He closed his eyes, then opened them, then closed and opened them again. The book was lying near the edge of the wall, open to a colorful picture of a deer standing in a clearing.

"Jared? Are you up here?" Her voice was closer now, probably coming from the bottom of the stairs. On legs barely sturdy enough to support his weight, Jared rose and picked the book up off the floor. He turned, shambled into the bathroom, then closed and locked the door.

THIRTY-SEVEN

TUESDAY, AUGUST 7TH

Jared rose early the next morning. Early enough that the neighborhood was cast in a copper hue. Watching last night's sunset had brought him no interest at the time, but witnessing this final sunrise seemed more worthwhile for some reason. Jared supposed he liked the fact that it reminded him of new beginnings. Even if it signaled an end for him.

Melody had joined him for a while, sitting beside him in a matching wicker chair and discussing the idea of going on a beach trip before summer's end. Listening to her talk of a future they wouldn't have had been heartbreaking. But soothing too.

She'd gone back inside about half an hour ago, yawning and puzzled at why she was so sleepy after getting a full night's rest. She'd been fast asleep by the time Jared helped her to the couch, the three milligrams of Lunesta he'd slipped into her coffee taking little time to do their job.

He'd pulled a blanket over her, then gave her a kiss on the forehead. A goodbye kiss that she wouldn't remember for a parting she would never understand. Then he'd returned to the porch and sat back down in the chair, soaking in the sunlight and breathing deep the cool morning air. From his experience with the sleeping pills, it would be at least a few hours before Melody woke up again. There was plenty of time to do what had to be done. And he was most surely not in a rush.

What was it, though, that had to be done? Could he even bring himself to admit it? The first part of his plan was easy enough to formulate and easy enough to accept. In due time, he would go upstairs and talk to Elena. He would yell, and scream, and threaten, and do whatever it took to make her talk. And then...

And then what? Jared couldn't say. Was there even anything that she could tell him that would change the equation he'd already solved? If she admitted to letting Ra'Tak in and promised that she could make them go away, then it would at least buy them both time—time to see if she was telling the truth. This, Jared thought, was the best-case scenario. The only scenario where they both lived to see another sunrise.

Was it likely, though? Somehow, Jared couldn't imagine it. For the first time ever, the future seemed just as certain and unchangeable as the past.

Yet was it possible that a single pull of the trigger could change them both? When Elena invited Ra'Tak in, she had poisoned the past and future alike. *They* had shown him this, forced him to witness the magnitude of what she'd done. But they had shared more of themselves than perhaps they'd meant to. Their work with her was not yet complete. She was the source of their grip on this reality, and, without her, it would slip.

Jared had spent a great deal of time contemplating what this might mean. If their work was not complete and the new timeline they'd woven not yet solidified, might the past itself revert the moment their connection was severed? Would Jared be transported to a world where his father had never killed himself and Ra'Tak had never entered any of their lives, all before his ears could even register the gun's retort? Did he even dare hope that his family might still be with him in this world?

This seemed like a lot to hope for and an even more dizzying thing to try and unravel. What Jared did feel strongly to be true was that it would change their future. It would prevent Ra'Tak from taking the rest of his family. It would prevent them from coming for each new generation until the day his lineage was snuffed from existence.

This was a belief that Jared intended to cling to until death. One he had no desire to confirm. If…if he did what had to be done and was still there holding the gun when he opened his eyes—the past unchanged—he would turn it on himself at once. No waiting around to see its impact on the future. There was nothing more he could do to save them if this didn't work. And nothing he could do to save himself even if it did.

Down the street, Jared could hear the bounce of a basketball against asphalt—the Morris's oldest boy practicing free throws like he did every morning. Jared had played himself at one time. In junior high and freshman year of high school, before his father's diagnosis.

What did it mean, he wondered, for a life to begin so normal and hopeful and then spiral into inexplicable hell? He supposed it meant nothing at all; supposed it was simply the way things were. He'd been born into a strange reality full of spiders and flies, and, for no reason other than piss-poor luck, he'd been caught in the web of what was surely the vilest spider of them all.

Jared checked his watch. It was twenty minutes past eight now. Elena would likely still be asleep, if she slept at all these days. By the way she'd looked ever since he got back from the hospital, it seemed that sleep wasn't something Ra'Tak allowed. Either way, the time had come. Jared rose from the porch chair, crept back inside and past the couch where Melody lay dreaming what would likely be her last pleasant dream, and started up the stairs.

His heart was thudding so hard that he wondered if it might explode and spare him the horribleness ahead. Tears had begun pooling in his eyes the moment he looked away from his wife lying asleep on the couch. By the time he made it to the top of the stairs and to Elena's bedroom door where the butterfly watercolor still hung—a heartbreaking reminder of childlike innocence and a time to which he so badly wished to return—it was all he could do not to sob.

With trembling fingers, he touched the waistline of his jeans where he had tucked the .38 revolver, making sure it was concealed by the hem of his shirt. Without a proper holster, the steel pressed cold against his skin. Its cylinder bit into the soft flesh of his underbelly with every step up the stairs, cruelly reminding him it was there.

Somewhere in the recesses of his mind, a voice long drowned out by voices dark and deafening cried out for him to turn around. It almost startled him to feel reason's tug once more, like hearing the voice of a dead relative. And Jared almost listened. But a compulsion whose current was far too strong to swim against now pulled him onward. Pulled his hand up from the hem of his shirt where the revolver lay concealed to the doorknob of Elena's bedroom door.

Gliding along, flowing forward like driftwood caught in an eddy's pull, Jared pushed open the door. He saw Elena lying on the bed, her eyes closed and her hair splayed across the pillow like golden strands of silk. He crept closer, holding his breath and measuring each step. In the dim glow that filtered through her closed curtains, he could see her eyes moving back and forth beneath her eyelids like fetuses moving in the womb. He wondered if they visited her in her dreams the way they visited him in his and felt a chill at the thought that they might be with her now.

"Elly," he said and nudged her shoulder with his hand. "Elly, wake up."

Elena stirred, and her eyes fluttered open. She rubbed them, then blinked at Jared. "Daddy?"

"Come on, Elly. We've got to go." Jared hooked his hands underneath her arms and hoisted her out of bed.

"What's going on?" She stirred a little in his arms, but she didn't resist like he feared she might.

Jared didn't answer. He hurried down the stairs and across the living room, never pausing to make sure Melody was still asleep on the couch, though the thought crossed his mind. Everything was moving so fast now. The stairs and living room and driveway outside their home all flew by in a blur. One blink of the eye and they were out the door and into the sunlight's glare. The next and Jared was fastening her into the Camry's passenger seat. The next and he had slid into the driver's seat beside her.

"Where are we going?" Elena asked.

"Nowhere," Jared said.

"Then why are we—"

"We're not going anywhere. Not yet. We just need to talk, okay?"

"Okay," Elena said, still sounding just as confused. Jared studied her intently, never mind not knowing what he was searching for. Was it a sign that she understood more than she was letting on? Or was it a sign that she was still in there somewhere and not Ra'Tak merely replicating her nature?

"Elly," Jared said, fighting to keep his voice from crumbling into a sob. "Elly, if you're still in there, you have got to talk to me, sweetheart. You've got to tell me why you did it and you've got to tell me how to stop it. Right now."

"Did what?" Elena asked. She sounded more scared now than confused and looked on the verge of tears herself. Or was she only pretending to be? Jared suspected that they might try to pull on his heartstrings in the end, try to change his mind, but it didn't make her quivering lip and wide eyes any easier to decipher or any easier to bear.

Jared shook his head. "No. Not this time. No more dodging the question. What did you do, Elena? You have to tell me what you did."

Elena only stared blankly back at him in response.

"Tell me what you fucking did!" Rage coursed through him suddenly as though someone had injected it with a syringe. If she didn't confess to him now, if she didn't fight back against whatever force compelled her not to, it would cost them both their lives.

Instead, Elena started to cry. Jared screamed and slammed his fists against the steering wheel, honking the Camry's horn sporadically, and Elena's cries turned into sobs. It was maddening not knowing if they were real or simply Ra'Tak's ruse. More maddening what they would cost either way.

"Listen to me, Elly," Jared said, trying to keep his voice calm. "Stop crying and listen. I know who Ronny is. I know what you did. And I need you to help me stop it. If you don't, baby…if you don't help me stop it…we are all going to die."

Jared expected nothing but more sobs and sniffles. More confusion and denial and pleading. This was the only outcome he'd been able to imagine when he'd played out this moment over and over lying awake in bed. So when Elena stopped crying as quickly as shutting off a faucet and flashed a weary, knowing smile, Jared's breath caught in his throat.

"I know this has been really hard for you, Daddy. But I promise that it's almost over."

"What does that mean, Elly?"

But Elena wasn't looking at him anymore. She had closed her eyes and slumped back against the seat, seeming to have fallen asleep in an instant. Jared reached across the center console and shook her shoulder hard. "Elly, tell me what that means!"

It wasn't her voice that answered. Instead, a dreaded voice that had mercifully left him alone this morning up until now made reply, sounding to come from the back seat.

That's right, Jared. It is almost over. It is almost done.

Jared jumped so hard that he banged his head on the sunroof. He whirled around, but the back seat was empty. He stared at the spot where the voice had come from for a moment, then turned back to Elena. Her eyes were moving beneath her eyelids again, he noticed, even more rapidly than before. This time, there was no question who joined her in her dreams.

"Wake up! Wake up, wake up, WAKE UP!" He shook her with both hands, hard enough that her head jiggled like a dashboard doll and bounced against the headrest.

With startling timing, the entire car shook too. A low rumble rose to a roar, growing strong enough to bounce the car against its suspension in an erratic pattern. Jared let go of Elena's arm, and she slid a little farther down in the seat. Her eyes were still closed, and the jostling of her limp frame made it look like she was suffering a seizure.

Overhead, piercing through the steady roar of the sudden quake, a clap of thunder boomed. Jared jumped and tore his eyes from Elena just long enough to glance out the car's trembling windshield. It was darker now than it had been before. The morning's feathery clouds had changed to thick pillars of gray and black that now blanketed the sky. A flash of nearby lightning flickered across Elena's pallid features, but no thunder followed it. Instead, a voice boomed down from the clouds in its wake.

We are taking them, Jared....

The work is done...

It's time to claim what's ours...

Still staring hopelessly at Elena, Jared saw something moving out of the corner of his eye. The front door to his home was open now, shaking even more violently than the frame it was attached to and swaying back and forth against gusts of wind that were rapidly growing stronger.

In front of it, standing near the porch's steps, were Grace and Emily. They stepped off the porch and onto the walkway in unison, strolling toward the drive where the car was parked in slow, coordinated steps. Jared darted his eyes to the right—to Elena's still sleeping form—then back to the older girls. They had stopped midway along the path, halfway between the porch and the drive. Their heads were craned down to the quavering ground at their feet, and their hands were at their sides. When they finally looked up, slow and in unison, Jared saw that their eyes were black. He moaned, then turned back to Elena.

"Wake up, Elly! For the love of God, please wake up!"

Leave her... the voice from the storm clouds bellowed. *She is Ra'Tak now...*

"Fuck you!" Jared screamed, turning wet, angry eyes up to the Camry's moonroof. He reached out and started shaking Elena again. She thrashed and jostled in his hands, but her eyes never opened.

Jared struck her. His palm hit the side of her face with a sharp smack, leaving a bright pink handprint that stretched from her ear down the side of her jaw. Still, she never stirred. He wailed and turned back to the path where Grace and Emily had been standing. But they were no longer there.

Frantically, he scanned from window to window, then checked the car's rearview mirror. Nothing. He looked again. This time, barely visible in the top left corner of the windshield, Jared saw a foot standing on the edge of their home's slanted roof. He bent over and tilted his head.

From the new angle, he could see Grace and Emily again. They were standing on the roof with their heels near its edge, facing away from him and toward the woods at the back of the house. The wind whipped at their hair and the hems of their clothing, and their arms were stretched out with the tips of their fingers pointed toward the sky.

Jared hurried a glance back at Elena. She was sleeping still, motionless save for the way the tremor continued to oscillate her. Outside, it had started to rain. A deluge of thick, heavy drops fell all at once, pounding the car's windshield. On the roof, he could see Grace and Emily still standing in place with their arms outstretched and their hair now matted down in saturated strands.

Beyond them, coming out from the woods where they faced, a dark silhouette approached. It rose above the trees, its misshapen head almost touching the black clouds above, making it difficult to tell where one ended and the other began. It lifted its gangly arms as it advanced until its six-fingered hands were stretched heavenward.

Something struck the car's windshield hard, lurching Jared's attention away from the encroaching nightmare, and a smear of blood and feathers appeared on the glass. On the hood, a pigeon flailed and flopped in its death throes, splattering blood from its shattered wing and brushing it across the rain-soaked hood with thrashing feathers as if it were creating a crimson watercolor. Beyond it, another bird nosedived from the sky, exploding against the concrete driveway like a feather-covered water balloon. Another, this one a rather large raven, crashed headfirst into the side of the house. It fluttered down to its feet and began to stagger forward, drunkenly flapping its dark wings as it tried in vain to take flight.

One after another, birds of all sizes and varieties plummeted from the sky. Hailstones of flesh and bone, striking the ground and car and roof of the house with wet splats distinctly audible over the earthquake's ongoing rumble and the steady rush of falling rain.

Jared covered his ears with his hands, then, finding that it did little to mute the bedlam, started tugging at his hair. "Wake up! Fucking wake up!" Strings of spit flew out from his lips as he screamed, one of them landing on the side of Elena's neck. Beneath her closed eyelids, her eyes still darted back and forth.

A buzzard crashed into the car's passenger window, shattering the glass before falling to the ground in a lifeless heap of charcoal feathers. Cubes of safety glass rained down onto Elena's lap, but still she never stirred. Jared was sobbing again, the long, heavy wails making it difficult to breathe. Streams of tears all but blinded him, turning the wretched scene into a kaleidoscope of blurred colors.

Without realizing that he had reached for it, Jared felt the rubberized butt of the revolver against his hand. He pulled it from his waistband, then, as if startled to see himself holding it, let out another wail. He looked from the gun to Elena and felt his stomach roil. A crack of thunder split the air. From within its echoes, Ra'Tak spoke.

Put it down...

It's too late to save them now...

You've already failed...

Jared screamed. Fear and anger, desperation and agony, all mingled together in his cries. Before he realized what he was doing, he pushed the .38's barrel against his temple and set his finger against the trigger. Jared squeezed his eyes shut and inhaled sharply, drawing what would be his final breath.

LOOK AT US WHEN WE SPEAK TO YOU! the voice bellowed, deafeningly loud. Like a child snapping to attention, Jared opened his eyes. Through the cracked and rain-soaked windshield, he could see four blurred figures floating in the air, their arms lifted toward the dark sky above. Lowering the gun from his head, Jared fumbled at the car's windshield wipers, finally managing to find the right lever. The blades squeaked across the glass, clearing his view. He saw Grace and Emily first. They stared down at him with black eyes that peered through strands of soaked hair fallen over their ashen faces. Melody and Timmy were on either side of them, levitating as well. But while Grace and Emily seemed to float in the air as if suspended by an invisible harness, his wife and son thrashed as if suspended by a noose.

Unlike the girls' dark eyes, their eyes were bloodshot and panic-stricken. Yet their lips were stretched unnaturally into wide smiles. Smiles that persisted even as their faces turned from red to blue and their legs began to thrash a little more sporadically. Jared looked away.

You die when we command you to, Jared…

Not a moment before…

Not until you've watched each one of them go before you…

Jared looked back at Elena. She was sleeping still. Even as Ra'Tak shook the earth and murdered her family around her, she looked peaceful. No different than she had looked so many times before when she'd fallen asleep in the passenger seat while Jared was driving, curled up with her knees against her stomach and strands of hair falling over her face.

Without warning, she opened her eyes—eyes that for the briefest moment were the same shining blue that had melted his heart the moment he first held her. But as a smile spread across her face, her eyes began to change. Dark tendrils grew out from the black of her pupils, cutting across the gem-like surface of her irises and carving trenches through the white of her sclera. They spread out like a virus, growing and multiplying until they had covered the whole of her eyes and only inky black orbs remained.

Looking into those black, soulless eyes, Jared felt the last few threads of sanity he'd been clinging to snap like broken bungee cords. Any trace of the person he'd once been was gone now, incinerated in a furnace of grief and horror. Now, only agony was left in the ashes.

Still staring into the dark gaze of the thing that wore Elena's skin, Jared felt his arm lift up as if moving on its own volition. No thoughts formed in his mind as he pressed the barrel of the revolver between the thing's black eyes. No memories of the daughter he had once cherished rose up to stop him. She was gone already, and so was the man who had been her father. Whatever remained of them both now, only death would cure.

VOLUME II

ONE

79 DAYS BEFORE THE WORK IS DONE

Fear. It was something they had not felt in a thousand years. The sensation was so new to them, so foreign, they almost didn't recognize it. They were Ra'Tak. Fear was what they inflicted. Not something that they felt. Yet when the little girl walked into their Quarry's bedroom, they'd felt a terror not known to them since The Fall.

Worse still, they couldn't determine *why* they were afraid. The small, fragile little girl stood in the doorway, looking at the bed where her father was sleeping and where Ra'Tak was gathered around, whispering into his dreams. She stared straight at them, and for a moment they had the most bizarre feeling that she could see them. But it was not possible. They were Ra'Tak. They had wandered through the cities and homes of men since the dawn of civilization, never once seen unless they wanted to be seen, never once spotted in their true form by mortal eyes.

But then the girl began to speak. She began to speak…to *them*…and the fear they'd felt when she first walked through the door started to gain a foundation.

"Who are you?" the girl asked. Her voice trembled, and Ra'Tak could tell that she too was afraid. "What are you doing here?" There was more defiance there now. They had to act quickly. They didn't yet understand why they feared this girl, but they trusted it nonetheless. They were Ra'Tak. Their instincts were never wrong.

Let's have a look inside, they said to one another. *See who she is. Make her forget. Then the Work can continue.*

Ra'Tak slipped away from the bed and toward the girl, their morphing shape creeping toward her like an advancing shadow. She followed them with her eyes—eyes that should have never seen what they were seeing—and Ra'Tak's dread grew stronger. They needed to see inside her. They needed to know who this girl was, then they needed to make her forget. The Work had to continue. The Work was all that mattered.

Ra'Tak advanced on the girl, growing larger as they neared her. Their dark form rose in front of her, grazing the ceiling. Shadows moved inside of shadows, and darkness itself seemed to radiate from Ra'Tak's shapeless form. And yet the girl did not waver. She stared at them with intense yet curious eyes. Was there not even a hint of fear behind those eyes? If not yet, there would be soon enough.

They poured themselves into the girl's mind, ready to learn who she was. Ready to understand why she could see them. And ready to make her wish she never had.

But for the second time that night, Ra'Tak felt something they hadn't experienced in millennia. Pain. A force of cosmic magnitude crashed into them, ejecting them from the girl's mind before they could even begin to wrap their talons around her soul. Its intensity, its power, had been immeasurable. Nothing—no mortal man nor spiritual being they had ever encountered—could compare.

Ra'Tak revolted back, shrinking a little in size. They were shocked and frightened. But also in awe. They were Ra'Tak. They had whispered into the minds of prophets, broken into the dreams of witches and holy men alike with never the slightest resistance. They'd waged battle with the forces of Heaven and rivalries with the forces of Hell. But never had they touched a fire as mighty and divine as this.

For a brief, terrifying moment, they wondered if it was Him. They wondered if He had returned to walk the earth as a mortal once more. Would they now be banished from the earthly realm as so many had been during those dark years of defeat over two millennia ago, purged from existence by Heaven's most holy flame?

No, they thought. It cannot be so. Whatever else she might be, she is mortal and mortal alone.

Still, they had to act swiftly. Their thoughts worked at a speed that would have been incomprehensible to the little girl in front of them. They calculated all the options, considered all the scenarios, and argued amongst themselves about the best way for the Work to continue—all in the time it took for the girl to blink but once.

They were powerful too. Almost certainly stronger than she, they agreed, in spite of the unimaginable force they had felt. They could challenge her, throw the full weight of their evil against her soul now that they knew she was no normal child. But that could not be risked. They couldn't let pride stop the Work from continuing, and to accept the peril of challenging this girl given what they'd just felt would be nothing but risky hubris. Besides, claiming her life was not how the Work was supposed to go. There were rules that had to be followed for the Work to continue. Rules that had to be followed for Ra'Tak to continue.

But they had a plan. A perfect, cunning plan that would solve all the problems this little girl presented. As powerful as she was, Ra'Tak could tell that her power was unknown to her. It rested beneath the surface of her conscious mind like the calm, dark waters of an underground lake—an impossibly deep reservoir, but one yet undiscovered.

Ra'Tak could also tell that this girl had the innocence and curiosity of the child she was. This was no spiritual warrior, no agent from Heaven that stood before them. They didn't have to enter her mind to know that. It was only a little girl. A little girl with the soul to rival an Archangel, to be sure, but with the mind of a child still the same. And though she had swatted them from her like a fly, it was not before they had gained the slightest fingerhold on her psyche. Just enough to do what they did best.

Before the girl could blink a second time, Ra'Tak transformed the way she perceived them. In her eyes, they took the form of a cartoonish dog, standing on two legs like a man. Swirling shadows collapsed into soft blue fur. The essence of evil itself formed into a pair of shining brown eyes.

"Hi there," Ra'Tak said, the voice that she heard come from the dog's grinning lips soft and cheerful. "What's your name?"

The girl stared into their warm, friendly eyes with a look of utter confusion. For a moment, Ra'Tak felt sure their plan had failed. For a moment, they readied for battle against the strongest soul they had ever encountered. And then the girl started to laugh.

Ra'Tak laughed too, and they wagged their big, furry tail back and forth in genuine excitement. "I'm Ronny," they said. "Ronny the big, blue puppy dog!"

Ra'Tak flashed the girl a giant smile that seemed to stretch on for miles, and she laughed again. "I'm Elena," she said.

"Elena," Ra'Tak repeated. "What a delightful name. I bet a girl with a name like Elena is going to grow up to be the prettiest, most wonderful girl in all the world."

The girl smiled a little, but there was concern creeping back into her features. "What are you doing here, Ronny?" she asked.

"Well, you see, Elena," Ra'Tak said, leaning in close. "I'm a very special puppy dog. Once every few months, I get to visit a new family. And then you know what I get to do, Elena?"

"What?"

"Then I get to make all their dreams come true! I get to grant their wildest wishes. Why, I've brought little children just like you along with their families to a world where the rivers are made of chocolate and the mountains are made of toys. And do you know what the best part is?"

"What's that?" the girl asked, spellbound curiosity already replacing the suspicion in her tone.

"You and your family are next! Why, you are so lucky, little Elena! Now that I'm your friend, your entire life is about to change!" Ra'Tak lifted the paws of the character they had formed, and a pink lollipop appeared between its fingers.

"Wow," Elena exclaimed—loud enough that Ra'Tak grew concerned she would wake their Quarry. That wouldn't do. They couldn't have him distracting her before their plan was complete.

"Shhh. Quiet now, little Elena. We can't have you waking up Dad. The truth is you weren't supposed to meet me yet. I was supposed to make your father's wishes come true first, and then you were next. There's an order these things have to be done in, you see, and now I'm afraid we might have messed the whole thing up."

Ra'Tak handed the girl the lollipop and sighed. There was worry in her eyes again now, but this time it was the worry that they had planted there. "I didn't mean to mess it up," she said.

"Oh, don't worry, child. I don't think you did. I think everything can still work out exactly like it's supposed to. But you have to do just what I say. Can you do that?"

Elena nodded.

"Good. Now, I'm very happy to have met you, little Elena, but your father is still the one that I have to take to the magical new world first, you see? He's the father, so he gets to go first. That seems fair, don't you think?"

Elena considered this, then nodded again.

"And then I'll come back for you," Ra'Tak continued. "I *promise* I will. But in the meantime, I need you to let me spend as much time as I need with your father without interrupting. Do you think you can do that?"

"Yeah," Elena said. "I can do that."

"Wonderful!" Ra'Tak said.

"Will I see you again?"

"Oh, I think you will, Elena. I'm going to be spending a lot of time around your home, so I think we'll become good friends. We can talk and play games, and I can make you all sorts of fun toys and tasty treats. But only if you always do what I say and only if you let me spend time with your father too. And then you and your siblings and your mommy and daddy and all your friends and family can come with me to a magical new home!"

Elena giggled, and Ra'Tak giggled too. "Run along now, little Elena," they said. "Go back to your room. There is work to be done with your father."

Elena started to turn away, then stopped. "What about the lollipop?" she asked, looking down at the large piece of candy in her hand.

"What about it?" A touch of Ra'Tak's anger slipped through into Ronny's tone. Their patience was wearing thin.

"I'm not allowed to have candy before dinner," the girl said.

"Ah," said Ra'Tak, trying as best they could to keep their voice warm and friendly. "Well then hide it away wherever you please and eat it later. Your parents won't be able to see it wherever you put it, dear. It's a special lollipop. Just like I'm a special puppy dog."

The girl smiled, then tucked away the mirage of a lollipop they'd formed for her and headed for the door. "Good night, Ronny," she whispered as she left.

"Good night, Elena," Ra'Tak whispered back.

TWO

TUESDAY, JUNE 26TH

Outside the Gordon home, on an afternoon atypically cool for a summer day in Georgia, a single monarch butterfly danced back and forth on the breeze, pumping its velvety wings until it had hovered its way down to the soft, orange petals of a marigold flower. It prodded the flower for a moment before finding the sticky nectar it searched for. Preoccupied with its prize, the butterfly didn't notice when a shadow loomed over it, blocking out what sunlight filtered through heavily clouded skies. Something moved behind the butterfly, and it brushed its wings once, ready to lift away at the first sign of danger.

Elena Gordon paused, standing motionless like a seasoned hunter. She had no intention of trying to catch the butterfly she had been stalking since she'd first spotted it struggling against the wind, but she did want to get as close a look as possible. Elena loved butterflies. She loved most creatures, for that matter—even the ones that weren't so cute and snuggly. Toads, beetles, and even the occasional spider were just a few of the backyard wildlife she had tried to move indoors at various times throughout her childhood.

But Elena was nine now, old enough to realize that some creatures are better left in the wild than adopted as pets. Case in point: butterflies.

Besides, her birthday was just a few months away, and she was still holding out hope that her gift from her parents would be a furry, four-legged friend. It didn't matter to Elena if it was a dog, a cat, a hamster, or anything in between. Any pet that she could call her own would be enough to send her to newfound levels of glee.

Of course, there was one dog that had already come into Elena's life. But he wasn't like any dog that she had played with before. He looked and talked like a dog from the cartoons that she watched with her little brother. That'd been pretty surprising, but also too enchanting for her to question it too much.

Since her first encounter with the big blue dog named Ronny, the two of them had spent a fair amount of time together. They'd drawn pictures, played games like Simon Says and Follow the Leader, and had even gone on walks. Ronny told her that she was the only one who could see him, and that had turned out to be true; there'd been plenty of times when he would be standing right in front of her parents, practically brushing up against them with the tips of his fur, yet they never noticed.

It was like having an incredible secret friend that no one else in the world knew about. For the most part, it had been delightful.

But... Elena thought and frowned at the butterfly. It was the only word that pushed to the forefront of her mind, but it carried with it things she didn't like to dwell on.

As much as it pained her to admit, there were some things about her newfound friend that she didn't find so delightful. For one, he insisted on spending a lot of time with her father. That didn't make a lot of sense to Elena, since her father couldn't see Ronny (and had actually become strangely upset when Elena mentioned him). But the one time she'd brought this up to Ronny, he was the one who got upset.

There was something else too. Something that Elena couldn't quite find a way to explain, even in her own head. She had always been privy to insights beyond the veil of what anyone else could access. Sometimes they came as memories of events she had not been there to witness or visions of events that had not yet happened. More often, they came as just a feeling in the pit of her soul. But they were always irrefutably certain, proven reliable time and time again.

Too young to give such anomalies any more than passing scrutiny, Elena considered this quirk of hers just another normal part of the human experience. When these flashes of truth did come to her, though, she tended to trust them. And the chill that she'd felt when she first stepped into her parents' bedroom the day she met Ronny had been something that Elena couldn't shake. Something else had been in that room besides Ronny and her father. Something that had drawn her there in the first place.

She'd sensed it from downstairs. She'd felt it enter her home the moment her father lay down for a nap, and it had struck her with a set of emotions that she had never quite felt before. It felt hateful and angry and dark. Before that night, Elena's own understanding of evil consisted of Disney movie villains and Scooby-Doo monsters. But what she'd sensed that day had changed her perspective.

Yet, frightful as it had been, something had pushed her forward. Something had calmed her fears. As though sparked by the darkness filling her home, a light inside her had begun to glow much brighter than ever before. It had always been there for as far back as she could remember—this thing that she had no words to explain—resting beneath the surface of her emotions and flaring only slightly, only when it needed to. That afternoon, though, as she approached her parents' bedroom door and the vile force leaking out from underneath it, her light blazed like a beacon—so bright she'd felt its warmth in her chest and seen its glow underneath her skin.

With each step that Elena took toward her parents' room that day, the dark presence behind it had grown increasingly intense. Yet her light had matched it at every step, outdoing the other by magnitudes so that all she felt was confident determination. By the time she eased open the bedroom door, this feeling had so entranced her that it almost seemed like dreaming.

When a dark presence like columns of suspended ink materialized before her and rose from the floor, twisting and oozing its way closer, Elena had only watched it come. When it leaned itself against the portal to her soul, attempting entry, Elena had felt no cause for worry. And when her soul had expelled it without the slightest trouble, she had felt no surprise. It seemed to her at that moment that she would simply burn this dark thing out of existence right then and there. Like a shaft of wheat tossed into a furnace, never to trouble her again.

But then the dark thing had vanished. It was gone, and in its place, Ronny had appeared. In spite of all she had just felt and seen, Elena couldn't help but giggle at the sight of this wonderfully silly-looking dog. Conscious thought—childlike thought—came rushing back to the forefront of her mind. And that's when Ronny had introduced himself.

The darkness she'd felt and the shadowy thing she'd seen were not hidden from her memory. But they did, by and large, evade her understanding. Ronny, while certainly not an ordinary thing, was at least something she could wrap her head around. The thing that had been there before him was not and was thus mostly disregarded.

And for a while, things had been mostly fine. In fact, for the most part, Ronny and all of the magical new delights he had brought into Elena's life had been impossibly splendid. He'd been the most amazing friend that a nine-year-old girl could ask for. He played all her favorite

games with her for hours on end without ever growing bored. He conjured up tasty treats like ice cream sandwiches and strawberry snow
cones and chocolate candies out of nothing but air anytime she asked,
and each time they seemed to Elena to be the most wickedly delicious
thing she had ever tasted. He was never cross like adults could be nor
cruel like children her own age sometimes were. Every time she saw
him—which had been increasingly often as of late—there was a smile
on his face and his fluffy blue tail was wagging.

He'd been smiling yesterday afternoon when he told Elena about a
new kind of game that the two of them should play, and his tail had
been wagging too. That brought Elena some comfort at the time, and it
still did now. But she hadn't liked the sound of Ronny's new game when
he described it.

It was in the woods. It *had* to be in the woods, Ronny explained. And
it had to be at night, sometime well after the sun had set and the rest of
her family were in bed. Elena didn't like the woods outside her home
very much, and she certainly didn't like them at night. The shadows
cast by thick clusters of branches sometimes fell against her bedroom
window when the moon was full and the curtains were open, and those
alone gave her a sense of unease. It didn't help that her father had seemingly come to dislike the idea of Ronny, so much as he knew of him,
quite a lot. The stern, worried conversations he'd had with her about
him were not far from her mind.

What troubled Elena more than all these things, though, was the way
Ronny had acted when he talked about this new game. He'd seemed
happy as always, that much was true, but much more serious than she
had ever seen him before. He had told her that this new game was
important, *very* important, and that their entire friendship—all the
wonderful things that were yet to come for her and her family—hung
in the balance. If she listened, if she did exactly what she was told, then

Ronny promised that all her wildest wishes would come true. If she didn't listen, if she failed to sneak out of her bedroom when the hour turned to twelve and follow the path he'd shown her deep into the woods until she came to the hollowed-out stump in the clearing, if she didn't wait by that stump for Ronny to arrive and if she didn't do and say everything he told her to do and say once she got there, then he would be forced to leave and she would never see him again.

Elena didn't want that to happen, and neither did Ronny. Still, the way she'd felt as Ronny talked about these things yesterday after-noon reminded Elena of the way it had felt approaching her parents' bedroom door those moments before Ronny appeared. She felt cold and anxious. Worst of all, it seemed that Ronny was the source of these feelings, so that by the time their conversation had ended, Elena was, for the first time in their relationship, happy to see him go. This time, when Ronny faded into nothing right in front of her, Elena was relieved, and she didn't find herself wishing he'd come back sooner rather than later like all the times before.

Having finally grown wary of the gargantuan figure that loomed closer and closer toward it, the butterfly pumped its dusty wings and caught the breeze, lifting up and away to find some other flower that offered a little more privacy. Elena sighed, but she didn't blame the creature. While she herself meant the butterfly no harm, Elena was old enough to know that there were things out there that wanted to eat it. The butterfly was small, and it had to be careful.

She looked away from the flower where the butterfly had been perched and toward the horizon, frowning as she did. The sun would be setting soon. Her parents and siblings would be going to bed soon after that. And then, after darkness had fully settled over the woods outside her home, Elena would have a choice to make.

THREE

42 DAYS BEFORE THE WORK IS DONE

The Trinity's dark antithesis, Ra'Tak functioned as one. Like Legion before them, they were many—yet united as one mind with one all-consuming purpose.

So rare were the times they disagreed that even their near-timeless existence was marked by only a scattering of such occasions. Yet dissent had roiled through their number ever since they'd first encountered the girl named Elena Gordon. And it pertained, as it almost always did those scarce times they clashed, to one of the Work's most delicate operations: the taking of a Conduit.

Only the most difficult chapters of their Work had ever required this measure—those times when their Quarry possessed an especially strong spirit and will to live. This time, it wasn't their Quarry that concerned them, but the girl and the ineffable spirit they'd felt in her necessitated all available precautions.

Completing the Rite of the Conduit—attaching themselves to the soul of one close to their Quarry and leaching its vitality—would instill them with the strength they needed to ensure the Work's completion no matter what obstacles the girl presented. The risks this came with made taking a Conduit a rare and controversial practice for them. This time, however, it wasn't *whether* they should take a Conduit that caused disagreement in their ranks, but *who* they should take.

Their Quarry's lastborn son was the safest choice. He would be the easiest to deceive into completing the Rite. And though his spirit was undeveloped, youth, they'd found, had a potency all its own.

But some of Ra'Tak had more ambitious aspirations. The power they'd felt from the girl frightened them, but it also fanned the flames of their bottomless lust. If they could somehow tap the spirit from which that power sprang, bleed it dry and consume every drop, there'd be no limit to the destruction they could unleash on Creation.

Taking her by force wasn't an option. Penetrating any further into her mind than the surface level that allowed only the most basic illusions was too risky to try again. But if they could trick her into *letting* them in, if they could earn her trust and convince her to complete the Rite entirely of her own accord, they would claim a Conduit unlike any they had taken before.

Lust and ambition had ultimately won the day, and Ra'Tak had set about executing one of their most precarious plans to date. For the past month, they had played the character of Ronny to near perfection, painful though it was; they were not as adept as their Master at duplicating sentiments that ran far counter to their being, and each friendly smile or kind word they fabricated burned much more than their pride—it stung like acid and singed their very essence.

Fortunately, these minor scars were already proving their worth. At the very least, their Ronny ruse had distracted the girl quite nicely and had allowed their Work to continue right on schedule. And a prize much greater than this was now right within their reach.

Still, the Rite of the Conduit was not a simple ritual. It required a specific set of actions, words, and thoughts from the mortal they chose—difficult, at times, to coerce even when they were able to enter their would-be Conduit's mind. Coercing it from the outside, with no control at all, would be even trickier.

But Ra'Tak had played many games with the girl since revealing themselves as Ronny. Some familiar, some made up, and some strategically strange. They had placed a special emphasis on games that required her compliance and had turned her obeying their commands into harmless fun. Now, she was ready for the most important game of all.

Getting her to the spot where the Rite of the Conduit must take place would likely be the most difficult task. There were only so many places in Creation suitable for such exercises, and the timing likewise had to be just right. In this case, it meant getting Elena to travel far into the woods behind her home sometime during the midnight hour.

Ra'Tak ran through their plan countless times, war-gaming every possible way it might go. It was shaky, at best, they realized—all hinging on the whims of a girl not old enough to bleed yet powerful enough to likely annihilate them if she were to ever harness her potential.

One way or another, be it taking her as a Conduit and claiming that potential as their own or some other measure yet to be decided, Ra'Tak would make sure that didn't happen.

FOUR

Elena pushed the back door closed as gently as she could manage, hoping the sound wouldn't be enough to bring her parents downstairs. Somewhere in the bushes that her mom had planted alongside the house, a chorus of crickets serenaded the crescent moon. Elena looked up at the sliver of light and frowned. It was doing little to illuminate the backyard where she stood. Even less to light the woods beyond it.

She had a flashlight, though, she reminded herself. She felt for it in her jacket pocket and suddenly found herself wanting to check one more time that it actually worked. But it was a silly thought; she wouldn't turn the flashlight on until she made it into the woods to make sure her parents didn't see, and she had certainly tested it enough times in her bedroom before building up the nerve to go outside.

There was no reason to be nervous, anyway, she kept telling herself. No reason to be afraid of the woods, even in the dark. There weren't any truly dangerous animals living in those woods. Ronny would likely be the only animal or person she saw. Elena still couldn't decide which of those two terms, if either, fit Ronny best, and that bothered her for some reason.

A great many things were bothering her, to tell the truth, and they'd been bothering her ever since Ronny first broached the subject of the new game he wanted to play in the woods. They'd bothered her so much that she hadn't eaten all day and was feeling faint as a result. But the one thing that bothered her more than anything else was the thought of letting her new friend down. So when the time had come— when the stretch of light underneath Mom and Dad's bedroom door had gone dark and the clock had reached midnight—Elena pushed aside all other worries and resolved to do as Ronny had asked her.

Nevertheless, when she came to the edge of the woods where neatly trimmed grass gave way to dark thickets of trees and shrubs, that resolve felt a little weaker. She stopped at the tree line. A gust of wind moved through the leaves and limbs and fluttered against the hood of Elena's purple windbreaker, carrying with it the earthy smell of topsoil and pine needles. It was a soothing scent, even if the way the breeze whined through the branches and the way they moved like shadowy arms had not been so soothing. Elena took a deep breath in through her nose, thought of all the fun games that she and Ronny had played together, and stepped into the forest.

She glanced back over her shoulder, but it was only to make sure one final time that her parents had not followed her out. Satisfied she was alone, Elena pulled the flashlight out of her jacket pocket and turned it on. Yellow light lit a weathered but recognizable path that cut through the thick brambles and snaked its way around the larger pines. On either side of it, though, at the path's edges where the beam didn't reach, Elena could see only darkness.

If this new game had to be played in the woods, why couldn't they at least play it in the daytime? The entire thing would not have been nearly so frightening if only the sun had been out to fill the forest with green-tinted light. Elena found herself growing frustrated. Frustrated with Ronny. Frustrated with all his rules and stipulations that didn't seem to make much sense at all. *This had better be a fun game*, she thought. *A really fun game.*

She was far enough into the woods now that when she turned around and shined the light back toward her home, all she could see was trees. A feeling struck her suddenly that she was deep in the belly of some forgotten wilderness. She knew it wasn't true, knew that she could sprint back down the path and be back in her bed in a matter of minutes. But the feeling only grew stronger with every step deeper into the forest.

None of the scant moonlight filtered its way through the branches here. The woods had grown so thick that they smothered all but the thin path she followed. Elena kept her light pointed straight ahead, not liking the look of the choked thicket on either side of the path or the way the flashlight's beam died against it.

It was only by happenstance then that another few minutes into her journey she managed to spot the clearing that Ronny had told her to find. Glistening strands of spider silk had been blocking the path, and the flashlight's beam had landed on the clearing as she'd tried to work her way around.

It wasn't large enough to call a gale. Just a roughly circular patch about the size of her backyard where no vegetation grew. Nothing save for a dead stump near the clearing's center and a patch of brown grass encircling it.

There were pools of water trapped inside the stump's several pockets, and a small, wrinkled leaf was floating in one. Elena picked it up by the stem, twisted it around a few times between her thumb and forefinger, then placed it back down in the black water.

Alarms began to ring somewhere in the wells of her mind. This wasn't a good place. It wasn't the darkness, or the woods, or the distance from her home; she had come to grips with these things already, and they were not what troubled her now. It was the place itself, this space in the woods where nothing grew from the ground but a long-dead stump.

It was a bad place and bad things came here. A place of rot and death where only rotten, dead things came. And she shouldn't be here.

Elena looked at her hands and saw that her skin had started to glow. A faint, silvery-white shine that could have been blamed on the moonlight if the moon had been more than a slim sickle obscured by the trees. Her body hummed like an instrument's string, and energy that beckoned her to run away coursed through her with every heartbeat.

"Hello, Elena," a familiar voice said. Ronny appeared on the stump beside her, a furry, blue mass where an instant before there'd been only air. His cartoonish eyes met hers, and his tail began to wag. "I'm so glad you've come! We're going to have so much fun!" Elena watched him without reply, and Ronny watched her back. His tail stopped wagging. "Are you hungry, Elena? You look like something's wrong. Why, I could whip up an ice cream cone or a slice of cake for you right now if you'd like."

"I'm not hungry," Elena said. Even if she was, Ronny's snacks were never filling for long.

Ronny considered this for a moment. "Very well. You've come all this way and I'm sure you're as excited about our new game as I am. Let's get started, shall we?" He looked like he was waiting for a response, but Elena didn't offer one. A gust of wind whistled through the trees and lifted a strand of hair from her shoulders. But the long, silky strands of Ronny's coat never moved.

"Elena? Would you like for me to teach you this new game or not? If not, I suppose we could both go back home. Although, if I go back to my home, I might not be able to ever visit yours again."

"Show it to me. Show me the game and then I'll decide if I want to play it."

"My my," said Ronny. "No need for such distrust, dear. It's a very easy game, and I'm sure you're going to love it. All you have to do is sit here on this stump beside me, close your eyes, and do what I tell you. If I tell you to say something, you say it, even if it's something strange or silly. If I tell you to do something, you do it, even if it's strange or silly too. Even if it's something that frightens you. Can you do that?"

"That doesn't sound like a very fun game."

"But Elena," Ronny said, his voice now low and serious, "the game is only the beginning. What comes next is the fun part. Now no more dillydally, little dolly. It's time for us to play."

"No," Elena said. "I've changed my mind. I'm going home."

Ronny's eyes widened. "Elena, you can't leave now! You've come all this way. And so much is at stake. If you will just play this one game, I will give you anything you want! One short, little game and the whole wide world is yours!"

"I'm sorry I won't see you anymore, Ronny. But maybe it's for the best." She turned away from the stump and pointed her light back toward the trail. But suddenly Ronny was standing in front of her again, materializing in an instant directly in front of her path.

"You can't leave, Elena. We've come too far."

Elena pressed forward. Ronny didn't move and instead seemed to grow larger—slowly expanding so that by the time she reached him, he was looming over her. But she didn't stop. She walked up to Ronny, then, still never slowing, walked straight through him, somewhat surprised to hear herself giggle a little as she did.

Up ahead, Ronny appeared in front of her again. Except he wasn't really Ronny anymore. He had swelled even larger, and his soft, rounded features had grown sharp and angular. Half-circle ears grew pointed and his cartoonish face narrowed into a snout like a wolf's.

"Stop!" Ronny snarled. "Stop or I'll hurt you! I'll tear you to shreds!"

"You can't hurt me," Elena said, her voice calm and level. Ronny roared and howled, dropping down to all fours. He snapped at the air, each clash of his fangs sounding like gunshots. He tore at the earth with thick, black claws. And when Elena reached his snapping jaws and crouched yet towering frame, she passed straight through him once more. Unharmed, untouched, unaffected. As if he was nothing but a mirage.

The thing that appeared in front of her this time bore no semblance to Ronny at all. This time, the thing blocking her path was the dark thing she had glimpsed surrounding her father's bed before Ronny appeared. The flashlight's beam seemed to die against it, snuffed out by its void. It spoke to her, but not in the way that Ronny had spoken. The dark thing spoke without words. It assaulted her with messages of hate and pain and violence. But each thought that it flung into her mind—each projectile of darkness—was scorched at once like paper airplanes tossed into the sun.

She pressed forward. She marched through the dark woods and toward the dark thing attempting to block her path at an almost casual gait. Entering these woods had been frightening. Leaving them, despite the fathomless nightmare now enveloping the path ahead, Elena felt no fear at all.

She walked through the dark thing as if it were only a shadow. And when she had stepped past the boundary where the flashlight's beam died against roaring, black flames, Elena saw nothing but light. Brilliant, white light so beautiful she couldn't help but smile.

There was noise coming from the world outside, from the world beyond her wonderful bubble of light. It roared like a tornado and screamed like all the souls of the damned. But to her, these sounds seemed distant. To her they sounded more like gentle waves splashing against the coast and angels singing soft songs down from the clouds.

She couldn't remember stepping out of the dark thing, couldn't recall the exact point at which her view had changed from breathtaking rays of heavenly light back to that of the woods and the path ahead. All she knew was that when it happened, the dark thing was gone. Ronny was gone.

Elena never felt the need to look back and make sure he wasn't following her. She strolled out of the woods with a smile on her face. And when she had made her way back inside and up to her bedroom and had crawled back under the covers of her bed, Elena Gordon slept without trouble and dreamed of beautiful things.

FIVE

41 DAYS BEFORE THE WORK IS DONE

Ra'Tak roared. A thousand conjoined spirits shrieked in unison, rage their only regard; rage stronger—*purer*—than it had ever been before.

They had retreated. Fled away to the bottom of some faraway crevice in a corner of the world long neglected by man. They had failed. And this time there would surely be consequences.

This was not how their Master mandated the Work proceed. Their charge since The Fall had always been simple and had always been the same. They were the madness that drove men to destruction. The catalyst for one of their Master's favorite delicacies: a soul so tortured that it ends its own life.

Their Master had marked the man named Jared Joseph Gordon as their next Quarry. His life, taken by his own hands, was the offering they owed.

But betwixt them and this offering for which no excuse would be accepted stood a mortal who confounded their ancient mind. How could a being so meek and feeble come to possess such power? If only they had the means to attack her frail little body instead of her impossibly guarded soul.

Licking their wounds in the darkness, they dreamed a collective dream of all the ways they might tear her asunder if only a physical form was theirs to possess. Perhaps the form of a wolf, or a lion, or some other wild beast. Perhaps the form of her own mother or father so they could savor the confusion and betrayal in her eyes as they carved her apart one piece at a time. They imagined her smugness melting into dread the next time she tried to stride through whatever nightmarish mirage they conjured only to find it solid and lethal instead of ethereal and benign.

But these were only fantasies. A physical form would never be theirs to possess. Not for one moment of their epoch existence had they ever truly experienced all the sights, sounds, and sensations of the physical plane. Even the ones whose minds they entered were never fully theirs to control.

For them, creating a vision, or a feeling, or a memory in the minds of the mortals they entered came effortless. But the bodies their Enemy had vexingly gifted these unworthy beings were entirely out of reach. Existing on a plane that Ra'Tak and those like them could observe and understand but never directly experience.

Or directly manipulate. Were it not so, they and their Master and his legion of the fallen would have devoured all Creation long ago.

But these beings they so despised were not wholly invulnerable. Some of their gifts also brought weaknesses: a soul, free will, and all that these entailed. A connection to the spiritual plane that went both ways—and one that Ra'Tak could enter.

Some souls were easier to enter than others. But never had they found the act even bordering difficult until now. That the girl's soul was impenetrable to them wasn't what worried Ra'Tak most. Attempting to take control of her had been a tantalizing gamble, but she was not needed for the Work to continue. Her brother could serve as their Conduit. The life force they could draw from him alone and the power it lent them would be more than plenty to drive their Quarry to madness. It was possible their Master might even choose not to punish them for the disruption the girl had already caused if they proceeded now with haste.

But it was what she might do to them if she turned that impossible power against them that frightened them to their core. Frightened them almost as much as the fear of failing their Master.

Almost. For even now in this refuge of defeat, there was no question that the Work would proceed. They dared not even consider denying their Master's demands. Consider it even a moment and he would hear it in their thoughts. And take it as nothing less than treachery.

They could not hide here for long. Time was not on their side. Every hour that passed, the girl grew more aware of her abilities. More in control. They needed to bring about their Quarry's demise and the Work's completion much quicker than anticipated. And that would mean assaulting him more violently than any mind they had destroyed in the past.

In other circumstances, there were parts of Ra'Tak that might have enjoyed the challenge. But too much was at stake now for any such amusement. Their eternal existence hung in the balance. An existence that, despite the hate and suffering they carried, Ra'Tak clung to rapaciously. And one they would defend with more ferocity than mortal minds could conceive.

SIX

THURSDAY, JULY 5ᵀᴴ

"Would you like some more tea, Mr. Fuzzybum?" Elena asked. The honey-brown teddy bear sitting across from her made no reply; he only watched her with glassy eyes. Elena poured him some more anyway.

It came out clear as water. No surprise, she supposed, given she'd filled the kettle from the tap herself. Before, when Ronny had played tea party with her, there had been real tea with cream and sugar and a little glass pitcher full of honey. There'd been real cookies, too. And real company. Mr. Fuzzybum, Arnold the Rabbit, and her doll Lisa-Loo—now all staring straight ahead with frozen eyes and stock-still limbs—had come to life in Ronny's presence and carried out the most fantastical tea parties a little girl could ask for.

Or so it had seemed, at least. Elena doubted now if any of it had actually been real. More likely that every bit was just as fake as the things Ronny had tried to scare her with in the woods. She'd fallen for the tricks out of amusement, like suspending disbelief at a magic show, but now the act was over, and reality had set back in.

Ronny had left. Almost two weeks had passed since she confronted him in the woods, and she'd seen no sign of him since. Yet despite all the wonders he'd brought, Elena was glad for him to be gone. It turned out he wasn't a very nice dog after all.

Besides, there was a new development in her life. One that interested her much more, she suddenly concluded, than a tea party with lifeless toys in attendance and lukewarm water in place of tea.

She rose from the floor and turned off the lights. She slipped into bed and got comfortable beneath the covers. It took only minutes this time before she started to drift; she was getting faster at it.

Elena felt the muscles in her limbs grow loose and heavy. There was a soft ringing in her ears that rose steadily louder. It reached a crescendo, then cut off sharply, ending in silence. She felt a sensation like that of falling, but only for an instant. Then she was back on the solid support of her bed, eyes open and looking up at her rainbow-colored ceiling fan. The only difference she noticed now (and all the times before) was that everything seemed a little brighter. As if some sourceless, golden light filled the room. She rose from the floor, turned around, and looked back down at where she'd been lying.

What had come as quite a surprise the first time she'd pulled this little trick now came expected. Elena watched herself still lying on the bed—saw her own closed eyelids and her own chest rising up and down with the rhythmic breaths of sleep.

Extending from the body she no longer seemed to inhabit—connecting her to it—was a braid of silver-white light. It looked as if someone had spun moonbeams into a cord. When she walked farther away, the cord lengthened. When she drew closer, it contracted. If it had a limit as to how far it could stretch, she had yet to find it. And she had already stretched it *very* far.

This marked the seventh trip she'd taken outside her body over the past few days. The first trip had been a total accident. She thought she was getting up to get a drink of water and had been stunned to look back at her bed and see herself still snuggled under the blankets.

She'd barely had time to notice the cord of light then before it snapped forward, retracting her back like the end of a spring-loaded tape measure. She'd flown across the room toward the bed at blinding speed. In an instant, she was back under the covers once more, awake and alert and reunited with her body.

The second trip had happened accidentally as well. This time, though, she didn't panic. And the cord of light that seemed to dictate how long she got to stay outside her body—even if it didn't appear to care how far she ventured—let her stay a little longer.

The third trip and all the trips that followed had each been planned. Dropping down into the special sleep that let her mind leave her body and go exploring was something that Elena picked up quite quickly. It seemed to her like swimming or riding a bike; a skill that clicks once and comes natural thereafter. She'd been thrown into the deep end that first trip outside her body but had quickly learned to tread water. By trip number five, she was swimming like a dolphin.

Now it was time for trip number seven. And trip number seven was going to be special. Elena looked away from her sleeping form and toward her bedroom window. It was closed, and the curtains were drawn, but it didn't matter. She glided across the room, stepped up onto its sill, then passed through it as effortlessly as she had passed through Ronny's various forms a couple weeks ago.

There was nothing but empty air to greet the soles of her feet when she stepped through the window, but she didn't fall. She hovered in place for a while and then ascended a few dozen feet into the sky. The sun was just a smudge of red on the western skyline, and to the east, she could see city lights against a darkening horizon. There were stars overhead, but only the few, especially bright bodies that were as of yet just dim pinpricks in a violet sky.

Elena lifted her eyes and focused on a white star that was close to being directly above her. For reassurance, she glanced one last time at the cord of light connecting her to her body. It drooped down from the center of her chest before curving like the bend of a hook and passing through her window, out of sight.

I hope it can stretch this far. I hope it doesn't break, Elena thought, then looked back up at the star.

With only a thought, she shot up like a rocket. Her house seemed to shrink at once to the size of a home an ant might live in, instants later growing so small as to be invisible. She could see the entirety of the North American continent below her now, its eastern seaboard and the ocean beyond engulfed in shadows. Elena paused at this point where the air grew thin and its color cooled from azure to black. Paused and floated, taking in the view just as she had done the trip before. Unlike the trip before, though, this trip was not going to end here at the edge of the world. This time, she had *much* farther to travel.

Earlier that morning, when Elena had soared up past the clouds for the first time to watch the sun rise over the planet's gentle curve, a voice had called out to her. It whispered softly from somewhere beyond the expanse above her. It sang the song of the stars and spoke words older than the universe itself. Words that Elena somehow understood and melodies that somehow seemed familiar. It beckoned her to come. Hearing that voice and its soothing, mystical song, Elena felt like a child hearing her mother's voice for the very first time.

Now, she could already hear it again, calling out across the infinite sea of space. It enchanted her at once just as it had before, resonated with something deep inside her in a way Elena couldn't quite define. Once again, it beckoned her to come.

"I don't know the way," she said, her own voice dying against the vacuum all around her.

Without ever speaking the words, the voice told her the way. Instructions came to her as inexplicable yet certain as whatever tells birds the way north. Surging with confidence that the voice instilled, Elena soared away from the earth like a meteor traveling in reverse.

She zipped across the empty expanse at a speed immeasurable. At a speed that nothing physical had ever traveled. So that by the time any time at all had passed, she had already passed the edge of all that was known.

Somewhere within the infinite so far from where she'd come it eluded comprehension, her journey came to a stop. Elena turned and looked back in the direction she'd come from. The silver-white braid still springing from her chest stretched across the star-spotted expanse, disappearing into the abyss. Seeing it there—knowing where it would lead her back to—brought her a wave of comfort.

She scanned the space around her, certain she'd arrived at her destination but with no idea what to do next. Every direction looked the same. Just emptiness speckled in the distance by faraway stars.

Only one of these stars caught her attention. It seemed close somehow. Close and small—as though it weren't a star at all but rather a pinprick in the darkness just ahead that let light from the other side shine through. And from somewhere within this tiny sphere of light, the voice Elena had followed here still sang its cosmic song. Still beckoned her to come.

Elena watched the speck of light begin to grow. It swelled larger until it engulfed the space in front of her like a blazing white star. With no hesitation, she descended into it.

Crossing its boundary brought sensations undiscovered in her nine years of life. The air sparked and fizzled against her skin like carbonated water. Tremors of pure, warm bliss ebbed and flowed in a rhythm as steady and constant as waves in the ocean.

All around, fractals of reflected light bounced from one mirror-like surface to the next, illuminating the prism-like world in a dazzling display of color. It was like being inside of a diamond held near the firelight. It was like being under clear water when the sun is high on a cloudless day. From seemingly all around, the voice that had guided her here still sang out, its timeless songs reverberating across the strange fabric of this new reality.

"Where are we?" Elena asked. Her words were echoed back at her repeatedly, seeming to harmonize a little more with the otherworldly chorus each iteration until they became a part of it. Like the notes of a backup singer fusing into the harmony.

Suddenly, the chorus changed. It grew warmer and gentler. And with this change in tone and timbre, new thoughts and feelings entered Elena's mind as if they'd been spoken there. They reminded her of home and her grandmother's house. They reminded her of the water park where she went for her birthday last year and the little nook in the school library with the purple beanbag chair. And together, these thoughts made sense. Together, they answered her question.

"We're in a good place," Elena said.

The chorus rose in confirmation. Elena closed her eyes and basked in it for a while. Soaked within its heart-tugging tones and the tingling charge of this unearthly world.

"Who are you?" Elena asked, her voice slow and drunken.

This time, the change in the chorus was much more dramatic. It rose to a powerful crescendo, sounding now as if angel armies had joined the symphony. Rumbling bass boomed from all sides of the world's shifting prisms, and ethereal voices sang triumphantly in melodies beautiful beyond Elena's measure. There were no concrete thoughts that entered her mind this time—no memories of places she'd been or people she'd met. The answer to her question was one that defied any comparison to things Elena knew and understood. And yet, some part of her understood it nonetheless. Some part much older and wiser to the ways of worlds beyond.

The being that lived in this particular world—that *made up* this world, as if the shifting prisms were its flesh and the beams of refracting light its blood—continued speaking to this subconscious part of her mind, instilling feelings that had no context. The chorus lifted at times, lifting her up with it and making her feel powerful, brave, and determined. Other times it lowered to a haunting, hollow tone that impressed on her a sense of grave danger. This nonverbal monologue and the roller coaster of emotions it instilled continued, it seemed to Elena at least, for a very long time. Despite how remarkable the whole experience had been, she couldn't help but feel a little flustered.

"Can you talk to me now?" she asked. "For real, I mean."

The chorus rose again. This time, the brightness of the light all around grew with it, intensifying from scattered rainbows to a blazing white flare that engulfed her entire field of view. The symphony of angelic voices and celestial sounds reached its final, jubilant note, then faded into silence. The light dimmed, and Elena's vision came back into focus.

But even before her eyes adjusted and she was able to see distant, snow-capped mountains—even before the song had gone silent and left the gurgle of a stream in its place—the first thing Elena noticed was the feeling of lush grass beneath her feet and the vibrant smell of springtime rain. She'd known right then that she was in a place much more familiar than the one she'd left.

"Now where are we?" Elena asked.

"We're in a good place still," a voice—a real voice speaking real words—replied.

Elena turned around. About twenty steps behind her was a small cottage with bright green moss hanging from the aged and knotted logs of its walls. Beside the cottage was the upturned ground of a garden where an old woman was kneeling. Elena watched her press the point of a small spade into the soil, turning up a wedge of earth before dropping a seed into the hole and gently patting dirt back over the top of it. "The same good place as before, actually," the old woman said. "Just dressed up a little different is all."

"Are you the same as before, too?" Elena asked. The old woman looked up from the seeds she was planting and smiled. Her wilted skin and wispy white hair weren't all that different from any of the elderly ladies Elena had met. But her eyes answered the question well before she spoke again; they were eyes that seemed each one to hold the entire universe within them.

"Yes, dear. Yes, I am." She stood up from the tilled ground and brushed the dirt off her dress.

Elena watched her, mulling over her words before speaking again. "He's the reason I'm here, isn't he? Ronny. I don't know if that's what he's really called. But I think you know him. And I think that's why you asked me to come see you."

"Does that bother you?" the old woman asked.

Elena considered this for a moment. "A little, I guess."

"You shouldn't let it bother you. The light may serve to purge the darkness, but the darkness does not define it."

Elena looked on with mild confusion. It made sense on some level—both what the old woman had just said and all that had been impressed upon her in the place she'd first arrived at. But not in any way that she could have explained out loud.

"I'm sorry, child," the old woman said, offering her a smile. "I'm speaking again in terms beyond you, and that's not the reason why we're here, is it?" Elena shrugged. To be honest, she wasn't quite sure why she was here. "Take a look around you, Elena," the old woman said. "Take as long as you like."

Elena did as she was bidden. Beyond the cottage burbled a brook that curled its way across the field, its water so crystal clear that she could see the bed of smooth brown and black stones lining its basin. Along its edges, sporadic cattails grew up from the underwater soil, their stems bent slightly toward the ground under the weight of seed-filled flowers that looked to Elena like corn dogs. Beyond the brook, a field of clover spotted with wildflowers spanned as far a distance as she could see before melding into the mountain-lined horizon. Above ice-glazed peaks, clouds like puffy balls of cotton decorated a perfectly blue sky.

"It's beautiful," Elena said, turning full circle back around to face her host.

"I'm glad you think so," the old woman replied, pausing a moment to take in the view herself. "I made it just for you." Elena looked at her puzzled, but the old woman only smiled in return. "Watch this," she said, the stars in her eyes gleaming a little brighter. "I saved the best part."

Elena heard splashing coming from the brook and turned back toward it. A pair of otters were playing with one another at the water's edge, diving in and out of the brook and letting the current carry them on their backs for a while at times before picking the game back up again a little downstream. Overhead, birds of all sizes and colors caught wing on the gentle breeze, calling to one another in shrills and whistles. Lower in the sky, a blanket of pink and yellow butterflies fluttered back and forth, rising and falling with each gust of air.

The sound of panting and the feeling of soft fur against her leg broke Elena's trance. She knelt and ran a hand across the velvet nape of a young collie. The dog licked at her appreciatively, then crouched to a playful position, its sleek snout flush against the ground and its wagging tail high in the air.

"What's her name?" Elena asked.

"Whatever you'd like it be," the old woman replied. "She's yours." Elena could hardly contain her glee. But the old woman's emotions seemed mixed, and Elena thought she could see what looked like tears clouding the glimmer in her eyes. "I made this place to be your refuge from the storm, Elena. For I'm afraid the storm you've been called to calm is one very dark and furious."

A feeling struck her, strong enough to pierce through her elation and musings of what she would name her new best friend. It was the same feeling she'd felt earlier in the strange place she'd come to first. One of urgency and danger. "You're talking about Ronny, aren't you?" she asked.

"You are wise beyond your years, Elena. Wise enough to make sense of an old woman's ramblings. I won't ask it of you anymore, though. From now until it is time for you to go, I want to be very clear and straightforward with you, dear.

"Something terrible has found you and your family. It is very old, and very strong. You know it as Ronny. You know it as the dark thing as well, and I know it by a foul name not worth speaking in this beautiful place. But they are all the same; a wicked thing that exists only to bring pain and destruction.

"*You*, though, Elena, exist for quite opposite reasons, and the dark thing has never encountered anyone or anything like you. I could smell its fear from across the universe—and I could see the blaze of your soul as well. That's when I knew that you were special. That's when I knew that a great light had been called to chase a darkness that's existed for far too long."

Elena fidgeted a little and took a heavy breath. It was starting to make sense to her now, the reason she'd been brought here and the purpose of this place; the abilities that allowed her to reach it and what she was meant to do with them.

The things stamped on her subconscious by the voice from before and the things the old woman was telling her now were coming together like a connect-the-dot picture. And it was a frightful picture they formed. "Why me?" Elena asked. Despite her growing worry, her question was more curiosity than any kind of resentment.

"That's something I've asked myself as well, child. You are just so young and have so much still to learn! But I did not question when one not much older than you was called to slay a Philistine giant, and I won't question your youth now.

"If you really want an answer, though, Elena," the woman continued, as her smile and the gleam in her eyes both returned a little, "know that the answer is this: you have been chosen because you are the most capable. I've told you that the dark thing is strong, and it's true. But you are stronger, dear. *Much* stronger. The moment it met you, it knew it had already lost. Everything that comes next is only its death throes."

"I don't feel very strong," Elena said. She thought of her father, then Thor and Superman. "Not really."

"You're here, aren't you? Do you think anyone else has ever been here? And trust me when I tell you that your ability to travel without the limits of a physical body is only the beginning. You've already shown the dark thing the strength of your shield, child. Now time to show it the sharpness of your sword.

"In the meantime, consider this place my gift to you. It'll be here when you need rest. And I will be here when you need guidance. I only wish that I was strong enough to offer you more, Elena."

Elena took a breath of clear, cool air and surveyed once more the world around her. It was a peaceful place, there was no denying. A place she would surely return to. But it was also a place that she now had to leave. Elena sensed this even before she saw the sorrowful look on the old woman's face.

"It was a blessing to meet you, Elena," she said. "God be with you."

Before Elena could respond, she felt herself whisked away as if yanked by a string. The serene landscape disappeared at once, giving way to blackness as she soared out of its sphere and back into the emptiness of space. Now, all that Elena could see was the cord of light that stretched out from her chest and across the dark expanse ahead. It glowed brighter now than before, looking more like a beam channeled from a star than a cord of spun moonlight. And it retracted her back across the heavens even faster than she had crossed them before.

As sudden as a sneeze, Elena was back in her bedroom, lying on her bed and staring up at the ceiling. The sound of her bedroom door flinging open made her jump. She sat up and turned around. Her father was standing at the door, and he looked upset.

"Daddy?" she said.

"Wake up, Elly. Wake up and get dressed."

"Where are we going?"

"We need to talk," he said, lifting her out of bed by her shoulders as though she wasn't moving fast enough on her own. There was a sternness to his voice that made her think she was in trouble, and her heart started to beat a little faster. "We're gonna go for a drive, Elly" he said. "We're gonna go for a drive, and you're going to tell me about Ronny."

SEVEN

33 DAYS BEFORE THE WORK IS DONE

Rain falls on the just and unjust alike. In a book they abhorred, this was Ra'Tak's least reviled line. Finally, amid what was quickly becoming a drought, the clouds had let loose on them. And it came without a moment to spare.

The girl had nearly told her father everything. She had nearly told *their* Quarry everything. This was a problem they had anticipated and one they had planned on dealing with. But it wasn't one they thought they'd need to fix so soon.

There were consequences, they'd learned long ago, to pushing the Quarry too hard, too fast. It made them unpredictable. Made the Work messy. The threat the girl posed had forced them to accelerate the Work's timeline, but pushing their Quarry to the point he whisked his daughter away in the dead of night and demanded answers from her was something they'd not predicted.

Desperate to prevent a likely unbreakable alliance from forming, they had appeared to the girl in the back seat behind her. Appeared in the swirling, shadowy form most true to their being.

They had spoken to her. Warned her to stay silent. They had told her that they would kill him if she didn't. That they would kill all of them. And as she watched them through the rearview mirror, Ra'Tak knew she didn't believe these threats—could tell she was on the verge of calling their bluff.

Then, at last, the rain began to fall. Some fool had stopped on the road ahead, just around the end of a narrow turn that the girl and her father were fast approaching. It was the perfect stroke of good fortune. An intervention of the sort they weren't capable of causing on the verge of causing itself.

Consider this a warning, they had said to the girl just before her father rounded the turn.

Her face smashing into the airbag as the two vehicles collided had brought them untold pleasure. But the blood leaking from her nose and the dark blue skin beneath her eyes had not been nearly so rewarding as the sudden, new fear they sensed in her. Fear that she had underestimated their abilities. Fear that she was wrong about their limits.

At the very least, this stroke of luck had bought them time. Time that they would use to set a new plan in motion. An unallowable alliance had indeed nearly come together. The disaster they had dodged and how narrowly they had done so was not far from Ra'Tak's collective mind. Now, in the place where this alliance had nearly formed, they would hammer a wedge.

EIGHT

MONDAY, JULY 9TH

"I don't know why I still invite you over," a sweet-pitched yet cutting little voice said. Lying on the floor, Elena turned to face the voice's source, Crystal Heaney—once a good friend of hers in second grade and now hardly more than an occasional playmate. "I have other friends, you know," Crystal said. She was sitting on the bed with her legs crossed, peering down at Elena over the top of her phone. "Friends that aren't so weird."

Admittedly, Elena thought, she had been acting a little weird today. Three days had passed since the dark thing caused the crash. The bruises on her face were already starting to fade, and her limp was growing less prominent. But the tightness in her chest—as if someone had set lead weights on her lungs—had only grown worse the more she'd thought of the dark thing in the back seat of the car and the way it had so easily put their lives in peril.

Today, this feeling had been worse than ever. Something was happening today. She'd been able to feel it the moment she woke up. It hung in the air like a rotten odor only she could smell and darkened the skies in a way that only she could see. It was something bad, that much was clear, and something Elena felt powerless to stop.

"Are you even listening to me right now?"

"Huh?" Elena said.

Crystal rolled her eyes, then went back to playing on her phone. Elena stared at the ceiling and frowned. Coming here had not been her idea. When she'd woken up this morning and sensed the something terrible to come, she had practically begged her mother to cancel. She wished now she had pretended to be sick, but the idea hadn't come to her. Lying had never been her first instinct.

Except now, telling the truth seemed too dangerous. She'd been so confident, so *certain*, that Ronny couldn't hurt her. It'd been a certainty that came to her in the same way as so many other certainties that had never once been wrong. But Ronny *had* hurt her. He'd hurt her and her father both. And next time, if she tried again to tell her father or her mother or anyone else about Ronny and the dark thing he became—the dark things he did—he was likely to hurt them again. Maybe next time much worse.

"Want to go outside?" Elena asked. Crystal's small, cluttered room was starting to make her feel trapped.

"And do what?" Crystal asked, incredulous. "It's literally a thousand degrees out there."

"We could put the sprinkler on the trampoline again. That was a lot of fun last time."

"Mom said we can't do that anymore. Jake tripped over the hose last time and fell off."

"Oh."

"Yeah. Little brothers ruin everything."

"Well, maybe we could…" Elena trailed off. She shivered, perplexed as to why the temperature in the room had suddenly dropped so dramatically. She could see her breath freezing in front of her and felt frigid air pricking at her skin like icy needles.

"Why's it so cold?" she muttered. The words were difficult to form. Trying to stand even more so, and she slumped back to a seated position after her first attempt.

"Are you nuts? I'm sweating right now," Crystal replied. Then, after watching her stagger, "Are you feeling okay?"

Elena heard the question. But the sound of it was all wrong—muffled and distorted like someone speaking underwater or with their face buried in a pillow. Her vision started to swim, the room suddenly blurring into an abstract watercolor, then coalescing into a blinding white light.

Elena blinked. When her eyes came open again, the light was gone. She was in a bedroom still, still sitting on the floor next to the bed just like before. But it wasn't Crystal's bedroom anymore. The comforter that hung down the edge of the bed was blue instead of purple, and a toy castle sat next to her instead of Crystal's floor mirror. It was Timmy's castle, she realized: Timmy's castle and Timmy's bedroom.

Elena stood, finding the task as easy as ever now, and noticed for the first time the familiar strand of light stretching out from her torso. Starting to make some sense of the situation, she scanned the room for her brother and found him asleep in the bed with the covers pulled up to his neck. She felt an instant of relief, then her heart sank. He wasn't alone.

A black fog hung over the bed where Timmy lay sleeping. It rose and fell in rhythm with his breathing, seeping in through the corners of his mouth with each inhalation and out again through his nose each time he exhaled. Timmy rolled over and ran a hand across his eyes, starting to come awake, and the black fog pulsed a little more rapidly. It was the dark thing, Elena knew. And this was the something bad she'd sensed coming.

Time to go, boy, a voice from within the dark thing said. Timmy opened his eyes and stretched his arms. He rose in bed, looked around the room, and, seeming not to notice Elena standing just a few feet away, pulled the covers off his legs. He stood up and looked around once more, yet again moving his eyes across her and back again without pause. Then he turned and walked toward the window. The dark thing followed him there.

"No!" Elena shouted. Timmy began to fumble at the window's locks. If he'd heard her, he didn't show it. But the same could not be said for the dark thing hovering around him. It froze at once, its shifting, ethereal form crystalizing into a rigid shape. "Leave him alone!" she cried.

Like a sheet of black rain falling from the sky, the dark thing dropped to the floor. It flowed across the carpet, advancing toward her feet. Tendrils rose from its inky surface and collapsed back down into the flood like misshapen waves as it drew closer.

Elena didn't move. Just as it looked like it was going to flow right over the tops of her feet, the dark thing came to a stop. It drew together, rising as it did into a roiling, black obelisk.

From the whirlwind of shadows, a familiar shape began to form. Limbs sprouted out from the column, and a dog-like head grew up from its tip. Dark tendrils sewed themselves together up and down its length as if weaving muscles onto its frame. Oil-like flesh solidified and sprouted blue fur.

"Noooooo," Ronny said, straining to shape the word with jaws not fully formed. He was much larger now than usual, and he stared down at Elena with one fiery red eye. The other hung from its socket by a glistening strand—smashed flat like a popped balloon and matted to the fur on Ronny's cheek. Out of nowhere, it reminded Elena of the time she'd gotten a lollipop stuck in her teddy bear's fur. Elsewhere on Ronny's face and body, only sparse fur remained. Patches of hairless, rotting skin dotted him like spots, and what fur did cover the putrid remains beneath was stained and darkened by mold.

From the darkness behind Ronny's empty eye socket, a lone moth crawled out. It took flight as soon as it found the exit, seeming eager to buzz away from its rotting host. But Ronny paid it no mind. Still leering down at Elena with one blazing red eye and one empty black socket, he opened his mouth and grinned at her, his jaws stretching impossibly wide to reveal rows of broken fangs, yellowed and stained black with blood.

"Go back where you came from now, Elena," Ronny growled. "Leave or we will hurt you."

"No," Elena said. "Not until you leave him alone."

Ronny took a step toward her, the fire in his eye flaring. He was close enough now that the deathly smell of him almost choked her. Beneath his human-like fingernails, something started to grow. Sharp points punctured the surface of the skin, growing wider as they lengthened and making a mangle of Ronny's fingers in the process until all ten digits were bloodied stumps supporting thick, black talons.

"Leave! Leave or we'll rip you to shreds!" Ronny snarled, and strings of brown drool fell from his teeth.

But Elena wasn't looking at him anymore. She was focused on Timmy, struck by a sudden insight the moment she'd spotted him over the top of Ronny's shoulder. It was one that came from that same unknown and unfailing source from which all her impossible insights sprang. This time, though, it wasn't just an insight that manifested in her mind, but a new capability. Like instructions downloaded from the heavens.

"Timmy," Elena said, her voice calm and confident. Timmy turned to look at her, his face scrunching in confusion as he seemed to notice her for the first time. "Timmy, grab my hand," she said, reaching it out to him.

"Stop!" Ronny roared. But his voice was quieter than it had been before, and he did not follow her as she walked across the room to her brother.

Looking down at her outstretched arm, Elena noticed that her skin had begun to shine again. It glowed golden-white, bright enough to fill the room and cast shadows on the wall. "Grab my hand, Timmy."

He did, and Elena closed her eyes. A rush of energy warmed her arm, spreading swiftly through her entire body and filling the darkness of her closed eyelids with light.

When she opened them again, she was still holding Timmy's hand, but they weren't standing in the bedroom anymore. A gust of wind laced with droplets of water and ice lifted her hair and brushed against her skin, stirring the thick fog that obscured all but the closest trees in the forest where they now stood.

"Sissy?" Timmy said, staring up at Elena and still holding on to her hand. "Sissy, where are we?"

"We're in a dream, Timmy. You're dreaming."

Timmy considered this for a moment, then asked, "Why are you here?"

"Because I'm dreaming too. Listen to me, Timmy. I don't think we have very much time." Thunder rumbled overhead, and the next gust of breeze was a little cooler than the last. "I'm here to wake you up. I need you to please wake up, Timmy. Wake up and play with your trucks, or go downstairs to Mommy, okay? This is a bad dream. It's a bad dream, you're sleepwalking, and you need to wake up right now or something bad is going to happen."

Thunder rolled again, louder this time. Timmy peered up at the fog-smothered sky, then back at Elena with new fear in his eyes. "He's coming back," he said.

"I know. That's why you need to wake up right now. You need to wake up right now, Timmy." Timmy started to cry, and Elena pulled him into a hug. "Shhh. Shhh, it's okay. It's going to be okay. Just wake up, okay? Wake up and it's all going to be alright."

"I can't, Sissy!" Timmy sobbed. "I can't!"

"Sure you can. It's easy. Just think about it really hard." Thunder boomed, loud enough this time that Elena could feel it vibrating the hairs on her arms. "Please, Timmy. I can't keep him out much longer."

The wind picked up, whining first, then intensifying into a constant shriek. Timmy covered his ears and fell to the ground, sobbing into the knees of his pants. Whirlwinds of fog circled around them. Then, after a final crack of splitting thunder loud enough to shake the very fabric of the dream where they both resided, the dark thing fell from the sky.

It tumbled through the atmosphere, leaving behind a trail like the tail of a black comet. It landed between Elena and Timmy with no register-able impact, rising at once into a tall silhouette with long, gangly limbs and a featureless face.

You're too weak, Elena, a voice said, coming from the shrouded sky above rather than the figure now standing between her and her brother. *Too weak, by far. And now he is ours.*

Elena watched the dark thing reach down and wrap its fingers around Timmy's head. It lifted him off the ground with one arm, dangling him in front of her. Timmy's eyes were clenched shut, and his body trembled in the air.

"LET HIM GO!" Elena screamed.

On the final syllable, a halo of light exploded from where she stood, driving the fog away in all directions as it expanded. It swept through the dark thing unimpeded, knocking it back violently and expelling Timmy from its grasp.

Elena flew to where the dark thing had fallen. Her skin glowed like molten silver and her eyes like white stars as she approached its cower-ing form. She stood over it, staring down into its black soul with eyes that continued to burn increasingly brighter.

The dark thing writhed beneath her gaze, wisps of smoke rising from its form. A single pale flame licked up from within the shadows, flickering away before another quickly took its place. Soon, its entire form caught blaze.

Just as it seemed she would burn this terrible thing out of existence right there and then, an explosion rocked Elena's senses. It knocked her off her feet and turned her vision dark. When her sight returned, she was back in Timmy's bedroom.

"Leave! Leave or we'll gut him!" Ronny's tortured corpse stood by the window, clutching Timmy in its claws. It snarled, unhinging its jaws like a snake and opening wide a mouth now full of gleaming, needle-like fangs. "Leave or he dies!"

Elena took a step forward, and the Ronny-thing roared. Power still surged through her like a current. Power and determination. But when the Ronny-thing lowered its dripping jaws around Timmy's head, she wavered. And fear leaked in for the first time.

Another explosion, this one even more deafening and concussive than the last, collided into Elena's mind like a shockwave of dark energy, smothering her senses. She struggled against it. Struggled to stay alert and keep pressing forward. But when the very air around her seemed to detonate into fiery darkness for the third time, Elena's mind shut down.

NINE

Pain rippled relentlessly through Ra'Tak's damaged being. Their very essence still smoked and smoldered where the girl had burned them. She had brought them to the brink of annihilation. One failed diversion from nonexistence.

They longed for rest, to retreat to another realm where the girl couldn't follow and heal their wounds. But there wasn't time to spare. The Work had to proceed.

Claiming the Conduit had required much suffering. Had been more difficult than any time before. But the outcome had been the same as always. They had won their first true battle with the girl just as they had won all battles before. And now, the Conduit was theirs.

They sank themselves into his soul like leaches, soaking in the life force they drew from him. Reward for executing their Master's will had never been theirs to demand, but they had always considered this the Work's wages.

With each minute that passed, Ra'Tak grew more confident. They had never entered a Conduit having been so badly damaged beforehand; to feel the energy they filched from it restoring their strength made the experience all the more gratifying.

And soon, they would take another.

It would not be the first time they had taken multiple Conduits, but it would be the first such occasion in centuries. Most chapters of the Work were easily finished without even requiring a single Conduit. But there had been rare occasions in the past where breaking an especially strong Quarry had required taking two.

This had always been a chilling risk. The Rite of the Conduit was one that sent ripples through the realms each time they performed it. And there were beings residing in certain faraway realms whose attention Ra'Tak dared not attract. This time, though, there was no other choice. One just as strong as these distant beings they feared had already found them. Their brush with annihilation had made the decision to take another Conduit one that needed no debate.

Before that could be done, however, their link to the first Conduit had to be finalized. They were free to draw from him for now, but unless the Rite was completed, the connection would never last.

Like breathing in, Ra'Tak absorbed the life force from the boy's soul. Like breathing out, they injected a dream back into him. A waking dream that would guide sleeping limbs to the place in the woods that Ra'Tak had prepared as their gateway.

The process was painfully slow. As always when the Work reached this tedious phase, Ra'Tak envied those of their kind who had once been allowed to truly possess the vessels that they could only hijack in the world of dreams.

The Conduit stumbled around the bedroom as though in a stupor, running blind hands along the wall until finally they fell upon the latches of his bedroom window. Getting him to open the window and climb out onto the ledge took a number of attempts that would have tried their patience even on a day that had not already brought so many trials.

They managed to lure him only halfway down the drainpipe before his grip relaxed and he tumbled to the earth below. Ra'Tak froze, an instant of terror sweeping over them; to harm him or any other in this state would be breaking rules that even their Master did not dare defy. But the boy staggered back to his feet on sleep-addled but unharmed limbs, and their panic subsided.

They cursed their carelessness. And the girl. And this chapter of the Work that had turned so wretchedly sour. Then they bid the Conduit to his feet and lured him down a zigzag path across the lawn.

By the time they led him out the gate and into the woods to the place where no new life sprouted from the ground, the day had almost ended. They positioned him on the rotting stump that marked the clearing's center. They guided his hands up toward the cloudless sky. They bid him speak the words.

And when the last dreamy syllable left his lips, Ra'Tak felt the familiar dark charge cascade through them. Never mind what others might sense it. Never mind their intention to do it again this very night in near reckless defiance of the cautions that had kept them safe this long. If they were to make the most of this risk they'd chosen, there was no time to dwell on its consequences.

Drawing in one final pull of vitality from the first Conduit they would take this day, Ra'Tak released themselves from his mind. The boy opened his eyes and squinted against the dying sunlight. Before his confusion could freeze into fear, Ra'Tak took it away.

They bid him go find his father, and he rose from the stump. There was a wobble in his step at first; they had drawn much from him already. Enough, it seemed, to have taken a physical toll. But soon the muscles found their strength and the boy was walking normally. Plodding obediently down the meandering path they'd set him on— one that would lead him to his searching father in due time.

Across the darkening woods, in the house where their Quarry lived, they could sense the soul of the one called Grace Gordon. A vapid, vacuous soul just like all the rest. One that made the astonishing spirit of the girl who shared her blood only more confounding. Yet a perfect soul for their needs.

Within the dark, sensationless world Ra'Tak inhabited, Grace glowed like a flame. Nothing like the inferno of the other, but a warm, inviting beacon that pulled them in like moths. Still basking in new-found strength from the first Conduit, Ra'Tak poured themselves into that glow with ease.

Even the great risk they were taking and the near defeat that had driven them to such desperation could not spoil the moment's ecstasy. Never before had they taken two Conduits in such quick succession. They could feel the strength surging through them like tidal waves as they drank greedily from her spirit, the flow of which only seemed to grow stronger the more they took.

They had underestimated this soul, it seemed. It glowed gently, but its well ran deep. Traces of that which the other possessed in profusion coursed through it like veins of gold, tasting sweeter than even the purest souls they'd devoured before. Drenching them in vitality they'd not felt since The Fall.

This was more than could be explained by how long they'd gone without taking two Conduits. Much more. It was only when they had tapped as much from her as they were able that clarity pierced through their lust. What miracle was this that they'd stumbled upon? What trap of His had they sprung?

And then it happened. Before they could answer these fearful questions, Ra'Tak saw the light. Saw it through Creation eyes. And their immeasurable thoughts crystallized into only wonder and fear.

They could feel the heartbeat in the Conduit's chest. They could feel the blood pumping through her arteries, her lungs enriching it with oxygen, and the countless other functions of her body all happening at once. They could feel the brush of fabric against her skin and the way the draft moved across every tiny hair.

Sights and sensations, sounds and smells poured in like a torrent. All the qualities of a world they understood but had never experienced materialized before them. They tried to focus on only one—on the buzzing white bulbs that the Conduit was staring up at. On the light flooding into a mind that for eternity had known only darkness. But even this was beyond overwhelming.

They screamed at the Conduit to shut her eyes. It was an action they should have easily forced given their current grip on her subconscious, but the focus required felt almost impossible against the assault of new sensations.

This should not be happening. This was not allowed. Endless fantasies of taking for themselves the gift that only His creation had been given evaporated against the weight of its consequence.

And yet…and yet here they were. Still existing, no word yet spoken from Him to erase them. Still *living*, indulging that which had always been forbidden them. Perhaps they were drunk on the power. Perhaps the pride of newfound life had clouded their sense of self-preservation. But for as long as this indignity would be allowed, it was an indignity they would relish.

They were assimilating quickly to the experiences of physical reality. Starting to integrate them into their being. Soon, they began to find a wicked pleasure in the qualia that had paralyzed them moments before. They craved more control. Craved the ability to satiate the appetites awakening in them like rising flames. But they were just passengers in this vessel. Free to experience through it. Free to draw vitality from it and free to influence the soul that truly occupied it, but little more. And even then, free only for now.

Suddenly, their vessel began to move. They felt the synapses in her muscles firing as she rose from the bed. They felt the rhythm in her chest pick up and spurts of adrenaline rush through her blood.

She had sensed them. They could hear the alarms ringing across her mind. Alarms that had no context, they were relieved to realize. No understanding to accompany them—just the blind fear of primal instinct. The very medium within which Ra'Tak functioned best.

The body they inexplicably found themselves inside bolted out of the bedroom and down the hallway, dragging Ra'Tak along with it, and they braced themselves against this new tsunami of sensations. The walls and floor rushed by in an onslaught of morphing colors and patterns. Floorboards creaked under the pad of frantic footsteps, machines whirred, and electricity buzzed through the walls. Then, as quick as her movement had started, it stopped. She froze in front of a door, her hand hovering near the metal handle. Behind it, Ra'Tak could sense their Quarry.

With as much focus as they could muster, they kept her frozen there a heartbeat longer. They wondered if this interaction should be allowed. Wondered if they should turn her around and wondered if they even could. It didn't seem likely. Against the determination they sensed within her, their influence was like a breath of wind against a mountain.

Unable to stall her any longer, Ra'Tak felt her knuckles rap against the door. There was the sound of a body stirring, then a fear-laced voice. A voice they loathed the instant it struck their vessel's ears.

"Who's there?"

"It's me, Dad," their vessel replied.

Hinges creaked and the door swung open. A rush of air stirred against skin that Ra'Tak wore like an ill-fitting cloak. Their Quarry stood at the threshold, searching his daughter's desperate eyes. Eyes through which Ra'Tak stared back.

Their hatred for him and all those they'd taken before him burned like hellfire. Yet to look into his eyes and see him in a way they'd seen no Quarry before stoked that hatred even hotter. They would end this creature's life in an inferno of torment if it was the last offering they delivered. But for it not being theirs to move, they would have thrown this body they inhabited at him right then in a maelstrom of flailing limbs and gnashing teeth.

"Dad, can we talk?" their vessel asked. The object on which all their limitless malice was focused placed his hand against a shoulder they were starting to consider their own, and they shrieked with revulsion.

"Honey, what's wrong?" he asked.

"I don't feel right."

"What's the matter?"

"I don't know."

He was holding her now. Holding *them*. They could feel the race of his heart against their shivering body, every beat an insult. Every breath a taunt. "Tell me what you're feeling, sweetheart. Tell me what's wrong."

Their body began to tremble more violently. Something was happening to it. They could feel it starting to shut down in a final, desperate attempt to reject their intrusion. With all the strength they could muster, Ra'Tak dug their talons deeper.

"I feel like something's inside me," their vessel said betwixt labored breaths. "In my head. Under my skin. Oh Dad, please make it stop!"

The spark of consciousness they'd hijacked was fading. The lights were starting to dim. And cold realization washed over them. Once more they had underestimated Grace Gordon's spirit. It might have been too weak to stop their invasion, but it could still burn the fields and salt the ground before it left. Sever its connection to her body and leave behind a lifeless husk as useless to them as all the others that littered so many tombs.

And they, amplified even by the life force of two Conduits, were helpless to stop it. Giving life. Stopping death. These were powers that only their Enemy possessed. They could do naught but watch as the spectacle of existence dissolved and the darkness returned.

The girl's lungs stopped drawing breath. The beat of her heart slowed to a halt. And in the darkness they'd been plunged back into, Ra'Tak could sense her soul rising up around them. Mocking them silently as it drifted toward a light they could not see. A portal they were not allowed to cross.

Rage engulfed them once more. This was more than a small setback. This was the loss of their second Conduit and a crippling disruption. Even more chilling was what might happen when the Archangels waiting to greet her soul on the other side of that light found out it was *they* who had sent her there.

Just when it seemed the gift they'd taken had forever slipped from their grasp, the soul that had tricked them out of it ceased its ascent. Ra'Tak quieted their screams and observed. Observed in fascinated horror as a miracle took place.

Grace's soul retreated, seeping back into the body it had left one spark at a time. Her mind reignited, flickering back to life as though someone had gently breathed on its dying embers. And when Ra'Tak searched the space and found a presence all too familiar there with them in the bedroom, they knew who that someone had been.

When the glaze already forming on Grace's frozen eyes melted away like frost in the sunlight, Ra'Tak awoke again behind them. Struggling to keep their focus against the returning torrent of stimuli, they braced themselves for a fight. Even in this strange world of colors and sounds where their conventional senses seemed to dull, they could still feel Elena's spirit there with them.

Fear washed through them, dousing both wonder and rage. Not even the Archangel Michael could command the dead to rise. Not even the prophets of old. They had worried that taking two Conduits might draw the attention of some being much stronger than they. But that being was already here. Their Enemy's champion had already been called.

Yet even power as profound as hers had its limit. And when the attack Ra'Tak dreaded never came, they realized she had exhausted that limit. Like a foul scent mercifully fading, the girl's presence dissipated until only the lingering simmer of the energy she'd exerted remained.

Ra'Tak considered going after her. In their strengthened state and her weakened one, now might be their best chance to strike. But the miracle they had witnessed kept them rooted in place.

It was a risk not worth taking, they decided. Certainly not considering the great favor the girl had inadvertently done them. She had saved her sister's life, but she had also returned their Conduit. And more than just their Conduit, the first physical vessel they'd ever been able to possess.

Still acclimating to the experience more and more with each instant that passed, Ra'Tak found their ability to exert control from the back seat of Grace's mind growing more adept. Forcing any action that wasn't her own volition was still well out of reach. But injecting themselves into the words and expressions she chose came much easier.

A little slip of the tongue here. A strange twitch of the eyes there. Nothing too conspicuous, but still fuel on the flames of their Quarry's fears. Effective as their methods had always been, they'd never had the luxury of bolstering the illusions and false memories they instilled with actual happenings. Even if its impact on their Work ended up negligible, Ra'Tak still relished the opportunity.

Grace smiled and wished her father good night, every memory of the events that brought her here wiped clean. And Ra'Tak tainted each gesture. Altered her aura just enough that their Quarry would know whose eyes stared back at him. Even from across the room, they could smell the terror on his skin. Such a ravishing scent, clouded though it was by that of their own fear.

Only time would tell if this night of so many wonders had been a victory or defeat. With power unlike any they had leached before still streaming through them and the experiences of a world forbidden unlocked at last, it was hard to feel anything except victorious. Yet they had witnessed power far greater. Power leashed only by the things that Elena did not yet know—that to give life to the dead was a feat worlds beyond casting out mere demons.

TEN

At the first ray of sunlight, Elena's eyes came open. It had been almost ten hours since she'd gone to bed, but the constant fever dream the night's sleep had been hardly felt like sleep at all. Her PJ's were soaked in sweat, and yet she woke chilled and shivering.

She considered lying down again and going back to sleep. It was an appealing idea, but her throat was raw and dry from thirst, and the water bottle she kept on her nightstand was empty. Besides, she did seem to be feeling a little better today than the past ten mornings since these symptoms began, and that was cause for optimism.

She got out of bed and walked to the bathroom across the hall, water bottle in hand. She stopped when she reached the sink and stared at her reflection in the mirror. Her face was pallid except for the dark half circles beneath her eyes, and her hair was tangled.

A classmate had told her one time when she hadn't been feeling well at school that she looked like she'd been run over by a bus. It'd been a cruel exaggeration then, but today, not so much. Elena glanced at the hairbrush near the counter's edge, then quickly decided that appearances were not her priority. Water was her priority, and the feeling that she might die of thirst before she could even get the bottle filled didn't seem so unrealistic. She filled it a quarter of the way, then downed it in two quick gulps before filling it again. Her body absorbed it like cracked earth, and it wasn't until she had emptied the bottle, filled, and emptied it again that her throat stopped screaming for more.

When she reached to turn off the faucet, something fell from the counter. Elena bent down and picked it up. It was her older sister's curling iron. She had borrowed it from her countless times before with Grace's permission. Seeing it now, though, Elena felt like crying.

Eleven days had passed since the dark thing took Grace and Timmy. She could still remember all that had happened that night clear and vivid. But where memory served her fine, understanding failed.

She had left her body again—that part was easy enough to accept by now—and had tried to stop the dark thing from taking Timmy. It had defeated her, and when she'd realized later that night that it was taking Grace too, it had been too late. Grace had somehow died. And Elena had somehow brought her back to life. She remembered doing it, remembered the effort it took and the pain it caused her, but she couldn't remember ever knowing *how* to do what she'd done.

It had been almost like a dream she wasn't really in control of. Arriving in Grace's room just in time to see the life drain from her eyes had sent her into a panic. And in that panic, something else took over.

Whatever it was, she hoped it knew what it was doing. She had saved her sister's life, but she had not saved her from the dark thing. Even with the walls between them, Elena could feel it resonating from Grace's bedroom, its own presence like a rotten aroma mingled in with senses sweet and familiar. She could feel it coming from Timmy's bedroom, too, though not in quite the same way. It was more muted there, though no less upsetting.

She felt like sprinting across the hall and down the stairs to get away from it as fast as she could, but the muscles in her legs were too weak. Instead, the walk past Timmy's bedroom was slow and painful. So slow that she couldn't help but stop when she neared his bedroom door.

She could almost hear it in there with him when she listened close, her ear against the door. And she could certainly feel the coldness of it on her skin. Elena's hand hovered near the doorknob, instinct screaming for her to rush in and save him. But after what had happened the last time she'd tried, she couldn't risk being so reckless.

And certainly not in her current state. Water had helped a lot. Maybe food would help some too. Elena turned away from Timmy's door and eased down the stairs, keeping a loose but steady grip on the railing. The kitchen was just around the corner at the bottom, and Elena remembered seeing strawberry Uncrustables in the refrigerator. Her stomach grumbled at the thought, and it seemed that food really was just what she needed.

But just as she'd finished pouring a glass of milk, a noise from the living room interrupted her—the sound of the front door opening. Elena sat the glass and her sandwich down on the table and walked out of the kitchen.

Her father was standing by the front door, looking aimless until he spotted her. She watched fresh fear wash through the valleys in his face long ago carved by the same and wondered just what the dark thing had done to him. It hadn't taken him like Grace and Timmy, Elena could tell, but it had obviously not left him alone.

"Where have you been, Daddy?" she asked and wrapped her arms around him. She wanted so badly to help him, and to let him help her. How different would things have already been if she'd managed to tell him all she'd intended to the night of the wreck? She'd been so convinced then that the dark thing couldn't hurt her. That it couldn't hurt either one of them and that there was nothing it could do to stop her from enlisting his help. Yet that night had ended with them both in the hospital.

"Just out for a drive," her father said. But strangely, it seemed to Elena that he wasn't actually sure. "Where's your mom?"

"Upstairs."

"And your brother and sisters?"

"Emily went to Violet's house, I think. Grace and Timmy are upstairs too."

"What have you been up to?" her father asked. Though he tried to mask it, Elena could hear the suspicion in his tone. Misplaced suspicion, she knew, but still so stinging to hear.

"Just about to eat lunch," she said and turned away from him. If he saw her sadness, he might have questions. Elena wondered what would happen if she answered them truthfully and imagined the worst. Imagined the monster she'd seen in Timmy's bedroom—the Ronny-thing—appearing behind her father and pulling his head off his neck like plucking an apple from a tree. Or another pickup truck, this one careening through the kitchen wall and smearing them both across the tile. Was the dark thing even capable of such things? Though some voice deep inside whispered that it was not, Elena couldn't be sure.

Her father followed her into the kitchen and sat down with her at the table. She could feel him watching her the entire time she ate. He'd poured a glass of water for himself but never touched it. He just rested there with his chin in his palms and alternated between staring at it and staring at her.

"We need to talk, Elly," he said the instant she swallowed the last bite of her Uncrustable.

"I know," Elena said. The words came out with no urge on her part to stop them. If anything, something was urging her to keep speaking.

"Something happened last week, Daddy. The night that Timmy got lost in the woods."

The chair creaked as her father straightened in it, his stare growing suddenly piercing. "What? What happened?"

"I don't know if I can explain it. But—"

"Try, Elly," her father said. "Try and explain it."

"It's going to happen again tonight." The words left her tongue almost the same instant as the realization struck. Another wave of the nausea she'd woken with rolled through her stomach.

"What's going to happen, Elly? Tell me. Right now. Tell me what's going on."

"I..." Elena started. Her father's jaw was clenched tight, and his gaze unblinking. "I think something is in our house. I think I might have let it in. I have a...*power*, I guess. But I couldn't stop it. It took Grace. And Timmy. And it's coming back again tonight. I know it is, and I don't know what to do." Tears blurred her sight, but she could still see her father staring expressionless at her. "Say something, Daddy. Please."

His lips didn't move. His eyes didn't blink. Not a single muscle in his face so much as twitched. Elena wiped away her tears with her sleeve and gasped when the terror frozen into his motionless features came into clarity.

"Daddy?"

"I think it's time *we* had a talk, little Elena."

The voice was not her father's, nor did it come from his paralyzed lips. It was Ronny's voice, and when Elena blinked again, she could see him perched on the kitchen counter behind her father's left shoulder. He slid down and padded across the floor on two legs. He pulled out the chair at the head of the table and hopped up into it, crossing his paws across his lap and fixing his animated eyes on her. The disfigured form the dark thing had taken the last time it presented itself as Ronny was gone, replaced again by the pristine fur and warm features that had once delighted her. Even still, they weren't enough anymore to hide the darkness beneath.

"What did you do to him?" Elena asked.

Ronny's ears flattened. "Nothing, Elena. Why, nothing at all. We just …put him on pause. That's a good way to put it. He's not in any pain, don't worry. *Not yet.*"

"What do you want?"

"Hmm," Ronny said and tapped a finger at the tip of his snout. "What do we want? That might be a little hard to explain to you. For now, what we want is to stop you from making a big mistake."

"You mean stop me from telling Dad about you."

"Oh, your father already knows all about us. We just don't want you to do something that gets you and your family hurt."

"You can't hurt me," Elena said with confidence she didn't have to fake. "You would have done it by now if you could. In fact, I don't even have to look at you if I don't want to."

With a thought, Ronny was gone—like blinking him out of existence—the chair she'd watched him pull out from the table now empty and unmoved.

Ronny sighed, his voice still something she'd decided to entertain for now. "You're right. We can't hurt you. Your body is outside of our reach and your mind…well, your mind is a fortress, isn't it, little Elena? *But…*" Ronny trailed off, letting the last, disembodied word hang in the air.

When he spoke again, his voice had grown more guttural. Like the voice of the dark thing when it was no longer trying to cloak its rage in trickery. And rather than coming from the empty spot on the chair, it came from all around.

"But the same cannot be said for dear old Dad. The same cannot be said

for Mommy dearest or your snot-nose little brother or your whore sisters! Their minds are like eggshells! Pathetic, fragile little things! Ripe and ready for us to devour!" Elena felt her skin flush warm and squeezed her hands into tight little fists at her sides. *"You don't believe us, do you?"* the voice continued, the question laced with mockery. *"Alright. Watch."*

Her father jolted in his seat, his body locking straight and rigid, and Elena jumped with him. Veins and tendons bulged from his wrists and neck, and panic blazed in his frozen eyes. The ghost of a moan leaked through his slack mouth, then a strand of drool fell onto his lap.

"What are you doing to him?"

"Dragging his soul through Hell. Bringing his darkest nightmares to life so they can kill him over and over again. If only you could imagine the pain he's in, Elena. If only we could show you."

"Stop it!"

"No. This is the consequence of your interference. You did this to him. And it won't stop until you do."

"Fine!" Elena shouted. "Leave us alone and I won't ever mention it again. Just leave! Leave and leave us alone!"

Her father slumped in his seat, his muscles relaxing and his chin resting against his chest. And since the dark thing had allowed that, Elena allowed it to show itself again.

Ronny reappeared in the kitchen chair, a wide grin exposing lines of teeth perfectly straight and white. "Now that's a start," he said. "But that still won't quite do, deary. You see, we have a purpose here. Some work to do. And we're not going to leave until we've done it.

"That doesn't have to be any concern to you, though, Elena. There's nothing we'll do here that's going to stop you from living a long, normal life. With your gifts, it might even be long and *extraordinary*. Your family too. None of them will even remember a thing once we're done.

What we have to do isn't always easy, but it is always for the better. You will all be better off for it in the end. Unless you keep messing things up, that is. Then…well then, we're afraid there's no telling what could happen."

"Do you promise you're not going to hurt them?"

"Yes," Ronny said with no hesitation. "It might not seem like it now, but we really are here to help your family."

"How do I know this isn't another trick?"

Ronny scratched his chin. "How about, as a sign of good faith, we make it so your father doesn't remember any of the dreadful things we just showed him? How about we even go ahead and give him a reasonably pleasant day? He deserves that, don't you think?"

Elena glanced at her father. His head was still slumped as if he was asleep, but through the tufts of his unruly hair, she could see that his eyes were open. "Okay," she said. "It's a deal."

"Wonderful!" Ronny barked and disappeared with a sound like that of a bubble popping. Elena heard her father suck in air and saw him moving from the corner of her eye. He looked a little confused, like someone waking up from a long nap, but otherwise relaxed.

Before either of them could say anything, Grace came into the kitchen. She didn't look well at all, so when she mentioned something about needing help upstairs, Elena felt obliged. Even though some murmur in her soul recognized it was another of the dark thing's tricks.

On her way out, Elena glanced again at the chair where Ronny…the dark thing…had just sat and wondered whether it knew—that it wasn't the only one capable of lying.

ELEVEN

18 DAYS BEFORE THE WORK IS DONE

Like spider lightning jumping between dark clouds, Ra'Tak cascaded from one desolate realm to the next. They needed to distance themselves from the girl. To recover the composure that yet another dance with death had shaken.

If the girl's determination to stop her father's suffering had triggered another transcendence, there's no saying if they could have survived. Their gambit had worked. At least for now. But to bluff so brazenly with stakes so high was starting to take its toll.

That there was no accessible realm, no matter how far away or barren, where they could escape her unnerved them even more. The Work was their fate, an unchangeable destiny. And the Work went through her.

In some dark realm devoid of time and space, Ra'Tak stopped their frenzied, aimless journey. They rested for a while in the comfort of nothingness. They dreamed a collective dream that all the realms were like this. No Heaven or Hell or Creation between. Just they and nothing else.

It was a reckless dream. How dare they even fantasize of defying their Master's will. They wondered if he could sense their trepidation even now with the gulf of a trillion dead universes between them and decided he surely could; could they themselves not still sense his fury?

With no choice to make, Ra'Tak returned to the realm of Creation. That yawning canvas, once like all the rest, on which their Enemy had painted His masterpiece. So many flakes they and their Master had chipped from it over the eons, and yet it still triumphed. Lights still spanned the darkness, the earth still coddled its creatures like a perfect crib, and beneath its blankets of clouds, their Quarry still lived.

Ra'Tak swooped down into him, both their reprieves now over. But what they had in store for him today was only gnawing unease. They had pushed him hard earlier. Hard enough to upset the Work's delicate proceedings if the memory of it had not been erased; drive a man mad too hard, too fast, and you risk reducing him to an empty husk unable to comprehend, much less carry out, the final act the Work demanded. They had learned this lesson before and would not endure their Master's lashings for it again.

Tonight, their plans involved another. Diligently, Ra'Tak sewed the day's poisonous seeds into their Quarry's mind. Just a few wounds for him to pick at while they left him. Then they drifted up through the ceiling and into the bedroom of his second-born child.

They gathered around the desk where the one named Emily Gordon sat, draping themselves over her. She shivered as though she felt them there—a disquieting idea. Was this soul special too, they wondered? They would need all the strength they could steal, and to take a third Conduit as bountiful as the eldest daughter had been would surely be advantageous.

But such spirits did not go quietly. How many more flares could they send soaring through the realms before someone took notice?

With tendrils like strands of smoke from a smothered candle, Ra'Tak seeped through her lips and nostrils and the corners of her eyes. They pricked at the countless doorways in her mind, not ready yet to force themselves in but creaking them open just enough to peer inside.

Lights glowed warm and steady behind each one. Traces of the gift that somehow ran through this bloodline comparable, they gauged, to what they'd found in her older sister. They wondered if the young boy they'd taken first might develop it too, given more time to mature, or if it had skipped him somehow. Realizing they didn't know how any of it worked, or even what it was, made the glow of those lights as chilling as it was alluring.

Ra'Tak retreated from her mind, careful not to disturb a single thought on their way out. They would wait until deep into the night to take their Conduit this time. Maybe if Elena was asleep, she wouldn't sense it happening. A small chance perhaps, given the foresight she'd demonstrated. But it was not the only ploy they had schemed.

Satisfied with the scouting they'd done, Ra'Tak drifted through the wall behind Emily's desk and into the adjacent bedroom. Grace was lying there in bed, her eyes closed but her mind very much awake. They could feel the turmoil in it, the distress of a soul invaded and beaten, crying out in ways her conscious self could only interpret as pain.

She recoiled when they entered her, but, to them, it had already become like slipping into a familiar dream. The avalanche of sensations no longer paralyzed them like it had at first. And they were starting to gain more control.

It was easier when she slept. They had spent most of last night testing their abilities, walking her sleeping body back and forth across the room, lifting her arms up and down like a marionette. It was still slow and unreliable. Sometimes they'd move left when they wanted to move right. Other times her muscles wouldn't respond to them at all. And anything more than a jostle would wake her and boot them out of the driver's seat entirely. They'd been practicing keeping her asleep but with mixed results thus far.

Still, Ra'Tak found even this modicum of control intoxicating. With more time to acclimate and the power of a third Conduit soon to be theirs, there was no telling what the limit would be.

They stayed there inside her for hours, her anxious thoughts like music while they waited. It was late into the night before she finally slept, their efforts to induce it themselves once again proving fruitless. They'd hoped to practice commanding her limbs once more before they set their plan in motion, but now there wasn't time.

They withdrew from her, their world returning to darkness and silence the instant the connection severed. Through the bedroom wall they hovered near—formless and invisible to anyone who might have entered the room—they could sense the soul on the other side. Emily Gordon was fast asleep now, stuck deep in some nightmare their earlier intrusion must have triggered.

For no other reason than the humor of it, they waited until her fear reached its crescendo. Until the moment when the nightmare becomes so vivid that the mind aborts back to the waking world. Then, just before her eyes flashed open, Ra'Tak struck.

They poured into her like rushing water, barging violently through the countless doorways of her mind, filling every crevice. Taking her was effortless and instant. Yet they realized right away that something was wrong.

There were bars on all sides of them and chains shackling them in place. Actual steel biting into actual flesh. They recognized the form they suddenly inhabited. A humanized dog with moon-like eyes and shining blue fur. It bound them to its flesh and bone as securely as the shackles binding its limbs, and every struggle to shed it was useless.

Screams of rage came out only as howls and whimpers, enraging them even more. Being bound to the form of the very character they'd projected was a purposeful insult. Someone was taunting them. And there was no question who.

Amidst thick clouds that smothered their view through the bars—as though the cage were suspended high in the air—Ra'Tak could see a circle of light growing brighter. They snarled and fought against the chains. Fought even more desperately than before to retreat from the dream she'd trapped them in, but still to no avail.

Clouds parted around the advancing halo of light, and the face of Elena Gordon came into view. A million threats, a million obscenities all left their drooling tongue as only barks and growls.

"Quiet, boy," Elena said. "You're being a bad dog." She took another step toward them, her glowing feet swirling the clouds as they lifted, and placed her glowing hands against the bars. How had they let this happen? They, the weaver of nightmares, trapped within one like a frightened child.

"Don't be too hard on yourself," Elena said, tipping her hand, whether she'd meant to or not, that she could hear the words they were unable to say. "I know what it's like to be tricked."

Confident now that she would see it, they imagined all the fury they would unleash on her family if she didn't let them go, picturing every gory detail of every possible way they would drive them to their demise.

"Not if you're trapped here," Elena said. "Not if I keep you here forever."

Ra'Tak realized what this implied but snuffed the thought before it could ever form, desperately hoping she wouldn't intercept it. Eyes like molten diamonds bored into them, and it seemed that no truth could possibly escape them. But her tone when she spoke again was still one of smug confidence.

"Maybe I'll let you out someday. I think everyone deserves a second chance. But it's going to take a lot before I can trust you again."

Thunder rumbled somewhere distant within the cloud-covered dreamscape. Elena's eyes didn't turn toward the sound like theirs did, but they could tell she'd noticed. The cage and the body she'd trapped them in might have been her making, but not everything here was under her control. This, after all, was not her dream.

Ra'Tak ended that train of thought before it (and, more importantly, its stowaway) could reach the conclusion they were hiding. So obvious, really. Such a silly mistake she'd made. A *child's* mistake. There was another clap of thunder, this time not so distant. That brazen conviction in Elena's blazing eyes started to waver.

"I could just kill you, you know?" she said. "I'm pretty sure I could if I wanted to. I'm being nice trapping you here."

Well then you'd better do it quickly, girl. Ra'Tak spat the thought at her like venom. *You don't have much time.*

Thunder boomed, deafeningly loud, and the bars of the cage rattled and shook. Slowly at first, then gradually faster, the world around them began to dissolve. First the cage, then the shackles, then blue fur and the flesh beneath. All evaporating into the air piece by glittering piece. Ra'Tak made sure that Ronny was grinning wild and devilish as he vanished.

She'd thought herself so clever, making this trap in her sister's dream. What a perfect way to disguise it from them. If she'd struck hard and fast when she'd had the chance (like they or any true warrior spirit would have), the victory could have been hers. Planning to trap them forever in a dream that would last only as long as her sister slept, however, had been a costly oversight.

Far too late, she launched at them like a missile, all fiery fervor and indignation. But they were already gone.

When Ra'Tak returned to the bedroom where Emily now sat up in bed—her thoughts spinning from a dream so strange and vivid and oblivious to all that was happening around her—Elena was waiting for them there. She burned even brighter now. Bright enough that her skin lit up the room and her eyes cut through them like twin torches. Already, they could feel her searing into their being.

Something bumped against the outside wall near the doorway, then the bedroom door swung open. When the scorching light that smothered the room only grew hotter, Ra'Tak feared their diversion wouldn't work. Feared that Elena was too focused to even notice her oldest sister stumbling through the doorway.

Scanning the bedroom through Grace's eyes, they could no longer see Elena's white-hot spirit. But they could still feel it, same as before. And she could still see them. In their agony, it was all they could do to keep the butcher knife clutched between Grace's fingers. They tried to raise it, to wave it toward the corner of the room where that fire burned the hottest so that she would see the moonlight flash across its blade, but they couldn't manage the focus required.

Just as it seemed their final contingency would fail, Ra'Tak felt a shift in the air. A trickle of fear—so sweet and familiar—began to douse the devouring blaze.

"No!" Elena screamed. They heard the word so clearly that they wondered how she'd formed it. She had noticed Grace at last and the knife they still strained to keep clutched in her hand. Ra'Tak readied themselves, their entire plan to survive this night hinging on being right about what she'd do next.

She flung herself at them. Ra'Tak could feel the heat of her rushing toward them like the blast of a furnace. She could see them there in Grace's mind, swirling behind her sleeping eyes. And she was coming to rip them out.

They waited until the last possible instant. Until the heat became so scorching that their concentration melted and the knife dropped from

Grace's hand. Until the very moment that Elena crossed the portal into her sister's mind.

Then they were gone, ejecting themselves from her like a pilot bailing from an aircraft the second before a missile strikes. Ra'Tak streaked across the room back toward Emily. They didn't know how long it would take Elena to search Grace's mind and realize they weren't there, but they knew they had to work fast.

Even more brutally than before, they forced their way into her. Awake now and coursing with adrenaline, Emily tried to resist them but couldn't even manage to slow them down. They tore through her defenses like a tidal wave through sandcastle walls, latching themselves to every neuron they invaded, forming the countless connections to their Conduit at a frenzied speed.

From somewhere outside where they worked, Ra'Tak could hear an approaching roar. They latched the links into place even faster, a million at a time. Sensations started flooding in as they took over, and when Emily turned to look at the specter blazing so brightly in the spiritual plane that its outline burned through into this one, Ra'Tak could see it too.

They should vanish, they thought. The initial connection was already formed, and their Conduit could be taken to the woods to complete the Rite at some later, safer time. All they had to do was retreat and leave Elena empty-handed once more, helpless to use all that power she possessed. But they were coursing with power too. Power unlike any they had felt before. Power that screamed to be unleashed.

Too drunk on delirium to think twice, Ra'Tak attacked. They crossed the space between Emily and where Elena's spirit hovered in an instant, a roiling, dark wave crashing into her.

There was an explosion of light and a tremor so powerful that it rippled through the realms. For the first time in time eternal, Ra'Tak's mind went dark.

TWELVE

Elena watched a dandelion petal let go its mooring and drift away on the breeze. In the distance, gray clouds gathered over the top of the mountains, staining an otherwise clear sky. "Is it going to rain here?" she asked.

"Not today, child," the old woman who had gifted her this place replied. "Those dark clouds are only a reflection of my sorrow for your loss. I'll take them away if you'd like."

"You can leave them," Elena said. "I'm sad too." She hadn't needed to tell the old woman what had happened to her siblings or about the defeats she'd suffered against the dark thing. The moment she'd arrived here, the old woman already knew.

They hadn't spoken much since then, spending most of the time sitting in silence near the brook's edge. Elena gazed down at her reflection in the water. She looked older, it seemed, than she had when she'd first visited this place two long days ago, and wearier for it.

"You are still going to win, my dear. Good is going to prevail. I know it hurts right now, but you must remember that."

"How?" Elena asked. "I've lost every time I've tried."

"Maybe you're trying the wrong thing," the old woman said. Elena lifted her head and looked at her quizzically. "Do you see the trout in the brook, dear?"

They hadn't been there before, but there they were now, gliding along beneath the surface of the water with their silver scales shimmering in the refracted sunlight.

"Yes."

"What do you think would happen if one of them jumped up on land and tried to beat you in a race across the meadow?" the old woman asked. "Who do you think would win?" Despite her dispiritedness, Elena giggled a little at the mental image. "Now what do you think would happen if you jumped into the water and tried to race one of them to the brook's end?"

As if to punctuate the point, one of the fish curled itself into a crook, then launched downstream, darting through the water at a rate Elena's eyes could barely follow. "You've tried to fight the dark thing on its terms," the old woman continued. "Terms of force and deception. And on those terms, it has won. You must fight it on your terms, Elena. Terms that don't look like fighting at all."

"What do you mean?"

"The dark thing does not belong in your realm, child. It is an intruder there, and the hold it has over your brother and sisters is the only thing giving it power."

"I've already tried to save them," Elena said. "I couldn't."

"You tried to stop the dark thing from taking them. You fought it while it did, and you fought bravely. But that is not the only way to save them. Nor your only chance."

Elena felt a stir of hope at this. "What's the other way?"

"The dark thing has attached itself to them. It has woven connections to their minds and sewn seeds of rot into their souls. But you can fix them, Elena. You can take them back."

"How?" Elena asked. But the answer was already coming to her before the question was even out. Like knowledge from the heavens spoken silently into being.

The old woman smiled softly, then lifted her head to let the sunshine warm her face. "Save your brother first. He's not as important to the dark thing, which means it won't be guarding him as closely. But once you save him, it won't have nearly the strength to stop you from saving the others. Then you can end it."

"You mean kill it, don't you?"

"Yes," the old woman said. "That is what I mean. When the time comes, you must not hesitate. Mercy is a virtue of God, and you should never be ashamed of yours. But so is justice."

"I won't hesitate," Elena said. "Not again."

"I know," the old woman said. But something about her starry eyes seemed distant now. Like they, too, had seen some secret knowledge. Elena reached for it, got a sense of something saddening her, but could uncover no more. She let it go and turned her attention back to the river. A breeze of the sweetest air moved through the grass, and Elena breathed it in deep. Songbirds trilled and whistled somewhere upstream, their songs and the gurgling water the only sounds in this place of solace.

"Can I just stay here a little longer first, though?"

The old woman smiled and wrapped a tender arm around her shoulders. "Of course, dear. You can stay as long as you like."

THIRTEEN

17 DAYS BEFORE THE WORK IS DONE

For the first time, Ra'Tak had seen the true darkness of death. Witnessed what it was like to cease existing. And even they could imagine nothing more awful.

It couldn't have been more than a second or two that they had slept. When the void lifted and their mind awoke, it seemed no time had passed. But they were beings that had never slept before. Now, they'd do anything to make sure they never slept again.

Their foolhardy collision into Elena's spirit had at least succeeded in driving her back to her body, even if it ultimately hurt them much more than her. By some mechanism Ra'Tak could not explain, it had also been strong enough to shake the physical plane. Though it alarmed them not knowing how such a thing could even be, this had created an opportunity. A chance to speed up the Work so they could get this dangerous chapter of it over and done.

Shaken themselves but still rippling with power, Ra'Tak had decided to set up a gathering. Their Quarry had been in Timmy's bedroom when the earthquake drove him to his knees. With three Conduits now theirs, guiding Grace and Emily into that room—making them disregard and then forget all that had happened before—had been as easy as moving pieces on a board. Making their Quarry see and hear them both as something else when they came through the door...even easier.

That had broken him. The fusion of delusion and reality was even more potent than they had hoped. The quake had been *real*. The girls being there in the room with him and neither of them seeming themselves had been *real*. That made the rest so much more real to him.

If there'd been any doubt left that he was only imagining it all, that night had shattered it. Now, the only obstacle left between him and the self-demise their Work demanded of him was his unwillingness to leave his family behind. To leave them at Ra'Tak's nonexistent mercy. It was an obstacle that they had encountered many times before, and they knew the remedy. They only needed to convince him that his family was already gone. That whatever effigies of them remained were just his tormentors in disguise.

Then, once they'd finished this difficult verse in an ode they'd been writing to their Master since the Fall of Man, Ra'Tak would leave this place and the girl that threatened their sacred continuance far behind. On to their next victim in some other place and time where she could never find them.

Even with power unimaginable still pulsing through them in wave after exquisite wave, Ra'Tak hastened its coming.

FOURTEEN

SUNDAY, JULY 22ND

When the numbers on her bedroom clock changed from 11:59 to 12:00, marking midnight and the start of a new day, Elena got out of bed. She'd been lying there for the past two hours, waiting sleeplessly for the hour to grow late enough that no one else in the house would still be awake. She could not afford to be interrupted.

Sneaking out of her room as quietly as she could manage, she tip-toed down the hall to her brother's bedroom door. On her way, she looked back at the closed door at the hall's end—the door to her parents' room. Her father would be in there now, and Elena hoped he was sleeping soundly. He distrusted her—more and more, it seemed, each day that passed. The dark thing had not taken control of him like it did her siblings, but it had not left him alone either like it had her mother. Whatever it was doing to him, it was taking a terrible toll.

Eventually, she would explain it all to him. But for now, trying to reach out to him again would only bring him more suffering. If she was going to save him, she had to save Timmy first.

That meant going back into the woods. Elena had seen clearly in a daydream (or a vision? She wasn't quite sure what to call it) just what she needed to do. Some places were special—her home, and her school, and the valley where the old woman lived. Other places—places like the clearing in the woods where nothing grew—held a different kind of power.

Elena pressed her ear against Timmy's bedroom door and listened, hearing only the whir of his ceiling fan. No sounds of clumsy bumps and shuffling feet like those that had come sporadically from her sisters' rooms the past few nights.

She eased the door open, slipped inside the room, and eased it closed again. There was more light in here than the hallway outside, the glow that filtered through the plastic, Scooby-Doo-shaped housing of Timmy's night-light casting the room in warm ochre. She spotted his silhouette on the mattress, his blue and red striped comforter pulled all the way up over his head. Elena knelt beside the bed and placed her hand on his back. "Timmy? Timmy, wake up."

The mass beneath the blankets rolled over. For an instant, Elena had the terrible idea that it was the dark thing hiding under the covers, set to explode the moment she pulled them away. But the dark thing wasn't there, she knew. It wasn't very good at hiding.

Another gentle nudge did the trick. Timmy pulled the covers away from his face and looked at her. There was fear in his features that dissipated only slightly when he recognized her. Elena could sense fragments of the nightmare he'd been having still hanging in the air.

"Put your shoes on, Timmy. We have to go outside." She was relieved when he didn't protest, but also a little disheartened. He looked so hollowed-out and submissive, sitting on the bedroom floor with sleep still pulling at his eyelids, struggling to twist the laces of his sneakers into the appropriate loops and knots without even bothering to ask her where they were going. Elena sat down next to him and helped him with his shoes.

"Follow me," she said. "But be really quiet, okay? Can you do that?"

Timmy nodded, his gaze so distant she wondered if he'd really heard her. She hadn't realized until now just how bad these past few days had been for him as well. She'd been too caught up in the more obvious changes in her sisters that, like the dark thing, perhaps she had neglected Timmy too.

They made it out of the house without incident, and Elena let herself exhale. She didn't know which would have been worse: being stopped by the dark thing or being stopped by her father. She couldn't really explain the shift she'd seen in him or why he no longer looked at her the same, but something deep inside urged caution.

The new moon left only the stars and the scatters of streetlights to illuminate their dew-soaked backyard. The thick darkness of the woods, neither would even touch. Elena waited until she and Timmy had made it out the gate and to the edge of the woods before she dared turn on her flashlight. The way the trees and brush swallowed its meager beam transported her back to the last time she'd visited these woods in the cover of darkness. With the dark thing waiting for her there.

Elena pushed ahead past the tree line but stopped when there was no sound of Timmy following behind. She turned the flashlight back around and shined it on him. He was standing unmoved at the edge of the woods. A limb blocked most of his face from her angle, but Elena could tell he was starting to cry.

"Timmy," she whispered, circling back to his side. "What's wrong?" Timmy didn't respond, but Elena knew the answer anyway. "It'll be okay. We have the flashlight, and I'm not going to leave you. I promise."

If she'd kindled any encouragement in him, it evaporated the moment he looked away from her and back at the abyss of trees and shadows ahead. Elena took him by the hand and squeezed it tight. "I won't let go. I'll hold it the whole way."

But that didn't seem like it was going to work either. There was an instant where Elena thought he would pull away from her and run back to the house. Instead, he pulled her in tight and buried his face in her side. "Something bad lives out there," he said. Elena could barely make out the muffled words.

"I know. That's why we have to go back. To..." *Kill it*, Elena heard the old woman say. "...Make it go away."

Timmy shook his head, his expression suddenly incredulous. "No. No, no, no, we *can't*. You have to do what it says, Sissy. You have to always do what it says, or bad things will happen. *Really bad* things."

"Timmy, listen to me," Elena started but cut the next words off when she realized they would do no good. Timmy was on the verge of hysterics, his mouth trembling and his eyes no longer seeing the dark woods before them, rather memories of the dark thing that had brought him there.

She had to start now, she decided. If she didn't, the only way to get him back to that clearing in the woods would be to drag him. Just as his head turned back to face the house his feet were soon to sprint toward, Elena wrapped her arms around his shoulders and closed her eyes.

Like diving into warm water, she crossed the gateway between her mind and his. There was a rush of air that swirled into a funnel, and she let herself drift down it. Stray thoughts—not her own and all of them fearful—whizzed past like bullets, a few catching up to her as she spiraled down, exploding into clarity.

You have to do what it says...

Bad things will happen...

I want to go back, Sissy...

Really bad things...

Elena swam deeper, pushing past shallow cognizance and into the deeper waters of memory. Here, innumerable windows lined every innumerable surface of the non-Euclidean space. Most were fogged by time and unimportance, but some were still clear, the scenes unfolding beyond them visible for her to see. She saw Timmy riding the merry-go-round for the first time at the Atlanta fair, the window through which the images came framed in sunshine yellow. Through another—its edges framed in crimson—she saw Timmy running across the yard and wailing in pain, a welt rising on his forearm with the rooted stinger of a honeybee jutting out from its center. There was another beside it where Mommy pulled the stinger out with tweezers and rubbed ointment on the swollen skin—this one framed in a softer, almost pink shade of red.

Then she spotted the windows framed in rot, an entire collection of them draped in oozing black. They were memories of the nightmares the dark thing had shown him, each pane of glass painfully clear so that there could be no suppressing the awful visions on the other side.

The breathing, black rot that ran through nearly all of Timmy's more recent recollections ran deeper too, like roots from a poisonous tree, tunneling through and beneath the windows of memory and into the doorways of identity below. The doorways to the soul.

This was from where she would have to save him: from the deepest parts of him the dark thing had corrupted. But only after she had taken him somewhere suitable to leave all that rot behind. For now, the memories were her focus.

Elena avoided looking through each rot-framed pane as she worked, having no need—and certainly no desire—to see the views they showed. They were things that a child should never have seen; that much she could sense without having to look. Experiences with no purpose but to tear made memories with no purpose but to scar.

One by one, she closed these windows. Turned each smokey, translucent pane into glimmering mirrors. Mirrors that, should her brother's thoughts ever stumble across them, he'd see only the best of himself instead. The rot still framed them when she was done, still snaked beneath them into the depths of the soul, but that, too, she would fix soon enough. And then what a sight to behold those mirrors would be. A thousand wounds the dark thing had inflicted turned into gifts she'd leave behind.

Elena was elated, almost to the point of giddiness. It felt wonderful saving her brother. The old woman had been so right; *this* was what fighting back on her terms looked like.

Leaving this place where the mind and soul of her younger brother took quasi-physical form was far less a journey than entering it had been—like sliding downhill after a difficult climb up. Just a thought and she was back outside, still clutching Timmy in her arms.

"We need to go now, Timmy," she said, smiling at him without having to force it. Timmy nodded, perhaps a little dazed, it seemed, but no longer stricken with fear. Elena took his hand, just as she'd promised before, and led him into the woods.

The stars were mere pinpricks between the black silhouettes of the forest canopy, the scattered rays from the streetlights on the other side of the house they'd left long smothered by darkness. Yet the woods glowed in a way that neither these nor the flashlight's dim beam could explain. It was like moonlight that beamed up from the ground and from the leaves all around instead of the sky above.

Even the clearing where no creatures, flora nor fauna, dared to live since the dark thing had turned it into their poisoned portal didn't seem nearly so eerie when they reached it. By the time the trees and bushes thinned and they could see the empty patch of earth ahead, it looked almost as though it were washed in morning light. As if their journey of just a hundred footsteps had taken the entire night and dawn was now warming the horizon.

Elena brought Timmy to the stump at the center of the clearing and sat down beside him on wood grayed by death and time. His hand still in hers, she squeezed it tight and promised him it would all be okay.

She closed her eyes and leaned into the whirlwind, spiraled down through thoughts no longer frenzied or frightful and into the windows of memory. Beneath this space defying description lay the doorways of identity, interwoven passageways to a galaxy of flickering lights, each one an individual essence of her brother's soul.

Elena knew the dark thing's rot would ruin the sanctity of this special place and had already braced for what she'd see. But when a surface like glassy water broke beneath her descending feet and the doorways of identity yawned before her, she felt a rush of sorrow.

The dark thing had corrupted everything and everywhere. Not a single doorway left secret and secured. Not a single beacon within untainted. The trails of rot that ran through the windows of memory had been only a vestige of what grew beneath. Here, it slicked every surface. To say she could smell the putrid steam rising from it in a place where even sensations of sight and sound lost most of their common meaning would not do justice the way it flooded her with disgust. She worried the feeling would grow so intense that the silver strand she still didn't control would impel a retreat to her body and leave her mission here unfinished; whatever the light-like mechanism connecting her spirit to its earthly host was, it had shown little tolerance for risk.

I'm okay, she thought, the words directed at it just in case it could hear them more than to herself. Not sure how much time it would allow her, Elena went to work.

The moment she tore the first tumor from Timmy's soul like a weed plucked from a garden and burned it away like the same, she knew that the dark thing had felt it. She could hear the echoes of its screams reverberating through the essence of itself that infected this place. She could sense it drawing closer, scorching through the realms back to the prize it was losing. This time, it was the dark thing that would be too late.

Removing that which had no place there proved effortless. The same light that seared away every connection the dark thing had formed and every corruption it inflicted only charged the soul beneath brighter.

Somewhere outside, she could feel the dark thing trying to force itself in. But the pathways it needed to travel burned too hot now to allow it entrance. It tested them once, then shrieked at the pain and futility.

Elena felt the dark thing retreat too soon, its sudden absence much more worrying than its fruitless attempts to stop her. She'd hoped it would burn itself up trying, driven by rage into the inferno too far to turn around, but now she sensed a new threat approaching.

When the last of its parasitical links had burned to withering ash, the dark thing let loose an anguished wail. It made her smile to hear it squeal like a spoiled child whose toy had been taken away. But a different noise turned her solemn again—a voice, real and recognizable, piercing through from the world outside.

"Elly!" her father cried, his voice distorted and echoing. "What the hell are you doing out here?"

Elena hurried a final check that no trace of the dark thing's fingerprints remained, then let herself drift away; up and out through the fantastical spaces of spirit and psyche and back into the cradle of her own mind and body.

Her eyes opened and then squinted against the rays of a flashlight shining in her face. Not the dull, yellow halo of the keychain flashlight she still clutched in her hand, but the white, sun-like flare of a much larger, LED light. Like the big aluminum one her father kept in his nightstand drawer.

For an instant, with only his black silhouette visible behind the glare, Elena thought he looked like the dark thing. And as he approached and she could feel his anger electrifying the air, she knew the dark thing had sent him.

He shouted and shook her, asked questions and made accusations she didn't understand. Behind his narrowed, accusing eyes, she could see the dark thing's fury. It didn't matter now, though, she assured herself. Getting her in trouble with her father was just another one of its tantrums. It wouldn't recapture the soul she'd saved.

Still, that didn't stop the tears from forming. Just before they swelled into puddles and she shouted something true yet more than she should have spoken at this time when the more her father knew, the more danger he was in, she noticed something at the base of the stump. Up from the carpet of yellowed bermudagrass and upturned soil, in this clearing where all life seemed quashed by the dark thing's rot, rose a single sprout of springtime green that had not been there before.

FIFTEEN

16 DAYS BEFORE THE WORK IS DONE

Deep within the darkest realm of all, in a place where no light or love has ever traveled, Ra'Tak met their Master. They cowered before him, not daring anything less than groveling capitulation. He that walketh the earth like a lion seeking whom he may devour seemed ready to devour them; they had disappointed him before—and had suffered the steepest of consequences—but never like this.

And now they were before him, begging for mercy from one whom mercy had never been given nor received. Pleading that the bitter cup the Work had turned to should pass from them.

There'd been no need to explain themselves. He that watches all Creation with one burning, hateful eye had seen their failures clear. Now that eye was fixed on them, the hellfires roaring within it looking liable to leap out and consume them.

The debt they owed would not be forgiven, their Master decreed. Instead, it was to be doubled. Such audacity, he rebuked while Ra'Tak quailed beneath his gaze, to bring back failure as their offering. So irreverent of them that they would think themselves safer in the flames of his unholy rage than those of a mortal's spirit. And as their penance, two lives were now owed instead of one.

They were not meant to succeed at this charge, Ra'Tak realized. Despair trickled through them like icy water, but still, they dared not entertain a single thought of protest.

They were to be a burnt offering. Set ablaze in the girl's holy fire as a martyr to their Master. To command that they return to her now—their power diminished by the loss of their Conduit and hers burning brighter than ever—with both her and her father's lives now their debt to pay could have no other reason.

Unless…

Their Master's gaze flared hotter, incensed that they would dare even hope. But Ra'Tak could hardly suppress it, for it wasn't them alone, they sensed, at which his fury blazed. Power such as the girl possessed was an insult to him more than any other—he that should have wielded the full power of their Enemy and was instead stripped of title and position. And, though Ra'Tak knew better than to dwell on such thoughts for more than an instant in his presence, power such as hers was also a threat.

Hide us from her, they implored him. *Blind her to us, and we will deliver her to your altar.*

Their Master watched them, his decision already made but letting slip no indication what it would be. Yet Ra'Tak knew their Master well. There could be no hiding his desire to see the girl snuffed from Creation, and if sent not here to this place of darkness and wailing, then sent at least to a place where she could no longer interfere. And with deceptions that only he of such infinite infernality could conjure, his will would be done.

SIXTEEN

SUNDAY, JULY 29TH

Something wasn't right. Elena had no grasp of what it could be that seemed so wrong, but the subtle sense of wrongness pervaded her thoughts like a distinct odor—foul yet faint and untraceable to its source.

One week had passed since she had saved Timmy from the dark thing's clutches. It had left that night and not come back. Or so it certainly seemed. She'd seen no sign of it in her siblings and had caught no hint of its unmistakable presence. She had planned to do for Grace and Emily the same thing she'd done for Timmy, but upon entering her oldest sister's mind the following night had found no trace of the dark thing's rot.

For the first few days, Elena assumed she had won and that things had returned to normal. She might have even gone on assuming so—might have ignored her slight misgivings and written them off as lingering paranoia—had it not been for her father. Unlike her brother and sisters, his condition had not improved in the days since Timmy's salvation. Something bad was still happening to him.

Whatever it was, Elena couldn't bring herself to look. Going into Grace's mind had not been the same as going into Timmy's. She hadn't found the dark thing there, but there'd been other things she shouldn't have seen. With Timmy still too young for much but bliss and inno-cence, the things she'd seen in him (beyond that which the dark thing put there) only brought her joy. Splaying open the depths of Grace's soul—laying bare every secret, fear, and desire—had brought dizzying revelation of just how invasive this ability of hers was. She'd avoided doing the same with Emily, content with just a cursory glance as confir-mation that the dark thing had left her too. The idea of going into her father's mind—feeling his fears and knowing whatever adult knowledge left his eyes so wild and his face so gaunt—brought too much dread.

What bothered her most of all was that he seemed to be frightened of *her*. He didn't look at her the same anymore. Even without a procliv-ity for such things, she could have sensed his distrust. It hurt to see the ghostly look pass over his face each time she crossed his path. It fright-ened her too. She had mostly avoided him these past few days. It wasn't hard to do; when her father was not in bed or at work, he was sitting in the living room recliner staring at the TV he rarely bothered to turn on.

That's where he was now. Elena had seen him earlier when she went downstairs for a drink. He had watched her every step with the vigi-lance of prey that had just spotted its natural predator. His gaze made her scurry back to her bedroom, the first bottled drink she'd blindly grabbed from the fridge in hand, as fast as she could manage.

Mom had gone to Aunt Laura's house earlier and had taken Timmy with her. She'd been spending a lot of time over there lately. It seemed she was avoiding Dad too. Avoiding all of them, maybe, and the gloom in this house she couldn't explain but clearly felt as well. Elena knew her mom better than most daughters of nine years and thus could not fault her too much. Some creatures survive by hiding, some by fighting back, and others by running away.

Mom had at least asked her if she wanted to come along, but Elena had declined. Now the rain was starting to pour again, and she wished her mom was home. Water snaked down her bedroom window, the sky beyond it already dark despite the hour as angry clouds hammered the house with wind and rain for the fourth straight day. The dregs of a hurricane, so the news had said, swept inland from the Gulf. They'd also said it should fizzle out by morning. Elena hoped that part was true.

A streak of lightning lit up her window, bringing the shadowy backyard into momentary detail. Elena leaned forward, squinting her eyes. She'd seen something moving through the window, something in the yard by the swing. But now all she could see through the rain-soaked glass was water and darkness. She rose and pressed her nose against the pane. When the view still wasn't clear enough for her liking, she flipped up the window's latches and pushed it open. Wind stormed in, flapping the curtains and spraying rain against her face. Shielding her eyes, Elena stuck out her head.

Grace and Emily were both in the yard, swinging back and forth in rhythm on the swing set at its edge. Wind whipped at their drenched hair and drove sheets of water into their faces. Yet even over the roar of the storm, Elena could hear them laughing.

Lightning struck somewhere close by, a whipcrack of thunder loud enough to rumble the walls hot on its heels. Was it safe for them to be out there? Elena had always been told to stay inside and away from tall objects during a lightning storm. Shouldn't her sisters know this too?

She started to call out to them, but then Grace looked up at the window and beat her to the draw. "Elena!" she yelled over the wind. "Come swing with us!"

Emily looked up then too and let go of the swing chain with one hand to give Elena a wave. For a moment, Elena thought about throwing on the pink rain jacket she had in her closet and rushing outside to join them; it wasn't very often that her older sisters invited her to participate in the fun that the two of them were always getting into, and Elena usually jumped at the opportunity. But the storm outside seemed too strong and violent a thing to defy. And something about the way her sisters ignored its fury and carried on as if it were a calm and cloudless day didn't sit right with her.

"I don't think it's safe to be out there."

"What?" Grace yelled, lifting a hand to her ear.

"I said I don't think it's safe to be out there!" Elena shouted as loud as she could manage. "You guys should come inside!"

"In a minute!" Grace shouted back. Elena watched them swinging for a few seconds longer, then backed away and closed the window. She was dripping wet from the shoulders up, and a puddle was already forming at her feet.

Worry gnawed at her stomach like hungry rats. Her sisters had never been the outdoorsy types, and finding them both outside on the swing would have been a little unusual even in weather not so wretched.

Something wasn't right. She kept coming back to this thought. Her father wasn't right. Her sisters weren't right. And the feeling of some dark cloud that hung over her—high and faraway yet smothering her world in its shade—wasn't right at all.

Frustrated, Elena flopped onto the bed, ignoring how wet she was getting the sheets. She couldn't fix what she didn't understand. For now, she resolved, all she could do was wait.

SEVENTEEN

9 DAYS BEFORE THE WORK IS DONE

Through the eyes of their Conduits, Ra'Tak watched the storm rage on. Being in the middle of its wrath—feeling rain drive against skin they coinhabited and watching the lightning flash around them—was electrifying. Seeing Elena stare out her window dumbfoundedly at them without the slightest idea who it was that stared back, even more thrilling.

Their Master had been true to his word. The scales he'd placed over the girl's all-seeing eyes had hidden Ra'Tak completely, freeing them to carry on with their Work unimpeded. And, in the days since their Master began rendering his aid, the Work had been going splendidly.

Convincing their Quarry that his own daughter was the root of his tremendous suffering was turning out to be a rather simple task. He had caught a sense of Elena's abilities even before Ra'Tak began manipulating him to distrust her and had wildly miscredited their source. With Ra'Tak weaving his dreams and whispering into his thoughts, it had not taken them long to turn him against her.

But driving their Quarry to fear his own daughter and resent her supposed betrayal was not nearly as difficult as driving him to end her life. Fear and betrayal were an important start, but there was still much to be done if they were to fulfill their Master's command.

A clap of thunder rocked the air, reminding Ra'Tak of the days when man thought thunder to be the bellow of the gods. Their Work had been much more challenging in those times—back when the ancients still believed in the dark things that stalked the night and knew how to take precautions. These recent trials marked the first time in a millennium that they'd been challenged.

In a way, it felt empowering to face such resistance again, at least now that the worst was behind them. They would be stronger for it when the Work was over. And what a trophy the girl would make when it was done.

First, there were matters to attend to with their Quarry. Before the sun set and the already blackened skies turned full dark, he was going to flee. The smell on his skin was like that of a deer the moment a lion explodes out of the brush. He was going to run, and, when he did, Ra'Tak was going to bring him back.

It did not take long for their prediction to come true. There was still some semblance of daylight left when they heard through their Conduits' ears a car starting in the driveway. As to where he was going, Ra'Tak would have known even if they hadn't been traveling along with him, privy to his every thought. He was going to see the only person alive he thought would believe him.

When the Work had first begun, long before they could have anticipated the challenges that lay in store, involving their Quarry's brother in the delusions they created for him had seemed a harmless way to give them depth. Like most they targeted, their Quarry for this chapter of the Work had a tortured past. His father's sickness and eventual suicide had not been their doing. Taking credit for it, though—going as far as to plant the memories in his mind and nurture them slowly back to life as if time had made him forget—had been their chosen foundation for this chapter of the Work. Feeding him words he wouldn't remember writing in a journal they told him was his father's had, at the time, seemed a brilliant touch.

Now it was just another complication. An imagined lifeline for him to reach for. And what would happen when that mirage shattered? When his brother knew naught of the memories their Quarry believed they shared. It was unpredictable, and the knife's edge the Work now balanced on left no tolerance for unpredictability.

They would intervene when the time was right, they decided. His half-baked intentions of what he'd do when he arrived at his brother's house—the reason for the revolver tucked in his waistband—could absolutely not be allowed.

That he was already willing to go to such extremes did encourage them, though. Him deflecting the suggestions they'd fed him about Elena onto his brother instead was an unfortunate diversion, but nothing they couldn't correct.

More than once on the winding roads slicked by rain and darkened by overcast skies, it seemed their Quarry might kill himself accidentally and bring a serendipitous end to it all. When the front bumper of his car strayed across the yellow lines and into the path of approaching headlights—80,000 pounds of instant death barreling toward him with all the speed its diesel engine could muster—Ra'Tak couldn't help but be hopeful; it wouldn't be the ending the Work required, but it would be an end. And so long as they had no hand in causing it, perhaps they would not be blamed.

When sometime later their Quarry pulled safely onto the dangerless gravel road leading up to his childhood home, Ra'Tak knew it wasn't to be. Now, the danger was theirs. Theirs and Jeremiah's.

A greeting at the door and a brotherly embrace soon gave way to accusations and denials. Ra'Tak could feel their Quarry's anger and his brother's confusion clouding the air inside the house like mixing smogs, each emotion matching the other's intensity step for step.

Then came the climax Ra'Tak knew well. That mental breakpoint when fear and rage boil into plasma and erupt in unchained violence. So often this rhapsodic moment marked the Work's successful conclusion—so often that Ra'Tak almost forgot their charge and let the calamity unfold.

But before their Quarry could draw the gun he clasped concealed beneath the hem of his shirt, Ra'Tak whisked his thoughts away. His fingers slipped from the handle. His lips mumbled something about being tired—just the line they'd hoped to coax with all the fatigue and confusion they pressed into him—then he stumbled away from the table. Off to the bedroom of countless childhood nightmares where they would have him all alone.

With the risk now past, Ra'Tak swelled with encouragement. Had they not intervened, Jared Gordon would have surely sprayed his brother's brain across the kitchen wall. They had felt the fire of his resolve just before they snuffed it out. To kill a daughter, especially with their encouragement, was not so far a leap from there.

The moment their Quarry's head hit the pillow, the moment he sank into sleep, and the moment that Ra'Tak met him there all blended together as one. The dream they'd prepared for him this time was to be especially vivid and cutting. A punishment for the rebellion that had brought them here and just the push the Work needed.

When his mind's eye opened to a dreamscape identical to the bedroom where he slept, he embraced it as reality. When Ra'Tak roared down at him from the heavens and filled his nostrils with smoke and sulfur, it didn't matter that none of it was objectively *real*. When his daughters entered the room, eyes darkened and smiles beaming wickedness, how they'd found him there or any other such rationale never crossed his thoughts.

The terror was real, and the hopelessness, and the sharp, pinching pain when his eldest daughter worked a knife across his throat. And when he woke from this dream and drove himself home—too broken and panicked to even question how his lungs still drew breath or what had happened to the ragged incision he'd felt open in his throat inch by agonizing inch—that's how he'd remember it. As real as memories can get.

EIGHTEEN

MONDAY, JULY 30ᵀᴴ

Peering through the blinds of her bedroom window, Elena watched a heart-rending scene unfold. In the front yard, two police officers were wrestling with her father. One of them had twisted her dad's arms behind his back. The other was fumbling with a pair of handcuffs.

The officers shouted orders. Her father screamed. From the doorway outside Elena's view, her mother was crying. It was such a loud and awful discord it made her want to cover her ears.

It had all seemed to happen so quickly. First the sound of her father storming into the house just before daybreak, shouting and crying and bringing them all out of bed. When he grabbed the knife from the block in the kitchen, Mom had ordered her and her siblings back to their bedrooms. But all except Timmy had stopped at the top of the stairs.

She'd watched her father put the knife against his neck, whatever words he continued to scream muddled by his sobs. She'd heard her mother start to scream too, then panicked pleas to a 911 operator. It felt like hours then and just seconds now looking back before she'd heard the sound of approaching sirens.

Her father looked back once as the officers half led, half dragged him toward their car, his gaze seeming to settle directly on the spot in the window where she'd pushed down one of the slats. Elena let go of the blinds and stepped away from the window.

Adrenaline-fueled inner voices shouted for her to do something, but none bothered elaborating what that something should be. She was just a kid, too young to have any influence on parents and police officers in a situation like this and old enough to know what would happen if she tried. Her abilities might have scared away the dark thing, but they couldn't make handcuffs disappear.

And had she even scared it away at all? Elena still felt no sense of the dark thing, not a whisper since she had saved her brother from its clutches, but *something* was still happening to her family. Something that every nerve screamed was its doing.

For the better part of an hour, she felt like doing nothing but lying in bed. Occasionally, she would close her eyes and probe the world around for some trace of the presence that had been so palpable just a few days before. Even though she sensed nothing, it no longer felt true that the dark thing was gone. *Hiding* was what it was doing. And hiding frustratingly well.

It was during one of these mental scourings that Elena felt a different presence approaching. One warm and familiar yet soaked in fear and sadness. She heard a timid rap against the door and welcomed her mother in.

The tears that had spotted her mom's face just before she opened the door were now damp spots drying on her shirt tail, but reddened cheeks and even redder eyes weren't so easy to wipe away. Her mom didn't even try to force a smile, and Elena was glad. She would have felt obligated to force one back.

"Hey, sweetheart. Are you okay?" Elena felt herself start to shake her head, then nodded instead. Mom sat down on the edge of the bed. "I know what happened must have been really scary and upsetting. I was really scared too."

"Is Dad going to jail?"

"No, baby, he's not. The policemen are just taking Dad to the hospital. So that the doctors can help him."

"What's wrong with him?" Elena asked, already knowing what she feared the answer to be.

"I don't know for sure. That's what the doctors are trying to figure out. But something is wrong with his brain, sweetheart. It's causing him to see and believe things that aren't true. That's why he did what he did today. He didn't do it on purpose."

"I'm not sure the doctors are going to be able to help him."

"Helping people like your dad is what they're best at. You don't need to worry about that. He's in good hands."

Elena started to say that wasn't what she'd meant, but something made her think better of it. "When does he get to come home?"

"I don't know that either, baby," Mom said and wiped her eyes again with the collar of her shirt. "Whenever he gets better."

Elena wished he could come home now. If the dark thing was hiding in him somehow, she had no chance of finding it with him gone. "Can we visit him?"

"Not yet, okay? We need to give Dad some time with the doctors first."

"I think he's in danger there." It was more than she should have said, Elena realized when she saw the worry already etched into her mother's features grow deeper. "I just think he needs us there with him, Mom. That's all."

"That's sweet of you, Elena. But this is for the best. Things are going to be different now. In a good way. This should have happened a long time ago, and it wasn't very brave of me to let it get this far. But Dad's going to get the help he needs now. And it's all going to be okay."

"I love you, Mom," Elena said. She could tell her mother needed to hear it, and there was no use saying what she felt: that it was *not* going to be okay. That the doctors were *not* going to help. That Dad—and all of them maybe—was in real danger.

"I love you too, baby," her mom said, leaning across the bed and wrapping her in a hug. At the touch of her skin, without even trying, Elena caught sense of thoughts unspoken. A mother's urge to take her children and flee the dangers she too could sense if not understand. A mother's instinct of what would happen if she didn't.

"Why don't you come downstairs with me?" Mom asked. "Your sisters are in the living room watching TV with Timmy, and I was thinking I could make us all some hot chocolate. I've already called into work, so we can spend the whole day together, okay?"

"Okay, Mom. I'll be right down. I just want to change out of my PJ's first."

When her mother left the room, Elena closed her eyes and searched even harder for the malefic signature that marked the dark thing's presence. But even in a house that fumed with fear and misery, she could sense no trace of anything as wicked as it.

"Things only hide when they're afraid," Elena whispered into the air.

There was no sign or response that followed, but she knew in her soul that the dark thing had heard her.

NINETEEN

ONE DAY BEFORE THE WORK IS DONE

For seven days and seven nights, Ra'Tak worked their Quarry's mind like wrought iron, heating and hammering it into shape; honing it to an edge ready to spill its first blood.

The isolation his stay in the hospital provided had been their panacea. Here, there'd been no one to interfere. No distractions to set his mind at ease. No innocent smiles on his family's faces spreading warmth over the monstrous mosaic they'd assembled.

In these seven days, they had spun a yarn for him. One woven with just enough truths to convince and more than enough falsehoods to complete their purpose. They told him of a poison flowing through his youngest daughter that had envenomed his future and past. Of an invitation that had sealed all their eternal fates. Of a bridge between worlds that only she held open.

They nudged him toward thoughts he thought were his own, then feigned worry when he arrived there. They convinced him that the act their survival relied on was instead the only thing they feared. Now, it was the morning of his release, and Ra'Tak had left no doubt that he would do what they required.

In a matter of hours, their Quarry was going home. They envisioned him as an arrow resting between a triangle of bent wood and taut string, ready to take flight. Though they'd still be there to guide his course once he left these padded walls, it hardly seemed necessary; once released, their arrow would fly true.

Yet the fear they feigned each time he thought of Elena and what he must do had not been entirely contrived. They had not returned to the house where she stayed since their Quarry left it, but they had felt her searching for them even with the distance between.

They had stilled their thoughts to a hush each time her feelers brushed across them—like a mouse frozen beneath the grass watching a cat stalk past. She never saw them, their Master's shroud remaining opaque to even the most piercing light, but there had to be a reason why she was looking. There was no doubt she knew that they were there.

Soaking in the inky depths of their Quarry's thoughts was the only thing that eased their worry. Feeling his resolve like iron bars around his heart gave them blessed assurance. Their victory would not be long coming, they affirmed to themselves as visions of their Quarry holding a gun to his youngest daughter's head cascaded through his mind and over theirs like icy, welcome waves.

They were Ra'Tak, a being whose past was measured in eons and whose future would be measured the same. Elena Gordon was a child, a mortal who burned too bright in her short time and whose life was now numbered in days.

TWENTY

TUESDAY, AUGUST 7TH

Through Elena's bedroom window, it appeared a splendid morning. The mockingbirds chattering raucously from the oak tree at the backyard's edge would have surely agreed. Between their flights in search of bugs to swallow or twigs for the nesting season soon to come, they bathed in the sunlight and preened their feathers with the insouciance of creatures that knew no worry. Elena watched them with envy. For her, all the glowing sunlight and bright blue skies in the world could not make this morning splendid.

Her father had come back from the hospital two days ago, and the dark thing had come back with him. If, that is, it had ever left at all. With the sense of it now unmistakable—even if untraceable still—she wondered if it had been hiding in plain sight all along.

Something still obscured it from her. In the nearly two weeks since the dark thing disappeared, Elena had come to a better understanding of the stifling fog that took its place. It was a fog that formed over only her. No one else could feel it, and the realization that it originated within her own mind had been one of the first things she'd discovered about it. It was cold—so noticeably chilling that she had taken to wearing sweatpants and long-sleeve shirts all throughout the day—and cold in other ways as well. Cold in the sense that happy thoughts came difficult and bad thoughts came uninvited ever since it formed.

At first, she had wondered if this was just the dark thing's way of covering its escape. Like a squid squirting ink to cloud the water before it swims away. But the more she explored this thing that shrouded her thoughts, the more a different comparison kept coming to mind. This wasn't the diversion of fleeing prey. This was the camouflage of a predator still on the hunt.

And now was the moment it pounced. Elena felt the tiny hairs on her arms stiffen and a chill in the air too bracing to have come from the AC vent. She heard faint sobs coming from somewhere, downstairs perhaps, and the sound of pacing steps. Something bad had already happened. Something worse was about to happen now.

Elena closed her eyes and cleared her thoughts. She fell asleep and then woke again in the same breath, rising from a body that still lay curled on the bed in one that knew no physical bounds save for the cord connecting the two.

More adept than ever in this form and in this plane, it took only picturing the faraway realm where the old woman lived for her to get there. A near-endless expanse passed by in an instant. Galaxies like bubbles in an infinite ocean trailed past in streaming filaments until she arrived at the spot of light that marked the old woman's domain.

Oblivion gave way to lush gardens the moment Elena crossed its barrier. The old woman met her there, facing her with her hands laced across her lap as if she'd been waiting for her arrival.

"You look troubled today, dear," the old woman said.

"I need help," Elena said. "Please. I can't do it on my own."

"Sit down, Elena. Sit down and rest with me for a while." Elena sat down in the short grass beside the old woman's rocker and took a long, deep breath. Her nerves still thrummed like instrument strings—piercing alarms still whined inside her ears—but the smell of wildflowers and wet grass was at least a little soothing. "If what you said was true," the old woman continued, "then you would have not been sent."

"I don't understand."

"The dark thing's day of judgment has come, dear. Today is the day God's will is done. And you, chosen by His hand to walk the earth in mortal flesh, are the instrument of that will."

"What if I don't want to be? Why can't God just do it himself?"

The old woman smiled, taking no apparent offense to the frustration that leaked through Elena's tone. "Your time as a mortal and inability to remember what came before have clouded your perspective, dear. You were once *grateful* for this holy mission. *Honored* to have been chosen."

Elena tried to think back as far as she could. She could remember the day her brother was born—this the first real event of significance in her then four years of life. She could faintly remember falling out of a tree and scraping her shin sometime before this. There were a few more faded reels in these deepest wells of her memory, then nothing. She'd heard others tell of the day she was born or the day she spoke her first words or took her first steps, but these were just stories she knew, not memories of her own.

And yet, when Elena thought back further than this—to a time predating even the womb—something stirred in her soul. "Show me then," she said. "Show me what came before and what I need to do now."

"I'm sorry, Elena. That's not my decision to make. Soon enough you'll remember. I promise this is true."

"Please. I just want to see it again. Just once so I'll know."

"There isn't time," the old woman said. Her expression grew more serious, as though she had heard even before Elena did the sounds of footsteps and stifled cries that came from another world far away and yet still right within reach. "You already know what to do. You already remember enough."

The creak of an opening door rippled through the realms and into this one where there were no doors to be found. Elena felt her vision start to swim as the cord of light coming from her chest stretched taut as a bowstring.

"We'll see you soon, child," the old woman said. Even with the colors of this place blurring and fading white, Elena caught a glimpse of something remarkable in the old woman's eyes. In them, she saw windows to a place and faces forgotten where the multitudes of those she once knew and loved watched and waited for her triumphant return.

The sensation of a hand grabbing her shoulder was what fully broke the spell. Her cord of light snapped her back to her bedroom and the body lying in her bed the instant her father's fingers grazed her skin.

His eyes were wide and reddened, and when she opened hers, his breath caught in his chest. Through her father's sweat-stained shirt, his heart beat hard enough to see each pounding thump. The hand he held against her shoulder trembled wildly, but his grip stayed firm.

"Come on, Elly," he said, the sound of his voice suddenly frightening her even more than his appearance. "We've got to go." Her father didn't wait for her to get out of bed. He lifted her up into his arms before she had the chance and carried her out of the room.

"What's going on?" she asked. But her father did not answer. Light as she was, he seemed to be laboring carrying her down the stairs. Once, his footing slipped and Elena braced herself for a tumble before he regained his balance. She realized then that if she struggled, she could probably wrestle free from his grasp. But Elena stayed docile in his arms. Her fight was not with her father but the thing that had twisted itself into his mind—a presence still cloaked and masked yet bordering unconcealable now so close and so blazing.

Her father carried her across the living room—hurrying a little faster, Elena noticed, past the couch where her mom lay sleeping deep enough to snore—and out the front door. Elena squinted against the morning's brightness.

By the time her eyes adjusted, her father was buckling her into the passenger seat of his car. He closed the door, then hurried around to the driver's side. Elena watched him sit down in the seat beside her without buckling his own belt, then heard the mechanical thump of the car's doors locking.

"Where are we going?"

"Nowhere," her father replied without looking at her.

"Then why are we—"

"We're not going anywhere. Not yet. We just need to talk, okay?"

Elena remembered what had happened the last time she tried to tell her father about the dark thing. Remembered the suffering it had caused him. But this time would be different. Her sense of it there with them in the car grew clearer every second. The veil around the dark thing grew thinner, like clouds evaporating in the sun, the harder she focused. Whether it dared reveal itself or kept trying in vain to hide would not matter; this time, she was going to destroy it.

"Elly, if you're still in there you have got to talk to me, sweetheart. You've got to talk to me right now. You've got to tell me why you did it and you've got to tell me how to stop it. Right now."

His words broke her focus. Elena felt the presence she'd been tweezing at sink back into the background of things more tangible. Nothing her father said made sense, but the way his eyes pleaded for a response made her throat grow tight. "Did what?" she asked, then bit her lip when it felt like she was going to cry.

This wasn't the answer her father was looking for. The tendons in his neck tensed as he shook his head and ground his teeth loud enough to make a sound like gravel crunching beneath treaded boots. "No. Not this time. No more dodging the question. What did you do, Elena? You have to tell me what you did."

Somewhere amidst the turmoil in his eyes, Elena caught another flicker of the darkness burrowed inside him. A cold flare of malignancy too piercing to hide. She gazed into it unblinking and willed herself to see it clearer. Just a bit more focus and the veil would tear. Just a bit more clarity and all the dark thing's defenses would fall.

"Tell me what you fucking did!" Elena winced as though he had struck her. Unable to stop herself, she started to tremble, and the tears that had only been pooling before began to drop. Something between a scream and a sob crept up from her lungs, but Elena pushed it down; now more than any other time in her life, she had to be brave.

"Listen to me, Elly," her father said. "Stop crying and listen. I know who Ronny is. I know what you did. And I need you to help me stop it. If you don't, baby…if you don't help me stop it…we are all going to die."

Even as he commanded her to stop, her father started crying too. And yet Elena felt a flutter of encouragement so relieving that it turned into a smile. He wasn't angry at her. Or scared of her. He was scared of the dark thing. And he needed her help.

"I know this has been really hard for you, Daddy," she said, holding tight to that encouragement and fanning it into determination. "But I promise that it's almost over."

Over once and for all. No more unrequited mercy. No more second chances undeserved. The instant Elena closed her eyes and let her spirit free, destiny flooded her soul. A thousand choirs of voices she'd long forgotten sang songs of jubilee. Light rushed in to fill the darkness. Love rushed in to quell her fear.

When her eyes opened, the dark thing loomed over her, letting go any hope it had of hiding. She had floated out of the car and up into the air high enough to see the roof of every house in their neighbor-hood. Yet its shifting, black pillars like myriad tornados still rose so high into the clouds that Elena couldn't see where they ended. Its roar rocked the skies like a thunderclap without end, and whips like black lightning snapped down at the treetops below.

All things meant to frighten and daunt—the dark thing's favorite ploy. But it would not work this time. Elena rose higher into the swirl-ing winds, up through clouds of chilled mist and into the thin, clear air above the peaks of the dark thing's tallest pillars. From here, she was the one who loomed over it.

Elena could feel a charge in the air growing sharper as it readied its attack. The light emanating from her skin blazed brighter in response, turning the clouds around to woven gold. Like sunrise on a shrouded horizon.

She closed her eyes and breathed deep the cold, ozone-scented air. She felt the warmth of sunrays unobscured by atmosphere against her shoulders. And through the whirl of racing winds, ethereal voices still sang their comforting songs. She could feel them all around her, just their presence there with her lending her strength.

A crack as loud as mountains splitting shook the skies. Elena's eyes opened—burning now like binary stars—just in time to see the dark thing streaking toward her. It shrank and narrowed as it sped across the sky, its transformation as swift as its approach. Columns large as thun-derheads condensed into a single, needle-thin jet. A streak of poisoned ink flying straight and fast as a bullet.

Its unworldly whine grew louder—a cacophony of hissing steam and shattering glass, bloodcurdling screams and the wails of tortured souls. Yet over all this, Heaven continued to sing.

The dark thing struck her. A sensation like diving into ice-slushed water shocked her senses and sucked the breath from her lungs. An instant stretched into an eternity. She felt its hatred and hunger for life, saw the scope of its history play out before her, and heard pleas of justice from the multitudes it had slain.

Supernovas detonated behind Elena's eyes, bursts of brilliance exploding on a radiant white canvas. She felt a twitch of pain and a touch of fear before the light swept these away. When its glow finally faded and Elena's vision returned, she could hear the distant sound of trumpets join voices now rejoicing.

Shriveled and smoldering, the dark thing fell from the sky. Streams of smoke trailed from its tumbling form. Showers of flame like burning phosphorus erupted from its core.

Elena followed it down, tracing the trail of ash to the spot in the driveway where it had landed. Her feet touched the concrete, and the dark thing writhed in front of them.

She took no joy in its suffering. No vindication in its defeat. There were no lessons for the beings that comprised it to learn. No need for parting rebukes. Just a destiny for them both to fulfill—one set in motion before the wheels of time.

One last burst of light was all it took. A wide and roaring torch that washed the dark thing in fire. Layer by wretched layer, Elena watched it melt into the air. When the burst subsided, a few dozen floating specks of black were all that remained, these too soon igniting and flickering away. It looked like a cloud of fireflies gone as quickly as it had appeared. Each spark and silent scream that followed another of the dark thing's members vanishing from existence until the last speck winked out and all of them were gone.

TWENTY-ONE

THE DAY THE WORK IS DONE

It was ending. *They* were ending. Ra'Tak could not bear the weight of this realization. Could do nothing to quell the terror that flooded in behind it.

Their Master had forsaken them. Left them to burn. Perhaps it had been their failure that he could not stand to witness. Or perhaps it had been his own.

Despite how painful these last few moments of existence had become, Ra'Tak still clung to them. Even a lifetime in scorching flame seemed preferable to them over the darkness fast approaching.

That an epoch of existence would end with them writhing at the feet of a child enraged them most. They who had stalked the earth unchallenged for a thousand mortal lifetimes to be vanquished by the meekest of mortals. Must they be made to watch their pride fall first before their demise? They thought of the one who sent her, His propensity for such things, and let hatred soothe their pain.

There would be no pride in this defeat. But there would be vengeance. Like a wasp picked up too soon after death when its synapses were still firing and its glands still full of venom, Ra'Tak would have one final sting.

Nothing the girl could do now would stop the trap they'd set. Its springs were groaning, just a hair trigger holding them down. The shattered mess they'd made of their Quarry's mind was like smoldering tinder ready to combust at the first breath of wind.

Just before the nothingness enveloped them and thought slipped into dreaded silence, Ra'Tak delivered him one last illusion. A vision of Elena opening her eyes—eyes empty and black as midnight pools.

They would not last to witness what happened next. They were fading too quickly beneath the flames. But a parting glimpse into their Quarry's thoughts was all the assurance they needed.

He had fallen over the edge and into the abyss. Plummeting down the chasm far past the point of no return. Just as their Master had ordered, two lives would be delivered this day. Just like every time before on their unblemished record, Ra'Tak's Work would be finished.

TWENTY-TWO

TUESDAY, AUGUST 7ᵀᴴ

Elena continued to stare at the empty air where the dark thing had been. But the way the sun seemed to shine just a little brighter, the triumphant sound of voices much farther away than even it yet somehow all around, and the glowing satisfaction of fate fulfilled rising in her chest all left no doubt; the dark thing was gone. Gone this time in the truest, most permanent sense of the word.

"Well done, my child," said one voice that thundered above the rest. Hearing it, Elena felt like weeping with joy. "Your work on earth is done."

What the words meant became clear the moment they were spoken. Yet the rapture in them left no room for fear and sorrow. Across the driveway, she could see her empty body sitting in the car and her father crouched over it, arms extended and holding something shiny in his hands.

"Welcome home," the voice spoke strong and gently, and so echoed angel choirs.

Elena closed her eyes. She felt the midsummer breeze against her face, its scent of cut grass reminding her of the softball fields from a few years ago when she used to play. While birds sang and squirrels chattered from the limbs of nearby trees just like they had back then, Elena reminisced on the best of those days. The day she caught the final out of the game because something had told her just the spot in right field where Lexi Masterson was going to hit it.

So much to miss in this life. But so much, too, to long for in the next. No more time left to breathe the world in deep and savor sweet memories. But all the time in eternity for the paradise calling her home.

There was a crack of sound, then a burst of light. Elena felt warmth rush through her body, a surge of exquisite energy entirely different from the pain she'd been expecting. The light and warmth quickly faded. Her vision and thoughts faded too until all was silent and dark. But only for an instant.

When her eyes opened again, it was like the first time she'd opened them at birth. She could remember that moment now, and all the moments that formed her brief yet purposeful life. What came before—a life eternal in both directions with this task on earth just a fleeting interlude—came back to her just as clearly.

She was still standing in the driveway, the pavement beneath her bare feet still every bit as real as it had been before, the breeze still warm and steady against her skin, and what few birds the gunshot hadn't scattered still chattering overhead. Yet everything had changed.

Her surroundings had taken on a near-translucent quality, as though the driveway and the grass and the walls of her house had all been painted on the surface of a bubble. Through the watercolor film, Elena saw lights racing back and forth. Bright green runnels flowed up and down through the trunks of translucent trees. Brown pulses traveled up from the earth to meet rivers of blue streaming across the sky.

Lost in the technicolor display, it took Elena a second to notice the one light that was missing. The silver cord she'd come to accept as part of her body each time she ventured outside her physical one was gone. Her eyes traced the path it should have followed, across the driveway and up to the passenger seat of her father's car. But something blocked her view.

"You did so well, dear," the old woman said, stepping in front of her. Elena recognized her then in a way she hadn't before. Like the face of a friend last seen a lifetime ago. "It's time to go."

The shapes and colors around her were fading faster. The lights beneath intensified and ran together into brilliant white beams. Even the old woman was fading, the form she'd donned dissolving into the background as the familiar spirit within glowed brighter.

The sound of the sprinkler spurts and birdsong and the AC unit's hum were all being drowned out by sounds indescribable. Voices and trumpets and the chime of mighty bells. Only one tone from this world she was leaving fast was loud enough to still be heard: the sound of her father's screams.

"Follow me, Elena," said her spirit guide. "I'll show you the way."

"I have to help him," Elena said. Clinging to the last remnants of dissipating reality had become a struggle. The muffled wails and knowledge of what her father intended to do were the only anchors she had left.

"Quickly then. And with restraint."

Floating across the melting landscape was like swimming against the current. Ignoring the beckon her soul cried out to follow took every ounce of will.

Even blurred and vanishing, the scene inside the car tore at her heart. Not the lifeless body in the passenger seat. She had no more use for it anymore. Felt free of it now, if anything. But the broken soul in the driver's seat was one she had to save.

Just as her father leveled the gun against his own head—just as the pull of realms beyond swelled too strong for her to resist any longer—Elena showed him the truth.

EPILOGUE

Dr. Alice Embry checked her watch, then slowed her pace down the gray tile halls of the Georgia Institute for the Criminally Insane. She was fifteen minutes early but still felt in a rush.

Anxiousness, she knew, was the culprit. One didn't need to be a licensed psychologist to know that. In fifteen minutes—or sooner if he was early like her—she was going to sit down with one of the hospital's most interesting patients. That was something bound to make anyone anxious. For more reasons than one.

"He's about as docile and agreeable as they come," Dr. Reynolds—the hospital's chief psychiatrist and an old colleague of hers from her time at Columbia University—had told her over the phone. "Still crazy as a loon, though, if you'll pardon my slang. I've worked with Jerry for nine years now, and he still believes his delusions just as strongly as the day they brought him here."

And my, what fascinating delusions they were. It had taken Dr. Embry half the night to read through the volumes of pages documenting the various religious delusions and grandiose delusions that led Jared Gordon to take the life of his own daughter. He had recounted it all in meticulous detail over the years. He'd even written most of it down. But while many had studied his case, no one had yet seized the opportunity to publish it. Already an award-winning author in the genre of true crime committed by psychotic offenders, Dr. Embry had a keen nose for opportunity.

What she didn't have a keen nose for was navigation. The orderly she'd spoken with on the first floor had given good enough directions to room 304, but she'd gotten turned around somewhere, and the door numbers were now ascending from 321. "Excuse me," she said, waving at a young Middle Eastern nurse a little farther down the hall. "Can you tell me how to get to room 304?"

The nurse glanced up from her clipboard of papers and gave her an appraising look. "Are you Dr. Embry?"

"I am."

The nurse smiled then and stuck out her hand. Dr. Embry shook it. "My name's Mariam. I'm on Jerry Gordon's care team. He should be waiting for you already. In room—"

"In room 304."

"Right."

"And how do I get there?"

"Sorry," Mariam said with a sigh. "It's been a long shift."

"Aren't they all."

"Just turn around and take the first hallway you come to on your left. 304 will be the room at the very end. It's the visitation area for this floor, so it is a big room. You shouldn't miss it."

"Thank you," Dr. Embry said. There was a renewed haste in her step knowing for sure that Mr. Gordon was waiting for her. The real possibility that he might bail on their meeting at the last minute had been lingering in her mind. People with his condition were prone to such impulsivities. But now the prize was at her fingertips, and she could hardly hold back her anticipation.

With directions that even a lab rat could follow, it didn't take her long to find the hallway she'd passed by earlier and the door marked "Room 304" at its end. There was no window in the door for her to peek through, but she could hear someone drumming their fingers against a table on the other side. A common nervous behavior. Maybe he was anxious too, she thought and found the idea relaxing. Found her mind easing into the familiar frame of doctor and patient.

She reached out and knocked on the door. The drumming stopped. Seconds passed, then a voice bid her come in. The room was like most visitation areas she'd seen over her twenty-eight-year career—about the size of a tennis court with a half dozen round metal tables and accompanying duos of chairs all bolted to the floor. Only one of these chairs was occupied. The man sitting in it wore beige scrubs, a little tattered at the hems but otherwise neat and clean. He had chalk-white hair and a matching goatee and eyes that—at least at first impression—were friendly despite their weariness.

"Hi, Jerry," Dr. Embry said, stepping into the room all the way and letting the door swing closed. "Is it alright if I call you Jerry?"

"Jerry's fine. It's what everyone calls me these days. I've honestly come to like it."

"Alright then, Jerry. My name is Dr. Alice Embry. You can call me Alice." Then, motioning to the empty chair across from him, "Do you mind if I sit down?"

"I don't mind," Jerry said. Dr. Embry smoothed her skirt and settled into the cold, metal seat. Why did they have to make these things so uncomfortable? It was like no one who built these places ever stopped to think that a few creature comforts might be more rehabilitating than empty gray walls and bleach-scented floors. And hard, icy chairs.

"I really appreciate you agreeing to speak with me, Jerry. Truly. Has Dr. Reynolds told you why I'm here?"

"I believe he said you were writing an article."

"A book, actually. If all goes well."

"Oh," Jerry said. "That means we'll probably be spending a lot of time together, doesn't it?"

Dr. Embry smiled. "I promise I'm pleasant company."

"Can we get started then? I don't mean to be rude, but lunch is at noon, and I usually take a nap after."

"Of course. But there's no rush. I plan on coming back other days, and we can talk over the phone some, if need be." She couldn't tell if this pleased or bothered him. He wore the expression of a man waiting on a bus. Patient and contented, yes, but also bored and tired. Dr. Embry placed her phone on the table and pressed the bright red "record" button at the center of the screen. "Why don't we start with the journal?"

"Dad's journal or mine?" Jerry asked.

"I was told they are one and the same."

Jerry sighed. "That's what everyone keeps telling me too. That it's all in my handwriting. That I wrote entries from my father's point of view right between entries of my own. That's not how I remember it, but..."

"But what, Jerry?"

"Jeremiah—that's my brother, if you didn't know—he swears to this day that he never sent me the journal. He's the only one who ever visits me now. I'm not sure how much I trust handwriting experts or even psychiatrists...no offense. But I do trust him."

"But you don't actually remember writing it? Not those parts anyway."

"I don't remember a lot of things. And there are a lot of things I do remember that didn't really happen."

"What about the second journal you started after you were committed? Do you remember writing it?"

"Yes. I was afraid I'd forget what she showed me. So I wrote it down. Funny thing, though, I still remember every bit of it just as clearly as ever. I think she made sure I'd never forget."

"You're talking about Elena?" Dr. Embry asked. Jerry bristled a little at the mention of her name. No surprise, that, but it could not be helped; if they were going to get anywhere worth going—or any-where worth *publishing*—with this conversation, it would have to get uncomfortable.

"After I...after she passed...Elly showed me the truth. She saved my life."

"And what truth is that, Jerry?"

A glaze seemed to pass over his eyes, then the slightest touch of a smile at the corners of his lips. "That there are more things between Heaven and Earth, Dr. Embry, than are dreamt of in your textbooks."

"Oh, I don't doubt that's true."

"You're religious then?" Jerry said, seeming to perk up a bit.

"Hmm, I don't know if that's quite the right word. I've strayed a long way from my Catholic upbringings. But I do still believe there is a God."

"What about the devil?"

"Is that who Ra'Tak was?"

Another name dropped, another emotional response triggered. This one even more visceral than the last. Dr. Embry watched Jerry's face turn the pale, sweat-slicked appearance of someone who is about to be sick. Remarkable, after all these years, the clinical side of her thought, but she resolved to tread with a touch more caution moving forward.

"Call them the dark thing," Jerry said. "That's what Elly called them. And no, they're not the devil. Just one of his manifestations, I think. Elly couldn't show me everything." Jerry paused then and dropped his eyes to the ground, searching for the right words, it seemed. "Some knowledge isn't meant for this life."

"A demon. Is that what you're describing?"

"*Demons*," he said, then added another clarification in the same mat-ter-of-fact tone. "Sometimes they work in groups."

"So Ra'...the dark thing... was a group of demons, working for the devil, and trying to do what exactly? What I'm asking is, what did they want with you?"

"They wanted me to kill myself. That's what they do. Or *did*. They drove people mad until suicide was their only way out. They'd done it thousands of times before."

"Yet here you are."

"Thanks to Elly, yes."

"Why then did you do what you did?" Then, when this didn't seem to get the message across, "Why isn't Elena here too?"

Jerry's eyes never moved, but they seemed to stare somewhere a million miles away. "They tricked me," he finally said. "They needed her gone, and they tricked me into doing it."

"Because they couldn't do it themselves. Is that right? In fact, I believe you've said before that the dark thing was unable to harm anyone. Physically, anyway."

"That's right."

"So all the things you experienced, you accept that none of them truly happened. That they were all just delusions and dreams."

"I prefer 'illusions,' Doctor."

"Care to explain the difference?"

"Illusions require an illusionist."

Dr. Embry contemplated this for a moment, then decided to switch directions. "I want to talk about your childhood next, Jerry. What age were you when your father was diagnosed schizophrenic?"

Jerry stared at her blankly. "You've read all my files, right?"

"I have."

"Then you already know the answer to that. What you're doing is fishing for quotes for your book. Which I don't mind, really. I'll give you all the quotes you need. What I want in exchange, though, is a real conversation."

Dr. Embry picked her phone up off the table and set it in her lap. For no reason other than to make a point really; she kept it recording, but the way Jerry seemed to relax a little told her the gesture had worked. "Alright then. What do you want to talk about?"

"I want to know what you think," Jerry said.

"What I think about what?"

"About what I've told you, and everything you've read about me."

"I'm not your doctor, Jerry. I wouldn't feel qualified to give an opinion any different than the one that Dr. Reynolds has already given you."

"But do you have one? A different opinion, that is."

"No," Dr. Embry said after a long moment's consideration. "I agree with Dr. Reynolds' evaluation. I think that you were suffering from a severe and unusual case of paranoid schizophrenia coupled with parasomnia from your night terrors. I think that everything you've described are classic examples of grandiose and religious delusions and that your improvement these past nine years is not because the dark thing is gone but because the treatment is working.

"I also agree that, once you realized what you'd done, you couldn't live with it. So you changed the story. You couldn't bear the idea that Elena was wicked, so you made her a savior instead. You couldn't bear thinking that what you did was your own free will, so you put the blame on destiny. That's why you wrote the second volume and convinced yourself that Elena had shown you all those things.

"This narrative you've created is just a defense mechanism. You accept that none of the horrors you witnessed actually happened. But you still blame this entity for them. Because to believe anything else would mean admitting that Elena is gone. It would mean that you—not the dark thing or God or destiny—were the one who killed her."

It felt good having all the cards on the table. Transparency, she decided, was probably the best approach. These things were nothing

Jerry hadn't heard from a dozen doctors before; no sense in her trying to pretend anything different.

And it wasn't like it seemed to shake him. The only thing shaking was his head, slow and confident. "She's not gone. There's a part in all of us that no one can kill." Jerry exhaled and closed his eyes. His lips moved as if uttering a silent prayer. "She talks to me sometimes," he said, eyes still closed and head still bowed. "She tries to make me smile. She helps the others too. Her mom and brother and sisters. They can't see her like I can, but she still helps them."

Dr. Embry started to speak but stopped when she spotted something odd. Though there weren't any windows in the room and none on the entire floor that could be opened, a small, yellow butterfly had gotten in somehow and lit on Jerry's arm.

His eyes were open again, and he was staring down at it, seeming careful not to move as it explored his skin with tiny feelers. A smile spread across his face. The butterfly moved slowly down his arm and across his hand before it finally fluttered its wings and took flight. Dr. Embry watched it meander around the room until it found a crease in the door and made its exit to the hospital's halls.

"She told me to tell you she likes you," Jerry said, a new sparkle in his dreamy eyes.

Though it was quickly ignored and soon enough forgotten, Dr. Alice Embry felt a chill run up her skin.

THE END

AUTHOR'S NOTE

Dear Reader,

I hope that you enjoyed reading this story as much as I enjoyed writing it. At the time of this publication, The Dark Thing is the only book that I have published, but there are many more to come (and some soon to come!). If you would like to be notified of these future releases, I invite you to sign up for my newsletter at johnashleyauthor.com. Or, come be friends with me on TikTok (@johnashleyauthor)!

Thank you so much for letting me share this story with you. If you want to help me share it with others, kindly consider leaving a review.

Until next time we journey somewhere dark and chilling together,

John Ashley

JOHN ASHLEY is a freelance writer and indie author who lives in Springfield, Missouri. What started as a love for ghost stories and Goosebumps books turned into a lifelong passion for all things horror, and writing horror books is the bloody, beating heart of that passion. When he's not writing, John enjoys watching sports, spending time outdoors, and hanging out with his wife and their three pets.

Printed in Dunstable, United Kingdom

70478378R00205